Hamelin
STOOP

Other Books in the Hamelin Stoop Series

The Eagle, the Cave, and the Footbridge
The Lost Princess and the Jewel of Periluna
The Ring of Truth

Praise for the Hamelin Stoop Series

"The author has a real gift. I simply could not put this book down once I started reading it."
- Nicholas, Amazon.com reviewer

"The characters in the series are engaging and relatable. The plot is interesting and keeps the reader involved. It's a book you want to keep reading to see what happens next."
- Monique, *Mountain of Grace Homeschooling* blog

"There were a lot of strong themes in this book of loyalty, trust, and obedience versus selfishness and dishonesty. I felt like my own character was being developed as I followed the choices of the different players in this story."
- Sara, Amazon.com reviewer

"Each book in the series builds on the others to intricately weave an amazing fantasy adventure that will draw the attention of both youth and adults."
- Teresa, Homeschool Review Crew

Hamelin STOOP

The Battle of Parthogen

ROBERT B. SLOAN

TWELVE GATES PUBLISHING

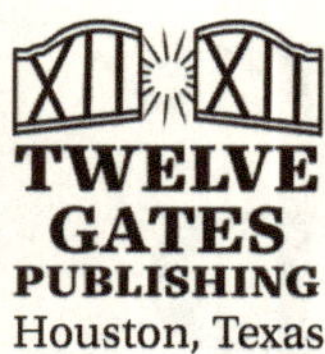

TWELVE GATES PUBLISHING
Houston, Texas

Printed in the United States of America. For purchase or more information, contact Twelve Gates Publishing at www.12GatesPublishing.com.

ISBN 979-8-9878571-0-6 (paperback)
ISBN 979-8-9878571-1-3 (hardcover)
eISBN 979-8-9878571-2-0 (e-book)

Library of Congress Control Number: 2023906394

Cover design and illustrations by Angela Merkle

041923

To Angela Merkle,

Editor and Friend

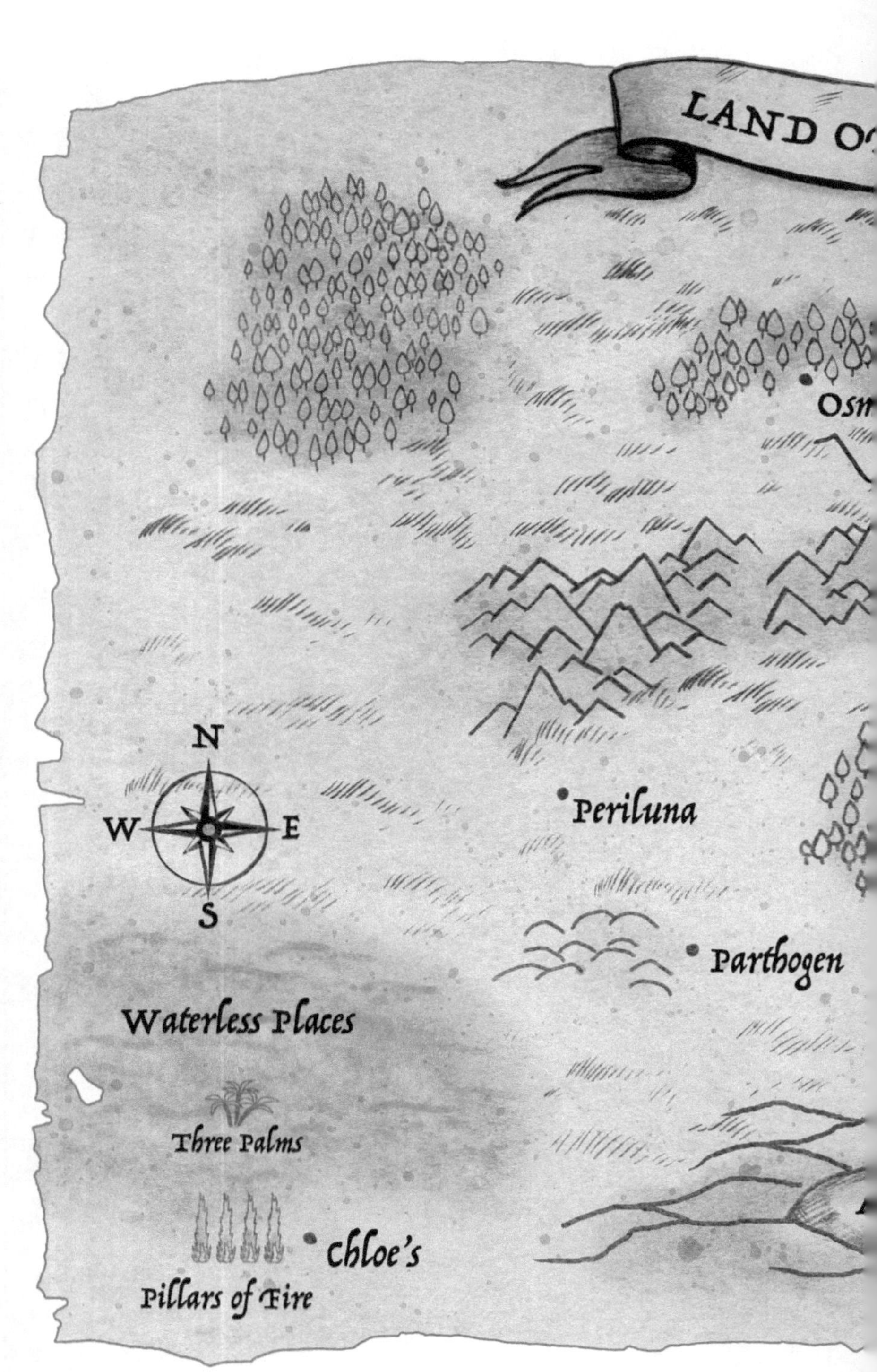

LAND O
Osm
Peppermint
N
W E
S
Periluna
Parthogen
Waterless Places
Three Palms
Chloe's
Pillars of Fire

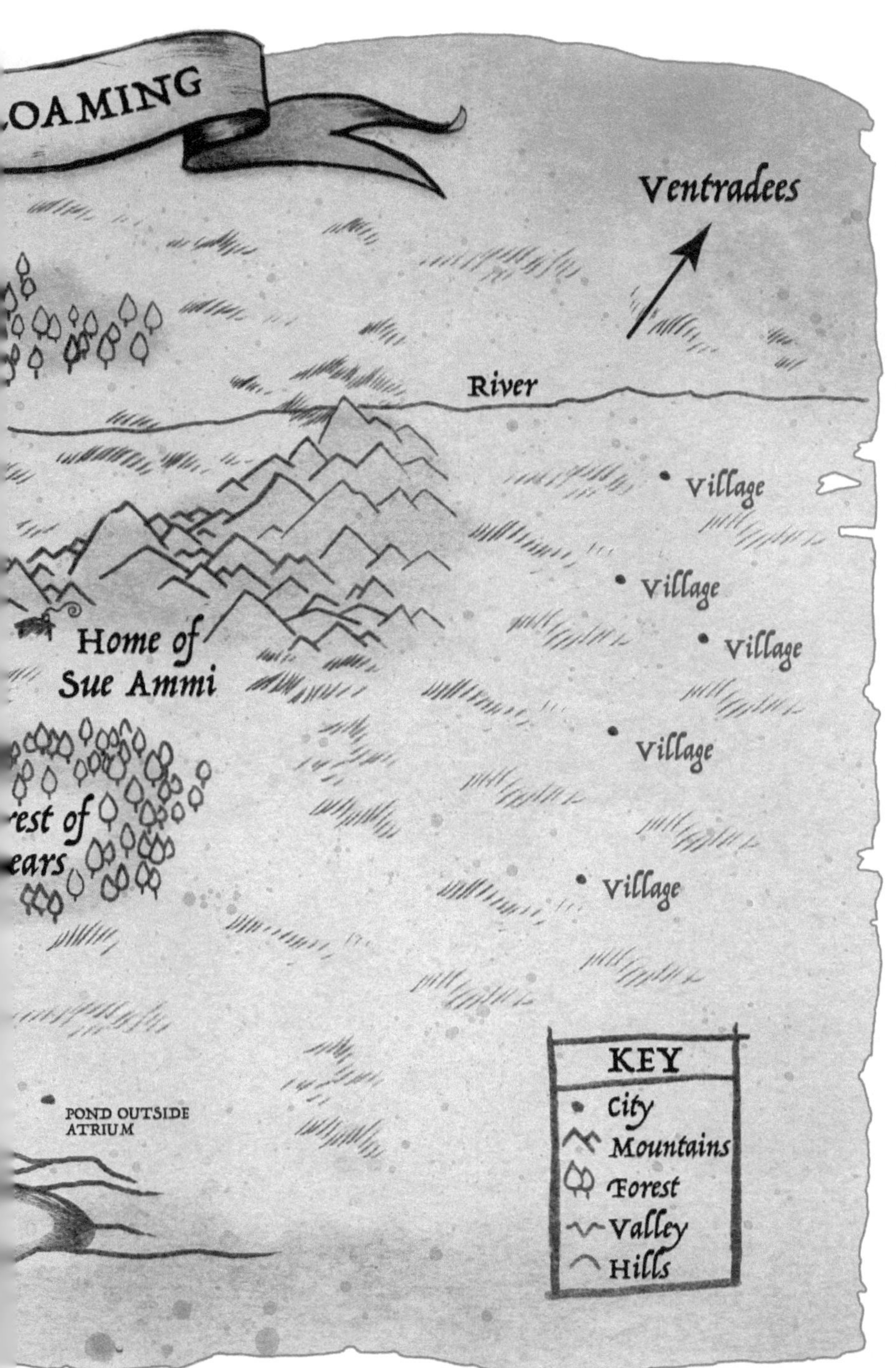
OAMING
Ventradees
River
Village
Village
Village
Home of
Sue Ammi
Village
rest of
ears
Village
POND OUTSIDE
ATRIUM
KEY
City
Mountains
Forest
Valley
Hills

Chapter 1

Deep Sleep and No Sleep

Where am I? Let me out! Her mind was working, but she couldn't move, not even to open her eyes. *Help!* an inner voice yelled, but no sound came from her throat. Only dryness there.

The darkness pushed against her, a heaviness pinning her on her back. Her mind frantically tried to conjure more pictures, but the darkness grew, and the scenes faded. *No!* she tried to scream, but still nothing came.

Am I in Ventradees? Did I die? Some people go directly there when they die. Her fears smothered her like a heavy cloud, now a massive stone, rolling and tumbling—and certain to crush her. But then an image of a boy took over. He hovered above her. *Who's that? I know him! Our friend from another world. He's strong, holding back the stone—Hamelin! Where is he? Didn't he ride off to Ventradees? Is he here? Can he save me?*

Underneath the boy was the last thing she saw before her world turned black—the side and belly of a white horse. *Oh! It's the horse that threw me, and Hamelin's still on it!* And then she remembered the last thing she felt, hitting the ground and her neck and head snapping back as everything faded. Hamelin, the horse, and some familiar voices—her sisters? Her father?

The darkness deepened as the sounds and pictures vanished. The pain in the back of her head grew and pounded, and she began to sink.

What's that? Something cool. It's like water, maybe wind, on my face. It feels good. Maybe I'm not in Ventradees. Are those voices again? Who's talking? They're so far away.

And then the smell of dirt, like a sweaty dog, hit her nose, and the weight of the pitch blackness fell upon her again and a painful sleep took over, until hands—old, rough hands—began pushing and scraping the side of her head. *Stop! Leave me alone!*

Layla watched her youngest sister, Sophie, who lay motionless in her bed—unconscious since being thrown from the back of a runaway horse earlier that day. She wouldn't leave the bedside, even though she had known Sophie in person for only a few days.

Layla had lived in Texas for more than twenty years and just days before had returned to the Land of Gloaming, with the help of several strange creatures, to be reunited with her family. And Hamelin Stoop, the twelve-year-old boy she had known since he was a baby at the Upton County Children's Home on the other side, had been a central part of it all.

As a four-year-old, she had been carried away from Parthogen on the back of a great white bull and had eventually ended up on a hillside just outside a mysterious cave, part of a passageway from Gloaming to Texas and the children's home.

But now she was back in this medieval land. Her father, King Carr, was still alive, though her mother, Queen Flora, was dead. At twenty-five, she was the second oldest of four sisters—the oldest, Charissa, was twenty-seven, and Eraina and Sophie were seventeen and fifteen. All four were princesses, though Layla knew little of what that meant. But she knew she had to stay near Sophie, to help as best she could.

Layla leaned over with her head touching Sophie's side, her hands clutching her sister's left hand and arm. Darkness filled the tent except for light from a flickering torch just inside the opening. The torch was small, but it added to the July heat and, worse, gave off a rotten-egg smell. Layla tried to stay awake to bathe her sister's warm face, but exhaustion overcame her and she fell asleep.

Patches of memories began to float through her tired mind—and sounds. Sounds of wind, which conjured up the storm on July 4 after the fireworks display back in Texas at the children's home. The very night Prince Lars of Periluna showed up and told her she had to come back to the Land of Gloaming...and later the swirling wind when she rushed home from Amy's house late at night—with all the city lights off—and she could feel the darkness.

And from the darkness red eyes emerged...then a long neck and more heads followed! And she saw the seven-headed snake on the ledge of the cave, the one whose hot breath had burned Mr. Kaley's arm.

But now, instead of Mr. Kaley yelling in pain, she heard a wheezing groan. The dreamy images fled away, and Layla woke up. It was Sophie. She was gasping, and then came a choking cough, followed moments later by breathing so faint that Layla could hardly detect it.

Layla again rested her head on Sophie's arm and desperately tried to think of a way to help her sister. She possessed some knowledge of herbs and modern medical practices, but she was no doctor, and what she knew was limited to what she had learned from living on the other side and especially from her job in a pharmacy. Though, strangely enough, she was also beginning to remember some of her grandmother's old cures. Things she had learned over here before being taken away.

The king's doctors had their own procedures in mind. They had recommended medieval practices that sounded frightening, and she had pled with her father not to allow such treatments. He was, however, listening more to them than to her.

Layla stayed with Sophie, afraid to leave her and determined to protect her. It grew late. Where was everybody? Gone to bed?

She glanced around the tent. They called it a hospital tent, but this bore no resemblance to any hospital room she had ever seen. In fact, it had been specially constructed for one person, the injured princess Sophia. The tent was larger than most others in the camp, to be sure, but except for some towels and pots filled regularly with fresh water, a few extra chairs for Sophie's family and closest friends, and the small bed Layla had requested for herself, the space was otherwise empty and plain. And dark.

Noises stirred outside the tent, and Layla lifted her head toward the opening. Who was that? Her sisters? No, those weren't women's voices. Then whispered words mixed with the shadows of what looked to be three men approaching the opening. They quickly stepped inside the tent and paused. The doctors. But where was her father? One of the men held what appeared to be a long razor, and another tried to hide other strange instruments beneath his long-sleeved robe—a hammer and a rounded metal spike! Trephining!

They approached Sophie's bed from the other side, heads down to avoid eye contact with Layla. The leader of the group, clearly the oldest of the three, lifted his face. "Princess Alathea, you'll have to leave."

She glanced back toward the opening—still no sign of her father. Surely he wouldn't allow—

As if reading her mind, the man spoke again. "We have the permission of the king. This must be done."

Layla stood. She leaned over and kissed her sister, then rubbed the side of her face and squeezed her hand. "Don't worry. I'll be back."

She glanced at the old physician but then lowered her eyes to the floor and circled around the end of the bed. She slowly walked toward the opening of the tent, stopped near the torch, and turned around one last time to look at Sophie.

The lead doctor followed her with his eyes as the man with the strange instruments moved to the other side of the bed. The old physician then turned his back to Layla and nodded toward the others.

She remained at the opening for an extra moment and took everything in. Was there nothing to do except watch her little sister suffer such poor treatment and likely die? Where was everyone else? She looked toward Sophie, but now her view was blocked as the practitioners of strange arts huddled around her sister's bed, bending over her.

She could smell the smoke from the torch as it cast its wavy lights and shadows across the room. She saw one of the physicians hold up a long razor—or was it a scalpel?—and test it with his thumb. For a moment she closed her eyes, but she opened them again, forcing herself to watch.

"I need some more light." The man with the razor leaned closer.

The light flickered and then grew brighter, and with no plans or thoughts beyond the next instant, Layla grabbed the torch with both hands and yanked it from its holder. Then with screams that shattered the night air, she gathered up her long skirt and ran toward the king's tent, crying out, "Father, please! Charissa! Eraina! Somebody *help!*"

Hamelin Stoop was back at the children's home. The last thing he had expected when he woke up that morning in the Land of Gloaming was that he would be back in Texas by that night, but here he was, sitting in the dark on his bed at the end of the long boys' room. He had just spent more than two hours explaining to Mr. and Mrs. Kaley, the house parents at the home, and Mrs. Eastland, their friend and his favorite teacher at the local elementary school, everything that had happened since he left in a flaming chariot almost two weeks ago, until earlier this very evening, when the Great Eagle had brought him back and angrily dumped him at the cave. He was so ashamed that he had sneaked into the Kaleys' apartment without anyone else seeing him. He hated telling them what had happened that day on the other side of the cave—especially the disaster he caused at the end of it—but he had to.

His mind raced, alternating between shame and anger. Everything was confusing. In the first place, he had no idea what he would say to others about where he had been, but the Kaleys and Mrs. Eastland told him not to worry about that. They had already explained to the workers and other children in the home that he was away visiting Bryan and Layla. Since everyone knew they were friends, though they didn't know Bryan and Layla were now in Gloaming, no one would ask any hard questions. He hoped they were right, but he didn't want to think about it. He sighed and placed his gloves of strength and the scabbard that once held the amazing sword—but now contained only the little hammer—in a wooden box at the foot of his bed and crawled under the top sheet.

One of the boys stirred somewhere in the vicinity of Paul's bed, but then things got quiet again. No matter; he couldn't sleep. He took out a book that Layla had given him, turned on a small flashlight, and tried to read, but it was no use. Even though he already knew the story, he couldn't concentrate and finally had to quit after reading the same half paragraph several times. All he could think about was what had happened that very day in the Land of Gloaming, the world on the other side of the cave. It all kept turning endlessly through his head, but more important than what had happened was why.

Everyone over there was excited about the return of Layla, the long missing princess who, along with her brother Bryan, had grown up at the children's home. Now, after many adventures, she was reunited with her royal family camped just outside the city of Parthogen, and Bryan was also in Gloaming, though no one knew exactly where. Layla's return only two days ago, however, had already stirred great emotion and big plans. Her three sisters had persuaded their father, King Carr, to present her publicly as a princess, and arrangements for the debut and formal ceremony, to be followed by a great banquet, were underway when Hamelin caused the catastrophe. The grand events would have lasted until late this very night, but the celebrations were no doubt canceled, and it was Hamelin's fault.

He had saddled and mounted a mysterious horse, an Arabian palomino, and pulled Layla's youngest sister, Sophie, up behind him, even though there was no bridle. And then for some reason—was it the surprise appearance of the eagle?—the horse bolted and raced away with his two riders. After two sudden starts and stops, Sophie was thrown and struck her head.

He had no chance to dismount and try to help. The horse bolted again, and the eagle flew after them at top speed, snatching Hamelin off the back of the runaway animal. The last thing he saw as the eagle wheeled in the air and flew him away was Sophie lying unconscious on the ground, with her family and others like Lars, Amy, and Fearbane crowding around. He would never forget the shock and fear on their faces as they looked at him and then back to Sophie's motionless body.

Guilt and pain flooded his head and chest, and he tried not

to think any more about what he'd done. But the scenes kept racing through his mind, and his frustration built. *It's not all my fault! What was I supposed to do?* Then he remembered that the eagle told him to think. But thinking was hard work. Besides, it was too hot to think!

It was late July, with hardly a breeze coming through the one open window in the boys' room, and he caught a whiff of something nasty. It smelled like trash, but worse than that. In a home with more than fifty children, plus several workers, a lot of trash accumulated every day, and it was not unusual in the stillness of a hot summer night to smell it—stale and stinky—through an open window. But this was worse. Whatever it was reminded him of burning rubber. Had Mr. Moore burned trash that afternoon? He closed his eyes, but the smell and the darkness combined to remind him of traveling through the cave.

Hamelin sat up on the side of the bed, and anger began to take over his frustration. He had never asked to go over there! He was only eight years old the first time he went, when the eagle practically forced him to follow him through the cave. On that trip, he failed to cross the footbridge, and the eagle grabbed him up from the ground and flew him back. *He sure does a lot of grabbing and snatching! Why didn't he just carry me across?*

He had, after all, tried to go back on his own several years later, but the eagle got angry and sent him away, saying he had to be summoned. Why couldn't he just make up his mind!?

Finally, Hamelin was summoned, and he did lots of great things in the Land of Gloaming, but apparently that wasn't enough. Just when everything was starting to go well and he wanted to look for his parents, once again in a surprise move the great bird flew him back to the Atrium and through the cave. That was last Christmas.

Who was telling the eagle what to do and ordering all these things? Why couldn't he just stay over there until he found his parents? His mind then turned back only a few weeks to the first part of July, when SueSue sent Lars to get him and Layla. But Bryan switched places with her at the last second, and she stayed while the three young men flew to Gloaming in a chariot of fire drawn by winged black horses. *I did everything I was supposed to do! I helped rescue Layla and then the eagle got mad again and now I'm back here!*

But he no sooner thought these things than he admitted to himself they weren't the full truth. The eagle, who served the Ancient One, took him away from Gloaming and flew him back today because, as the great bird put it, he was out of control. And to top it off, the eagle told him it really wasn't his horse to ride. And now Sophie… He took a deep breath and tried to do what the great bird said to do, which was think, but it was harder than he expected.

The outside smell and the weight of the darkness both grew stronger, conjuring another scene, partly old and partly new, that now flashed through his mind. He could see himself back in the cave, standing at the edge of the chasm, stuck in place, with one foot forward on the rope bridge as he stared into the bottomless pit. And the smell hit his nose again—hot tar or maybe burning rubber.

He heard in the distance a roll of thunder, unusual for that time of year in West Texas. Then he remembered the surprise rainstorm that July night when he had first gone to the cave a little more than four years ago. Was he being summoned again? Was it already time to go back?

Hamelin quietly rolled out of bed and put on his clothes. He slipped out of the room, down the stairs, and out the front door, making sure the screen door didn't make its characteristic thwacking noise. He briskly walked north on the road toward the hill where, halfway up, there was a ledge and an opening to a cave that led to another world.

Chapter 2

The Sisters Act

AYLA'S SCREAMING BROUGHT EVERYONE RUNNING. HER sisters Charissa and Eraina were the first to rush to her side from their nearby tent, followed by her close friend Amy and Lars, the Prince of Periluna, as well as various soldiers, including Fearbane. Her father, King Carr, emerged from his large tent with servants following. He took the torch from Layla's hands and put his hands on her shoulders. "What's the matter, my dear?"

The words tumbled from Layla's mouth. "Father, the doctors came to do trephining, and I know it's something practiced here, but please! You can't do that to Sophie. It's very dangerous and—"

The three physicians stumbled out of the darkened hospital tent and made their way to the king.

"Sire, please excuse this disturbance. We are only doing what you permitted, and the Princess Alathea—"

"Father, I beg you, listen to me—"

"Please, Father." Charissa took up her sister's cause. "We

are amazed at how much Layla knows, and since she comes from a world more advanced with medicines and cures and has spent so many years there, shouldn't we pay attention to her ideas?"

"But, Sire," said the lead physician, "there's not much time. Princess Sophia barely clings to life, and we have our instruments ready in the tent—"

While the doctor made his plea, Layla slipped away from the group to hurry back to Sophie's tent. She strode through the opening and paused to let her eyes adjust to the torchless darkness. She listened for Sophie's breathing but detected only her own—and something else. For a second, it brought to mind an old memory, or at least the fragment of one...the image of a dog that snarled and leaped at her. But no dogs were in this tent. Surely.

She took three steps toward Sophie and again thought she heard a low, threatening noise. And then another sound—hurried steps—just behind her at the opening. She angled her body back to her right and expected to see her father. But silhouetted there were Eraina and Lars.

Eraina's hands gripped the special scarf from SueSue that allowed her to see what others couldn't. She peered into the dark past Layla toward the far end of the tent, near the foot of Sophie's bed. Her voice came through the stillness, a soft but insistent monotone, "Layla, go to your left, and crouch behind the bed."

The tone said it all—there was no time for questions. Layla took two steps and fell to her knees in the same movement, then twisted her shoulders and head back toward Eraina.

Eraina pointed. "Right there."

Now came Lars's voice. "I don't see anything yet. My eyes haven't adjusted—"

"There! Two o'clock!"

In that split second, Layla saw the form of a huge wolf dog springing toward Lars. As the snarling creature flew through the air, the prince, wearing his special shoes of speed and balance, leaped straight up from his standing position and delivered a thudding, two-legged scissor kick to the dog's head and body. A breathy howl followed. Lars then set himself, preparing to deliver another blow, but the dark, motley-colored half-breed shot past him toward the opening. Just as his body reached halfway out the tent, however, a barking yelp erupted, and by the time Layla, Eraina, and Lars got outside, the growling animal lay twisting and squirming with his neck pinned under Fearbane's boot. After that, it took only seconds for soldiers to tie the thrashing animal's legs and muzzle his mouth. What everyone knew must be one of Landon's dogs lay helpless on the ground.

The outrage and chaos of the moment soon settled. A torch was placed in the holder near the opening, and the dog was dragged away. The king dismissed his physicians and ordered a guard to be posted at the hospital tent. He then summoned Fearbane and Lars to his quarters, and Charissa and Eraina also followed. Layla returned to Sophie's bedside, but before she sat, footsteps and another voice came from near the opening. "Layla, come on back to the girls' tent." It was Amy, and behind her stood the guard.

Layla shook her head. "I'm not leaving Sophie."

The tall, burly soldier took a step closer. His deep voice sounded confident. "I promise to stay here all night. Princess Sophia will be safe."

With further encouragement from Amy, Layla finally agreed to go to the girls' tent.

Charissa knew that she and Eraina were not invited, but she didn't hesitate to follow her father, Fearbane, and Lars. Eraina was right behind her. This wasn't the first time either of them had been in their father's special tent, though it had been a while. Its layout hadn't changed.

His quarters were spacious and—for a place in the woods where a battle could break out—it was nonetheless well appointed and befitting a king. It contained not only a hand-carved bed with quilted blankets on the opposite side from the entryway, but also chairs and small writing stands around the walls. A long conference table with lamps, maps, and other drawings on it dominated the middle of the room. Carr had another, even larger, tent available for war councils, but this one, even though it was the place he slept, was often used for important strategic discussions regarding the camp and his kingdom.

Charissa watched the king take the middle spot on the other side of the table, across from those who had followed him. Fearbane and Lars stood close to the table, while she and Eraina remained a few steps away, somewhat to the side.

Carr noticed his daughters but turned toward Fearbane. "What do you suggest we do with the dog?"

"As much as I would like to take my sword and finish the creature off, I think it best, for various strategic reasons, simply to send him back."

Carr then shifted his body toward Lars, but before he could say anything, Charissa stepped toward the table. "I would send him back as well. In a bag."

The king abruptly turned his head. "Do you mean to say you would kill him?"

"I would."

"But, Your Majesty," said Fearbane, "that seems unnecessarily cruel."

"And perhaps vengeful," said Lars.

Charissa took a step toward the table. "I would answer both points similarly. In the first place, cruelty is always unnecessary, and my advice has none of that in it. I did not say to send him back piece by piece. One fell stroke and one bag will do. What I seek is justice. And if justice—putting things right—requires a payback for the wrong that Landon has done, because it is deserved, then I would say it is necessary and not cruel. As to the word *vengeful*, I prefer *retribution*, but call it what you will. A measured vengeance is a just response to an outrage committed."

"But the dog didn't *kill* anyone," said Lars.

Eraina huffed. "Not because he didn't try!" She stepped forward, and her voice was not quiet. "He leaped at you, head high, and who knows what would've happened if you hadn't deflected the attack? You know full well how vicious Landon's dogs are!"

Lars shrugged.

Charissa took another step and put one hand on the king's table. "Besides, all of us know that the unexpected death of the queen, our mother, precipitated Landon's treachery. In retrospect, is it possible he, somehow unknown to us, contributed to her death? And who can measure the pains that have had to be endured by the families of our kingdom because we've been exiled out here? Have babies died in these camps because we didn't have the comforts of our homes in Parthogen? Were there illnesses not prevented or injuries not healed?"

"But we shall get our revenge for these terrible things," said Fearbane. "It's only a matter of time."

Charissa snapped her head toward him and glared. "I see that you now admit a proper time and place for the word *revenge*, when *you* use it. But leaving that aside, the time for deterrence is already upon us."

Lars lifted his hands and turned his palms up. "But surely that wasn't an attack on us. He's probably just a scout, right?" He looked at Fearbane and then the king.

"You could be right about that," said Charissa, "but when confronted, that scout attacked. And what was he doing in Sophie's tent? Eraina, did you see the dog enter the tent?"

"No. The first I saw of the creature, he was already there. Sniffing around Sophie's bed!"

Carr sat down and put a hand to his chin.

Charissa put another hand on the table and leaned in toward her father. "Then we may presume he had already sneaked in while Layla was with Sophie. It's no accident that just after Layla has come back—which Landon surely knows—his dog was snooping around that tent. Whatever that scout intended to do, it was at least preparatory for something worse."

Eraina moved closer to her sister. "I agree. We need to send Landon a strong signal that—"

"Your Majesty," said Fearbane as he also crowded closer to the table, "we are *preparing* for the day when you give the signal to attack, but this is *not* the right time. It seems to me, with all due respect to the princesses, that killing the dog will only provoke Landon."

"*Provoke Landon*?!" Charissa felt her eyes grow big and a deep breath fill her chest. She pivoted toward Fearbane and pushed her words out slowly. "He has *attacked* us, and if we do not respond in some measured way, we encourage him to do more. A proportional response will deter him, at least for now, if only because it will make him think again before sending dogs to sniff around our camp and our sisters."

Fearbane shook his head. "We agree that Landon must have a day of reckoning—"

Lars leaned forward, about to speak, but Eraina jumped in. "A day that you earlier conceded we could call *revenge!*"

"So we concur," said Charissa, "that he deserves retribution, but you're only saying not now? I'm *not* counseling an all-out attack, at least not yet. I'm saying we must do *something*. For the sake of our sisters, our house, and our father's kingdom."

Fearbane blinked and swallowed. "But the question of timing is important, and right now, all the benefits of withholding our retaliation lie with us. Again, we don't want to provoke an immediate response from Landon. He has the advantage of maintaining a defensive posture from an elevated position behind city walls. We will need the element of surprise. He will never attack us, but a hasty response from us now will encourage him to be better prepared."

Charissa put her hands on her hips. "Or it will embolden him to do more the next time he sends his dogs! No, I tell you, don't think he's not already prepared. He knows the fourth princess has returned. He also likely knows that Sophie is near death. I'm guessing he sees these things as providing both a necessity and an opportunity for attacking."

Charissa looked at the king. "You didn't invite me or Eraina to this conversation, Father, so perhaps we've already said too much. But I have said all that I intended. Anything further would be repetition. Obviously, you will do what you believe best, and we will follow your lead."

The king took a deep breath as several long moments passed. Finally, he looked at Fearbane. "Release the creature, but make sure Eraina watches as he returns to the city."

Charissa stared at Fearbane and saw her sister give Lars a withering look at the same time. She bowed to her father, and Eraina followed her out. She hated sounding argumentative in her father's presence, but being king didn't make you always right. And she feared he wasn't.

Chapter 3

The Tree

H*AMELIN!"*

He heard a voice he remembered, a man's voice, and it drew his mind to the pond in the Atrium of the Worlds, where he gazed at his reflection, at first handsome but then wavy and distorted as the water began to ripple.

"Hamelin!" He heard it again, and this time he felt something hard against his left cheek. He was lying on a rock floor, and it wasn't in the Atrium. He opened his eyes and found himself outside, staring at the gray-blue light breaking in the east. Then he remembered. He was on the ledge.

"Hamelin! Are you up there?"

Stiff and sore, he sat up and squinted against the bright morning sun as it all came flooding back. Last night he had slipped away from the home, climbed the hill, and waited at the opening of the cave, hoping to be summoned. He also recalled how mad he had gotten at himself because he had come completely unprepared—of all things forgetting his special gloves and the scabbard! But still he had waited here, until he had fallen asleep.

"*Hamelin*!" It was Mr. Kaley.

"Yes!" He yelled down the hill. "I'm up here on the ledge."

"Can you come down? Mrs. Kaley and I want to talk."

Hamelin's first feeling was embarrassment that he had sneaked out at night and now was being brought back like a little kid who had run away from home.

"Just a minute. I'll be there."

Within ten minutes, he made his way down the brushy hill and found Mr. and Mrs. Kaley standing at the bottom, with Mr. Kaley's sedan parked just across the road.

He looked at his feet, expecting to hear a scolding word from one of them, but Mr. Kaley just nodded at him. "Are you okay?"

Mrs. Kaley put an arm around his shoulders and mumbled something about him sleeping outside without a blanket.

Hamelin walked with them to the car, stiff and hungry, hoping he could still get some breakfast back at the house. But they didn't get in the car, only pausing there for a second while Mrs. Kaley reached in and brought out a blanket and a big picnic basket. They led him across the shoulder of the road and into the woods beyond.

"We know you're tired and need to get back to the house," said Mr. Kaley. "But we've got some things we want to talk about and something to show you. It's probably an odd time to do it, but when we woke up this morning and realized you were gone again, we knew we couldn't wait any longer."

"Besides, you must be hungry." Mrs. Kaley held up the basket. "And there's a good place for a breakfast picnic just ahead."

They seemed to know exactly where they wanted to go, so Hamelin followed as they walked further into the woods, angling a little bit back toward the house. Ten minutes later, they came to a big mesquite tree.

"Here it is." Mrs. Kaley nodded at the tree as if it were

something very special. "I mean…it's a good spot…shade and even a slight breeze."

Hamelin followed her gaze and noticed some markings on the trunk. A memory stirred. He trained his eyes on the mesquite. "That tree. It's the one where the ants stung me, and those markings are initials. Right?" He leaned in toward the trunk.

Mr. Kaley took a step closer. "Yes. It's the one you told me about after you got back from that hike. You went for a walk in the woods, but then, as we know from your later story, you were also looking for the cave."

Hamelin nodded. "That was the time I thought the eagle was trying to lead me around the north side of the hill. I made it into the cave, but the eagle had to save me from a huge bobcat. He got really mad and said I had entered the wrong way and that I wasn't summoned."

"That's also when you tore your jeans and I sewed you that extra big pocket." Mrs. Kaley smiled.

"After the eagle saved me, I came into the woods and sat against this mesquite tree and fell asleep, but when I woke up, I had ants all down my shirt. I got a lot of stings."

Mr. Kaley pointed toward the carved initials on the tree. "You said that you remember these, but can you tell me what the letters were?"

Hamelin's eyes narrowed. "I remember that they looked like the initials of a boyfriend and girlfriend, since there was a plus sign between them."

"Well take a close look." Mr. Kaley tilted his head at the trunk of the tree. "These letters—"

Mrs. Kaley cleared her throat. "Can we slow down a little? I brought this big picnic basket out here, and this is going to take some time to talk about, so let's just have some breakfast first."

Hamelin was ready to hear more, but his hunger won out,

so he and Mr. Kaley helped her unfold the blanket. It took several minutes to lay out everything, which included muffins, soft breakfast tacos, toast and jelly, coffee for Mr. Kaley, and some hot tea for her.

Hamelin decided to try some of the hot tea, so she poured it for him and said she had a special way of preparing it for breakfast. She winked and added some cream to Hamelin's hot mug. The color and smell reminded him of candosheen, though he knew it wouldn't be the same without SueSue's special spices. But it tasted good going down, even on a July morning.

Although Mrs. Kaley had packed a big basket, they had eaten only some of the breakfast tacos when Mr. Kaley started again. "So can you read these initials, Hamelin?"

Hamelin answered with no hesitation. "JSK plus JSK. Whose are they?"

Mr. Kaley glanced at his wife and took a slow breath. "That's a big part of the story we want to tell you. When we finish, you'll know."

Mrs. Kaley reached over and patted Hamelin's forearm. "It'll take a few minutes. It's a story we've wanted to tell you for a long time—and now we realize that we probably should have talked sooner. But we thought keeping everything to ourselves was for the best, especially for you. We love you, Hamelin." Her eyes moistened.

Mr. Kaley took a sip of coffee, laid his cup down, and began. "It all started about thirteen years ago. We became estranged from our only child, a son, when he was twenty years old. He didn't do well in college his first few semesters—he never really wanted to go to college—"

"No, he wanted to join the army," said Mrs. Kaley, "and fight in the war, but we wouldn't let him, and the war ended in 1945, just months before he turned sixteen. So he stayed in high school."

"And finished," said Mr. Kaley. "He went on to college but did poorly. I warned him he was going to have to pay his own bills if he didn't pass his courses."

"He came home for the Christmas holidays of his sophomore year," said Mrs. Kaley. "He was staying out every night and had told us that he was probably going to fail all of his classes."

"Even on Christmas Eve he was out late," said Mr. Kaley, "and by the time he dragged himself out of bed on Christmas Day, I was pretty mad and said some things I shouldn't have. Before I knew it, we were in a full-blown shouting match. He left home late that night and just vanished. I still blame myself."

"There's blame enough for all of us." Mrs. Kaley squeezed his hand.

Mr. Kaley reached for his coffee and paused to let Mrs. Kaley fill the cup again, but it was too hot to drink.

She handed Hamelin a small basket of warm breads. "I know Mr. Kaley probably wants some more toast. How about a buttered muffin for you?"

Hamelin took the muffin, and Mr. Kaley reached for a slice of toast.

Mrs. Kaley covered the muffins with a small towel but then picked up the story. "For months, we didn't have the slightest idea where he was. Eventually one of his friends told us that he was still in Texas but somewhere farther west. We didn't know exactly where, but at least that gave us a general idea.

"Then after several months, he wrote us and said he had a job as a maintenance man. The letter was postmarked from Midland, Texas. We tried to locate him, but it was just impossible. Then almost exactly a year after he vanished, he showed up at our door. We were thrilled to see him, of course, but we were in for quite a surprise. An attractive young woman with beautiful blond hair, two to three years younger than he, was with him. He explained that they had gotten married the previous May and she was about three months pregnant. We were taken aback, but we were also overjoyed to see him—and to meet her. They stayed with us for several days, and it felt like old times again."

Mr. Kaley smiled and took a sip of his coffee. "He and I reconciled. I apologized for the things I had said and told him how pleased I was to have him home. He seemed happy to be there."

"We tried to find out about her and her family," said Mrs. Kaley, "but she was very shy and reluctant to talk about her past." She passed Hamelin another muffin and nodded at Mr. Kaley to continue.

"She also appeared fearful, sometimes looking around or over her shoulder—almost like she was being chased. Our son thought it was just her shyness and insecurity. But even he admitted that he was starting to wonder if someone was following them."

"Then late one night," Mrs. Kaley said, "I noticed two very big, strange-looking men down at the corner of our street. I didn't think too much about it until I saw them there again the next morning."

"That's true," said Mr. Kaley. "I saw them too, and our new daughter-in-law began to grow more and more nervous. Our son and his wife had been with us for about four or five days, and we had enjoyed a wonderful Christmas, but then, just before New Year's, I heard some loud clattering outside. It was after midnight, and I thought it was an animal, so I didn't go look. But the next morning, when we got up for breakfast, they were gone. They had packed up their few belongings and slipped away. They just vanished."

"We were so heartbroken..." Mrs. Kaley's voice cracked.

Mr. Kaley refilled her teacup and waited a few moments

before continuing. "I jumped in my car and tried to find them. I drove all through our little town of Coleman, but there was no sign of them. They didn't have a car, so we don't know how they left, but they were gone."

"But," began Mrs. Kaley again, "don't forget to tell them what you saw outside."

"Yes. I looked all around the house and found footprints from at least two men. Two big men. Whatever noise we heard the night before they left, they must have heard too. We think it spooked them and they decided to run."

Mrs. Kaley dabbed at the corners of her eyes with a napkin. "We called the sheriff and the highway patrol, and they did their best to look for them, but they had no clues to go on. We finally did hear from the sheriff's office that a young couple was seen hitchhiking on the highway early that same morning, going west, but no one knows if or when they were picked up."

Mr. Kaley sat up straighter. "But I was more determined than ever not to lose my son again—and also his wife, who was pregnant with our grandchild. Since he told us she had been raised in a children's home, I got to thinking that maybe they could be tracked using that information. We didn't know her maiden name, but we hoped her first name would help us. We got lists of every orphanage or children's home in West Texas and began to make calls. We even took weekend trips and sometimes stayed for days just visiting all the children's homes we could find.

"But no one knew anything about them. And since they were a married couple—not missing children—the authorities were no help. For years, we would look in spurts, almost despairing, fearing something terrible had happened to them. But even though the years began to mount up, we never gave up hope."

"Finally," said Mrs. Kaley with a note of excitement in her

voice, "we came across Mr. Moore. It's another story how we met him, but he confirmed that he knew our son and that he had worked for Mr. Moore at the home several years earlier for about six months. He also said that our son seemed to have eyes for one of the girls, a pretty blond, and that they had both disappeared late one night shortly after her high school graduation. It was obvious that the two of them had run off together."

"From there," said Mr. Kaley, "we were able to ask a few questions, and we learned that our son's girlfriend had come here to the home when she was just a young girl about twelve years old; they found her wandering on the road one day."

Hamelin's eyes grew wide. "So what was her name?"

"I'm almost done with my story," said Mr. Kaley. "And then you'll know." He took a long sip of his coffee. "We kept looking for anyone who might know them, but the trail grew cold again. No one except Mr. Moore gave us much information, and we didn't want to attract too much attention around town.

"So when the Stephensons left a little over three years ago, we quickly snapped up the job as house parents. We hoped it would give us the opportunity to pick up some more clues about them and where they had gone." Mr. Kaley looked at his wife.

"So by now you can probably guess who she was," said Mrs. Kaley.

"Was her name Johnnie Smith?"

The Kaleys nodded.

"And what was your son's name?"

"Jonathan Simonton Kaley," said Mr. Kaley.

"He was named for his father," said Mrs. Kaley. "But we didn't want to call both of them John, so we used our son's middle name, Simonton. And then that got shortened to Simon. And that's what we called him."

Hamelin again glanced toward the tree. "So JSK stands for Jonathan Simonton Kaley, and then the other *JSK* stands for

Johnnie Smith Kaley?" Hamelin took a deep breath. "And they came to this very spot…"

Mr. Kaley lifted his chin. "It sure looks that way. After you left the first time, during the Christmas holidays, I remembered your story about a mesquite tree with some initials on it, and so Mrs. Kaley and I came out here looking for it. And when we found this tree, it confirmed what we already thought about our son and who his wife might be. They must've come out here more than once as a favorite meeting spot."

"How can you tell that?"

"Because it looks to me like it was originally JSK plus JS, and then the final *K* got added at a different time. Look—" He pointed to the initials.

Hamelin peered closer. "It looks like the other *K* was carved later. It isn't the same size, and it doesn't look quite as deep as the first letters."

"I'm thinking the same thing," said Mr. Kaley. "It's only a guess, but maybe the first time this was carved they were boyfriend and girlfriend, and then later, when they were married, the other *K* got added."

"But I thought they got married after they left here. So you think they came back? When?"

Mr. Kaley shrugged. "Maybe when they were being chased. Anyway, that's a good question. But whenever it was, it looks like they were in a hurry, because they didn't take the time to make the letters look the same."

Hamelin's body and then his head felt lighter as he stared at the initials. The letters grew sharper, and everything else blurred, and he felt like he was being carried back in time to another place, someone else's memories, memories that were connected to him.

Mrs. Kaley coughed and began packing the basket.

Hamelin's gaze finally broke, and he turned to Mrs. Kaley.

"So if your son worked at the home and he married Johnnie Smith and she was expecting a baby..."

Mrs. Kaley paused, but in an instant the words came tumbling out. "If she was three months pregnant when we met her that Christmas, then she would've had her baby sometime in late June. You were left on the screened porch in July. So if she's the one who wrote that note, then Johnnie Smith is your mother, our son is your father, and we're your..." Her eyes glistened, and she didn't try to wipe away the tear that rolled down her cheek.

"Grandparents," said Hamelin. "And maybe they carved the last initial, the *K*, right before they left me on the stoop."

Everything stopped—the sound of birds, the slight breeze in the air, even the sensation of his own breathing. The Kaleys were staring at him, and it looked like Mrs. Kaley tried to smile but wasn't sure of herself.

For most of his life, Hamelin had secretly hoped this moment would come. When he'd find out who his parents were and maybe even meet his grandparents. He'd tried to imagine it but never really pictured it. Whatever he had expected, it was nothing like this. And now, with no warning, under an old mesquite tree in the woods just north of the children's home—after a bad night's sleep near a cave on the side of a hill—he found out. At least a big part of it. He learned his parents' names and that the Kaleys were his grandparents. And they'd been at the home for more than three years. He stared at them. Three years, and they never told him.

And then certain feelings started to crowd his chest and fill his mind with other thoughts. He knew the Kaleys were there—and maybe he should say something—but his eyes couldn't focus. His surroundings faded away, and the Kaleys seemed a long way off. He didn't know what to think, but he knew what he was feeling, and then the words popped into his mind, and in his head they sounded loud. *Why didn't you tell me?* He looked away and could feel his jaws tighten. Maybe they didn't want him.

Mr. Kaley put a hand on his shoulder. "We're sorry we didn't tell you sooner. It's not because we didn't want it to be true, but it's because we believe it *is* true. We think you even look like our son, Simon, though we didn't get to know our daughter-in-law well enough to know if you resemble her too."

"And," said Mrs. Kaley, "we wanted to protect you."

"Protect me from what?"

"From the same men who were chasing our son and his wife," said Mr. Kaley. "If your parents hid you at the children's home, they did it to protect you, so you wouldn't be captured with them. They did it because they love you, even though it was painful for them."

Hamelin stared at the Kaleys and then glanced down for a moment. When he lifted his eyes again, one last thought came to his mind. "So if my mother wrote that note, it means the two big men that were chasing them were Ren'dal's trackers."

Mr. Kaley nodded. "But your parents saved you before they caught them. And that makes me very proud of my son, because I know for sure that he has grown up, that he's a man now, in spite of his immature behavior as a college student. Never forget, Hamelin, that the mark of a real man is that he sacrifices himself to do what's right, especially to protect the ones he loves."

For a brief instant, Hamelin remembered the times others had called him a man—not only King Carr on his twelfth birthday, and more recently Hargis, but also the eagle back on Christmas Eve, after his first journey to Gloaming. He looked at the tree and then turned toward the cave. He felt a sudden impulse to run back up the hill to the ledge, but he resisted it. The eagle had told him to think. He took a deep breath. Apparently there was more to being a man than turning twelve or even taming a horse.

Chapter 4

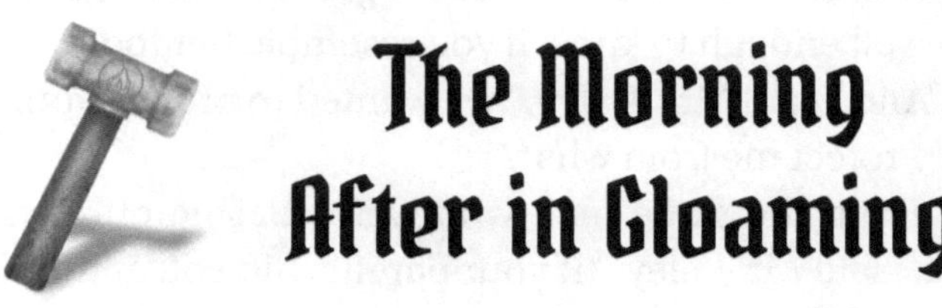

The Morning After in Gloaming

THE TENT WHERE LAYLA SLEPT WAS LARGE ENOUGH TO accommodate the four sisters and Amy. And her bed was comfortable enough—really more than she expected, especially since they were living as an outdoor army in the woods. She was, however, a princess, even though it felt strange to think of herself that way.

But she couldn't sleep. Sophie still lay near death in the hospital tent, and all Layla dreamed about when she occasionally dozed off was the doctors approaching her sister with their strange instruments. So in spite of assurances that nothing else would happen to Sophie that night—at least no more treatments from the doctors—Layla continued to worry. Had she come so far with Amy and the eagle, on the backs of the lion and the great white bull, and survived the attack of the ratsnake just to arrive here in time to see her sister die?

She rose early, while it was still dark, and tried to be quiet and quick. But putting on a bulky dress suitable for a princess slowed her efforts. Finally, she got ready without waking anyone and started making her way toward the hospital tent. At least she could still wear the outdoor shoes she had brought from the other side. They were easier to walk in than her princess slippers and helped her hurry along the path. Within a few minutes, she was able to resume her place at Sophie's bedside, talking to her, patting her hand and arm, and bathing her face.

Shortly after sunup, Layla heard her two other sisters, plus Amy and Lars, talking quietly outside the tent. She knew they would want an update about Sophie, so she stepped outside.

Charissa was the first to see her. "Please tell us you have good news to report."

"Some maybe, though not much. But before I go into that, can you tell me what happened last night after Fearbane caught the dog?"

Eraina frowned. "Charissa and I are not happy about that. We argued against it, but Fearbane followed orders from Father and released the dog."

She shot a glance toward Lars but continued. "I watched him run toward Parthogen, and another dog joined him on the outskirts of camp. So at least two of Landon's despicable creatures must've been prowling about."

"But we do think there were only two," said Lars. "Your father ordered a thorough search of the camp, and I'm sure they're gone for the moment."

Eraina sighed loudly, and Charissa turned again to Layla. "You said you may have a little good news to report?"

Layla shrugged. "Her breathing is faint, and I'm afraid her coma seems deep. But I don't think she's paralyzed. Although not moving much, she does have some reactions in her arms and legs."

Layla took in a deep breath, her lips began to quiver, and within seconds she buried her face in her hands and burst into tears.

Charissa stepped closer and patted her cheek, allowing her sister's head to rest on her shoulder. "Layla, please don't cry. You're working so hard to help Sophie. We don't know what we would do without you."

Layla sobbed. "But I don't know what else to do...those doctors are coming back...and the treatment they're going to try is barbaric...and it could kill Sophie. Can't we do something to stop Father from listening to them?"

Eraina wrapped her arms around Layla's shoulders, and the three of them stood there for long moments. "We'll do everything we can, but Father means well and is determined to do the best he knows—"

"But we know so much more from the other side about medical practices!" Layla looked toward Amy. "Tell them!"

Amy nodded and at the same time nudged the three sisters toward a nearby table. "Layla, you're hardly sleeping, and you haven't eaten anything. Why don't we just sit down for a few minutes. Maybe you all can think of something."

"But we've got to protect Sophie! We don't have time to sit here."

Amy patted her friend on the hand. "Layla, you didn't spend all those years on the other side for nothing. You learned things. Lots of things. So now it's time to think and remember. Why don't you tell your sisters how you learned about medicines and such things, things that they wouldn't know over here. Maybe it'll help you think of something."

They sat at the table, and between sobs Layla did her best to explain. "I've always been interested in health, so I got a job in a pharmacy on the other side while I was a college student. That's a place where medicines are compounded. I heard the pharmacists talk with doctors and also with people who needed medications and other kinds of help. So I learned a lot just by watching and listening."

She paused and looked at her sisters. "I know this sounds strange—but I also learned some things from our grandmother. I still remember her, and even more of my memories are coming back. I may have been only four years old when I was taken away by the white bull, but I have some memories of being with her when she was very old and confined to her room. I went there often and sat next to her. She told me lots of things about herbs and medicines and even strange stories about cures. I listened to her for hours. I wish I could remember more, but I think she must've influenced me a lot. Did you all ever hear her talk about medicines and treatments? And when did she pass away?"

Layla looked to Charissa for a reply, but her eyes were closed and her head turned.

Eraina shifted closer to Layla. "She was already gone when I was born, but how wonderful that you got to listen to her stories and learn things from her. Father sometimes mentions his mother, but I'd love to hear anything you and Charissa remember."

Charissa brushed a tear from her cheek. "Even though I'm the oldest, I didn't spend as much time with her as you did, Layla. She passed away not long after the white bull carried you off, and I missed my chance to be around her. Everything in those days was so sad. I should've spent more time with her, and now I regret it. While you were listening to her, I was more fascinated with the talk of kingdoms and armies, horses and battle plans. Father probably wanted a son instead of a daughter as his oldest, and I sensed it, but for whatever reason, for years I followed him around. Before...before I became so fascinated with clothes and jewelry that I quit listening to Father."

Now it was Layla's turn to pat her older sister's shoulder. "You shouldn't feel bad about spending time with Father. I missed years of that and will never recover them. All of us have our own stories and interests. You were just doing what your heart told you to do. Someday your fascination with kingdoms and battles will pay off.

"And who knows? I'll probably have to relearn some old lessons myself about riding horses into battle."

Charissa smiled, and everyone sat quietly for a few moments.

"Which makes me wonder," said Layla, "about Hamelin. I mean, why was he on that horse, with Sophie behind him? I've known Hamelin longer and better than anyone else here, even though you've had recent, intense adventures with him. But I've known him since he was a baby, and I don't understand what he was doing. Did it have something to do with his parents?"

Layla glanced around, but everyone was quiet. So she didn't wait long for an explanation. She stood and looked toward the hospital tent.

"I may be able to explain some of that," said Lars. "But it's a long story."

As Layla and then Eraina moved away, Charissa rose to join her sisters, but paused. "Lars, the story of the horse may be more involved than you think."

<hr>

Landon took pleasure in controlling his dogs. He also grew accustomed to the signs and smells of animal waste—wet, dry, and piled—that stained the cobblestone streets and walkways of Parthogen and attracted maggots and flies. The dogs, wolves, and half-breeds, with whom he mysteriously communicated, freely roamed the city most days and nights. Their rancid odors, made worse by the heat and stillness of late July, hung in the air, repulsive to all except Landon.

The people who had remained in Parthogen after Landon's takeover of the city regretted their earlier decision to support his disloyalty to Carr, but Landon's charm had convinced them that life would be better under him. Only later did they realize they were now little better than slaves in their own land, with no opportunity to escape. They tried to maintain their homes and their work to take care of children and elderly parents, but life grew harsh. They were required to clean the streets and courtyards of the city, but even then what was swept up was difficult to dispose of or wash away. But they didn't protest, except in whispers to one another, fearful that their words would be reported to Landon through his soldiers or other spies.

Landon hurried early that morning to the special kennels he kept for his canine creatures to make sure they were well fed and rested over the next couple of days and especially to hear a report from the two prized scouts he had sent to Carr's camp. He was eager to learn the reason for the massive banquet held there two nights earlier. He had summoned all of his creatures, and he expected the scouts to return.

He stood outside the entry and watched as they raced into the kennels from every direction, barking and yapping, no doubt glad to have the special treatment they anticipated. As his numerous packs scurried around him, Landon scanned the scene near and far, watching for his scouts. He also listened within his mind, hoping to hear whatever instinctive thoughts they might already be projecting toward him.

And then he saw them bringing up the end of the stream of canines racing toward him. He sensed they were prepared to report on their discoveries, but unlike pets who joyfully greet their masters by leaping into their arms, these two creatures, mixed breeds, slowed down and then stopped before they reached Landon. The larger one had a slight limp. As always, they kneeled with their forepaws stretched out and their heads bowed, unsure whether they would be rewarded or punished.

What happened? barked Landon. *Why are you limping?* He stared at the larger dog.

They averted their eyes as, with muffled howls and guttural whines, they yipped the story of what happened.

Landon understood their message and was furious. He responded with low, growling snarls that morphed into a yapping rant.

You should have been more careful, but they will pay! He glared at the two dogs, who remained before him with heads down. Finally, he changed the subject. *And what about the loud festivities? That's what I sent you there to find out. Don't tell me you didn't learn about that!*

The two creatures responded in a series of barks, conveying what Landon had expected, that the great banquet had been held to celebrate the return of Carr's long-lost daughter, the princess Alathea. He had already been told that she was alive, and now his scouts reported her successful journey on the back of the white bull, the defeat of the poisonous rat-snake in the meadow just south of the camp, and other things they had managed to learn from the banquet and the movements around the camp.

The dogs then fell silent while Landon reflected—angry that the missing daughter was back and that Carr and his people would now try to fulfill the prophecy regarding the four thrones.

I knew she was alive, and now it is left to me to prevent them from occupying the four thrones!

The larger of the two scouts then risked interrupting his master's thoughts with additional growls and even barks, this time even more animated than at first.

The surprising news that Landon had not expected was that one of Carr's other daughters—the youngest, Princess Sophia—had been injured. She fell from a horse just yesterday and now lay hovering between the edges of death and life. Further, that the boy of great strength had been carried away to the south by the eagle and was no longer around.

Perfect. That gave him more time to carry out his special plans. The dogs needed to be rested, but until then the scouts could continue to work.

He looked back to his two animals as they continued to kneel but raised their heads and eyes to meet his, awaiting his instructions.

Go back into Carr's camp and learn anything else that you can. Especially if they are developing any plans for an attack, though I don't expect it now. Carr will be too worried about his ailing daughter. Your job is to give him something else to worry about. You now have permission from me to seize a target of opportunity. If the daughter who is near death can be finished off while no one is looking, then do it. Or if another daughter, especially the one who has just returned, is vulnerable and exposed, eliminate her. I don't mind if it's painful, but just be sure you do it quickly. He held the eyes of the leader. *No more mistakes. And stop limping!*

Landon's two scouts scampered away. He ordered his other creatures to be well fed, penned, and allowed to rest. They would soon have plenty of work to do.

Back at his quarters in the castle, he sat for a long time and reflected. He knew he was under orders to tell Ren'dal everything he learned, but the memory of Ren'dal's pretentious letter made him smirk.

No need to tell his so-called brothers that the missing princess was back since she would soon no longer be a problem. And why bother talking about the boy of great strength? For now, he was gone, but they didn't need to know any of that. Let them worry about his whereabouts. Who knew where he was anyway? After all, his plans required the utmost secrecy. He'd show them. But especially his father. Chimera would soon see that he, Landon, should be his favored son—the one he should appoint as leader—and not Ren'dal.

Chapter 5

Morning, Afternoon, and Night

AFTER THEIR OUTDOOR BREAKFAST, HAMELIN AND THE Kaleys returned to the children's home. They agreed to keep the Kaleys' story and the likelihood that they were his grandparents a secret, but it gave Hamelin a lot to think about. For the rest of the morning, he wandered around the grounds of the home—frustrated and at times even angry. But mostly confused. Now what should he do? Would this help him find his parents? Or hurt his chances to go back? Why did he even get on that horse?

Near lunchtime, he found himself next to the barn where Mr. Moore usually kept his old tractor and also had his tools and workshop. He could hear a motor running and some crackling noises. Mr. Moore must be welding something inside.

Hamelin enjoyed watching him work, but as soon as he walked in, the older man turned off his welding torch and lifted the guard from his eyes. Mr. Moore's skin was fair but weather-beaten. His head was mostly bald, but he showed traces of what once might have been reddish hair. He wiped the sweat from his face and smiled at his young friend. His blue eyes sparkled.

At first Hamelin was afraid Mr. Moore was going to ask about Bryan and Layla, but the older man always seemed to sense when it was good not to ask a lot of questions. That was one reason Hamelin liked to be around him, in addition to the fact that Mr. Moore knew a lot of interesting things.

"Morning," he said. "Looks like it's going to be a pretty hot day—could raise blisters on a lizard. Might be a good day for swimming."

Hamelin shrugged. "Maybe. But I just thought I'd see what you were doing. Okay if I stay in here?"

"Sure, but I got to finish up this welding. Remember, don't stare at the light."

Hamelin had noticed that people always looked away whenever a welding torch was lit and gave off a popping flash. But he also knew that even after the flare, they didn't look without eye protection. "You told me once before that it can hurt your eyes," said Hamelin. "Why is that? Is it the flash?"

"Well, the glare can burn your eyes, that's for sure; but it's not just when you light it up. It's everything—the sparks, the light, even the heat if you get too close. They all kind of go together. Welding and metal cutting take heat, and where you have heat, you can have light and sparks. You have to be careful with your eyes when it comes to welding."

Mr. Moore pulled his eye guard back in place and leaned over to restart the torch. It popped. Hamelin walked to a corner of the workshop and sat next to a cardboard box and a couple of old work gloves that Mr. Moore had pitched there. He leaned back against the wood framework of the old barn and just watched, taking care not to stare at the light, though he could feel the heat from the welding torch. Even from a distance, it warmed his face.

Hamelin kept his eyes closed, and soon his late-night activities—especially climbing the hill—and his uncomfortable sleep on the rock floor of the ledge caught up with him. He wanted to think more about his parents and the Kaleys but started to doze off.

As he sat half asleep and half awake, the heat and the blowing sound from the acetylene torch created a dream-like memory that drew his mind back to the Atrium—when he had stood hot, thirsty, and dazed, looking at his reflection in the pond but also hearing the whooshing of the eagle as the great bird flew at high speed in a circular fashion, his wings pummeling the air.

Suddenly Hamelin heard a different noise—a big pop as Mr. Moore turned off the torch—and his vision of the eagle and the Atrium vanished. He opened his eyes and remembered where he was. The sound of blowing wind had stopped, but he felt something light and fluffy on his forearm, right where his elbow rested on the cardboard box.

It took a second for his eyes to focus, but then he saw it. A large brown spider, with a black line on its back and other markings that looked like a violin pointing down its body. "*Yi!*" yelled Hamelin as he simultaneously whacked the long, fluffy-legged creature away from his right arm with a single backhanded swipe of his left hand.

Mr. Moore rushed over. "Did he bite you? That looked like a fiddleback. You feel anything? Because if he bit you—"

"No, I don't think he bit me."

"You'd know if he did. Those things sting bad, and are poisonous. If you got bit, it'll flare up real quick, and there'll be a big spot there. It doesn't hurt?"

"No, I'm okay."

Mr. Moore stared at Hamelin's arm. "I got a good look at him—or her, I should say. "Definitely a fiddleback. And big enough to be a momma spider full of eggs, ready to give off a bunch of babies. It's that time of year here in Texas. I shoulda thought of it when you sat down. I've seen a few here in the barn. They like to make their webs and hiding places in sheds, especially around old wood. Could have been in that cardboard box. I better do some spraying."

"I've never seen one before," said Hamelin. "Never even heard of them."

"A lot of people haven't. But you'll find them here in Texas and Oklahoma. They usually don't come after you, unless they think you're bothering them. But if they get you, they can make you really sick or even..."

"Anyway, you sat down next to some gloves. They like to hide out in old clothes and shoes. Good thing you wasn't bit, because before you know it, you'd start sloughing off a big chunk of skin. They're bad."

"What kind of spider did you say it was?" asked Hamelin.

"I called it a fiddleback, but I think the right proper name is brown recluse. My daddy told me they have six eyes, but I never got close enough to one to tell. Whatever you call it, you don't want to mess with it. And that was sure a big one."

"Is it still around here anywhere? I wouldn't mind squashing it if I could."

"Don't worry about that," said Mr. Moore. "Ain't no shame in stayin' away from something bad. Just let 'em be. No sense looking for 'em and stirring 'em up when you're dealing with spiders like that. Of course, if one jumps on you, then you gotta swat him away hard—just like you done. My dad always said a good man does what he's supposed to do without picking a fight. 'Course, if the fight comes to him, then he'll do what he's got to do."

———⊙———

By the time Hamelin got back to the main house, lunch had already started, and he was surprised to see Mrs. Eastland talking to Mr. and Mrs. Kaley at one of the tables. She knew about Hamelin's journeys and for years had assisted others, including Layla, in traveling back and forth to Gloaming. She helped Hamelin when she could as part of her work for the Ancient One, who was the rightful ruler of Gloaming, in spite of the treacheries of Chimera and his sons.

As soon as lunch ended, Mr. Kaley gave him a nod and tilted his head toward their apartment. Hamelin waited until most of the other children had left the dining hall before making his way to the Kaleys' living room. The door was open, and Mrs. Kaley waved him in. The three adults were already seated around the coffee table.

Mrs. Eastland smiled at Hamelin and said only a quick hello before she began talking. Hamelin noticed that she spoke a little faster than usual. "The Kaleys told me about your night on the ledge," she said. "I know you must be tired, but I had to come back here to give you a message. After you told us your story yesterday evening, about how the eagle brought you back and said you might not be called to Gloaming again, I went home and did my best throughout the night to listen for any messages from the other side. I wasn't sure what to expect, given what you had said, but to my surprise I did pick up some vague instructions. I'm confident you'll be going back, and I wanted to tell you to be ready."

"I hope I can go back," said Hamelin, "but I'm not sure they'll want me. I really messed up."

"I understand," she said. "And you explained what happened. We all appreciate how bad you must feel. But I also know what I heard. I don't know much beyond that, but I'm very confident you're going to be called back."

"I'm surprised that you would hear anything this soon," said Mrs. Kaley. "Are you sure?"

"I admit that what I've been told lacks detail," said Mrs.

Eastland. "I don't know how or when, but I'm sure I was told that Hamelin would be returning. I'd like to stay out here for the rest of the day, if I can, and maybe even spend the night. I think there's something about being close to the cave that may help me receive communications from the other side. I just need a quiet place where I can be by myself."

Mr. Kaley looked at his wife. "I think we can help with that."

"Of course," she said. "We have a guest room right here in our apartment, and you're welcome to it for as long as you need it. You can just stay in the room, and we'll even bring you your meals whenever you want. Sometimes the kids can be a little loud, and the swimming pool is on our side of the house, so there may be some outside noise, but we'd love to have you."

Mrs. Eastland's face brightened. "That's no problem. I can close the doors, and I'll be able to concentrate. Remember, I'm a schoolteacher, and I'm used to children's voices." She looked at Hamelin and smiled. And as bad as he felt because of what he had done, it seemed like approval.

Hamelin was tired even though it was still early in the afternoon. He considered taking a nap, but Billy and Charles persuaded him to go swimming. He was glad to hear he would be returning to the other side, but after what the eagle had said, he figured it wouldn't be soon.

Swimming with Billy and Charles reminded him that he should talk to Paul, but he pushed the thought away. That would give him something to do tomorrow, though he found himself wondering just what they would talk about, since Paul would find it hard to understand anything as strange as his story.

By the end of an afternoon of swimming, Hamelin was exhausted. Supper was good, but he didn't eat much. And when it was over, he made his way upstairs without talking to anyone. His plan was to read a little bit and then fall asleep early. He was looking forward to a good night's rest.

⸺ ⟨◉⟩ ⸺

Layla woke up startled from a late nap. The fragment of a dream had been floating through her mind, but it darted away as she blinked her surroundings into reality—and now she couldn't remember it. After speaking with Amy, Lars, and her sisters, she had returned to Sophie's side and stayed there all afternoon. Finally, Charissa and Eraina had insisted she take a short rest in the girls' tent before returning. But her long hours of caring for Sophie since the accident two days ago had left her exhausted. She had fallen asleep, and now it appeared to be past sundown and the light was fading. No one had come back to the tent to get her. Where were they? Her worries grew when she noticed a shadow lingering outside, then drifting away.

Was that an animal or a person? An old memory about a dog passed like a dark cloud through her mind. She groped toward the nightstand near her, found the ring her grandmother had given her, and slipped it on.

She took a deep breath and hurried toward the hospital tent. On the way, the horrible tools for trephining that the doctors had brought to Sophie's bedside popped into her mind. Her father had not yet agreed to the procedure, as far as she knew, but Sophie hadn't improved, and she had seen the doctors whispering to him. But he had promised that nothing more would be done to Sophie that night—Wait! When was that? Last night? What time was it now? She quickened her pace as her mind raced with fears.

She remembered reading about trephining in one of her medieval history books. It was a primitive treatment, and she had once even heard the pharmacist where she worked say something about it in jest. But however she had learned the word, it was an ancient practice now agreed to have been misguided at best. Scraping or drilling a quarter-sized hole in someone's head to relieve pressure after a trauma—or to allow bad spirits to escape, as some suggested—was dangerous!

The darkness was falling rapidly, but Layla made her way with the help of light from the tents scattered here and there in the camp. She could also see a partial moon just above her to the east, but its light didn't help. Suddenly she caught a glimpse of movement on the ground a short distance ahead of her. What was that? Whatever it was crossed in front of her and vanished in the shadows. Did it slip behind her? She paused momentarily and turned around but saw nothing except a big soldier turning away from her. Where had he come from? Surely he was one of theirs

Her mind jumped back to the darkness of that miserable night nearly two weeks ago in Abilene. Whatever moved, it was way bigger than a rat! And it didn't look like a snake! And then she remembered last night…Landon's dog… She tried to smile at herself, but instead she felt a chill in her back. She started to run, but her bulky clothes slowed her down.

The tent where her little sister lay unconscious was just ahead. She could see lights inside and the shadows of several people moving around. Then everyone stood still, and some-one seemed to be leaning over Sophie's bed.

They can't be trephining! She opened her mouth to shout *"No!"* and tried to run faster, but she sensed something rush-ing at her from the side. It brushed against her right leg, and then she felt a sharp pain in her ankle.

The effect was immediate. She lost her balance and had just enough time to thrust her hands forward to brace for a stumbling fall. Before she hit the ground, something else—a creature of some sort—gave off a loud, sustained snarl and slammed hard into her shoulders from the left side. It was a glancing blow, but it was close enough for her to hear the snap of teeth. She also felt hot breath and smelled animal fur, followed by the sting of a gash at the base of her neck. Whatever it was flew on past her and hit the ground at the same time she did, rolling away from her, but not far.

She scrambled to her hands and knees and swung her right arm wildly in the direction of the attacking animal. *"No!"* she yelled at the very moment she heard a snarl followed immediately by voices and people coming toward her. She looked in the direction of her attacker and from somewhere had enough light to see. A wolf dog! And then a smaller canine came slinking out of the darkness, stopping just behind the other.

The approaching voices grew louder, and the smaller of the two creatures backed away into the shadows. The larger dog, however, lowered its chest and back legs. Then with a loud, sustained growl and its forelegs outstretched, it leaped toward Layla, its full body silhouetted against the available light, its maw drooling and teeth glinting.

In that instant, she raised herself to her knees and slashed her right arm in a karate chop toward the flying assailant. She felt her hand scrape against the creature's sharp teeth, and a split second before its jaws snapped shut on her hand, a tall, solidly built soldier, racing toward the point of attack, slammed his halberd broadside into the wolf dog's body. The animal howled as the force of the blow knocked its head and body away from Layla. The soldier then drew his sword and struck again. And again.

Carr and his physicians emerged from the hospital tent and rushed toward Layla. The wounds on her foot and neck needed bandaging but were not deep; her right hand was bloody but not mangled. The soldier's halberd had landed just in time, as had the sword.

More voices and steps—shouting and running—came from all

directions, but they weren't needed: the dog lay bloody and life-less on the ground, gaping wounds in his neck and body. Several soldiers arrived just before Lars, Amy, Eraina, and Charissa. Meanwhile, the tall soldier who had saved Layla vanished.

Carr's physicians rushed Layla into the tent, but before she would allow them to wash and bandage her wounds, she hurried to Sophie's bed and looked especially at her head, then lightly touched a small bare spot where it had been shaved. She turned to the king and spoke, in a voice that surprised even her for its boldness.

"Father, surely you weren't going to allow them to do trephining, were you?"

King Carr dropped his eyes before looking into Layla's. "My dear, I would do anything, even give my life, to protect any of you, my daughters. So I must listen to my physicians, who tell me this procedure has to be done."

"Father, please! I know these physicians are men of great experience and knowledge, but I have come from a world—and there's so much I can tell you about it—that is several centuries ahead when it comes to matters of medicine. You must believe me when I tell you that this is no longer done there. She could suffer infection and brain damage. We realize people in the past thought they were doing the right thing, but we now know so much more. I beg you, don't do this to Sophie!"

The king looked at his physicians. "We have enough to concern us tonight with taking care of Princess Alathea, so please attend to her. We will discuss what to do with Princess Sophia later."

As the physicians treated Layla's wounds, Carr caught her eye. "I understand what you're telling me, but Sophie must show some improvement soon. According to my doctors, we don't have a lot of time. So if there is something you know that can help, you must do it."

"Father, I promise you. I'll use everything I've learned from the other side of the Atrium, as well as the wisdom of your mother, my grandmother, to bring Sophie through this."

Just as the king kissed Layla on the cheek and turned one last time to kiss Sophie, Fearbane entered the tent. They whispered briefly, and within another minute Fearbane brought in the soldier who had rescued Layla. She recognized him immediately but didn't speak, because of the doctors still bandaging her hand.

"Your Majesty." The tall young man removed his helmet to reveal a head of dark hair. "I ran to catch the other dog, but he escaped. He hightailed it back toward the city walls, so I am confident he was one of Landon's creatures, but I believe there were only two."

"You did well to protect the princess," said Carr. "Please tell us your name."

"My name is Justin."

"And your father's name?"

"I come from the family of your loyal subject Gilbert. My father no longer lives."

"Wasn't your father a craftsman from a village on the outskirts of Parthogen?"

"Yes, Your Majesty."

"His reputation survives him. He was a craftsman of great renown, especially known for his faithful service to his many friends. All of the families there remain loyal to us."

"My father's last wish," said Justin, "was that I should come here to serve you, my king."

"You have already well fulfilled your father's hopes. We are much in your debt for the service you've rendered to our family."

The soldier dropped his eyes. "I only wish I'd acted sooner, before Princess Alathea was attacked. I was doing my best, as instructed by Commander Fearbane, to watch out for her. But..." He stole a quick glance at Layla.

"I tried to stay nearby, though not so close as to embarrass my lady. I followed her as she hurried toward this tent, but I failed to prevent her injuries. The wolf dogs who attacked must have been hidden in the shadows. I am grateful for Your Majesty's praise of my actions, but I never detected the creatures by either sight or sound until...I'm sorry."

"I understand your regrets," said the king. "But we are still grateful to you. Landon bears full responsibility. What else can you tell me about the events of tonight?"

"Princess Alathea was rushing toward this tent, and I was keeping up, though there was only enough light for me to see shadows in the darkness. Too late I saw something dart toward her—most likely the smaller wolf dog—and nip at her heels.

"Then the princess stumbled and began to fall. That's when the big creature came out of the darkness. I heard him before I saw him. He snarled and knocked her down, and even then it was so dark it was all hard to see."

"But you must have seen well enough to strike that first blow," said the king. "It was well aimed and very timely."

"Yes, Your Majesty, especially once the light appeared—"

"What light?" Layla had heard everything and couldn't stop herself from asking.

"I'm sorry, my lady," said Justin. "I confess not to know its source, and at that moment I didn't have time to consider the question. But it was a new light that enabled me to see well enough to act."

The tall man looked away and slightly up, apparently weighing his thoughts. Finally he spoke. "I'm afraid my words will sound odd and perhaps even confusing. But now that I think about it, it's almost as if..." He lowered his eyes.

"It's all right," said Carr. "You've acted bravely, so we trust your words. Please tell us what you saw."

"I mean no disrespect to Princess Alathea, Your Majesty," said Justin. "But what I observed was this. Once she was knocked down, a faint light—maybe it was more like a glow—began to shine all about her. And that's when I could see well enough to know that the wolf dog was about to strike again. So I rushed toward her for all I was worth and swung my halberd."

"Just in time," said Layla. "And your words are neither embarrassing nor disrespectful. What you've described is not completely unknown to me, but you've given me some new things to think about."

Carr again expressed his thanks to the tall soldier and sent him on his way.

He then turned to Layla. "I'll be interested to hear your thoughts about these matters. But for now you need to rest."

"I'll try, Father, but I'll be staying in this tent tonight, watching my sister." She let the physicians finish their bandaging and then placed a chair next to Sophie's bed and took her by the hand. The king again kissed his two girls and left.

Layla's attention was focused on Sophie, but she couldn't help wondering about the light that had shone from her. She had noticed it as well after she'd been struck from each side and knocked to the ground. And she remembered a glowing all around her when she had spoken to the seven-headed snake on the ledge—before the serpent struck. And then there was the light in the meadow that had momentarily delayed the rat snake's attack and enabled her friends, especially Hamelin, to defeat the strange creature. But this time was different—it was only after she was attacked and wounded that the light had come. What did that mean?

Layla squeezed her sister's hand, but there was no response. Sometimes Sophie's skin was clammy, but now her forehead felt hot. Layla dipped a soft cloth into cool water and gently bathed her little sister. As she did so, the ring her grandmother had given her caught her eye, and she tried to remember more of what that wise woman had told her, but it was no use. It only made her wish that she were with her now to advise and help—which certainly was impossible.

Chapter 6

Late at Night

KING CARR LEFT THE TENT, LOST IN THOUGHT. IT WAS night, but his people weren't asleep, and he understood their restlessness. Word of the attack against Alathea had spread rapidly, and additional torches and watch fires lit the camp everywhere. The hour of decision-making was approaching, and the weight of that burden pressed on his mind. He had not taken many steps when he heard an animated, at times loud, conversation between several people. The voices were familiar. The sounds led him toward his quarters, and just as he passed between two tents of soldiers, he veered left and saw four people just outside his tent. Even in the dark, he could tell who it was: Charissa, Fearbane, Eraina, and Lars.

This was not casual talk. Charissa's arms were extended with palms up, and although Fearbane occasionally nodded in deference to the princess, his voice grew louder. Eraina looked up and saw her father. She cleared her throat, and they paused.

"I can guess what you are discussing," Carr said with no hint of a smile. "Something to do with tonight's attack on Princess Alathea?"

"You are of course correct, Sire," said Fearbane. "Princess Charissa and I are having a spirited disagreement, but I do concede that she was right earlier. I should have advised a stronger response last night when Landon's two scouts showed up and one of them was prowling in the hospital tent."

"But now you don't agree on what to do next?" asked the king.

"We agree that something must be done, but, as before, we are of different minds as to the strategy. I am suggesting that we indeed send the carcass of this creature back in a bag, demonstrating to Landon that we are not to be trifled with."

"And what say you, my daughter?" said the king.

"It's not enough." She bit off her words. "That might have been sufficient last night, but the stakes are higher now. Once again there were two dogs, and one of those wolfish creatures made an all-out attack on our sister Layla. None of us dares to imagine what would have happened if that brave soldier hadn't intervened. Indeed, the loss of one dog for Landon is completely disproportionate to an attack by two dogs on a single person, especially a princess. And there's no telling what else they might have done had they succeeded against Layla. They were, after all, once again lurking around Sophie's tent."

Fearbane shrugged. "But are we sure that Landon knows what his dogs did? If he doesn't, then he would never perceive our response as justified."

"He knows *exactly* what he sent them to do," said Charissa. "Those wolf dogs wouldn't dare disobey him by doing any more or any less than he either permitted or commanded."

Fearbane looked toward the king. "But this still is not the time for an all-out attack. If we do more than send back one carcass, then he will likely escalate his efforts. As things stand right now, he'll never start an attack—"

"Are we so sure?" asked Charissa. "You keep saying that, but Landon's actions don't match your speculations."

"My lady, I'm not speculating—"

"Nor am I! I know for certain that he just attacked our family!"

"But, my lady, you can't allow this to be personal—"

"Of course it's personal! Those are my *sisters* his dogs have been coming for—but it's more than that. When the attack involves two *princesses*, then Landon is not just attacking two young women—as cowardly as that is. He's striking at members of the *royal family*, the rulers and representatives of Parthogen. He knows exactly what he's doing!"

Eraina abruptly pointed her index finger toward Fearbane. "And he knows the four thrones prophecy just as well as we do! Of *course* he knows what he's doing! This was an attempt to destroy the hopes of our people by voiding the prophecy of seating four princesses on their thrones!"

The volume of irritation in Charissa's voice rose. "I agree with my sister! Landon is trying to win the conflict before it ever starts, by killing at least one of the four future rulers of Parthogen."

Carr took in a deep breath and let it out. He turned toward Fearbane. "How do you respond to that?"

"I am sworn by duty, loyalty, and devotion to protect all of you, and your people, so my words are only differences of strategy, not intent, but I still maintain that this is not the time for an all-out attack."

Charissa exploded with a sighing groan. "Once again, you misunderstand my words! I am not proposing a frontal assault, at least not now. But I'm not willing—nor should any of us be—to let one defensively slain dog stand as compensation—as justice—for what Landon has done."

"Besides," said Eraina, "our people are now fearful. They've lit extra fires and torches all around the camp and want to know what we're going to do. If we don't respond..." She looked at her father, her eyes pleading.

"But killing one of Landon's dogs *is* a response," said Fearbane. "And sending it back with an armed contingent and leaving the bloody carcass at the city gates will certainly send him a message."

Charissa looked at Fearbane and shook her head. "But it's the wrong message! It's weak and not proportional to an attack upon our household, the seat of our government, and thus our kingdom itself! It will invite another attack!"

Charissa then turned to her father. "Eraina is right. Our people have great hopes for the future, and now they are fearful. Compassion for them demands a response—to protect and encourage. We must do something that measures out justice for what Landon has done and also adds a new level of deterrence to prevent any further outrages on his part."

The king studied Charissa's face. "You and Fearbane agree that something must be done. We've heard his proposed action, my daughter. What do you suggest as a necessary response?"

"I say that we make use of Eraina's ability to see great distances and Lars's gifts of balance and speed to launch a limited attack, but one that hits at the heart of Landon's power."

Carr wrinkled his forehead. "But his powers lie as much with his dogs and the influence he has on them as with his soldiers."

"I agree, Father. So we can't do something that simply puts a few of his soldiers at risk—and we certainly should not endanger the people in Parthogen. Some of them are still loyal to us, but they are trapped there, captive to Landon's treachery once he took over the city. But whatever we do, it must be secretive, quick, and forceful. And it must hit Landon hard."

Fearbane appeared eager to respond, but Carr raised his

hand and looked again toward Charissa. "You'll have to be more specific."

"I would threaten Landon's dogs. He depends upon them. He has some kind of strange, dark connection with them and is able to order them around. They were key to his ability to capture our city years ago, so the dogs are where we start. First, I propose that Eraina be ready to tell us when the dogs are not penned up. Can you use your special scarf to do that?"

"Of course." Eraina spread the scarf SueSue had given her over her head and looked toward the city. "I can tell you right now that the kennels are poorly built wooden pens on the north side of the city, downwind from the prevailing southerly breeze, and I can see at any time what Landon is doing with his dogs. At the moment, he has them penned up, but I can easily let you know when they're loose in the city."

Charissa turned to Lars. "Are you willing to take some risk?"

He came forward a step. "Not only willing, but eager. What do you have in mind?"

"At this point, my thoughts are preliminary and require further discussion, but I would suggest that, once we know the dogs are roaming around Parthogen, we have a small contingent of well-armed soldiers create a disturbance in the southwest, just outside the city gates and far away from the pens.

"Lars, with his unusual skills, can then sneak over the city walls on the northeast side, throw the carcass just outside the kennels, and set fire to the pens. None of the dogs will be harmed, not even the carcass, but Landon will get the message—that his dogs are not safe from us. We'll depend upon Eraina to watch it all so that these moves are well-timed.

"Once Lars escapes back over the walls, the diversion at the southwest corner can cease and our soldiers return. There would be other details to work out to make sure the strategy is sound and minimizes risk to our soldiers and Lars, but something of this sort will do what we want—Landon will get the message. He'll know that he is vulnerable—and especially his precious wolf dogs."

The king lowered his hand and looked toward Fearbane. He saw something in his face he seldom observed: doubt. "What do you think of this plan?"

Fearbane cleared his throat, glanced at Charissa, and then turned to the king. "Sire, I must admit that Princess Charissa's ideas have merit. With your permission, we can see what our chief strategists think as to the details."

Carr looked at those around him and knew the time for listening and gathering opinions was over. They were counting on him as king to make a decision, but he didn't feel like a king. In fact, at that moment he didn't want to be king. He glanced back toward the hospital tent, where he knew Layla was taking care of Sophie, and he longed to go there and sit at Sophie's bedside. To escape... And then he looked again to those near him—to Eraina, Charissa, Lars, and Fearbane. They were searching his face, waiting for him to speak. But he didn't see princesses, the young prince, or even his own commander, who was older than the others but still a young man to Carr. He saw the children they had once been, and in that moment he wouldn't allow himself to be the king. He was a father.

His vision narrowed, and though an inner voice tried to argue—to make him see other people, the families and the soldiers who were depending on him as their ruler—he shook his head to chase the thought away. His feelings overtook his mind, and anger—or was that resentment?—rose in him. He hadn't asked to be king! Nor had he chosen it. The role was his by birth. But being a father...he had gladly chosen that, hadn't he? Did anything else matter?

Long moments passed. Finally, he took a deep breath and shook his head. "I'm sorry, but I cannot bring myself to order such a retaliation. Only a few days ago we were all full of joy when my Layla returned, but now...such provocative action seems risky...and this plan exposes Prince Lars to much danger—"

Lars took a half step toward the king. "But, Your Majesty, I would gladly—"

Carr put a firm hand on Lars's shoulder. "No, brave prince. We are too vulnerable. I can't risk provoking a war that would require us to move Sophia while she barely clings to life. And the risk to my other daughters also is great. Landon has demonstrated that he's perfectly willing..."

Carr ducked his head. But then lifted his eyes toward Charissa. "Your thoughts are bold, my dear, but I cannot order even their consideration."

"But, Father. We know you love us and want to protect us, but there are others... Your subjects, their families, Parthogen itself, and the whole land of Gloaming must be considered."

Carr lifted his head and straightened his shoulders. "Landon will not attack us." His voice was firm, almost loud. "He has all the advantages of walls and the high ground. And his supply lines are intact. And Sophia is...so now is not the time to act. My mind is made up."

Charissa raised her hands to object but took a deep breath and stopped herself. "We will of course defer to your wishes... Father."

As the king walked away, he ordered Fearbane to double the guard around the hospital tent and provide special protection for Charissa, Eraina, Amy, and Prince Lars. Then he whispered more instructions to Fearbane. Charissa took a deep breath and walked toward her tent, waving away Fearbane's attempt to escort her. Eraina followed her sister. Lars offered to find a torch and assist the king, but Carr declined his company and made his way to his tent, alone and in the dark.

Late that night, Eraina found it hard to sleep, and she sensed that Charissa was still awake in the bed next to hers.

Eraina whispered. "Things have changed so much in just two days."

She heard Charissa roll over and continued. "We were celebrating the return of Layla, planning her debut as a princess. Hamelin was with us, and we could hardly have been more hopeful about the future. But now…"

Charissa sat up. "Now Sophie lies near death, and Layla won't leave her bedside, even though there's still no response from her. Hamelin has been taken away, and we have no prospect of his return. And Landon gets more aggressive by the day…and our father is unwilling to respond."

"Speaking of Father, did you by any chance hear what he whispered to Fearbane?"

"I did." Charissa clipped her words, and her voice betrayed notes of emotion, even pain. "He told Fearbane not to engage me in any more strategic conversations."

Eraina took a deep breath and let it out. "We need some good news…soon."

⸺ ⟪◉⟫ ⸺

Hamelin lay in bed reading *The Hobbit*, the book by J. R. R. Tolkien that Layla had given him last Christmas. He couldn't remember exactly why he hadn't finished it, but he recalled thinking back then that maybe he was too old for it. Now, however, as soon as he picked up the book and started to read, it transported him to the Shire and the world of hobbits.

He read for long minutes and then remembered the expression Layla had used, something about "hearing the horns of Elfland." But instead of Elfland, he couldn't help thinking about the Land of Gloaming, the other world he had gone into—one that was real, not like the world of Bilbo Baggins.

But then he stopped. *How do I know that? I would've thought the Land of Gloaming wasn't real either, until I went there.* He needed to think, so he laid his open book on his chest and closed his eyes.

He began to relive his adventures of the past four years—starting with the night he ran away from the children's home after everyone forgot his eighth birthday. The storm, the cave, the eagle, the bridge, plus recovering the jewel and rescuing Charissa. And only recently defeating the rat-snake and helping Layla return to her family in Gloaming.

But these moments of excitement brought to mind other things, some terrible mistakes he had made. Worse than just mistakes. What he had done was wrong. And he knew it. His breathing grew shallow and rapid, and even with his eyes still closed, the darkness in his mind grew blacker.

He had been really stupid. He'd messed up so bad that he would never go back to Gloaming. If he ever traveled to other worlds again, it would only be in fairy books.

Then Hamelin thought of the eagle's last words. The great bird didn't say he would never go back. He said maybe this would turn out to be "a painful mercy." What did that mean? What was he supposed to do now? And then he remembered that the eagle also told him to be quiet and think. He put away the book and turned off his light.

But it was hard to be quiet and just think. Other thoughts and scenes kept interrupting. He saw himself losing the sword to Romulus and then, even worse, he remembered Sophie and his foolish actions with the horse. It was painful. *Where's the mercy in that?* Maybe there was still hope, but he couldn't feel it. Still, the eagle always chose his words carefully. He closed his eyes and tried to think some more.

And in the quietness of his thoughts, he knew the truth. That if he didn't go back, it was his own fault...there was nobody else to blame. He hadn't listened. He had heard others speak but hadn't liked their words, so he had done everything he could to twist them to suit his plans. He had done that even after SueSue's warning. And he had done it again after learning about the special papers in the saddle bag. Sophie had spoken wise words, as usual—and he had just used them to do what he wanted.

*But I want to find my parents, and I want to know my real name...*and he realized this was where he often went off track. SueSue said he could maybe find his parents, but there were things that came first. He tried to focus on all the other things he was supposed to do, the tasks she had given him—to help his friends with their quests against Chimera's sons, to keep the scabbard away from the sword, and throw the hammer at just the right time.

He thought he heard a low rumble of thunder in the distance, but sleep was finally overtaking him. His last thoughts were about how much he wanted to prove to the others that he really was a man.

Chapter 7

The Wee Hours

HAMELIN HEARD THE CRACK OF LIGHTNING AND THE HEAVY rain, even before he woke up. It was the second loud clap of thunder and the wind rattling the windows that made him open his eyes and quickly sit up. The boys' bedroom was still dark, and he figured he must have slept for a couple of hours. The sounds of the wind and rain grew louder, followed by another crack of lightning. That one was close.

He quietly made his way outside the boys' bedroom. The suddenness of it all reminded him of the July storm almost exactly four years ago, when he first found the cave. He looked over the railing from the second floor and saw that he wasn't the only one curious about the extreme weather. Mr. Kaley was standing at a window in the foyer, looking outside. Hamelin slipped down the stairs and joined him.

"I've always liked watching a storm blow in," said Mr. Kaley. "There's just something about seeing the sheets of rain and the water beginning to run along the ground."

Suddenly a jagged bolt of lightning lit up their entire view.

Hamelin pressed his face closer to the window. "What's that out there in the yard?"

"I don't know," said Mr. Kaley. "It almost looks like a scarecrow."

Another crack of lightning hit, and they both leaned forward to detect what was in the front yard.

"It looks like somebody standing out there in the rain," said Hamelin.

Mr. Kaley jerked open the front door and then stepped outside onto the front porch. Then another lightning display lit up the western sky, and Hamelin pointed at whoever it was, standing with arms outstretched and looking to the right, to the northwest. "I think it's a woman!" He ran out into the rain, and Mr. Kaley followed.

Hamelin approached the figure, and she turned toward him. It was a woman with drenched clothing and her hair stuck to her head and face. She looked skyward but then lowered her head and arms, and their eyes met.

"Mrs. Eastland!" yelled Hamelin.

At the same moment, Mr. Kaley spoke. "Virginia, what are you doing out here? You're soaking wet! Let's get you inside to—"

"I've been listening."

"But you said you had to be in a quiet place," he shouted as another loud peal of thunder rolled across the skies.

"I did say that, and that's what I've always done before, but this time I heard something...the thunder."

"I'm sure everybody in the county has heard it! But—"

"But there was a voice in it. And now I know."

"A voice? We've got to get you inside," said Mr. Kaley. "I'll go get Margaret." He hurried back to the house.

Mrs. Eastland turned to Hamelin and put a hand on his shoulder. The rain continued to pour, but she seemed completely undisturbed by it. "I've received word that you're being summoned."

"When?" asked Hamelin.

Before she could answer, Mr. Kaley returned with an umbrella, followed by Mrs. Kaley in her nightgown and robe. She touched Mrs. Eastland's forearm. "Virginia, come with me! We've got to get you some dry clothes."

"Hamelin's being summoned again."

"No one can go anywhere in this rain!" said Mrs. Kaley.

"He'll have to. I've heard from the other side, and there's no time to waste."

"Well...maybe John can take him to the hill as soon as it's light."

"No! He has to go now."

"This is no place to argue," said Mr. Kaley.

Mrs. Kaley put her arm around Mrs. Eastland. "Let's get inside."

"I'll go inside, but this is a matter of life and death."

They hurried up the porch and into the house. Once in the foyer, Mrs. Eastland stopped. "No further!"

The four of them stood for a moment, dripping all over the floor. Mrs. Kaley touched Mrs. Eastland's hair. "You're soaking wet, Virginia! You'll get sick!"

Mrs. Eastland wouldn't budge. She stared at Mr. Kaley. "Now. Life and death."

Mr. Kaley paused only a second more before he told Hamelin to get ready and asked Mrs. Kaley to pack him something to eat.

She tried to object, but Mr. Kaley met her eyes with his. "Margaret, Virginia didn't say whose life is at stake. We have no choice. Hamelin has to go, and we've got to help him." She shook her head as she rushed off to the kitchen.

Hamelin ran upstairs and changed clothes. He put on a pair of blue jeans, a long-sleeved cotton shirt, and a pair of walking shoes. Then he strapped on the scabbard, felt the outside of it to make sure the hammer was still there, and stuffed his pock-etknife and his special gloves into his pockets. A couple of the boys stirred in their beds as Hamelin changed.

"What's all the noise?" someone muttered.

"A storm," said Hamelin as he rushed away.

By the time he charged back downstairs, Mr. Kaley and Mrs. Eastland were standing on the porch. The rain had slowed but was still steady. Moments later, Mrs. Kaley joined them and handed Hamelin a backpack. "I wanted to pack more, but you've got a sandwich in there and a canteen of water."

"He'll need it all," said Mrs. Eastland.

Mrs. Kaley kissed Hamelin on the cheek, and he and Mr. Kaley sloshed through the muddy yard to Mr. Kaley's pickup. They were surprised that Mrs. Eastland came with them, but they didn't object. Hamelin sat between the two rain-soaked adults, and in spite of sliding some on the slippery road, Mr. Kaley quickly got them to the foot of the hill.

"Hamelin, I've started keeping a flashlight here in the truck. You should take it."

"I won't need it. The eagle always provides the light."

Mrs. Eastland patted his knee. "I think you'd better take it. The eagle's not going to be there."

"Is the chariot coming again? It has a lot of light."

"No. You're going through the cave, but you're supposed to go a different way...and you'll be on your own."

"By myself? How will I know the way?"

"You'll have to figure that out as you go, but you have a canteen and some food. And now the flashlight."

"Are you sure it's okay to use it? I thought you could only use a special light in the cave."

"All light belongs to the Ancient One." She stepped out of the pickup, and Hamelin jumped out.

"Bye!" He yelled over his shoulder as he turned on the flashlight and took off into the woods.

But he hadn't gone far when he heard Mrs. Eastland shout, "Please take care of—" And then a crack of lightning covered the words. But then the voice returned. "Tell her I love her!"

Hamelin was glad he had the flashlight. It was the middle of the night, and the climb was already harder than usual because of the rain and mud. By the time he made his way up the hill and onto the ledge, his shoes were caked, and his hands and pant legs were drenched and muddy.

He immediately noticed that the big boulder had rolled back tight against the opening, so he pulled on his special gloves. The slippery conditions made it harder to move than before, but he soon rolled the stone away. He crawled inside and, even with the flashlight, was struck by the darkness of the cave.

On previous trips, he had gone to his right around a wall and then back to the left. But Mrs. Eastland had mentioned going a different way, and he hoped there was one, because he was already dreading the narrowness of the path the eagle had taken. He stood just inside the opening and pointed the flashlight in all directions, high and low.

Something caught his eye, a short path off to his left. He remembered seeing it before, when the eagle brought him back about seven months ago on Christmas Eve. The path ended at a corner, but just above it was a smooth, arched crack in the adjacent wall of rock—a crack that ran to the cavern floor and outlined what could be a door. The eagle had admitted that the path led somewhere but didn't say where.

Hamelin walked to his left and stood in front of the crack. He pressed hard in various places along the wall inside the arch, but nothing happened. Then just as he was about to give up, the wall moved slightly. He stepped back and then reached forward again with both hands and pushed. Once it budged, the rock wall inside the crease hinged open like a door. He pulled his gloves on tighter and instinctively patted his side to make sure he still had the scabbard. Then he picked up his backpack and, shining the light in front of him, stepped inside. As he swung his backpack into place, it barely brushed the door, which then softly shut behind him. He didn't bother to see if he could open it from this side. There was no turning back.

Mr. and Mrs. Kaley lay in bed, but neither of them could sleep. She turned her face toward him.

"I'm so worried about Hamelin. I just don't know what to do. Is there anything?"

"Honey, you know as well as I do there's nothing we can do at this point except wait. Of course, we can check with Virginia. Maybe she'll get some more messages from the other side, but those are apparently few and far between."

"It just seems like there must be something else we can do."

"Well, there is, and I'm afraid it's what we both already know. It's what we told Hamelin earlier today. We have to do our job. We have a lot of children to take care of here at the home, and it's important work. So in the morning, when we get up, we'll just start again with our routines."

She sighed. "I know you're right...which reminds me, it's time to spray for spiders again."

"What makes you say that? There's always spiders out here in the country."

"But we don't want them in the house!" she said with a loud whisper. "Especially those brown recluse spiders. I saw a small one tonight among the old clothes when I ran to the storage closet to fetch that backpack for Hamelin. I just hope there's not another one, a big one in the closet somewhere."

"I'll tell Mr. Moore to spray for spiders in the house. Those fiddlebacks can be bad."

Hamelin used the flashlight to scan his surroundings, sweeping its beam widely left to right. On two of his previous trips, he had depended on light from the eagle to lead him through the cave. His third trip, via the flying chariot of winged horses, had taken a route not possible from the ground.

In front of him lay a path that appeared different from the very beginning. On the walking trips, the eagle had early on led him toward his left as they gradually descended—until he found himself shuffling for hours along a narrow ledge, squeezed against a cavern wall. He had ended up crawling, able to stand only when things opened up just in front of the dark chasm spanned by the footbridge he had failed to cross on his first journey. Even the memory of that place churned up a sinking sense in his chest and stomach as he imagined falling from a great height.

For now, however, he found himself on a slightly broader path, with underground landscapes that pressed in all around him when his beam of light hit them. The musty smell he had detected on earlier trips rose up stronger here, and the mixture of dirt and moisture reminded him of an underground cellar. Even more noticeable than the smells was the feel of his surroundings.

There was something about it all, taken together, that reminded him of the Forest of Fears—especially the heaviness of the air and his difficulty in drawing a breath. And then there were the shapes and the constant sense of movement at the corners of his eyes. The mineral formations all around him were every bit as varied as the trees and other growth of the forest, and although stone still, Hamelin told himself, they nonetheless darted and jumped as he moved the flashlight in all directions, creating a dance hall filled with jerking shadows. Stalactites, stalagmites, and whatever stood beyond them produced shaky movements as he stepped into uneven spots, making the flashlight bounce to the irregular rhythm of his hands and swinging arms—and the glistening walls wink at him with glinting mineral eyes.

He remembered Mrs. Eastland's saying there was no time to waste and realized he was walking slower than he should. But why was he breathing in short, shallow breaths? What was it about the Forest of Fears that SueSue had explained? That it took your fears and magnified them? Was that true for this forest of formations? SueSue had also said it was hard for him to be alone, and this cramping darkness didn't help. Whatever it was, something had squeezed him the moment the door shut behind him, closing him in its grip. He picked up his pace and tried to stay focused on the ground in front of him.

The path trended downward. He wondered what turns he would take if he had to make choices. But the trail between formations was obvious, and he continued with no decisions for at least an hour. About the time he was ready to drink from his canteen, however, he reached what looked like an intersection, a footpath crossing in front of him from right to left. He paused. This would be a good time to stop and think.

He swung the backpack off his shoulders and unzipped the big pouch in the back, where Mrs. Kaley had put the canteen and what looked like a white plastic bread bag. That's where his sandwich would be. He pulled out the canteen to take a sip and realized he didn't recall the cave being this hot before. He had last walked through it in December, so maybe that's why it felt hotter now, though he thought it would be cool underground all the time

It didn't take him long to decide. He knew he wasn't going to turn left, because the path that crossed in front of him looked narrow and he didn't want anything resembling the one that had previously led him toward a cavern wall with a narrow ledge. And if that was the same path, he shouldn't go to the right either, because it might circle him back to the entrance to the cave.

After determining to go straight, he returned the canteen to the pouch, but when his hand touched the inside, he felt something soft stuffed in the bottom. What was that? He pulled it out and saw in the flashlight beam that it was a sock. A white gym sock, obviously left there by the previous owner of the backpack.

Hamelin then had an idea—he would drop the sock on the path at the intersection, weigh it down with a handful of pebbles, and use it as a marker. If he started walking in circles and got back here, he'd recognize the spot. He then zipped up the pouch and, after hoisting the backpack onto his shoulders, set off again.

The path continued downward but soon flattened out and stayed that way for an hour. Hamelin hoped he was moving fast enough, but he also tried not to miss any possible turns along the way, though having only a flashlight didn't give him a lot of perspective about his general surroundings.

The path then moved from level ground to a steep descent, and he had to push back on his legs to keep from running, which made his pace slower. Finally, the trail flattened out again, and although it had some curves and twists, going forward appeared to be the only option.

The air grew hotter as he continued, and he could feel the sweat, or something, trickling down the back of his neck. So he used his thumbs to pull the straps of the backpack away from his shoulders and swung it to the ground. By this time, he had been up for hours with almost no sleep, and he had to have a breather. He touched the back of his head and neck with his right hand and noticed that the glove came away damp with sweat.

He directed the flashlight ahead and saw that he might soon have to make another decision. So before he pulled out the canteen, he picked up the backpack in one hand and walked forward to what proved to be a fork in the road, where one path veered left and the other rounded a cavern wall and took a sharp right.

The same reasoning he had used before made him want to take the right-hand fork, but as soon as he stepped into it—to shine the light as far as he could to see what lay ahead—he was hit by a hot blast of wind that smelled like burning rubber. It immediately reminded him of standing at the footbridge over the dark chasm, and it was the same smell he had detected more than once when the eagle had flown him over the chasm back to the opening. To make matters worse, that fork seemed to lead toward a narrow shaft.

Surely I'm not supposed to go that way! He stepped back and returned to the shelter of the wall. He'd have to think.

Chapter 8

 # Decisions

HIS BODY WARNED HIM NOT TO MAKE THAT TURN TO THE right, while his head told him to go that way. To be safe, he decided to mark the spot in case he changed his mind and had to come back. He looked around for something to use but couldn't find anything as distinctive as a white sock. Then he remembered the bread bag. He pulled it out and decided this was a good spot to eat the sandwich. He was tired and hungry anyway.

Mrs. Kaley had only had time to throw a piece of ham between two slices of bread, but it still tasted good. He kept his mind on the fork in the road as he ate and after a short time retrieved the canteen and took a sip. Not too much—he had to save it. He didn't know how long the trip would take. He laid the canteen down and, using his gloves, scraped up several handfuls of pebbles and put them in the bag. For good measure, he even used extra strength in his fingers to break off a chunk from the rock floor and stuck it inside as well. He rolled the bag up around the rock and left it there in the path. It would be a good marker.

Okay, here I go. He figured he had to take the right fork. If that bad smell led to the chasm, that probably meant, one way or another, it was the right direction and he could find a way out. As far as he knew, only two places ahead of him had openings in and out—the Atrium, which wasn't far from the chasm, and the entrance that both Layla and Lars had come through when traveling up a river. Both had said the river had some foul water flowing into it, so maybe the bad smell would lead to it.

He stood and shoved the canteen into the backpack. As he removed his hand, he felt something brush against his wrist just above the glove but below his long-sleeved cotton shirt. It felt odd—light and fluffy and almost like a cotton ball with feet. Just as a possibility began to register in his mind, a sting like fire exploded on his wrist, and for the first time since he had entered the cave, he heard a voice. It was his own. A scream.

His cry of pain was so loud it surprised even him as it echoed throughout the cavern and rolled back at him. He instinctively flipped his left hand toward his burning right arm as the flashlight, which he had carefully placed on the cavern floor, revealed what he had suddenly feared.

A spider! And worse, it was a very big version of the spider he had seen in Mr. Moore's shop. *A fiddleback!* He stepped away from it, and the spider jumped off into the darkness, moving toward the left-hand fork. Hamelin grabbed the backpack with his stinging right hand and, with the flashlight in his left, ran several steps along the smelly fork.

But there was no way he could go far. The pain was terrible. He directed the light toward the hot spot just above his wrist, where a red circle was already forming and a chunk of skin was burning away. Mr. Moore said that could happen with a brown recluse, and now here he was watching it with his own eyes on his own arm.

Hamelin yelled again. And though the word *ouch* by itself wasn't enough, as a wail it was loud and long enough to express the awful stinging, now made even worse by the throbbing that had already begun. He grabbed the canteen again, and this time he checked to make sure no spiders were in the pouch. He didn't see any, so he poured some of the water on his arm, trying to cool it off. He stood there and shook his arm, but nothing would ease the pain. And then he realized he couldn't waste the water, but *oh!* his arm was on fire! He stumbled forward down the path, and the smell of burning rubber and the blowing heat added to the nausea he was beginning to feel.

He stopped again and took several deep breaths, then shook his arm repeatedly, but still nothing helped. He was gasping. He had to think, but the pain dominated everything, even his mind, raising panicked questions but offering few answers.

What should he do? He couldn't go this way now! Hadn't Mr. Moore said people sometimes die from these bites? This was crazy. He was supposed to be going to the other side, but no one had told him which path! Just a different way. And now he was stung! This was different all right! No guide, no eagle, no chariot! He was on his own.

He took in a deep breath, held it for a second, and tried to slow his rapid breathing as he slumped to the ground. Then the beam from the flashlight grew weaker. The batteries! He immediately switched the light off and sat in the darkness, hoping the spider wouldn't come back toward him. Probably the spider was smart enough not to go where it smelled so bad! He couldn't even muster a smile at his own joke.

Hamelin tried to hold his right wrist with his left hand, but he had to avoid touching the wound. It stung like nothing he had known before, worse than any wasp or bee. He felt like a gasping, helpless child and wanted to cry, but he knew that wouldn't help.

The eagle told him to think, so he began to think and calculate. He had just enough water to go back, and the way was marked! He could save the batteries and get to the house, and Mr. Kaley would take him to the doctor. Shouldn't he do that? He sat still in the darkness, his arm on fire and his mind screaming at him. But he could only hunch forward in a protective ball, rocking his upper body within a womb of black silence. And there was no answer except the answer of pain. Was this what Ventradees felt like?

The word *Ventradees* made him think of Sophie, because she had told him what it meant. And now Sophie too, if she was still alive, was buried in a womb of darkness In that moment, he knew what he had to do.

For a second, he flashed the beam down the narrow shaft to get his bearings, then quickly turned it off. He hoisted the backpack over his shoulders, got to his feet, and, with his arm stinging and throbbing, began to move to where the heat and the smell of hot tar rushed at him in nasty gusts.

He had no idea what time it was back at the children's home, but he knew he'd been in the cave for hours. It had to be getting near sunrise. The time really didn't matter, though it gave him something to think about while trying to take his mind off the pain. His body pulled at him, begging for sleep, but the burning and throbbing in his right arm wouldn't allow it, and he was afraid to try anyway because of the air. He couldn't stay in this acrid tunnel of heat much longer, so he had to keep going.

Within an hour of being bitten, waves of nausea had rolled over him, and he had vomited up the sandwich and what little water he had in his stomach. His head ached and felt light all at the same time. It reminded him of having fever, which brought back Mrs. Frendle's voice from years ago telling him to drink lots of fluids. But he couldn't.

He let himself sink to the cavern floor and took only a tiny sip from the canteen. Then he switched on the flashlight for just a few seconds to check for any changes in front of him—but for at least the next forty to fifty yards, the path remained a downward tunnel. Images of traveling through the waterless places with Lars moved through his mind, and he instinctively reached for the canteen and took one more drink before returning it to the backpack and zipping up the pouch. No owls or anything else would take his water this time.

He shook his head, not sure if his thoughts were making sense anymore. It was time to get moving, but trying to stand up seemed like too much, so he began to crawl. Mrs. Eastland's words about the urgency of his trip, and it being a matter of life and death, gave him a little more energy, but he stayed on his hands and knees. Then another blast of hot air filled with the smell of burning rubber hit his nose. He tried not to breathe it in, but he already had a mouthful before he could get his left hand up to his face. Another wave of nausea rolled over his stomach, and he stopped to heave up the water he just drank. He wiped his face and mouth on his sleeve and continued crawling.

He remembered that he and Lars, when they thought they could go no farther in the desert, had somehow made it to Parthogen. But this was, if possible, even worse, and he began to feel hopeless. He was still on his knees, but weakness pushed him to his elbows, his face to the floor. Even the dirt carried the smell of hot tar.

Then for the first time in a while, he thought he heard something. He lifted his head. A humming sound. He listened again and was almost certain he heard, above the hum, something like a faint human voice—or was that voices? He lowered his head again. He must be feverish...hearing things. He kept going. For how long, he wasn't sure.

And then he felt it. A breeze. Something about the wind changed. It still carried the awful smell of burned rubber, but not as much, and not as hot. He crawled forward another ten yards and was sure he could hear voices. He couldn't detect any words, but the sounds were there, faint and jumbled.

He switched on the flashlight and saw that the walls on either side suddenly ended about ten yards in front of him. He pointed the beam directly ahead, and it vanished in the darkness, into an open space of some sort, an area that he hoped would offer a bit of relief from the heat and the smell funneling up through the shaft.

Hamelin struggled to his feet and, by counting paces, stumbled to the end of the walls. The end was obvious, however, because of the change in temperature and odor. The wider area diluted the worst effects of heat and smell that the shaft had compounded. He rounded the corner to his left and sat, his back against the cavern wall. Now he could at least breathe again. He took another sip from the canteen. Maybe the nausea would stay away He closed his eyes...just a moment's rest.

⸺⸺◉⸺⸺

The long horizontal branch squeaked as the Watcher of the Tree, the River, and the Pond wound its injured body around its accustomed place in the habitat stolen ages ago. It had been a three-day journey back to the garden after that painful battle with the bull and his friends in the meadow—made a day longer because of the wounds sustained.

What was that? It could hear an intruder in the distance...the sound of a servant of the Ancient One. The snake-rat knew it hadn't the strength to leave the tree for an all-out attack, nor did it wish to summon its familiar creatures. This enemy was strong and needed greater measures than brute force. No matter. Its best—and oldest—tactic was a disguise. It required only the strength of its mind to effect its dark wonders.

⸺◈⸺

The pain in Hamelin's arm woke him up. Though it wouldn't let him sleep for long, even a few minutes had strengthened him. The burning was still there, but it was focused in the spot on his wrist where some flesh had fallen away. The throbbing up and down his arm continued.

He switched on the flashlight once more, and it barely cast a beam. He quickly turned it off, trying to preserve its fading energy, but in its last split second of shining, the perimeter of the light caught something white and fluttering a few feet off to his left. He leaned over and crawled until he felt something paper-like that was apparently caught between two small sta-lagmites. He was careful not to tear it as he lifted it away from the formations.

By the feel, he knew it was more than a piece of paper. An image of the scroll given to them by the servants of Simannas came to mind. What did they call it? The prophecy? He could tell it had the same firm ends that would unroll. Maybe if he gave the flashlight a few minutes, it would recover enough power for an up-close look, assuming the scroll-like object was in a language and script he could understand.

He forced himself to wait ten minutes. To use every moment of light possible, he unrolled the ends of the object and had it ready. When he pushed the switch on, there was a small, weak beam, but up close it was just enough. The scroll obviously was a map. He turned the flashlight off after a second or two.

How did it get here? Then he remembered—SueSue had given Lars a map when she sent him through the cave by himself to fetch him and Layla. But by the time they had flown back in the chariot and gone through the waterless places, Lars didn't have it. Was that what he and SueSue were whispering about in her dining room? That he had lost the special map, and she just said they'd "have to accept it"? Could this be that map?

Hamelin waited another five minutes, hoping for one last small surge of energy. He turned the flashlight on and, as quickly as possible, got his bearings on the map. It showed a river of tar and what looked like some kind of opening upstream that led toward other rivers. Was that the way out? Suddenly his thoughts were disturbed by a thudding sound, like something hitting land. He waited, tried the flashlight again, and then saw something long and slender. Maybe a boat. And maybe this was the river of tar. It certainly smelled like it. The light faded, and he turned it off, though he was pretty sure he wouldn't get another look.

He stuffed the map into his backpack, struggled to his feet, and made his way toward the thudding object—taking care not to step into something he couldn't get out of. Within a short space, he could feel the ground getting soft, and then he again heard the sound. At the same time, he heard more humming, and the voices now sounded like human voices, crying and groaning. He felt sorry for whoever it was, but the noises also gave him the creeps.

He shuffled closer and then with a groping motion of his right foot felt something solid. He leaned over and, despite the continued throbbing in his right arm, used his gloved hands to confirm that the object was indeed a boat. He climbed in, then felt around on the floor and found a pole. The simple craft was tied off by a short rope looped around a rock at the river bank. He untied the rope and tossed it in the boat, pushed off, and found himself floating on a surface of hot tar. As long as he could endure the pain, he still had strength in his hands to pole himself upriver.

Hamelin was exhausted, and his right arm continued to burn and ache, but getting out of the hot tunnel gave him a new motivation to pull hard on the pole, as did the disquieting voices that seemed to float up from the river of sludge and echo off the canyon walls. Was this the abyss the eagle had flown him over before? In spite of the pain—and maybe because of it—he poled furiously, and the farther he went, the river became easier to navigate and the voices fainter.

Without realizing exactly when it happened—and at first thinking his eyes were adjusting to the dark—he began to see his hands on the pole, followed by his feet standing in the bottom of the boat. And then at a distance, he could see minerals sparkling off the walls. Somewhere light was getting in.

And then he began to hear something, perhaps the noise of water falling—or maybe it was more sludge. But something up ahead was crashing and sloshing, and the sound resembled a waterfall more than anything else he could think of. Time proved him right. As he approached, a few drops splashed on his face. The substance was warm but not hot, and though it felt like water, it was oily and shared the same odor he had been smelling for hours.

Whatever it was, he had no intention of passing through it, so he quickly steered to the left bank, jumped out, and tied the boat off around a rock. More light was available, so he could tell he had apparently reached the end of the canyon, with the falls in front of him and behind them a rock wall. He looked up and followed the line of the falling water to the high point where it spilled down from a river or stream above. But something was different. When he continued to lift his eyes upstream from the point where the water began its descent, he spied a big hole— maybe ten feet in diameter and almost like a chute—through which the warm, dark water was shooting. What lay behind the opening he couldn't tell, though he could detect light on the other side of it. Probably another cavern.

He had apparently come upstream to the beginning of the

river, at least this lower portion of it, and maybe that explained why the water got thicker and more stagnant the farther downstream it went. But he had no idea about the voices and the heat.

Hamelin was drawn to the light, so there was nothing else to do but climb. He moved ahead to the wall that bordered the falls on the left, away from the warm water flowing from the opening above. He checked to make sure the map and flashlight were secure in the backpack along with his canteen, patted the scabbard on his side, and pulled his gloves up tighter. The throbbing in his arm was constant and the sting on his wrist like fire, but he had come to accept these as the pain he had to endure to keep going. Whether it would ever stop, he didn't know, but he couldn't change that, so he pinched his fingers into the rock and began to climb.

In a strange way, scaling the wall gave him confidence. It was one thing he knew he could do well after so many hours—in fact, days—of frustration and doing so many other things wrong. His confidence almost misled him at one point, however, because despite his strength, he failed to anticipate how slippery the walls were from the oily water splashing over them. But he figured out how to adjust his grip and within five minutes had scaled the wall and reached the opening. There was now no choice: he had to go head on into the cascading river. After a single step, he was chest deep, and the surging force of the warm, heavy waters immediately stalled his progress. He tried again to step forward, but the rushing stream and the oily rock floor beneath him swept his feet and legs from under him, and he plunged chest and face first beneath the choppy waves. He flailed wildly with his arms, grasping nothing, and so braced himself to be repelled backward over the edge of the waterfall. But with the swirls of crashing water all around him, just before he expected to fall, his left foot bumped against a rounded underwater boulder and slowed his backward slide. The left side of his body then brushed against it, and he instinctively grabbed at it, pinching it as it reached his upper torso.

Hamelin held on with one arm, creating simultaneously a deep five-fingered grip for his left hand while also pulling his body close to the rock and squeezing a similar grip with his right hand. The water crashed all over his face and pushed against his chest, but the strength in his hands allowed him to regain his balance, survey his situation, and even take a few good breaths.

It became obvious that he would sooner or later still have to go through the chest-deep waters into the opening just above the chute. The safety of the two-handed grip versus the risk of slipping on the oily rock floor convinced him of what he had to do. He used one hand to tighten the straps on his backpack, took a deep breath, and lowered his upper torso under the water, using his hands the same way he would climb a wall, pinching finger grips in the floor of the waterfall and pulling himself head first upstream, hand over hand against the descending flow. The main challenge would be to hold his breath long enough.

The water was just deep enough that he couldn't put his head above it and still maintain his grip, but the finger holds he was making felt much more secure than the slippery rock floor beneath his feet, so he began to muscle himself forward and up the falling river.

He could hear the roaring of the water swirling and rushing around him in his shallow path beneath the surface, and at one point, he thought he could detect a certain rhythm in the crashing stream above him. Was it saying something? It was slow going, and he wished he could open his eyes, but he couldn't, given the oily nature of the water. He pulled himself forward hand over hand as fast as he could, but that also, combined with the pounding of the water above him and against him, took more energy and made his chest ache for a breath sooner than he expected.

As the water hit just above him, he remembered reading somewhere a story about a man swimming in the ocean who was suddenly overwhelmed by huge waves breaking over him, holding him down beneath their weight. It was like being buried alive, but not with dirt.

Hamelin thought his lungs were about to explode, but he knew he had to continue as long as he could. Just when he was certain he couldn't go any farther, he felt the rock floor in front of him start to move up. The sound of the falling river grew louder, and he knew he was only inches away from breaking the surface, though he had to remember not to breathe immediately, since the force of the rushing water would then be hitting him directly in the face.

He reached up with his left arm and yanked violently with both hands, breaking the surface of the water and finding the rock side of the opening. He pinched a grip in it with his left hand and lifted his entire body up and to the left. He then plunged the fingers of his right hand into the wall just above his left and pulled again, while also turning his back to the hard flowing river. The air exploded out of his lungs, and he took the most welcome breath he had had since a similar experience coming out of the waters of death and life in the Atrium.

He climbed through the opening and into what was, as he had expected, another cavern. He waded through the dark water for a short space, but the room soon opened up enough for him to step out onto a bank. The burning, throbbing pain in his arm reasserted itself, but he did his best to think about where he was. This area had considerably more light, and for the first time in many hours, he could see his surroundings.

Which reminded him of the map. He pulled it out of the

backpack and was relieved to find it still dry. He gave it a thorough look. And then he started to remember the stories he had heard from Lars and Layla about their journeys, trips coming from the direction opposite of his. How each had come to the side of a domed hill—no doubt another part of the same mountain that concealed the Atrium of the Worlds—and entered, traveling upriver.

He studied the map, trying to connect what he was seeing there with the stories they had told. He looked around. Where was he? And then it hit him. Everything was so obvious that he had missed it. He looked around some more and realized the jigsaw pieces from their stories matched the map in front of his eyes. But more than the map, the spot where he now stood made all of it fit together. There was the rocky area like a patio, exactly the way Layla had described it. And just beyond it, to his left and upstream, he could see that a single river came flowing toward him into the smooth rock space she told about and there divided into two.

One of the rivers flowed to his left, behind him and down the chute he'd just come through, but the other one was there! Just across the way, on the other side. That must be where Layla had lost her ring! And somewhere over there she had drunk from the waters of forgetfulness, which flowed into the sludgy waters where he'd been. Why had she done it? Then he remembered. The white bull had told her to. Probably on purpose, to make her forget.

Hamelin knew not to drink yet, but he was dying of thirst and eager to try the pure water he expected to find just ahead. He plunged across the dark waters, over the patio, and across the next river on the other side. But even that water appeared murky, though not as bad as what he'd been through. He then headed farther upstream, and in spite of his exhaustion and the constant burning on his arm, his memories grew sharper.

First, he found the dark underground stream that polluted the single river before it divided and sent most of the bad water down the chute. He could tell that the river was untouched above the dark springs, but to be safe, he hurried even farther upstream, where the water was as clear and pure as any he'd ever seen. He splashed some on his face and, even before drinking any of it, felt strangely refreshed. The burnt rubber smell was gone, and the water was cool, so he waited no longer and cupped his hands to pull big gulps into his mouth. The water more than quenched his thirst. It cooled his body from the inside and soothed the aches that burned his muscles and joints.

And then he noted something very strange. When water dripped down his face and neck, some of it touched the wound on his right arm, and the pain stopped. He instinctively plunged his arm back into the water and then pushed up his right sleeve to stare at the place where the spider had bitten him. The very spot where a huge chunk of skin had died and sloughed off was now pink and fleshy again. The wound was healing rapidly.

Hamelin laughed out loud, and his laughter echoed across the cavern of the rivers. He pulled his canteen from the backpack and poured out the remaining water before plunging the canteen into the river and filling it. And then he drank and refilled it. And again splashed it all over his face and neck. And for good measure, he kept his hands and forearms in the water. A soft breeze stirred, bringing a coolness that covered his damp skin just as a restful warmth flowed through him. He lay down and within seconds was taking deep, drowsy breaths.

Chapter 9

The Voice, the Garden, and the Ball of Fire

SOMETHING WOKE HIM UP. A VOICE. IT REMINDED HIM OF Layla, but it sounded almost like an echo bouncing off the cavern walls. It didn't make sense, but the words sounded like "No, Hamelin!"

He shook his head and took another sip of water to help him wake up. He couldn't stay here, as pleasant as it was. He pulled out the map and did his best to reconstruct the stories and directions that Layla and Lars had given.

From this point, it shouldn't be hard. Both of them came upstream, so the way out had to be back toward the patio and on down that other river to the left.

He again glanced at the map, and that's when he heard it—what sounded as much like a lullaby as anything else, sung by a voice as soft and gentle as the wind that had just refreshed him. It wrapped itself around his head and shoulders and filled his chest. The voice sounded familiar, like that of a sweet singer he had heard before.

Come to me, dear child,
rest in your garden.
Sleep and don't fret while
I protect you.

You are a warrior,
mighty in battle.
No need to fight, for
you have come home.

Yours was the striving,
Healing has come now,
Though yours the bleeding
Hear this sweet song.

Stay here, O Man Son,
o'er all the others.
Your work is now done.
No charge to heed.

Undisturbed stillness,
peace without moving.
Hear 'neath the branches
only my voice.

All you can want grows
full in my garden.
Feel yourself floating
in my sweet air.

He then remembered something else both Layla and Lars had mentioned. That there was a garden, a beautiful garden that each of them had longed to enter. It was up there, just a little farther upstream. Maybe he could take an extra minute and go there...if it was so beautiful...like the song said. Besides, he would still be next to the pure water He gathered up his things and moved toward the garden, drawn by the singer and the song.

The song continued to guide him upstream, with no need to consult the map. The journey didn't seem far, but Hamelin paid no attention to its length, though the cavern itself changed, opening up and surrounding him with trees of differing sizes and shapes. The light increased so that the varied colors in the leaves and barks grew as alluring and entrancing as the song.

As the lullaby continued, he recalled Layla's description of this beautiful cavern and remembered she had seen the garden somewhere nearby. The farther in he walked, the more he recognized the voice—it sounded like Mrs. Regehr. In his mind, he could see her—the face that had so often looked down at him, lovingly putting him to bed in his earliest years before he turned five and was moved to the boys' bedroom.

Even as he walked, the lilting tone of the song made him drowsy, and he realized how tired he was and how little he had slept since he left the children's home in the middle of the night. Surely it was almost morning by now. He stopped to listen and sat down for just a moment, closing his eyes as the voice continued.

> Shards of the morning,
> pieces of sunlight,
> daytime bringing,
> soon showing the dawn.
> Still time for resting,
> bathing in moonlight,
> cling to the darkness,
> halting the day.

The soothing voice faded, and he lay down, feeling an enveloping warmth that matched the end of the song. He dozed but then heard a squeak, perhaps like the hinge of a closing door, and his eyes popped open. How long had he been there? The light was gathering.

He sat up and found himself at the gate of a beautiful garden, and just on the other side, in the garden itself, stood a tree with rotting fruit scattered on the ground beneath it. Just as his hunger pushed him to enter and try the fruit, a cloud of darkness rolled along the ground, rushing to cover it.

Something drew his eyes upward, and he spied, in the boughs of the tree, a ball of burning light the size of a man's fist. The fire grew until it covered the entire upper branches and leaves, but the tree wasn't consumed. Then he heard the squeaking noise again, louder, and the sound of the lullaby tried to start, but it failed, collapsing into a croupy cough.

Hamelin's mind stirred from its stupor, and he got to his feet. And then a small voice spoke to him. "Shhh, dear child. Don't fret."

"Who are you?" asked Hamelin.

"I am like the eagle."

"But your voice doesn't sound like the eagle's."

"I am a guide and a messenger."

"So you're going to take me to Parthogen?"

"Don't worry about that right now. It's a long journey, and you must rest. You must be quiet for a while."

That's what the eagle told me, but he also said I'm supposed to think.

The voice answered Hamelin's thoughts. "You think too much. You should take your rest."

"But the eagle—"

"You must not always listen to the eagle."

"But you said you were like the eagle," said Hamelin.

"But I know so much more than the eagle. You must listen to me."

Hamelin heard it again, something in the voice. But this time the final words ended with a hiss, followed by the squeak.

More than the eagle? Even SueSue discussed things with the eagle.

"We can talk about these matters later," said the voice. "But you must be hungry."

SueSue was always saying that.

"So take something to eat. Here on the ground is good fruit. Take it and eat. Then you can rest again."

Hamelin searched the ground for an eatable piece of fruit, but it all looked rotten and bruised.

"Don't concern yourself with that," said the voice. "There are good bits here and there that you can nibble on. Besides, a little bad spot won't hurt you. Just satisfy yourself for now. Then you can rest."

Hamelin picked up a piece of fruit and turned it over in his hands, looking for a good place to bite. As he searched, his thumb plunged into a soft spot and squirted some of the juice on his shirt. It stained immediately, and Hamelin felt his chest burning at the very spot where the juice hit.

"Don't worry about that," said the voice. "It's only a small stain." And now there was a distinctive hiss.

Hamelin noticed that the ball of light was getting larger and approaching. His mind took him back to Mr. Moore's workshop, where the welding torch had exploded into a shower of flames. He remembered not to look at it directly.

"You can look at me," whispered the voice. "Come closer and see my fire. I know you want to look." Hamelin turned his head and closed his eyes.

"But I said you can look at me. Come, share my beauty,"

said the voice in a whisper that shifted to a hiss and ended in a squeaky snort.

Hamelin took a step back.

"Come closer!" The aura of fire widened and moved nearer.

"I'm thirsty," said Hamelin.

"Yes, take a bite of the fruit. It will quench your thirst." But instead of the fruit, Hamelin reached for his canteen and put it to his lips.

"No!" squeaked the voice. "The fruit is so much better!"

The fiery ball came still closer, and Hamelin grew uncomfortable from the heat, his mind rushing all the while. He pushed himself to think. Something was wrong. The voice was not Mrs. Regehr's, and definitely not the eagle's And the blazing light— the eagle's helped him see. This fiery ball burned his eyes.

He filled his mouth with water from the canteen, and as he did so, he heard other words: "Sometimes a man's just gotta know when to fight and when to run." There was no mistaking that voice—it was Mr. Moore's.

The ball of fire jerked closer, and without thinking, Hamelin spit out the water. Where it touched the flames, they were quenched and momentarily parted. And in that instant, behind and within the spot he had doused, he saw a figure—a grotesque creature with a crushed cheek just above a crooked mouth.

Hamelin stared at it. The body was bruised and swollen, and the head was caked with dried blood. But even the distorting marks on its serpentine body, administered by the white bull's horns and hooves, and the wound in the side of its rat head where the flat rock had struck it couldn't conceal its true identity. Fastened around the branch of a tree, the creature didn't coil its upper body, but it did snap its blood-matted head and neck forward with a hissing, fang-flashing strike.

Hamelin jumped back, grabbed his backpack—his canteen still in his hand—and ran to the river bank and raced downstream. He didn't look back but could tell from the waning heat behind him and the sudden loss of his shadow in front of him that the ball of fire had disappeared.

The creature's spewing and hissing rose over the padding sounds of his shoes on the cavern floor, but the angry noises grew fainter the farther he ran. Within ten minutes, he reached the spot where he had stopped to drink, upstream from the dark underground spring. The burning in his chest was getting worse, so he fell to his knees, took off his shirt, and plunged it into the water. Still holding the shirt, he ducked his head in the river, and when he came up, he used his hands and arms to splash and wash his chest.

The burning stopped as he again immersed his shirt and then pulled it on sopping wet. After several long gulps, he patted the scabbard, made sure the canteen was full before returning it to his backpack, and double checked that he had the map and flashlight. Then he got up and ran downstream for all he was worth.

Following the flow presented no challenges with respect to direction. He came to the smooth rock patio, where the river divided, and glanced at the oily fork of the river shooting off to his right and down the opening he had climbed through earlier, but he knew he should follow the branch on his left. That would, he hoped, lead to the entrance both Layla and Lars, many years apart, had come through.

He continued downstream for quite a while, running and jumping along the riverbank as fast as conditions would allow, trying to make good time but being careful not to twist his ankle or otherwise stumble and fall. Any injury could prove disastrous.

He had been foolish to go upstream to the garden after refilling his canteen and discovering the healing powers of the water. Time was critical, and he now knew what he should have realized before—that this special water, which had healed his arm, would be of great value to Sophie. She was no doubt the reason for Mrs. Eastland's urgency in sending him to the cave during a hard thunderstorm in the middle of the night. It was her life that was at stake.

The more he thought about Sophie—and how it was his fault that she was injured—the harder he pushed himself, trying to make up for the time he had lost by going in the wrong direction, talking to the rat-snake, and dozing off.

Strangely enough, though the water continued to flow downstream, he was almost certain the riverbank was moving upward. The water was gushing forward from a powerful source, and even the air seemed different. Somewhere along the way the oily smell had vanished.

It had to be well past sunup by now, so he looked eagerly for signs of light, still hoping he'd find the opening Layla and Lars had used somewhere in front of him. The journey stretched out, and his mounting fears that he had made a wrong turn— or missed one!—approached panic. If anything, the walls that bordered the river seemed darker, and he stopped. Should he go back and look for another path? Maybe a few minutes more, but he'd have to turn around soon.

He walked forward, and the river bent ever so slightly back to his left. Then something in the distance sparkled. He quickened his pace, and pinpricks of light winked at him. The walls grew lighter, and he started running. The dots of light swayed, and his eyes and brain together reinterpreted what he was seeing: it looked like short rays of light streaming through some kind of curtain ahead. Which reminded him of the moss-covered opening Layla had mentioned when she described how the bull had taken her into the cave!

As he approached the dark covering speckled with light, he saw that the river disappeared at the base of it. Was this another waterfall? He continued forward cautiously, and what looked like a moss-covered wall came closer. He extended his arms and hands for protection and realized that the cavern narrowed, with the walls on both sides getting closer, which forced him to step into the river. The water proved to be deeper than he expected, and he found himself wading just above knee deep, but he was careful not to let the water touch his shirt. He moved steadily onward but slowed down as he reached what he hoped was the mossy curtain.

It was. He pushed it aside and stepped through, emerging into broad daylight. The brightness of the sun after so many hours in the cave forced him to look down and squint. A wave of exhaustion passed over him, but this was no time for sleep. He took a deep breath and slowly opened his eyes. The warmth of the sun reminded him that his shirt was still wet, so he proceeded with his plan. First he removed the backpack from his shoulders and pulled the bottom of his shirt up to his chest. Then he balled up a fist-sized portion of it, stuck it to his mouth, and lightly squeezed. He didn't want to waste even a drop of the special water in the canteen, so he sucked on his shirt instead.

He then looked around to get his bearings and realized he was outside what must be the dome that enclosed the Atrium, but there was no time to explore. His destination was Parthogen. He studied the map for several minutes.

The way to Parthogen corresponded to bits and pieces of Layla's description of her journey on the white bull. The directions looked simple enough, though he knew things were never simple in the Land of Gloaming. It looked like a trip of at least a day and a half under normal conditions, but he was hoping to make it in less time. Sophie—and everyone who loved her—was depending on him. Wearing his gloves, he swung the backpack around his shoulders and set out.

Chapter 10

Stirring Memories

L AYLA TIPTOED INTO THE ROOM WHERE SHE SPENT SO MANY hours. The room was dark, but the flickering lamp outlined the wrinkled face of someone sitting up in bed. Even as a four-year-old, Layla had learned to take care not to wake or startle the old woman, so she approached slowly and looked closely to see if the dark eyes were open. Her grandmother's steel-gray hair was well brushed against her head and braided on the sides in thick strands that lay back on the pillow and fell gently to the tops of her shoulders. Layla came to the side of her bed, and the old eyes slowly opened. "It's all right, my dear. I'm awake. Come closer. I have something to tell you."

"Yes, Grandmother. What is it?"

"I like it when you come to see me, and you may come anytime. But I may not always be awake when you come. Sometime, perhaps soon, I will fall asleep and go away, and you won't see me again."

Layla began to cry. "Please don't leave me, Grandmother. I want you to stay with me. I want you always to be with me."

"I will be with you, but you may not see me."

"But if I can't see you, how will I know you're with me?"

The old woman smiled faintly. "There's a lot more around you than what you can see. I'll always be with you, in your memories, in the faces of your family, but also in special ways that can stir your mind and memories."

"But I want to see you..." Layla tried to hold back her tears, but she broke into sobs.

"Here, my dear. Take this." She removed a beautiful gold band from her left hand. "It's not me, and you should never think of it as me, but it comes from my finger, and now I'm putting it on yours. Think about how it feels, and remember this moment."

The old woman slid the ring on Layla's left hand. "It's too big for you now, but your father can fix it to fit your finger. It will remind you of me and the things I've taught you that can help others. When you wear it, you will remember that we were once together and that we still belong to each other—and that I promised I would be with you."

"It's so beautiful," whispered Layla.

"This ring was given to me by my mother, and I've worn it for a long time. But soon I won't need it, so I give it to you. Now when you feel it on your finger, you can think of it as the touch of my hand. The senses of the body can stir the mind and the heart."

The frail old woman placed her other hand on top of Layla's and pulled her little hand to her face, touching the wrinkled old skin. "Wear the ring to remember me."

Layla began to weep again, and her crying brought her father into the room. He placed a cup of hot tea on a small end table and gently led her out, and the old woman, his mother, closed her eyes.

"Daddy," she said while holding up the ring, "see what

Grandmother gave me? She said you could fix it so I could wear it now. Can you?"

"Yes, my sweetheart. And I will, so you'll always be able to remember your grandmother." The king patted his daughter's head.

⸻⟨⦿⟩⸻

The hand on Layla's head continued to pat. She opened her eyes to find herself still seated next to Sophie's bed, where she had evidently fallen asleep with her head and upper body lying next to her sister. She quickly raised up to check Sophie's breathing and then turned to see that it was her father's hand on her head.

And then she smelled something. She didn't recognize it, but it was something strong and familiar.

"What's that? That smell?"

"It's an old herbal tea that I still drink occasionally. Your grandmother drank it all the time and said it helped her stay alert. I thought you might want some after a long night. It's a special mix, so I had some made."

A young attendant holding a tray with a saucer and cup came a step closer. The girl was a pretty blond, thin but not delicate, obviously accustomed to work and the rigors of life in Carr's camp. Layla thought she recognized her as one of Sophie's ladies-in-waiting. The girl held out the tray, and as she did, she nodded at Layla and smiled.

"What's your name?" asked Layla.

"I'm Allison, the gardener's daughter. Sophie and I are...I mean, I'm in service to your sister Princess Sophia, but..." The young girl faltered, and tears filled her large blue eyes.

"What Allison is saying," the king said gently, "is that she is more than a servant to your sister. She and Sophia have played together all their lives, and they remain close friends. Ali is like family to us. I knew she would want to see Sophia, so I asked her to help me with the tea."

The old, familiar smell of the herbal tea stirred something in Layla's mind. And then she began to remember snatches of the dream she'd just been having. Something about feeling and remembering. What else was it? It was something important. If only she had time to be quiet and think.

But then Charissa, Eraina, and Amy entered the tent. "Layla," said Charissa. "We're worried about you. You can't stay in here all the time. You've got to get some fresh air and rest."

"I've rested some. I fell asleep with my head on Sophie's bed."

"Any change in her?" asked Eraina, looking at her little sister.

"Not that I can tell. Her breathing is still faint, and I don't yet see any signs of her waking up." Everyone stood silently around the bed and looked at Sophie.

"My dear," said the king. "I know you're trying very hard to help your sister, but I also have to do the best I know to do, even if it is something old and primitive by your standards. If there's no change by the end of today, I'll ask my physicians to return tonight, and I'll have to let them do what they think best."

"I understand." Layla lowered her head and looked at her hands. There was the ring. And the smell of the old tea again caught her nose. She took a sip and put it down. Then once again stared at the ring, but this time she touched it with her other hand and rubbed it around her finger, and as she felt it, her mind stirred. She began to remember. She wasn't sure if it was the dream or an actual memory, but some of what her grandmother had said came back to her. Something about senses and memories.

"I've got an idea," she said. "Maybe we can help Sophie remember."

"Remember what?" asked Eraina.

"Remember us. Remember herself. That she belongs here with us. Sophie is in there somewhere. We've just got to bring her back."

"How can we do that?" asked Charissa.

"I know what I'm fixing to say is strange, but just trust me. I learned these things from our grandmother. We've got to affect Sophie's senses and try to stir her old memories."

"You mean things like touch and smell and hearing?" said Eraina.

"Exactly. So tell me, what did she like to hear? Any special music?"

"Yes—" said Allison. "Oh, please excuse me...I don't mean to interrupt. I know you're not asking me—"

"But we are," said Layla. "Tell us what you're thinking."

"Songs. Silly songs. Sophie and I sang them growing up, and even still, when no one else is listening, we sing the ones we loved as children. They always make us laugh."

Eraina smiled and touched Ali's shoulder. "I've heard you sing before, when you thought nobody was listening. And you're right. You always make Sophie laugh."

Layla stood and clapped her hands. "Look, here's what we do. I want you to think of those old songs, Ali, and I want you to stay in here and sing to her. I know it sounds odd, but stay close to the bed, and sing your favorites, especially the old childhood tunes you and Sophie sang together.

"Go ahead and start. We'll step outside to talk about other ideas. And, Father, we'll also need your help."

They hurried outside the tent and could already hear Ali singing.

The king listened while the girls talked rapidly, and within minutes they had decided to try several things. Amy would find Lars, and they would go to the stables to get a blanket used on Sophie's horse—something with a rough feel that would also smell like her horse. They would even get her saddle.

Charissa remembered that Sophie loved the smell and taste of chicken and dumplings. During her childhood, her favorite dumplings had been made by an old cook who, though now retired, still lived in Carr's camp. Charissa hurried away to find the cook and ask her to prepare the best batch of chicken and dumplings she'd ever made.

Eraina began to walk away. "Where are you going?" asked Layla.

"I've got an idea. I know something that Sophie used to love to touch when she was very little. But I've got to look for it. I'm not sure where it is, but just leave it to me."

"Father," said Layla, "what about you? What did you and Sophie do when you were by yourselves—when Charissa was gone and Eraina left to find her?"

"We used to read together. We both love the *Enchiridion*, but at first I was so grief-stricken, I couldn't read. So she used to read it to me before bedtime. And then, once I began to feel better, she asked me to read it to her. We did that every night until the girls came home."

"Then that's what you need to do, Father. Let Ali sing for a while, and when she needs a rest, you read aloud to Sophie from the *Enchiridion*—from your favorite passages and then hers. And when you've read a while, let Ali sing some more, and by then maybe the others will be back." Layla saw a spark of hope in her father's eyes as he left to get his copy of the *Enchiridion*.

When he returned, he and Ali rotated singing and reading for the rest of the morning, and even though Sophie showed no big signs of change, Layla noticed that her breathing grew deeper. Charissa found the old cook, who promised to have the chicken and dumplings ready that evening, and Amy and Lars brought the horse blanket and saddle into the hospital tent for Sophie to smell. They spread the blanket on her upper body near her face and rubbed her hands against the fabric. At one point, Lars even gently held the saddle close. They continued these activities throughout the afternoon. Layla also expected to use whatever Eraina went to get, but the hours went by, and she was nowhere to be seen.

Chapter 11

Anger, Uncertainty, and Fear

WHEN REN'DAL BECAME ANGRY, IT WAS HIS CUSTOM TO look for someone to blame; and when he found them, it gave him pleasure to order punishment. If the trackers Thurel and Procker had been anywhere near, his fury would have called for Snardolf.

But his trackers seldom came to Gloaming, and they knew better than to appear in person before Ren'dal. They sent word to Katris regarding the escape of the missing princess through the cave, and she had just reported it to Ren'dal in his chambers. He rose from his ornate chair and kicked it. Katris backed away and waited before she briefly mentioned their reasons, but Ren'dal accepted no excuses.

"Did you not deliver my message, Katris? My latest instructions were very clear. They were to dispatch the girl but, above all, make sure she didn't return. And now they have failed me once again. If they ever come back here..."

She nodded deferentially and waited for him to sit. "Certainly you would be justified in punishing them, Master, but for now you need them for your work on the other side. They are often incompetent, but they have also sometimes succeeded."

Ren'dal snorted and slouched in his chair, but his anger soon welled up again.

"And what of Landon? Has he provided any updates? He's supposed to keep me informed as to what's going on in Parthogen. If the girl has made it to this side, she could well be there by now. If she *is*, and he hasn't *told* me..." He stood as he slammed his fist on the arm of his chair.

Katris took another step back. "Perhaps now is the time to focus on the boy warrior, the one whose name is Hamelin. You gave instructions to Tumultor and his people that the boy should be found and brought to you. But I've heard nothing about him, Master."

"Tumultor also has no excuse! The boy can't simply have vanished. He has to be here somewhere. He was with the Prince of Periluna and one of Carr's daughters, so he may have gone back to Parthogen—which is also something I expect to know about from Little Landon!" He sat in his chair and crossed his arms. "Contact Tumultor and find out if he's learned anything from Landon about the young warrior. Our little brother is under strict orders to keep us well-informed and of course to undertake nothing without explicit orders from me!"

Katris bowed and slipped away.

———⋘◉⋙———

Parthogen lay northwest of the dome, though Hamelin's initial path, according to the map, would take him mostly north, following the general terrain of the river before it weakened into a creek. The creek then ran northwest along a line of trees into some heavy woods that in turn led to the meadow southeast of Carr's camp—the meadow where they had fought the snake-rat.

For a fleeting moment, Hamelin considered going directly northwest, which would cut some distance off the trip, but he also remembered SueSue's warning about staying on the path when he, Lars, and Eraina had first traveled to Osmethan. The map indicated the route to take, so he dismissed the idea of a shortcut.

With a long day of walking ahead, he started off, following the river as it rushed down and away. The water was blue, reflecting the midmorning sky, though he could still detect signs of tar in it. He was determined not to drink any of it, for as long as possible, though it seemed to get clearer the farther he went. He remembered how it had affected Layla as a child and that Mrs. Eastland had referred to strange "waters of forgetfulness" somewhere near Gloaming. But Layla had drunk from the dark underground spring back in the cave. Surely the water would purify itself before long. Still, he wasn't taking any chances—he had to stay alert, so he would rely on his shirt and try to save the water in the canteen.

He planned to go as far as he could before nightfall, though a lot would depend on the terrain, any problems he encountered along the way, and how quickly he could get to the thick woods. He made good time the first hour or more, and before long the river narrowed into a creek that flowed through the middle of an orchard. He was relieved to find some shade from the heat, especially to slow the evaporation of the special water from his shirt.

A beautiful tree with melon-sized fruit caught his eye, and he remembered that Layla had eaten something similar on her childhood journey, finding it very satisfying. However, his experience back in the garden—and his fear of anything touched by the oily water from the cave—stopped him from eating it. So once again he pulled a portion of his shirt up to his mouth, squeezed it, and took in drops of the good water.

Feeling refreshed, he started again without resting, following the creek.

As the hours dragged by, the weight of exhaustion began to pull on his shoulders, back, and legs. At times he found himself closing his eyes and almost dozing as he walked. More than once he stumbled. His pace grew slower, and his body begged for sleep, but he forced himself to press on, to get the water to Sophie.

A couple of hours before sundown, he reached the heavy woods leading to the meadow just southeast of Carr's camp. The creek he'd been following had already played out, and as he feared, the timing was all wrong. He didn't want to enter the woods now, because he had no chance of getting through them before dark. On the other hand, he couldn't wait until morning to continue his trip. There was no time to waste, so he decided to go on. If he slept at all—and he wanted to stop for at least a couple of hours—it would have to be in the woods.

He wrung a few more drops from his shirt and swallowed— still surprised at how much strength the water gave him. Then he strode into the woods in the remaining daylight.

———◈———

Less than three hours after entering the woods, Hamelin found himself in pitch blackness. The thickness of the trees made it impossible to discern the path shown on the map and also blocked the sky. So getting his bearings by finding the north star and a few constellations, as Mr. Moore had taught him, wasn't an option.

Exhausted, he plopped down. Why didn't he just stay outside the woods and rest! And that's when he heard it. Something like an animal's whimper of pain combined with a low growl, and it sounded close. And then he heard a thrashing noise, followed by silence. He sat completely still, unsure of the direction of the sound, but he thought it came from somewhere in front of him and to his right. He listened. Nothing else.

He was exhausted, but he couldn't risk falling asleep. Whatever it was remained silent for long minutes, and he slowly began to relax. But then he again heard some kind of noise. It was coming closer—at first a sniffing sound and then harsh breathing, almost a snort. Whatever the creature—surely it wasn't the rat-snake—it inhaled with a choking rattle, as if struggling to breathe. He wondered if it was a wild pig, which would account for the snort. He remembered how dangerous they were back in Texas. Deadly in fact. The sound came closer.

And then he thought of the flashlight. Maybe after not using it all these hours, a few more seconds of energy had stored up in the batteries. He pulled it out of his backpack and waited. Then he heard the sound again—and now it was a lot closer! He turned the flashlight on and pointed it in the direction of the noise. A weak beam streamed out and hit what looked to be a nearby pair of eyes close to the ground and then a movement of white. Whatever it was whined as if afraid of the light. And just as the beam faded and vanished, the creature backed away.

Hamelin continued to listen and heard several more groaning whimpers. They weren't closer, but they didn't sound farther away either.

There was now no way he could move, much less sleep. He had to stay awake and listen. Then he remembered what the eagle had told him to do when he was being quiet—he was supposed to think. This was as good a time as any to think. Maybe it would help him stay awake.

His mind turned especially to all the people who had helped him back in Middleton and at the children's home. He thought about the Kaleys and Mrs. Eastland. And Mr. Moore. And what the eagle had told him—that he was out of control. So maybe he should try to get things back in order, back in the right place in his mind. He had once heard Mr. Kaley call that discipline.

And when he thought of the eagle, he also remembered that the great bird had called him a man and bowed down in front of him, because he had fought the bear and the monsters in the pond. Which reminded him of what King Carr had said on his twelfth birthday—that he had showed great courage.

But then he remembered what Mr. Moore had said—that a man had to know when to fight and when not to. And Mr. Kaley had said that a man would sacrifice what he wanted for the sake of his family and do his best to help those he loved. Why so many ways to describe a man?

He heard the noise again, a kind of choking growl, but it didn't come closer. As he sat there quiet and thinking, he pledged to himself that he would try to be the man all the people he cared for wanted him to be. Not selfish, which made him think again of Sophie and what he had done. The pain of that rolled through his chest, and he swallowed hard.

⸻ ⟨◉⟩ ⸻

Though he tried to stay alert, he must have dozed off. How long he didn't know, but the snorting noise came again and startled him awake. Now, though the sun wasn't up yet, the morning light was beginning to gather, and he could see a little.

He waited a few more minutes and then stood. He noticed a path bending through the trees, and judging from where the sun would rise off to his right, he knew that he was facing north and that his journey would lead him around to the northwest. He listened and watched for the creature that had made the noises during the night, but there was nothing.

Maybe it had slinked off. He started walking on the path, and then he heard a thrashing noise and saw movement about ten paces to his right, followed by a snarling sound of warning, the kind of growl a dog might make.

He froze and looked to his right. And there it was, just a few paces away, lying at the base of a tree, watching him. Only its chest moved with each shallow breath. It was a big white dog. Hamelin stood still for long minutes and stared at it, and a faint note of remembrance came to him. It was a dog, but it also had some wolfish features, and then everything clicked in his head. It was the big white dog, part wolf, that had led the pack when he, Eraina, and Lars had traveled through the Forest of Fears to SueSue's house. Probably also the leader when the pack had chased them up a tree during Hamelin's first journey through the Forest.

But the white canine didn't look ready to pounce. He kept his eyes on Hamelin and gave out a breathy snarl but otherwise made no effort to move. Hamelin took a small step forward to get a closer look. The wolf dog then tried to move away, but he was in obvious pain.

After limping a few paces, the hobbled creature turned back toward Hamelin, who could now see the right side of the animal's face. The jaw was swollen, and Hamelin guessed why—he had punched the leaping dog in midair with a last-second roundhouse blow to the head from his gloved left hand. And now the mouth and jaws of the once strong animal were disfigured and stiff, locked shut. His body was thin, his ribs showing through his skin.

"You're starving, aren't you? And you can hardly move I guess you've come out here to die." Hamelin, realizing this was his chance to get away from one of Landon's canines, started walking at a quick pace, glancing back twice to make sure his former attacker wasn't following.

That's when he heard another whimper of pain. Hamelin paused. Something pulled at him, and he turned around to look at the creature one more time. The white dog didn't move, though his eyes were fixed on Hamelin. Then his head lifted an inch or two.

Hamelin took a deep breath and started back, muttering to himself that he didn't have time for this, but he knew he couldn't leave the dog to die if there was anything he could do about it. He remembered the water he was saving for Sophie and then thought of something else.

He got within a few paces of the animal and slowly kneeled. The boy and dog continued to watch each other as Hamelin took off his backpack. Checking again to make sure the injured creature wasn't about to spring at him, Hamelin, in one swift motion, stripped off his shirt.

"Hey, boy, just be still for a second more. I promise not to hurt you." Hamelin slowly inched forward on his knees, and the dog didn't move, though his eyes glanced between Hamelin and the shirt he now held in one hand off the ground.

Hamelin got as close as he dared—within two to three feet—with one hand ready to knock the dog away if the animal should snap at him. He stayed still, however, and Hamelin leaned over and held his shirt above the creature's head. Then using the strength in both of his gloved hands—and risking the exposure of his midsection if the canine did lunge—he squeezed the shirt. Two drops came out and landed on the misshapen mouth. The white dog pulled his head back but also stuck out his tongue and took in the drops. His eyes brightened.

"See, that's okay, isn't it? I'm just trying to help. Stay still, and let's see if there's any more."

Hamelin wrung the shirt again, and this time three drops came out and landed on the dog's snout, then rolled down his jaw line. The creature's mouth opened wider, and his tongue took in the drops. After several seconds, the dog lifted his head and neck slightly. Hamelin twisted the shirt once more, and now the animal, already gaining some energy, clearly understood the process, raising his mouth to take in the drops as Hamelin squeezed them out over his head.

Then the dog began to move, and Hamelin jerked back, raising one arm to protect himself. However, the animal only straightened his front legs and sat up.

Hamelin slowly reached over and held his hand several inches away to let the dog smell him. Then he squeezed a drop of water into his hand and held it out. The dog licked it and quickly backed away, now standing on all fours, tail wagging.

Hamelin got to his feet. "Come here, boy. Let's see if I've got any more." He held the shirt up high and squeezed it with all the power his gloved hands could muster. A few last drops formed, and as they started to fall, the white dog moved closer and let the healing water drip on his tongue.

"I think that's all. There's no more for you or me in this shirt. I've got more, but I'm saving it for another friend. Maybe that will hold you for a while." The white dog turned away for several steps but then looked back. Hamelin put on his shirt and grabbed his backpack. The dog barked—and almost sounded friendly.

"I've got to go now. I hope you understand."

The big dog jumped back. Hamelin turned around and hurried down the path. As he walked, he tried to keep his eyes on the creature, but the now scampering white patch disappeared into the woods.

Chapter 12

Parthogen, the Castle, and an Old Secret

BY THE TIME ERAINA REJOINED THE OTHERS IN THE HOSPITAL tent, it was well past sundown, and her mood matched the darkness outside. She sat just inside the opening and watched while Ali sang softly at Sophie's bedside. When the song ended, Layla signaled for her to pause and looked toward Eraina.

"Did you find what you were looking for?"

Eraina sighed and shook her head. "No. But have the other ideas worked? Have you seen any changes?"

Charissa widened her eyes and nodded. "There have been several times when she responded and we became hopeful. Her breathing improved when Ali first sang and Father read to her. Then the horse blanket and the saddle had some effect. Her head turned a little from side to side.

"But we really got excited about an hour ago, when our old cook brought the chicken and dumplings. It smelled just like we remembered it. Sophie stirred and wrinkled her nose. So Layla put a bowl of it close to her face and touched a little bit to her mouth, and she licked her lips and turned her head toward it. But she couldn't take any of it. And since then...nothing."

Layla stood and sighed. "If you have anything new to stimulate her senses, it might help."

Eraina shook her head. "I'm so frustrated! I had a great idea for something that could stir a deep memory for her, but I can't find it. It must be..."

"What is it?" asked Amy.

But before Eraina could answer, the head physician entered the tent and approached their father. They whispered together, and after several minutes of conversation, the physician left.

Carr cleared his throat and hesitated at first, but soon his voice grew firm. "I've given permission for the physicians to return in the morning and—"

"But, Father," said Layla, "we've had success with what we're doing, and—"

"I know. It's very encouraging, and you are to be commended, my daughter, for what you've done—what all of you have done." He looked around the room. "But the physicians maintain—and I think they are correct—that even with the success we've had, it's still limited, and we don't want Sophie slipping back into a deep sleep. Her stirring has given us some hope, but that's one of the very reasons my chief physician says we must act. We now have greater opportunity for success if the doctors follow up with their methods. I know it's not what you want, but I've given them permission to return first thing in the morning, before she drifts further away from us. If there's no more change, they will proceed with their methods. I hope you understand."

Layla took a deep breath and pursed her lips but said nothing. She returned to Sophie's side and bathed her forehead with a wet cloth. Amy approached Layla and patted her shoulders, staying near. Eraina stood while their father left the tent, but as soon as he was gone, she signaled for Lars to meet her outside. Charissa noticed and followed.

Eraina and Lars strode out of the earshot of passersby, but Charissa quickly caught up. "I know you've got some kind of idea, Eraina, and I have no doubt you're going to try something—maybe something very risky. So you might as well tell me what it is. Whatever you're hoping to do, you don't have much time."

Eraina glanced around. "I'll describe it quickly. I'm going to need Lars to help me, and I want to use the plan you mentioned earlier about creating a diversion in the southwest part of the city, so we can do something else on the other side."

Lars leaned closer, eyes wide. "You want to burn down the kennels?"

"No, but I want a diversion so we can do something else in that general vicinity. So you and I can climb over the walls in the northeastern area of the city, go into Mother's rooms in the castle, find a certain dress in one of her closets, and bring it back here."

A soldier walked by, and Lars waited. "Why do you want an old dress?"

Charissa touched Eraina's forearm. "I think I can guess. You're looking for that special dress Mother looked so beautiful in. It had layers of silk, and she wore it on very special occasions. It's the one—"

Eraina's face lit up. "Exactly. It's the one that Sophie—well, no time to explain now. But you remember what I'm talking about. If Sophie could feel that old dress again, who knows what deep memories and feelings it could bring out of her?"

Lars shrugged. "I don't know what you're talking about, but I'm with you, whatever you want to do."

Charissa stepped closer. "But I don't think you can use my earlier plan. You'll need a diversion all right, but we can't use any of Father's soldiers. They wouldn't help without Fearbane's permission, and Fearbane would go to Father. We don't have time for that, and he probably wouldn't allow it anyway."

"So what can we do?" said Eraina.

Just then a man and two small children came close, and the man pointed out the first stars of the evening. Charissa gestured with her head and led them all back toward the girls' tent. Just outside it, she pulled Lars and Eraina close. "Remember, as much as Landon has turned the minds of his dogs and wolves, they weren't originally made that way. They are the Ancient One's creatures, and they still have traces of goodness in them. We can use that, and it will require only you and Lars to do it."

Charissa explained her idea, and within minutes, Eraina and Lars were nodding. The plan was set. They would move that night.

⸻⊙⸻

Dressed in dark clothing, Eraina and Lars crouched low as they made their way toward the city walls, just north of the central gates. It was well past two o'clock in the morning, which meant sleepy guards and roaming dogs.

She repeatedly used her special scarf to see at a distance—and even through the walls—to evade the watch guards and any wolf dogs that might be slinking around nearby.

They reached the base of the thick walls. Eraina remembered stories of how many years and men it had taken to quarry, transport, and shape those huge, smooth, rectangular stones. They made the city a fortress. She touched the beautiful stones, mortared into place, and realized how as a young girl she had taken their protective strength for granted. But this was no time to reminisce. They moved to their right and continued farther north until Lars found a safe spot for Eraina to sit. It was at the bottom of a tower built into the wall and extending from the ground to the top. The base of the tower jutted out from the wall and created a small corner where Eraina could lean back and find some protection on two sides.

Lars reviewed their plans. "I've got the bag with you-know-what in it, plus some rope. No matter what happens, unless you are in danger, don't move from this spot. Keep a sharp eye out, and if anything goes wrong, return to the camp. I'll come back to get you, but if you're not here, I'll know you've gone back. I can easily get there on my own."

"I've been using my scarf to look south along the wall, inside and outside the city. Things appear calm, so you should be able to get to the far corner and then from there to the southwest without much trouble."

"Keep an eye on what I'm doing. And if all goes as Charissa predicted, you'll hear the noise, and I'll be back soon. Then we'll get over the wall."

Eraina watched Lars race away into the night. She followed his movements closely though she could do nothing to help. Even watching him made her pulse and breath quicken. As planned, he made it to the southeast corner of the city walls and went back to his right. She then used the scarf to look diagonally across the city and once again picked up his shadowy form still moving along outside the wall until he reached the southwest corner. He scrambled up and over the wall and dropped to the ground with the bag still in his hand.

Then he grew more cautious. He tiptoed toward an outer road that circled the city and stood there. She knew what he was looking for—one of Landon's dogs. And it didn't take long for three of them to appear. They were constantly guarding, but they may also have been attracted to the smell. Lars opened the bag and gently emptied the carcass of the dog Justin the soldier had killed a day earlier, when the two creatures had attacked Layla.

The three wolf dogs inched closer, heads down. Eraina could see their bared teeth and knew they were snarling. Lars slowly backed away from the dead creature. He would run if he had to, but he was trying not to bolt and startle the dogs into chasing him. He wanted them to ignore him and come near their fallen comrade.

Sure enough, they initially kept their eyes on Lars but soon were sniffing around the body. Two of them began to whimper, and what Charissa had expected began. One of them sat back on his rear legs, stretched his neck and snout toward the night sky, and howled—wolfishly long and loud. Eraina could hear it even in the distance. And then another dog began to cry mournfully, and she realized exactly what Charissa had explained to them.

The wolves themselves, with instinctive pity, would create the diversion through their howling, a collective sound of canine grief she had never heard, much less expected, even though Charissa knew of it and had described it. The animals were grieving for their dead pack member. And then other wolves and wolf-dogs approached, sniffing and then howling. And an even louder, wailing chorus of cries filled the night air. Still others came running, followed by soldiers rushing to check on the cause of the ruckus.

Lars had long since faded into the darkness back toward the city walls. Eraina saw him scale the wall, land on the outside, and start his return toward her, while the wailing grew more intense. She did her best to ignore the animals as they plaintively howled, but it was hard not to feel sorry for them.

Still carrying the bag, Lars came running up at top speed, but he was barely breathing hard.

They didn't need to say a word. Lars's confidence was evident as he pulled the rope—with a hook on the end of it—out of the bag and looped it several times in wide circles around his left arm. On his first try, he threw the hooked end to the top of the wall, where it wrapped around a rail that supported the upper tower.

Eraina then watched as he bent over slightly with his hands on his knees, and she knew what to do. She hopped on his back and held tight as he gripped the rope in both hands, leaned back, and put his right foot up against the tower, where the wide grout between the stones offered good places for toeholds.

Eraina leaned forward to help him stay balanced, but he amazed her with his steadiness—even after many occasions of seeing him run and jump using the shoes of speed and balance SueSue had given to him. Lars pushed with his feet and pulled with his arms, and soon they reached the top of the wall.

Lars let go of the rope, and Eraina's stomach turned over as they were momentarily suspended in midair, but he grabbed the edge of the tower battlement and steadied them both.

Eraina sat on the top of the city wall, leaning back on her arms and trying to catch her breath, but Lars never stopped. He pulled the rope up and then dropped it onto the other side, and they descended. For the first time in years, Eraina found herself inside the city walls of Parthogen.

They made their way toward the castle, and as they went, Eraina scanned their surroundings. The night was pitch-black, but with the aid of the scarf, she could make out every heart-breaking detail of the trash and animal waste littering the cas-tle grounds. And even though the kennels were some forty to fifty yards back to their right, farther to the north, and there was no breeze, the pervasive smell of the dogs—their hair, sweat, and waste—burned their noses.

As she thought of the dogs, Eraina instinctively looked toward their pens—though she knew the animals had run toward the diversion far across the city—and something caught her eye. She detected movement in one of the kennels, where a wolfish creature had evidently seen them, or smelled them, and stood peering at them through the mesh fence.

She continued to stare, and though some distance away, the half-breed dog actually looked familiar, reminding her of the one that had escaped after attacking Layla the previous night. Eraina had caught only a glimpse of it later as it slipped out of Carr's camp, but this dog was clearly similar. She was surprised it didn't bark, but perhaps that was because the howling in the southwest continued. But why was this dog penned up?

She expected Lars would find a way to get them both over the inner wall that surrounded the castle, but she was surprised to see that the courtyard gates were open and unguarded. The soldier stationed there—surely there would be one?—must have gone toward the noise in the other part of the city. Fearbane never would have allowed such undisciplined behavior.

They came into the courtyard, and Eraina immediately noticed the dismal state of the lawn and the once beautiful gardens. Her mother, Queen Flora, had taken great pride in the rich greenness of the courtyard and the magnificent sprays of color that filled the surrounding flowerbeds, but it all looked untended and—worse—in places dug up and wallowed over. The dogs.

She and Lars looked at each other in silent disbelief as they approached the unguarded doors to the castle and saw the extent of the neglect and disorder. Her father never permitted such lapses in maintenance and security. But now, in the quietness of the night, with only the howling of the wolves in the distance to be heard, they easily slipped into the castle.

Even without the scarf, Eraina would have known her way around. The lamps on the walls, usually trimmed low for the evening, were mostly out, although a few flickered here and there, allowing her to see dirty floors, tattered fabrics covering the windows, and scratches on the once ornate fixtures—and her Mother's beautiful furniture! Plus, everything smelled.

She and Lars crossed the ballroom and came to the elegant stairs that led to her parents' luxurious bedrooms and dressing rooms. Just as they took their first cautious step up, however, Eraina detected movement above them in the hallway that looked out over a balcony rail into the ballroom.

Someone was up there, and Eraina put her hand on Lars's forearm. They waited as she stared at the figure. It was a woman in a nightgown, her once black hair mostly covered by a nightcap but brushed out and flowing in long gray locks that touched her shoulders.

"Who's there?" the woman asked sharply. The voice confirmed for Eraina that the person was Judith, her mother's chief assistant, best known as the steward and keeper of the queen's wardrobe for as far back as Eraina could remember.

"Identify yourself!" barked Judith as she stepped toward the balcony rail and peered over it toward Eraina and Lars. "Speak now, or I will scream and bring fury down on you!"

"No," Eraina whispered loudly. "Please don't! It's me, Judith. It's Eraina."

"Who else is there? Who's with you?"

"A friend. I promise you. He's a friend of my father and our kingdom."

The woman hurried to the head of the stairs and stood there, squinting down toward the two young people as they resumed their climb. They paused a few steps from the top so Judith could get a good look. She gasped. "It *is* you! *Little Flower!*"

Eraina raced up the last few steps and threw her arms around the older woman. "I've missed you so much, and it's so good to see you—but there's no time to talk. I need your help."

Eraina whispered in her ear, and Judith knew exactly where

to take her. They hurried down the hall to a huge hand-carved wooden door. It was locked, but once it was opened and they stepped inside, Eraina immediately recognized it as her mother's dressing room. Unlike everywhere else, it was still clean. The dresser, the full-length mirror, a cosmetics table, a frame for fitting dresses, a small couch, and two straight-back chairs—everything was still just as Eraina remembered it.

Judith sighed. "It needs a good dusting, and I'm certainly glad your mother is not here to see it...though of course... but it's been all I could do to keep the dogs away." She almost sobbed but took a deep breath and recovered control of herself. She lifted her hands in a palms-out gesture that implied surrender. "No time for crying."

Lars stayed back as a lookout while she led Eraina into a huge walled-in closet filled with beautiful dresses. Judith quickly spied exactly the one that Eraina wanted. It was a long formal gown, royal blue and trimmed in gold with puffy sleeves and a thin waist, but gaining in fullness as it reached the floor.

Eraina reached under the dress and felt the fabric. "That's it for sure. Multiple layers of petticoats and satiny silk. Just what I remembered. May we take it? We need it for Sophie. I don't have time to explain now, but it's a matter of life and death."

Without saying a word, Judith took the gown, folded it carefully, and placed it in a soft leather bag, which she tied at the top. She and Eraina hugged again, and Eraina kissed her on the cheek.

"I would've gone with you, Little Flower," said Judith, her voice quivering. "But—"

Eraina patted her hand. "I know, but there wasn't time, and we barely made it out ourselves. I'm sorry you were trapped here. Thank you so much for protecting Mother's things. Take care of yourself. One day our family will be back, and you will be restored to us."

Just as Judith's eyes again began to fill with tears, Lars stepped into the closet. "I heard something."

Judith cupped her left ear and then with a finger to her lips motioned for the two young people to follow her. Strangely enough, she pushed some garments out of the way and stepped to the back of the closet. Moving the clothes revealed some shelves holding ornamental containers on the wall to her right. Several looked like jewelry boxes, but one of them was a small wooden box that Eraina recognized, though there was no time to ask about it. At the very back of the closet was the arched outline of what looked like a door, built flush to the wall with no handles. Eraina didn't recall that.

Judith repeatedly ran her hands over the wall and pushed on it, but it didn't move. A nearby male voice—apparently someone was now in the dressing room—grew louder.

Judith turned around and motioned to Lars, keeping her finger to her lips while also pointing to the spot where she wanted his help. Lars braced himself on his left leg, raised his right leg so his foot was chest high against the wall, and pushed. The door was no match for his strength, and it hinged open with hardly a sound.

She stepped aside and waved them through the passageway, gesturing to Lars to close the door behind them. The voice in the room grew louder, and Judith hurried toward the front of the closet. Eraina, just as she stepped through the opening, lifted the small wooden box from its shelf and slipped it into the garment bag with the dress. Lars used his shoulder to push the door, and as he did so, they could hear Judith loudly scolding someone. "What do you think you're doing here in the queen's dressing room? You know better than—!"

The last thing they heard was the man saying something about intruders in the castle grounds.

"Well, they surely wouldn't be in here! If I ever catch you

here again, I'll report you to your superior, and if he tells Landon, he'll feed your hide to his dogs!"

The voices faded, and Eraina looked around the pitch-black area to get her bearings. They were at the top of a steep flight of stairs, but with her vision and Lars's balance, they had no trouble descending as she led the way. Eraina noticed that they were leaving prints on the dusty steps. No one had been in this secret passage in a long time. She couldn't help wondering if her mother had ever used these stairs. They were obviously put there by her father—or one of his forebears—for an emergency escape, though Eraina had never heard about them.

They made it down the stairs, but the distance seemed longer than Eraina expected for a single flight of steps to the ground floor. They reached a landing, where they found another door, though instead of opening into a downstairs room, it put them at the end of another long hallway. Eraina peered through the walls and discovered that they were under the ground floor, in a tunnel that led from one end of the castle to the other.

She looked ahead and could see where they would exit the castle, so they hurried on until they came to a short set of stairs that led back up a half flight and ended on a small landing with a plain door.

Lars pushed on it with his right leg, and it opened to the outside, where they found themselves behind some thick bushes in a formerly well-landscaped area on the north side of the castle. The kennels would be forty or fifty yards in front of them, and the wall that they had climbed—with the rope still dangling from it—would be back to their right.

Eraina took a deep breath, realizing that the preparations someone had taken many years ago had now saved her and Lars. One quick dash to the wall and they would be over it and back to safety. They stepped from behind the tall shrubs and hurried toward the wall. But then several things happened at once.

Far back to Eraina's left, a torch bobbed in the air as a soldier carried it toward the kennels and the lone dog still there began to bark. Then from their right, another torch moved toward them, held by a soldier leaving the main entry to the castle. Was it the one who was upstairs in her mother's dressing room? Too late to step back into hiding!

"Who goes there? Halt!" The second soldier hustled toward them.

Eraina tapped Lars on the shoulder. "You better run ahead. See if you can divert him."

"No. Just jump on me piggyback style. I can still outrun him. How heavy can a 'Little Flower' be?" He crouched.

Eraina punched him in the upper arm. "You do *not* have permission to call me that." She hopped on his back, holding the leather bag.

But by this time, the second soldier was almost upon them.

"Stop! Who are you two? What are you doing out here this time of night?"

Lars began to run, and though he wasn't at his usual speed, he was easily faster than their pursuer. His idea was working—until the soldier yelled to his partner at the kennels.

"Open the gate, and let the dog out!"

Within moments, the first soldier yelled, "Sic 'em!" and the wolf dog tore after Lars and Eraina, growling with every step and quickly closing the gap.

The race was on, and it was going to be close. In fact, by the time they could get to the wall, grab the rope, and start up, it looked like the snarling wolf dog would be on them.

Chapter 13

The Wall, the Dress, and the Hourglass

ERAINA YELLED AT THE TOP OF HER LUNGS. "THE *WALL*! IT'S right there! Can't you *see* it?"

Lars charged ahead without slowing.

She pounded on his neck. "*Stop*! We have to stop and fight! The *dog*—!"

"*Brace yourself*! Hold the bag up, and bury your head in my back!"

Eraina had no idea what he meant by that, but she did know she had to take care of the bag. She pulled it to her chest and looked up. They were going to hit the wall!

The dog, with teeth bared, launched itself toward them. Just then, Lars leaped like a long jumper off his left foot and crashed into the wall with his right leg extended. As he did when he sprang off the head of the giant earthworm in Periluna, he timed his leap perfectly. His speed, balance, and the angle of his leap combined with the upward push of his right leg against the wall and catapulted them straight up. He never even tried to grab the rope. They landed on top of the wall, and in one motion Lars clutched the rope, yanked it up, and flung it to the other side. A thud and a loud, wailing yelp sounded from below.

Eraina at the same moment slid down his back, her legs weak as she also realized that her neck hurt, her nose was bleeding, and her top lip was starting to swell.

The pain grew as she realized why he had yelled at her to brace herself.

"Lars…" Her voice revealed exactly how she felt, dizzy and woozy.

His left hand went to the back of her neck as he helped her lie down on the top of the wall. She squeezed the bag up against her chest and arms. She thought Lars was asking how she felt, but there was a ringing in her ears.

Then for several seconds, things went dark, and Eraina wasn't exactly sure where she was. "The dog…"

"Don't worry about him. He's worse off than you. He just missed us and smashed into the wall full speed, head and chest first."

Eraina smiled and rolled onto her side. She glanced down the city side of the wall and tried to focus on the dog, who was limping away. But then she noticed the two soldiers with the torches running toward them. One of them held a short spear and was preparing to throw it.

"We've got to go." She tried to get up but couldn't.

Lars supported her neck as he raised her to a sitting position and, facing her, put her head on his shoulder.

She wrapped her arms around him and hugged the garment bag between them.

Then holding her with his right arm, he grabbed the rope in his left hand and from a backward squatting position, just as a spear flew over their heads, began to rappel down the wall.

They made it to the bottom and could hear the two soldiers shouting on the other side. Lars said something about their having to keep going before archers got to the top of the city wall and started shooting, so she held on to him and stumbled forward as quickly as she could. They went about a hundred yards and stopped.

Eraina was breathing heavily, and she half slid and half dropped to a sitting position in the open field between the city and Carr's camp.

She glanced back at the top of the wall and tried to see if any archers were gathering, but even with the scarf, her vision was blurred. She knew it was possible for the archers to take up hidden positions behind loopholes but unlikely that they would spot them in the darkness.

Lars was staring at her and frowning, so she frowned back. "Don't even think about leaving me here to go get help."

"What if you need a doctor and shouldn't be moved?"

"Just give me a minute, and I'll be ready." And she was. She held the bag, and Lars held her, and together they made it back to her father's camp.

Lars got her to her tent, and Charissa, who was still awake and waiting, jumped out of bed to help. Several ladies-in-waiting hurriedly joined in, while Eraina, clutching the bag, pulled Charissa close to her and tried to explain about the dress and the box.

Charissa started her reply, but Eraina closed her eyes, and a dizzy darkness overtook her.

⸺ ❈ ⸺

It was an hour before dawn, and Layla returned to the girls' tent. Charissa was there, sitting next to Eraina's bed, and Amy was asleep across the room, but the other beds were empty.

Layla glanced at her sleeping sister. "Did she find what she was looking for?"

"She did. She was looking for a certain dress of our mother's, and she found it. She and Lars apparently had several adventures getting there and back, but they made it."

Layla walked over to Eraina's bed and looked at her. "Oh my goodness! What happened to her?"

"Lars told me a good bit of the story, but the quick version is that after they got the dress, they had to run for it. Lars was carrying her because they were being chased by soldiers and one of Landon's dogs and she whiplashed her head into Lars's back."

"No kidding. It looks like she busted her lip and bloodied her nose."

"She looked worse when she first got here, but we cleaned her up. She wanted to take the dress and the music box she found straight to Sophie, but she either passed out or fell asleep."

Layla nodded and stifled a yawn at the same time. "It's better anyway to try during normal waking hours. On the other side of the cave, we refer to sleep as occurring during our circadian rhythms. But whatever you call them, this morning may be our last chance."

Layla spied the wooden box next to Eraina's bed and pointed. "Is that what you were referring to? It looks familiar."

"It should. You probably heard it when you were a little girl. Our mother used to come to our rooms on most mornings and tell us, 'You may be princesses, but you still have to get up. There'll be no lazy children in my house.'

"And then she would open the music box. Once it began, we knew it was time to wake up and get to work. She would give us a few more minutes to lie in bed, but not many."

"Perfect," said Layla. "Maybe it will stir the memory to wake up."

Layla leaned over Eraina and gently touched her shoulder. "Since she had a blow to the head, we probably shouldn't let her sleep too much for now. Let's start the music box."

Layla lifted the lid, and it began to play a soft, lilting tune with the feel of a slow dance that gradually began to pick up. Layla listened, and within a few moments, tears filled her eyes. "I do remember it."

Eraina stirred. Her eyes popped open, and she sat up suddenly. And just as quickly, she groaned. "Oh my head. And my nose!" She touched her hand to her face.

"I don't think your nose is broken," said Layla. "It looks straight. You may have a headache for a while, and it'll take several days for that busted lip to get better, but it will."

Eraina moaned again. "I'm not sure what you mean by a busted lip, but we've got to get the dress and the music box to Sophie."

Layla helped Eraina out of bed. "We've still got time before the physicians arrive. I just came from the hospital tent, and there was no sign of them. But I left Ali there to keep an eye on things. We'll get the dress and the box to Sophie. In the meantime, let's put a soft, wet rag on that lip, and you can wash your face. Some cool water will help your headache too. So while you're at it, make sure you take a good long drink."

⸺⸺◈⸺⸺

Layla, Charissa, Eraina, and Amy took the dress and the music box to the hospital tent before sunup, just as light was gathering in the east. Ali was sitting at Sophie's bedside when they arrived, and she jumped up to make room for them.

Layla took charge. "Let's try them one at a time. First, I think we ought to let the music box play for a few minutes and see what it does. Then Eraina can bring the dress close."

Layla placed the box in a chair next to the bed and lifted the lid. The music started. She motioned to the others, and they all tiptoed a few steps away and watched.

Charissa's eyes glistened as she whispered. "Sophie loved

this dress, especially the soft undergarments, and she used to get close to our mother at the oddest moments. She did that more than once, but the time we all especially remember—which became an often repeated story at the dinner table—happened when Mother put on a magnificent royal ball, one of her biggest ever. She and her staff worked for months, making special preparations and following the highest protocols. On the night of the ball, Mother was wearing this beautiful gown with all of its silk and satin layers and petticoats.

"The event was in full swing, with royalty from all over Gloaming present. Sophie, who was about two years old, was supposed to be in bed, but at some point, right there in the ballroom, Mother looked down and there was Sophie, sitting at her feet in her bed clothes and snuggled up with her head against Mom's leg—with her right thumb in her mouth and her left arm reaching under the dress to feel the soft materials. The fabrics were like her blanket, which she apparently couldn't find that night.

"At first Mother was mortified, but then she just began to laugh. She swept Sophie into her arms and took her upstairs to bed, stayed with her for a few minutes, and kissed her good night again. That was our mother."

The music stopped, and they looked intently at Sophie, but there was no response. Charissa stepped toward the box. "I just remembered something." She then moved it to the other side of the bed and placed it nearer Sophie's head. "That's more like where Mom used to put it in Sophie's room." Charissa restarted the music. The young princess rolled over in bed toward the box and took a deep breath. And another deep breath.

Layla nodded at Eraina. "Okay, now the dress."

Eraina carried the beautiful gown to the bedside and brushed it against the side of Sophie's face. She then placed her sister's hand at the bottom of the dress so she could feel the soft fabrics underneath. Moments passed, and Sophie breathed deeply again as something like a smile flickered at the corners of her mouth.

The music box stopped, and Charissa quickly wound it up again. Sophie stirred.

And then an abrupt voice, stern and loud, near the opening of the tent but just outside, broke the quietness of the moment. It belonged to the head physician.

"...so please, Your Majesty, do not allow any more delays. The princess Sophia's life is at stake. The longer she—"

By this time, their father and the gaggle of physicians had entered the tent and seen everyone gathered around Sophie.

Charissa stepped away from the bed. "Father, please! The dress and the music box are working. Sophie is stirring. Please give us just a few minutes longer."

"Your Majesty," said the old physician, "that is all the more reason for us to begin our work."

The doctors hurried toward the bed, but none of the girls moved to give them room.

Their father stayed back, watching the five young women protect Sophie. He looked at Ali. "Bring my hourglass."

She hurried away.

Everyone stood quietly, watching Sophie, but her movements had stopped. The sisters turned to face the doctors. No one moved, except Charissa, who crossed her arms.

Ali soon returned, handed the hourglass to the king, and then backed away.

He gestured to the three doctors, who followed him toward the door of the tent. At the opening, he paused, then placed the hourglass on a small table and inverted it. The grains of sand began to fall.

He turned to his daughters. "When the sands run out, if she's not awake, we must let the physicians do their work."

The three sisters, Amy, and Ali watched them leave and glanced at the hourglass but then turned to Layla.

The weight of their eyes pulled on her neck and shoulders, and she tried not to let her own vanishing hopes show in her face. They, and Sophie, were depending on her. She straightened up. "Okay, let's start over again. First the music box, and then the dress. Amy, go get Lars, and ya'll stay ready with the saddle and blanket. And, Ali, be prepared to sing."

From time to time, the black curtains parted, and figures—familiar faces—appeared on the distant stage. For a brief while, the voices and sights of the performers—who were they?—came regularly, but now there was mostly darkness. She knew it was no good shouting, but still there were the brief scenes. *Where am I? Am I alive? Will I ever go home?*

More voices—harsh voices off stage—and then the curtains parted again, and the figures returned. There was the pretty lady with her beautiful dress, and she could hear a music box somewhere. She wanted so much to open her eyes, but they were too heavy. And then—was that her horse? He rushed by and disappeared, but she could smell him. And the songs and the book were there too. But now everything—the people, the sounds—grew more distant, their performances jumbled and more hurried. And the curtains, those black clouds of blindness, jerked open for shorter and shorter periods.

She was missing someone and longed to see him. Hamelin. The strong boy who had saved so many—would he come to the stage? Could he find her in the audience and save her?

And then very slowly the curtains closed again and the people were gone and the voices stopped. *Please*, she tried to shout again—*please open the curtains!* But nothing came out of her mouth.

Chapter 14

Racing the Hourglass

NOW THAT THE SUN WAS RISING, HAMELIN MADE BETTER time going through the woods, but after days of very little sleep, he continued to stumble at times, finding it hard to focus his eyes and stick to the center of the path. His body and then his mind begged him to sit down for a moment, but he feared he would fall asleep, so he willed himself to keep going. He did, however, take off his backpack and shirt and try again to squeeze out some water, but nothing came—not a single drop.

Within an hour, he staggered out of the woods and found himself in a meadow. He paused and through bleary eyes recognized where he was. It was the field where they recently had fought the rat-snake. Realizing he was getting near Carr's camp pushed him to go harder, but fatigue and the rising July sun to his right held him back. And he could hear a dog barking. It was a long way off but sounded like it was getting closer.

Was that Landon's dogs again? How many? And this time

he didn't have Lars and Eraina to help. He fell to his knees and began searching for rocks to throw before he had to start fighting the dogs with his bare hands. But he found only a few.

He heard other noises, but he couldn't focus enough to tell what they were. He stacked the rocks he had, then removed his backpack and put it in front of him. It wouldn't protect him, but he could move better without it, and he especially wanted to know where the canteen was at every moment. He stayed on his knees and rested his head on the backpack, trying to gather some strength and prepare for a fight. He tried not to close his eyes.

The sounds drew closer, and then he thought he recognized the source. But it couldn't be...horses? The barking stopped, and the sounds of horses' hooves grew louder. And then human voices yelling. Were those battle cries? He looked to the northwest, and riding straight toward him were two men shouting and waving their arms. Glare from the sun kept him from detecting any colors. He grabbed a rock in each hand and rose, trying to focus on his targets. He drew back his right arm.

"Master Hamelin! Master Hamelin!"

Who was that? They knew his name. His eyes finally focused. It was Fearbane's scouts! His two best, Les and Mac. Hamelin sank back to his knees as the horses came charging alongside him. The scouts scrambled down, and Mac got to him first.

"Master Hamelin, please forgive me for saying it, but you look terrible! We've got to get you back to camp. You need some food and rest."

"No! Take me to Princess Sophia!" He grabbed wildly for his backpack.

Les had already picked it up but handed it to him.

"Hurry! I've got to see her."

Mac got Hamelin on his horse and held him in front. They rode hard to the camp, straight to the hospital tent.

After the interruption and the starting of the hourglass, nothing worked. The music box, the dress—nothing. Ali sang some more, and Eraina rubbed Sophie's hand against the fabrics under the dress. Lars held the saddle next to her, but she didn't stir. The more they looked at the hourglass, the faster the sands ran through, and the girls knew their father would delay no longer.

Even before time was up, Carr returned to the tent with his doctors. His face reflected a mixture of dread and resigned determination for them to start the procedure and get it over with.

"I'm sorry." He looked at his three daughters and the friends standing around the bed.

Lars inhaled slowly but walked away, and Ali ran to the other side of the tent and buried her face in her hands.

Charissa, Eraina, and Amy slowly made room around the bed for the physicians to approach, but they refused to leave the tent.

The king stood on Sophie's right side while the three doctors moved to her left. Layla gave them some room but squeezed in as close as she could.

One of the physicians shaved a small spot on the left side of her head, and Ali gasped to see her friend's hair cut away. The old physician then nodded, and a second doctor stepped forward with a leather pouch containing the tools they had seen before. One of them resembled a small hand-turned drill, and another looked like a screwdriver with a blunt, quarter-sized head that would serve as a punch. He also had a small hammer.

The head physician looked at the king, and the king took a

deep breath and looked again at his youngest. But just before he gave his final consent, he paused and cocked his head to one side as if listening to something.

A sudden commotion rose just outside the tent. There was shouting accompanied by the sounds of horses' hooves. Did someone yell Hamelin's name?

The king turned toward the door of the tent, and just then Fearbane stuck his head inside.

"Your Majesty. It's Master Hamelin!"

At that moment, Hamelin stumbled into the tent, his arms stretched out, holding a canteen.

Layla ran to him. "Hamelin! It's you! I can't believe it! Where—?"

He pushed the canteen into her hands. "Give this to Sophie."

"But she's in a coma."

"Layla, just do it. It's special water. It's from the cave. Near the garden, just up from where you lost your ring. Hurry."

In her mind's eye, Layla could see the very spot and understood. She grabbed the canteen and pushed her way through the physicians back to Sophie's left side, while the king pulled Hamelin to her right hand.

Layla moistened a fresh cloth with water from the canteen and touched her sister's face with it. "Hamelin, hold her hand."

He took Sophie's right hand in the palm of his own.

Layla dabbed more water on her sister's face.

"She squeezed my hand. Use more!"

Layla twisted the cloth and let it drip on her lips.

The sleeping princess took a big breath, the biggest anyone had seen her take in days. Her lips parted.

"Hold her head up."

Hamelin hesitated, so Layla placed his left hand behind Sophie's neck and repeated her instructions. Layla then took a small spoonful of the water and put it to her sister's lips. She drank and then groaned slightly.

Hamelin put his mouth near her ear. "Sophie, I'm so sorry. It's my fault. Please wake up…"

"Raise her up a little higher. Let's see if she can drink more."

Layla pushed Hamelin's left hand to the back of Sophie's right shoulder and pulled his right hand to the left side of her face to support her head. But as she touched his hands, she felt them grow suddenly warm, and a second later the muscles in Sophie's back began to tighten.

Layla gently put the canteen to her sister's mouth, and the young princess stretched her lips and drank, first one sip, then another—and with Hamelin still holding her, she reached up with both hands and took the canteen, helping Layla press it to her lips. She drank long and deep. She then stopped and took a full breath, and her eyes popped open—clear and sparkling blue.

Her gaze landed on Layla and stayed there for several seconds. And then she looked at her sisters, Hamelin, her father, and everyone else around her.

"Did I miss the party?"

Their father laughed and Charissa cried—and Eraina, Amy, Ali, and Lars cheered.

Layla held out the canteen to offer Sophie another sip when she glanced at Hamelin and saw him step backward and begin to sink. "Daddy!"

Her father caught him just before he hit the floor.

Chapter 15

A New Start

W HEN HAMELIN FIRST WOKE UP, IT WAS LATE AFTERNOON, and he was in a bed in the hospital tent, and Layla was bathing his face. She gave him a drink from the canteen, and he fell back asleep and slept hard.

The next time he woke, it was the following morning, and the first thing he noticed was how good he felt. He instinctively touched his arm where the spider had bitten him, and there was no soreness at all. In spite of all he'd been through, his whole body felt strong. The next thing he noticed was the buzz of energetic voices outside the tent. The people in Carr's camp sounded especially upbeat from all the good news that was circulating. He took a deep breath, and the smells of breakfast filled the air. That's when he realized one more thing—he was starving.

Memories from yesterday, especially his arrival in time to get the special water to Sophie, flooded his mind and made him as eager to see her and all his other friends as he was to eat. His clothes were clean and neatly folded next to his bed, so he dressed quickly and made his way outside to the long table where he expected to find both friends and food. The sounds of their voices met him just as he caught sight of them.

The first person he noticed was Sophie, out of bed and sitting at the table, eating breakfast with Layla, Eraina, Lars, and Amy. They were laughing at some story she had just finished. She then lifted her long blond hair to the side and pointed to the shaven spot on her head. "But at least I can cover that up!" Everyone laughed again.

Layla was the first to spy him. "There you are, you sleepyhead! You must think you've been through something hard recently, staying in bed this long!" She gave him a wink, and everyone stood and came toward him, hugging him and patting him on the shoulders. They then led him to the table and shuffled their dishes to make room for him.

He had been gone for less than a week, but it seemed like ages since he had seen his friends. He looked around the table and began to apologize for causing Sophie's accident, but she wouldn't allow him to finish. "Hamelin, I can only imagine what you've been through to get that water. Besides, I let you pull me up on that horse, and I shouldn't have. So I bear responsibility too. Please, no more apologizing. All of us have made mistakes and need forgiving, so that's done."

Being forgiven felt even better than the special water, but Hamelin knew he needed to say more. Being forgiven also meant being honest.

He tried to start again, but his eyes fell on Eraina, and he couldn't help looking surprised. She looked different. Then he remembered that in the hospital tent the previous morning, her face had looked terrible, her upper lip swollen and bruised. But now she looked great.

Eraina smiled. "You're staring at me, Hamelin. But that's okay. That amazing water you brought not only woke up

Sophie but healed my nose and mouth. Layla put a few drops on my face, and I'm fine now!"

Layla winked at her sister and turned to Hamelin. "And it helped you as well. Once we got you to bed, we gave you a sip, and you slept like a rock."

Charissa then joined them at the table and came straight to Hamelin. "I know others have said this, but thank you for what you did. You were so exhausted when you got here, it had to have been a terrible trip, wherever you came from. The last we saw, the eagle snatched you up and…well, we don't have to talk about that. You must be starving."

Eraina jumped up from the table. "I can take care of that." Within minutes she returned with two servants, who supplied Hamelin with more than he could eat—oatmeal, eggs, toast, butter, honey, and some kind of freshly squeezed berry juice.

The others resumed chatting, but he had hardly taken a few bites when he stopped and looked down, his hands in his lap.

Layla was the first to notice. "You'd like to talk about it, wouldn't you, Hamelin?"

"I would. Sophie asked me not to apologize anymore, but I really need to say some things, if it's okay."

Everyone fell quiet, waiting for him to continue.

"When the eagle yanked me off the horse, he took me all the way back to the Atrium and through the cave, and he told me to go home. He was mad at me and said I was out of control and had really hurt Sophie. He wouldn't even tell me if she was going to live. He just said I needed to be quiet and think."

Hamelin looked at the youngest princess. "I'm really sorry, Sophie." She nodded, and a single tear rolled down her face.

He then told the whole story. That after returning to the children's home, he wanted to come back so bad the first night that he climbed the hill and slept on the ledge. That the Kaleys found him on the ledge and provided a special breakfast. He even mentioned the tree and the initials and explained at some length what the Kaleys said about their son. He briefly debated with himself whether he should reveal that the Kaleys were probably his grandparents, but he decided they wouldn't mind, since these friends already knew so much of his story and he was on the other side of the cave anyway, so he did.

He described Mrs. Eastland standing in the rain and lightning, telling him he was being summoned as a matter of life and death and that he'd have to make the trip by himself.

Lars shook his head and widened his eyes in amazement, apparently wanting to ask how Hamelin managed that, since he had made the same trip himself, though with a map and a torch. Hamelin nodded at him but went on to talk about the flashlight, the other entrance, the spider bite, the heat and nasty smell of the tunnel, the darkness, the map he found, and how he finally climbed up the wall and made his way upstream to the pure water that healed his spider bite. He finished by telling about the garden, the rat-snake within the ball of fire, and the song that nearly charmed him. He was quick to say he never should have allowed the song to lure him in, though, in the end, he was able to get the water and bring it back.

He then briefly described the encounter with the dog, which they all found both puzzling and amazing. Lars was eager to hear more about the map—and Hamelin promised they would talk about it—but everyone else was more interested in the water.

"So what you brought wasn't water from the pond in the Atrium?" asked Charissa. "That was the water that helped several of us, but you're talking about a different place?"

"Yes. It's water from the spring that Layla and Lars drank when they came through the cave another way."

"And is there any more?" asked Amy. "I've been feeling a

little out of sorts myself lately." She tried to force a smile but then brushed away a tear.

"If it wasn't for your mom," said Hamelin, "I wouldn't be back here. And the last thing she said to me was to tell you she loves you."

Layla reached across the table and patted Amy's hand. "Your mom is a great person, and I wish the water could heal homesickness, but we just kept giving it to Sophie and then some of it to Hamelin and Eraina. And Father dabbed some on my wounds, so we used almost all of it. There was just a swallow or two left this morning, but I ended up pouring it out. I offered it to Sophie, but she said it smelled." Layla shrugged.

"I really wasn't kidding," said Sophie. "I guess a gift from the Ancient One is not supposed to be hoarded." As soon as she mentioned the Ancient One, they knew she wasn't teasing.

Hamelin took a sip of his berry juice. "I know I'm talking a lot, but I want all of you to hear a little more. It might be important.

"The horse I got on is the Arabian palomino Lars and I came across when we traveled through the waterless places. That horse saved our lives. And the saddle we brought back was his.

"When he came back a second time, I thought it meant he was mine. Sophie had told me that Hargis had cleaned up the saddle and found some papers hidden away in it. One special page said the one who rides this horse will go to Ventradees and conquer. So that's why I got on him and was about to ride away. Sophie told me the eagle was coming and tried to stop me, but I said she'd have to get on the palomino with me, and I pulled her up. I never intended to take her all the way with me, but as you all saw, the horse bolted. I just wanted to go to Ventradees, where my parents are, to find them and rescue them. I know it's not a good excuse, but that's what I was do-ing, and I'm really sorry that I caused so much pain."

Sophie got up and walked over to Hamelin. She stood beside his chair, leaned over, and hugged him. "Everything truly is okay. I am fine. The Ancient One has protected us all. And now you're back." She patted his shoulder.

Hamelin stood and awkwardly returned her hug. "But, please. Just one last thing. The eagle also told me the palomino wasn't my horse, though I might ride him again. The eagle said he was really for Charissa."

Charissa didn't appear surprised. "I've never told this, and I wasn't trying to hide it, but I just don't like talking about those terrible days when I was held captive in that dark basement and house for such a long time. Well…that Arabian is the horse I escaped on. I stole him from Tumultor. So I don't know what all that means, but that's how he was in the desert. He must have been there for a long time until Hamelin and Lars found him."

"More mysteries to think about," said Sophie, but she quickly raised one hand to signal a pause, glanced away, and then looked back, raising her eyebrows as if she had a secret to tell. She was clearly ready to talk about something else, and she began in a whisper.

"I had hoped we would be having Layla's presentation as a princess either today or tomorrow, but Father has other things on his mind. He says he wants me to get more rest, and I can tell his thoughts are elsewhere. So don't be disappointed, Layla, about your party, but we're working on it, right, girls?"

Layla rolled her eyes and shook her head. "Oh, I'm not disappointed."

Charissa leaned forward and lowered her voice. "We remember your fears, Layla, about coming over here and being presented as a princess. But I should tell all of you—and this is why I was slow to join you this morning—that Father's mind is definitely elsewhere, that he's focused on the implications of everything that's happening. Since Layla's back and Sophie's now awake—not to mention that Hamelin has returned—people are stirred up again. They're full of expectations that at last the days of fulfillment are playing out—that we will soon be able to recover our capital city. Father has to weigh all of these matters and make some serious decisions."

Eraina stood. "So you think Father and Fearbane are planning the big attack?"

"I don't know. They're not including me, but we will know more soon. Father told me he wants all of us in the next hour to gather in his big tent, where he holds his special councils. He's thinking about something bigger than a princess party."

Hamelin was glad the king was considering next steps. He knew he had a part to play in whatever was going to happen, especially if it was finally the big battle to recapture Parthogen. And his recent struggles, not to mention the eagle's words years ago that he was entering a war, meant there could be more suffering to come, even worse than a spider bite. If something happened to him, would there be anyone to rescue his parents?

Chapter 16

A War Council: Interruptions and Mysteries

WHEN THEY GATHERED IN THE KING'S MAIN COUNCIL TENT, Hamelin was surprised to see a large group already there, including Carr's most prestigious advisers, as well as several of Fearbane's top military leaders. Judging from the used dishes and the scattered positioning of the chairs, they had been there for quite some time discussing battle plans to retake Parthogen.

Like Carr's other strategic planning tent, this space featured a conference table in the middle, though this one was larger and could seat at least twenty-five. The well-lighted room also accommodated many others, with smaller tables, desks, and chairs loosely spread around and open places available for standing near the outer walls.

Writing supplies covered all the desks, and the large table especially was filled with maps, books, and drawings related to the capital city and its surroundings, particularly Carr's camp to the southeast and what would be the battleground between his camp and the massive city gates. Also prominently placed on the central table were two copies of the *Enchiridion*.

Hamelin expected that he, the princesses, Lars, and Amy would be assigned places at the smaller tables or stand along one of the outer walls, but the king's leading men—lords, nobles, and commanders—stepped away from the conference table and fell silent as Hamelin and his friends entered. The king and Fearbane stood behind the table discussing something in low voices, but Carr paused and nodded that they should take the chairs just opposite him.

Carr then gestured for everyone to be seated as he continued to stand.

"I'm glad each of you is here, as I have some important words to share. This is an unusual mixture of persons, consisting of not only my advisers and military leaders but now also members of the royal family and their close friends. To those who have just joined us, let me explain that we are assembled for what can justly be called the solemn work of a war council. The highly significant events of the last several months—including the joyous return of Princess Alathea and the awakening of Princess Sophia in the last few days—have led to this council, which was convened very early this morning. We also welcome the return of Hamelin Stoop.

"We have devoted ourselves to the consideration of battle plans and tactics, but now it's time for something more than maps, drawings, and strategies. It's time for a decision. I am strongly inclined to proceed with our plans for an attack on the forces of Landon, who currently occupies our beloved Parthogen. But I cannot overlook the role of the Ancient One in bringing us to this moment. He has led the mysterious and legendary wise woman, Sue Ammi, to guide my daughters and their friends, giving them special gifts—gloves, shoes, and a scarf—to aid them in their quests. Furthermore, the Ancient One has used powerful creatures—an eagle, a lion, and a white bull—to accomplish his plans."

As soon as Carr referenced the powerful creatures who had worked for the Ancient One, a dog started barking outside the tent. Though it was loud and insistent, such a noise normally would not command attention while the king was speaking. However, because of recent events involving Landon's wolf dogs, Carr's family—especially Layla and Eraina—looked at each other and stirred uneasily in their chairs.

The barking grew more intense, and the king paused in his remarks. Fearbane made a short, sideward move with his head, and two soldiers standing near the entrance immediately left to check on the disturbance.

Carr began again. "My daughters and their friends have told us of their experiences, and as we've listened to their stories, we've seen that the words of the *Enchiridion*, as strange and as difficult to interpret as they may seem, have been validated. What we were all taught as children from those great texts provides insight into these deep matters.

"Therefore, many of us have come to believe that the days of fulfillment are upon us. Expectation fills the air around us with a growing sense that the famous four thrones prophecy of the *Enchiridion* is now coming to pass and we must strike soon to recover our capital city. That of course is a moment long awaited and earnestly hoped for.

"But honesty demands that I pause to remind us that months ago, just after Charissa was rescued from her many years of captivity, I hastily gathered our troops to retake Parthogen. Were it not for my daughter Sophia's wise counsel—not to mention her shrewd maneuver regarding Alathea's old horse—we would have attacked.

"Had we done so, as my counselors and our soldiers will recall, the subsequent rains would have created a disaster. I was too hasty. But recently, after two vicious attacks by Landon's wolf dogs, I have been too slow."

The barking outside the king's tent continued but was now intermittently mixed with snarling growls. And along with the dog's threatening noises came the cries of men and women scrambling to run away, though others sounded like they were approaching.

Loud, authoritative voices could then be heard, and fragments of shouted commands suggested the angry animal was being surrounded. Two more soldiers rushed from the tent, and Fearbane quickly followed.

Carr tried to hold the attention of those in the council and slightly raised his voice. "Princess Charissa counseled a quick and proportionate response in both instances, but I failed to act. As your king, I understand full well that it's up to me to make any final decisions, but since I have previously been both too hasty *and* too slow to respond, I ask for your help. I call upon you to think with me about these grave matters that affect us all, and I especially call upon my children and their friends to speak."

The king sat down and waited. Eraina stood. But before she could speak, Fearbane reappeared just inside the tent. "Your Majesty, we believe this is one of Landon's dogs, but we need Hamelin to come join us."

Hamelin jumped to his feet and glanced at the king, who nodded his approval as Hamelin hurried to catch Fearbane.

The first thing Hamelin saw outside the tent was a group of soldiers surrounding an angry white dog. The creature turned in every direction and alternately snapped and barked, warning the soldiers to stay away.

Between the dog and the ring of soldiers, however, stood two men Hamelin recognized—Mac and Les, Carr's trusted scouts. They were apparently attempting to keep the soldiers away from the animal while also trying to calm him. Les held out both arms, signaling for everyone to stay back, and Mac slowly approached the white wolf dog, who continued to bark and growl.

And then something clicked in Hamelin's head—this dog was the one he had helped back in the woods! The very dog who had been near death but was dramatically healed by the drops of water he squeezed from his shirt.

Hamelin pushed through the crowd surrounding the soldiers and then cautiously made his way through the soldiers as well. He stood some distance from Mac and Les, who were still eight to ten feet away from the wolf dog. The angry canine saw Hamelin's approach, and the two of them—boy and dog—fixed their eyes on each other.

As the crowd, the soldiers, and Mac and Les stood watching, the big white animal stopped barking and continued to stare at Hamelin. Hamelin slowly dropped to one knee, leaned forward, and held out his right hand.

"Come here, boy. It's me." He kept his hand extended, and the soldiers and bystanders hushed.

The dog raised his head ever so slightly and cocked it to one side while keeping his eyes fixed on Hamelin. Several moments passed, and then he crept forward a few steps, cutting the distance between them in half. Mac and Les moved away.

"That's it, buddy. It's me. Everything's okay." Hamelin clicked his lips together in a smooching sound. "Come here, boy." He got on both knees and extended his arms.

The wolf dog yapped once and suddenly bolted toward Hamelin.

Several soldiers raised their swords, but no one had time to strike.

The dog jumped and planted his forelegs on Hamelin's chest, while proceeding—with whining noises—to lick his friend's face.

Hamelin laughed and rolled on his back as the dog pinned him down and continued to smother him with kisses.

Hamelin hugged him in return and with repeated pats on the head and back coaxed him to follow all the way to his tent, where he arranged a comfortable place with food and water close by. After more kisses and petting strokes, he gave him the name Buddy, and the wolf dog in response licked and nuzzled his hand.

Buddy closed his eyes, and Hamelin stepped outside and found Les and Mac. "Why did you send Fearbane to get me?" he asked. "Why did you think I might know this dog?"

Mac stepped forward. "I guess we never told you the full story, Master Hamelin."

"I remember that before you found me, I heard the sound of dogs barking. But I could hardly focus on anything. What happened?"

"First of all, there was just one dog, and while we were out scouting south of the camp, near the meadow, he came running up to us. He didn't try to scare our horses. He just moved back and forth like he wanted us to follow him, with all kinds of funny little barking noises. So we stayed with him until we could see someone—which turned out to be you—in the distance."

"Then he just disappeared," said Les. "But we got to you, and that's when we found you ready to throw rocks, but you stopped. Didn't you see the dog?"

"No, I couldn't see straight. I just heard barking and thought it was Landon's dogs coming to attack. And then I heard and saw you all riding up, but I never saw him."

"Well, be glad he led us to you," said Mac. "You were about to collapse. We might've found you eventually, but we wouldn't have gotten to you when we did if it hadn't been for him. For some reason he wanted to help you."

"That's another story, but really he and I have met several times. We used to be on different sides, but we're on the same team now." And then he remembered he needed to get back to the council. Could he leave Buddy by himself? Would Buddy stay calm, or would he go back to fighting others in Carr's camp, as he was just doing?

Hamelin stuck his head back in the tent, and Buddy was asleep, so he decided to get back to the king's tent. Carr was going to make a big decision, and he knew Layla feared something would soon trigger the four thrones prophecy. And then he also remembered—and it filled his chest with dread—that according to Layla, when the four thrones were filled, a warrior would die.

Chapter 17

The Council Resumed: More Mysteries

Hamelin missed very little of the council. As soon as he and Fearbane left the tent, the king called for a break, and the discussion resumed only a short time before Hamelin returned. The king was seated, and Eraina was standing, responding to her father's request for comments that would help him make a decision, and she had just mentioned that the four thrones prophecy was a good place to start.

"Because if we are wrong about it, then we are likely misunderstanding other things as well—which doesn't mean we shouldn't fight to recover our capital city, but if we do, it won't be in fulfillment of the four thrones prophecy. It'll be a great success if we win, but we can't expect other details of the prophecies to follow if we don't get that one right."

Sophie didn't stand to speak, but she was obviously listening very carefully. "Everyone knows that Eraina and I have disagreed about the four thrones prophecy, but I like the way she has put things, and I think we should at least begin there. I suggest someone should read it but we hold off our discussion of it until other texts and ideas—maybe even some stories that we haven't heard yet—have been talked about. That might give us a bigger picture of the famous prophecy. Then, after that, we can come back to the specifics of the prophecy."

The king pushed a copy of the *Enchiridion* toward Charissa. "Would you read the prophecy aloud?"

Charissa easily found the key text and stood to read. "Pay heed to the words of wisdom, for ferocious beasts will come to take the land, but when the living ones, true heirs of the king, are reunited and the four thrones filled, the evil creatures will be overcome. The power of the usurper and the warrior will be eclipsed. As he turns, so will he be turned."

Charissa looked at her father. "Since Sophie advised us to talk about some other passages, and since we are considering an attack, I think we should also discuss the warrior texts. We know some new things about them based on what Layla and Amy have told us about Bryan and his brother, Michael. From what I understand, the term *warrior* played a big role in why Bryan came to Gloaming and in turn how and why Layla came back and Amy joined her. Those references appear significant but also hard to understand—for example, are the usurper and the warrior we just read about the same person? Layla, can you help us?"

"I do know several of the warrior passages, and I can point them out for us." Layla then found the different places in the *Enchiridion* that referred to a warrior, and one of Carr's scribes began to write. When all the texts were finally copied down, they passed them to Charissa, who quickly scanned them and cleared her throat.

"Okay, here's what it looks like when we put these pieces together." She hesitated and glanced at Hamelin but resumed reading. "'A warrior will come to prepare the way of the mighty man. A young man will come with hands of strength, fit for battle. A strong warrior will oppose him to the point of death. He will'—and now we see that our copy has an alternate reading. The word is either *take, receive,* or *sheath.* Anyway, it says, 'He will take—or receive, or sheath—the sword that kills and shines once again.'"

Hamelin started to stand but settled back in his chair when Charissa continued. "And there's one last citation in reference to the sword." She paused again but didn't glance at Hamelin. "'It will pierce his body, and the sword of light will slay the usurper.'" Charissa's voice cracked as she finished the composite reading. No one spoke, and Hamelin stared at the ground, but he could feel the eyes of all in the tent looking at him. They probably expected him to say something.

A long moment passed, and he sensed that someone stood. He glanced up. It was Sophie.

"I know all of this sounds terrible, especially for Hamelin, but we shouldn't panic. There's a lot we don't know—a lot!— and it influences greatly how we interpret these prophecies. It looks like there are at least two characters involved—maybe more—and that they will fight. I have to admit that the reference to the 'young man' who will come with 'hands of strength' sure sounds like Hamelin. But who are all these other warriors? And who is the 'mighty man'? As for the 'usurper,' you would think it describes Landon, or Ren'dal, or even Chimera. It's all very unclear. And speaking of the 'warrior' and the 'mighty man' mentioned in the earlier texts—are those references to the same person as the 'young man'? And whose body will be wounded by the sword? I can't even figure out who's holding the sword anyway!"

Sophie's comments caused a low hum of chatter to fill the tent as the advisers and other leading men made notes and discussed her remarks.

Eraina moved toward the table, and her eyes found Hamelin.

She raised her voice to quiet the talking. "Hamelin, I think this would be a good time for you to remind all of us—a few of us know, but most don't—about the sword. Go over it again for everyone's benefit. Explain how the sword shines and kills."

Now Hamelin knew he had to say something. He stood, took a deep breath, and started. "The first time I came over to the Land of Gloaming, I was brought here by the eagle and met up with Lars in the Forest of Fears. We then found Eraina and joined her on her mission to rescue Charissa. We fought Landon's dogs but finally came to SueSue's house. She gave Lars his shoes, Eraina her scarf, and me a special sword and scabbard. I already had the gloves from the eagle.

"When she first showed us the sword and its scabbard, they were separate. But as soon as she put the sword in its sheath, it flashed, and she warned me I could draw it only once and that when I did, I couldn't hold onto it too long. She said it would bring death.

"I knew I had to use it at the wedding, when we were trying to rescue Charissa. I pulled it out of the scabbard, and immediately it started shining and whirring. I threw it and helped the eagle in a fight he was having at the top of the dome against one of Chimera's evil creatures, a bear. It hit the bear, but when it fell back down, it stuck in the huge rock and stopped the waters that the people of Osmethan were drinking to keep them young.

"As we ran from the wedding hall, Charissa was wounded. Later, the scabbard got in my way when I was trying to help her, and I didn't know I was supposed to bring it back to SueSue, so I left it with the servants of Simannas, an older man and woman who helped us."

The king nodded. "We have heard of the Great Rock, the waters that flow from it, and how you rescued Charissa by going back through the pond. And we know that the story gets more complicated, so tell us the parts that have to do with the sword and the scabbard. What happened next?"

"The Great Eagle took me away through the cave, but after some months I got back here to Gloaming, and Eraina, Lars, and I went back to SueSue's house. She then sent the three of us to Osmethan to get the scabbard. Once we got it, we were supposed to come straight back to her house without the sword, which was still stuck in the Great Rock. We learned it would make its way back to her one day and that when she decided on the next user, she would put them together again."

"So that's how the sword could shine again," said Charissa. "SueSue would hand it on to another user?"

"Yes. She said that at some point the sword would be put back in the scabbard and get its special powers back. But that's when I messed up really bad. Before we left Osmethan, I pulled the sword out of the stone, and then Romulus got it. It was terrible."

By this time, Charissa was standing. "So where is the scabbard now?"

Eraina spoke up. "SueSue wanted Hamelin to keep it a while longer, especially with the hammer in it."

He patted his side, where the scabbard was under his clothing.

Charissa continued. "What about the sword, since the stranger Romulus has it? Is it just an ordinary sword?"

Hamelin shook his head. "It doesn't have its special powers now, because it hasn't been put back in the scabbard, but SueSue said it's still an unusual sword. But if we get it, we should not resheath it, even though I have the scabbard. That's for her to decide. She said it's needed to defeat Chimera."

Carr's advisers began to talk among themselves again, but he called them to order. "We must remind our people of the sword and that it's in the control of others, possibly Ren'dal. But there's still something else we need to know—you have mentioned a hammer. What is this hammer you're referring to that's still in the scabbard?"

Hamelin then explained that the hammer was small, that he had found it in the Atrium, and that he had put it in the empty scabbard. But when SueSue learned that the hammer was in the scabbard, she wouldn't let him take it out. It had to do with mixing the Ancient One's weapons with a weapon from somewhere else. She said the sword could not be returned to its scabbard, especially with the hammer in there. But she also said Hamelin would know when he was supposed to take the hammer out, though she didn't say how he would know. Just that at the right moment, he would.

Hamelin took his seat, but Amy immediately stood. She waited for the king's permission to speak, but Carr's eyes soon found hers. He nodded.

"Your Majesty, as painful as it is, this discussion of the sword and hammer still brings us back to the question of the warriors and who they are. As Charissa just reminded us, the sword shines and kills, and then shines 'once again.' So someone's body is going to be pierced, and because of it, the sword will 'slay the usurper.' Is there any way to sort these characters out?" Amy remained standing, but she looked toward Layla, who shrugged.

"I agree with Sophie. The references to the warriors and the others that could be a warrior—like the young man with hands of strength, the usurper, and the mighty man—are all related, but it's hard to know who's who. I studied the *Enchiridion* on the other side, and I thought I understood some things, and especially that Hamelin was the warrior prophesied. But Bryan convinced me there's at least two warriors who fight each other. So that's why he took my place—not just for my sake but also to protect Hamelin and, now we also know, to find our brother, Michael, who is apparently Romulus."

"And Your Majesty," said Amy, "there's one more important

fact. Layla's father on the other side, Robert Trott, wrote in some notes that Simannas called Michael a warrior. So we think Bryan fears that Hamelin and his brother, Michael, are the ones prophesied to fight. And that's why he came here. To prevent that."

Carr took a deep breath and stared at the table for long moments, before looking up at Hamelin. "If this latter point proves true, we shall do all in our power to protect you."

Hamelin figured he should stand, but all he could do was lift his chin. "Thank you, Your Majesty. I'm grateful for your help, but the eagle told me a long time ago that I was summoned here to fight. I just wanted to find my parents, but the eagle gave me the gloves, and SueSue gave me the sword. They both said I have to do my part in the Ancient One's fight for a kingdom."

Carr nodded. "That fight is also ours."

"And if I end up in a fight with Romulus, which I hope doesn't happen—and I won't start it—I hope everyone remembers..." He looked at Layla, and his voice crew softer. "That Bryan and Romulus are Layla's brothers."

Layla buried her face in her hands and couldn't hold back a sob. Carr paused, and Eraina hurried to her sister's side and stood next to her, patting her shoulders.

Carr looked at Layla and Eraina and then to Charissa and Sophie. He then fixed his eyes on the table covered with maps and battle plans and slowly clenched and loosened his fists. He took a deep breath and nodded once. He then signaled to Fearbane, and the two of them strode out of the tent. Other close advisers followed.

Hamelin didn't move. He rested his elbows on his knees and his head in his hands, vaguely aware for several minutes that people around him were leaving. Had his friends left? Had they stared at him before walking out? Had any of them passed by and patted him on the shoulders? He wasn't sure. For a second he glanced around, but wherever they were, they were gone now. Carr and most of his advisers had left, and those remaining had walked to the other side of the tent, away from him. But he picked up snatches of their conversations, especially certain whispered words—the very ones that were running through his head—*sword, hammer, sheath, warriors,* and *strong hands*. He also occasionally heard his name, but he knew he wasn't supposed to.

He wasn't accustomed to thinking about death, and though the idea had gone through his mind ever since he came upon the footbridge for the first time, it hadn't connected inside him in the same way as now. He often thought about his parents and their possible death, but somehow death seemed so much closer now. SueSue had said the sword would bring death, but hearing it talked about so fearfully by his friends made it more real, almost certain. The ancient book prophesied that someone would die from a special sword, and it seemed like it was the sword SueSue had given him. One of the warriors would surely die—someone like himself.

What was originally an idea or even a word now felt like a weight, or maybe it was a dark, heavy shadow. But whatever it was, it was growing in his chest. It could actually happen...to him.

He tried to push away the fear of death, but he knew that's what he was feeling inside. And the fear brought questions. What was death like? Like going to sleep and never waking up—or just falling off into darkness, into nothing? Was it like slipping off the footbridge into the abyss and, as in a dream, never really hitting bottom? Or maybe actually falling away into a deep pit and hitting sharp rocks at the bottom? Did it hurt? It had to—but for how long?

The four pillars of fire that he had seen at Chloe's house,

after being flown through the cave in a chariot of winged black horses, had been called the pillars of death, but he hadn't connected that to himself. Other people were walking through them. But now—was he also going to die? What would it feel like to have a sword plunged into his body? Lars had said that Simannas had died the death of the good, but that wouldn't be his death. He had already messed up too much for that.

And then the other possibility filled his mind, something just as terrible. What if he didn't die in the fight but killed Michael instead? He would be hated by Layla and Bryan, and it would destroy their family. How could he show his face anywhere or anymore?

He wasn't sure how much time had passed, but he eventually heard the spirited voices of men and heavy footsteps approaching. He looked up and saw Carr, followed by Fearbane, striding into the tent. Other advisers and leading men were close on their heels. His friends followed, returning to their places around the table. Hamelin remained seated.

Carr seemed anxious, but determined. He rapped his knuckles on the table and raised his hand. The room quickly got quiet.

"We have spent a long time talking, but as a king, I must finally make decisions." He glanced at his children and then at Amy, Lars, and Hamelin. "I thank you for your comments and for the discussions we've had, but the time for talking is over. We face perilous times, and we must not allow others to set the timetable of our actions. All of us understand the threats that we face, and though some of those threats remain distant at this time, we cannot wait for them to get closer."

What was he talking about? What threats were distant? Was he talking about Tumultor? Ren'dal? Or...was it Romulus?

"There are terrible possibilities before us, and we must do all in our power to prevent them. The time has come!"

As Carr emphasized his last words, he clenched his right fist and hit the pad of his hand against the tabletop. Fearbane and his other top military advisers stood as one and cheered his decisive words.

What was going on? The king had asked for their advice, and they were talking about serious matters, but suddenly it seemed like the decisions had been made.

The king placed his fists on his hips and exhaled, and his grim determination filled the room. Now almost everyone was standing and cheering. Hamelin looked at his friends, and Eraina and Sophie slowly stood but didn't clap or shout. Lars and Amy followed, and then Layla stood but rubbed her eyes and cheeks as she looked down. He also stood out of respect for the king but fixed his eyes on Charissa. She remained seated, slowly shaking her head. Finally, amid the loud and sustained noises of approval, Charissa did stand, but only to leave the tent with everyone else still there.

Chapter 18

Questions and a Portent

CHARISSA STRODE AWAY FROM THE TENT. ONCE THE APplause for her father's words started to die out, she heard a loud male voice boom over the rest, and the cheering started again. She needed some fresh air and time to think—and especially wanted to talk to her sisters. They were likely stuck at the council tent, but she didn't feel like waiting. She grabbed her bow and arrows and headed to the archery range at the southeast edge of the camp.

Once there, she had no interest in practicing, so she continued on past the range into the woods. Maybe a change of scenery from the camp and its bare ground, tents, and rough tables would help. Even though she knew it was against camp protocol, especially for her as a princess, she walked on alone, looking for a place to sit down and think. Long minutes passed.

A twig snapped. She whirled toward the sound and in an instant had an arrow nocked and the bowstring drawn. "Step into the open with your hands up, or you'll be picking these feathers out of your chest!"

A tall man emerged from the shadows of a large birch. It was Fearbane. "Sorry, I didn't mean to startle you."

"What are you doing out here—besides following me?"

"I just... I only wanted to talk."

"*Talk*? *Now* you want to talk? We've had plenty of chances to talk, but you and my father have been very clear you don't want me involved in any of it! And there's apparently nothing more to talk about anyway! His mind is made up!"

Fearbane took a step forward. "Let me explain."

"That's close enough. I'd hate for you to get too far away from the camp. You should be back there with all the others cheering my father's plans to attack!"

"He's my king. I'm obligated to support him."

"But you're not obligated to agree with everything he says. Supporting him may mean telling him what he needs to know, not just what he wants to hear!"

"He's very determined to protect his family. And so am I."

"That's the problem. His obsession with protecting his family made him back away from my proposed retaliatory actions. And today the same emotions are pushing him to attack! Which is it?"

"But you can't blame a father for worrying about the safety of his family."

"I can when it clouds his judgment! Besides, he has obligations that go beyond being a father. He's the ruler of a great kingdom, and he will be neither a caring father nor a wise king if he allows his judgment to be compromised. The best thing he can do for his family is to protect his kingdom—the kingdom entrusted to him, to which we also belong!"

"Princess Charissa, may I at least accompany you back to the camp?"

"Why? So you can protect me? I think it's *you* who need *my* protection! Who taught you how to walk in the woods?"

Fearbane swallowed hard but stifled a smile as she tromped past him and back toward the camp.

———※———

When Charissa arrived at the girls' tent, her sisters and Amy were there, and to her great surprise, so were Lars, Hamelin, and her father. He stood when she walked in.

"I asked your sisters for permission to wait here with them until you returned. I also asked Prince Lars and Hamelin to join us."

"Did you send Fearbane to find me?"

"I was worried about you." He looked around the tent. "About all of you. I noticed you were reluctant to stand, and it could not have been more plain that my daughters were not pleased with my decision. Could we discuss this?" He motioned toward the chairs and beds.

Charissa remained standing. "Father, with all due respect, our feelings about your decision don't matter. You've made up your mind, and your military leaders and chief advisers support you, so there's nothing more to say."

"My dear Charissa—and I speak to all of you—what you think does matter to me. There's no one I trust more, and no one has done more than each of you in your own way to restore our family and bring us to this critical point. Your opinions matter—"

"Then why did you decide without hearing them all?"

Several long seconds passed, and Carr's face looked tired and old, showing the signs of years of decision-making. "Much is at stake for our people, including the families still in the city. Many of them did not want to stay with Landon. They were simply trapped inside when his dogs turned violent and he captured the city. Our people suffering with us here in this exiled kingdom long to retake Parthogen and be reunited with their loved ones on the other side of the city walls."

The king had been looking mostly at Charissa and his other daughters, but now he stood and extended his hand toward Hamelin.

"But more than that—how could I do anything that would unnecessarily endanger this young man who has done so much for our family? He joined Eraina to rescue you, Charissa, and then took you through the pond for healing. He also gave us hope that Layla was alive and encouraged her to come home to us, and then he endured the painful trials of returning through the cave by himself and bringing the water to Sophie."

He walked over to Hamelin and touched the gold chain around his neck. "When I presented this to you, it was not just a birthday gift. It was a chain passed to me by my father, who received it from his father, a practice going back many generations. With this chain, I brought you into our family and made you a brother to my daughters and a son to me."

And then he looked at Lars and Amy. "And how could I do anything to endanger the two of you? Lars, Prince of Periluna, you are as dear to me as your father, my friend King Elwood. He and I shared many adventures together as young men, princes of our respective realms. And now you have risked your life for my daughters and my kingdom. And Amy, you left your mother and life on the other side to accompany Layla on the journey to Gloaming and then here to Parthogen, carried by strange creatures, and you have already fought a wicked monster from Chimera."

He paused and slowly looked at each person.

"I will not endanger any of you beyond reason, though the Ancient One has by different paths brought us all to this moment. My men long to retake their city and return to their homes, but in addition to considering their eagerness, I have concluded that we must move quickly. There is danger for us all, but we know from our council that Hamelin has been summoned at even greater risk. It appears that he is the warrior who must fight another warrior in fulfillment of prophecy. And if that other warrior is Romulus, who has the sword, then one of them will die. That would bring unbearable grief to Layla's heart and to all of us, and divisive ruin to our family. I am doing all in my power to avoid that."

The king moved to the middle of the room and spoke with new energy. "For now, Romulus and Bryan are still distant. That's why I have decided that we can't wait. If Hamelin and Romulus don't fight each other, perhaps the Ancient One will lead us another way. If we act quickly, we can retake the city without precipitating a fight between them. I understand that my decision appears hasty, but I hope you know that I must protect all of you and our kingdom."

Everyone looked at Charissa. "Father, thank you for explaining why you have acted as you have. We readily agree that your intentions are true and good, but please allow me—I know you are in a hurry to proceed—at least to mention a few concerns." Carr nodded.

"Are we sure we can maneuver circumstances in such a way that we avoid one of the Ancient One's prophecies? Besides, if we don't know what the different warrior prophecies mean, then our plans to avoid their outcome could have the opposite effect. We might hasten the fulfillment! Surely it would be worth the effort to try to understand these things."

Carr shrugged. "I accept your point, though more in my head than my emotions. My instincts are still racing and driving me to move forward. But I will do my best to listen. What else do you think we need to understand?"

"Please remember that we began our council by agreeing to hold the four thrones prophecy until the end and then come back to it. But we never did, and there's a lot to consider. First, we've always read it to mean the four thrones will be filled and then the evil creatures will be overcome. It seems now—by attacking the city so that we can fill the four thrones—that we are reversing the order."

"But we can't get to the thrones until we retake the city. Surely that's obvious?"

"But, Father, your proposed order of events may be logical, but it is not obvious from the plain language of the prophecy. Isn't it true that a prophecy can have its fulfillment in surprising ways? And speaking of that, is it possible that the four thrones in our castle are not the ones referred to in the *Enchiridion*?"

Eraina shook her head, but her eyes reflected uncertainty. "Sophie and I have had this very discussion, and though I still think the four thrones of the prophecy are those in our castle, I admit that your question is worth reconsidering."

Charissa looked around the room. "Several of us have been to the Atrium of the Worlds. My life was changed there, and I will never forget what I saw..." She lifted her face and peered into the distance. The scenes of near death and healing that day filled her mind, and even the memory of them stirred her body as she momentarily relived it all—from fighting strange creatures while coming through the waters of death and life to emerging from the pond in the Atrium. She could again feel herself clinging to Hamelin's neck and shoulders from behind as the eagle pushed them through the water, and once more she sensed the great bird's sharp talons in her back. Such a painful way to be healed! And then she remembered her lungs nearly bursting before they broke the surface of the water and seeing a magnificent throne standing above and beyond them. Though she hadn't recalled the full scene in time to answer Eraina's earlier question, she now knew that it was possible for someone to sit on that throne.

In fact, for a brief instant, she had seen a human figure sitting there. Though the morning sun shining from an opening above and behind her had created a radiant glare and made the figure hazy, there was no mistaking his momentary presence.

The Great Eagle had then deposited them at the side of the pond, where they sat dripping but laughing with joy and feeling more fully alive than ever before. She had known then that she was herself again, though really not herself. She was a better self than she had ever been—her true self. Her body and her mind felt clean and right.

In her mind's eye, she could see it all—the Atrium and the plant life vibrant with color all around the room at the base of each wall. And formed out of each of the four walls was an elevated throne, high, huge, and magnificent, and while she wouldn't call them ornate—because there was no handcrafting, metal work, or precious stones on them—each had a beauty that reflected a plan and a purpose, beyond anything that human craftsmanship could have done. And yet they somehow seemed unfinished—was it their emptiness?

The base of the room was square, but as she gazed higher, the Atrium took on more of a circular appearance, and above each throne and connecting them was something like an ocean of water—oh, yes, Hamelin had said the eagle called it "a crystal sea"—that converged above the thrones and rose to the top of the dome-like ceiling. And at the top was the opening to the sky straight above them. The great cat had brought her down through that years ago.

She hadn't thought of it before, but now in her memories she somehow knew that she had stood in a unique spot, where earth and the upper realms of the skies met.

No one said a word while Charissa peered into the distance. The scenes raced through her mind in a matter of seconds, and her body trembled from reliving the soaring impact of those moments in the Atrium of the Worlds. She blinked slowly, and her gaze refocused on her sisters and father. "Could those formations be the four thrones of the prophecy?" She sat down, needing to think.

Layla stepped over to her and touched her on the shoulder. "I first read about the prophecy when I was still on the other side, and I imagined they were four ornate thrones that kings and queens would sit on. But when I got to the Atrium, I had the same impression as Charissa, that the formations on the walls were shaped like four giant thrones—and the four thrones of the prophecy immediately came to my mind."

Amy nodded. "They hit me the same way too."

Eraina couldn't remain seated. "But there are four mysterious thrones in our castle, and we can't rule them out! They were left to our family long ages ago and, according to the stories we've heard, were brought here by the envoy of a great king. Father, hasn't the word always been passed down that they were the four thrones of the prophecy? And that they would one day be filled? Besides, who could possibly fill four hidden thrones in a cave? Surely we cannot lightly pass by such an ancient tradition."

Eraina's question hung in the silence, until Layla spoke. "I don't know how to answer all that, though I certainly agree that we have to respect a long tradition of interpretation. But we still have to admit that prophecies can be hard to decipher."

Layla glanced toward Hamelin but then looked to the king. "I have some of the same worries as you, Father, but I'm not sure if avoiding a fight will prevent the death we hate even to consider. According to one of the texts in the *Enchiridion*, a warrior must die when the fourth throne is filled. That's the reason I didn't want to come. So, even without a fight between Hamelin and Romulus, just retaking the city and filling the four thrones could mean that a warrior will die by some other means. And maybe it's a different warrior."

Carr let out a frustrated sigh. "There's so much to consider. I'm not sure we have time or even enough information to unravel all these mysteries and puzzles."

Layla turned her palms up and scrunched her shoulders against her neck.. "And we haven't even begun to discuss why SueSue sent Lars through the cave to the other side."

Lars tilted his head, and his eyebrows rose in a slow arch. "It's a long story, and I've told it to most of you, but I'll try to be quick. SueSue sent me to get Hamelin and Layla over here, because something called "the tremors" was getting close. Apparently this is a series of troubles that will get worse and worse and then ignite not only various battles but finally a great battle. Right, Layla?"

"That's right. And the tremors would be started by something called 'the detestable thing.'"

The king shook his head and waited. Long seconds passed in silence.

"Father," said Sophie, "we have raised so many issues, but you bear the burden of deciding." She glanced toward Charissa.

"Sophie is right. Even with these questions, we will support whatever you decide, Father."

He stood. "I've learned over the years that you have to have enough information to make a sound decision, but if you wait to get all the information, you'll be too late." He walked toward the opening of the tent and then turned back to face everyone.

"I also know it's possible to be too hasty, and I want to avoid that. But recently I was much too slow. I should have retaliated against Landon, though I was fearful then of putting all of you in danger, especially Sophie, who was still in a coma."

Sophie smiled. "Thank you for protecting us all, Father. But remember what Hamelin and you both said earlier. That this is the Ancient One's fight. If it's his fight, it's also up to him to give you what you need to make a final decision, so you won't be either too slow or too fast. You said it yourself. He has summoned all of us to this moment. Perhaps now we must wait upon him."

"I understand your words. I'm sure they are wise, but I don't know how we wait for the Ancient One." He paused, and then his voice filled with emotion. "Years ago I let Landon deceive me, and I was too slow to recognize his treachery. Had I been wiser and not waited, perhaps Flora…"

He turned away to face the opening. His shoulders dropped. Eraina rushed over and with her arm around his waist leaned her head against him, but within seconds her head lifted, and her back straightened. She moved her hands to grip the ends of her scarf and peered into the distance.

She took a step outside the opening and turned. "Lars, Hamelin, anybody, come with me!"

⸺◉⸺

Hamelin and Lars quickly caught up with Eraina, still staring north into the distance, and strode with her from the tent. Hamelin had often seen her use the scarf, and he strained his eyes to detect anything in the northern sky. And then his stomach twisted into a knot. Though he could see nothing now, he remembered what had happened the last time he'd looked into that sky. The eagle had been coming, and that had led to the disaster with the horse and Sophie's terrible fall and injury. The sight of the great bird arriving from the north again would mean only one thing—that he was being taken back to the other side.

But why now? He hadn't done anything wrong, had he? Of course he'd done nothing wrong one time earlier either, when the eagle in a surprise appearance returned him to the children's home on Christmas Eve. So what was it now? Eraina stopped and stood still. Maybe she wasn't seeing the eagle after all. Maybe there was something else. He looked at her. Hoping.

Lars was also eager to know what she was seeing. He leaned close to her. "What is it?"

Eraina unrolled the scarf and spread it over her head. As she did so, Hamelin glanced back and saw the others catching up—Layla, Charissa, and Amy, and even the king, with Sophie next to him. Fearbane too. Several soldiers and some onlookers tried to join, but Fearbane waved them away. Everyone looked worried.

Eraina gripped the ends of the scarf in both hands, and her eyes narrowed. She turned her head to Lars. "It's the eagle, and he's coming this way."

Why didn't she look at him too? He was standing right next to Lars. Was there something she didn't want to say? Hamelin dropped back a step.

The others gathered around Eraina.

"She sees the eagle," whispered Lars.

Everyone looked toward the northern sky, but still only Eraina could see anything. She began to give updates.

"He's flying toward us, and he's looking directly at us."

Hamelin's chest felt heavy, and his breathing grew rapid. He put his hands on his knees. His throat was dry. Surely he wouldn't have to fly a long way without a drink of water.

And then, even worse, Sophie must have been thinking the same thing. She whispered to her sister, but Hamelin still heard her.

"Is he coming to get Hamelin?"

"It's like before. He's coming at us and getting lower."

Hamelin wanted to scream, *"No!"* But he knew it wouldn't do any good. And he knew what he had to do now. He separated himself a few more steps from the group and turned his back. He lifted his arms so the eagle could pick him up from behind, the way he usually did. He couldn't believe it was happening again now. He'd just gotten here!

Then Eraina shouted with a happy energy in her voice. "*Wait*! I don't think he's... He's going too fast to—and he's too high!"

The eagle suddenly burst into view, and everyone could see him with the naked eye. And within seconds, they heard a powerful whoosh as the great bird flew above them and passed by.

But the magnificent creature produced more than a sound. The drafting forces created by his high-speed flight stirred powerful gusts all around them, and everyone's clothes flapped in the winds as they turned to the south and craned their necks upward. Within seconds, the eagle was barely visible.

Charissa took a few steps in that direction but stopped. "What's he doing now?"

"He's banking and arcing left, to the east. Now he's a long way...but wait! He's sweeping north again... It's like he's making a giant circle. You should be able to see him." She pointed as everyone turned.

Hamelin's fears returned. So maybe the eagle would grab him from the other direction? But would that mean he was heading north to Osmethan? Or...*Ventradees*?

Eraina kept her arm extended, pointing at the eagle as he flew back northward toward them. But once again the great bird flew over them, pummeling the air with his powerful wings and heading into the distance. He was soon out of sight to all except her, but the torrents of wind he had stirred up continued to blow, gusting and swirling in all directions.

"What does it mean?" Layla shouted over the noise of the rushing currents.

"It is a portent," said Sophie. "The Ancient One is moving, stirring things up."

Chapter 19

A Strange Plan

It wasn't the first time Layla had seen the eagle. She had of course seen him only a few days before, as had everyone else, when Hamelin's horse bolted and threw Sophie. But then there was no time to think about the unusual creature. After the accident, she had focused all her attention on her sister. But now, actually her fourth time at least to see the great bird, something else happened—seeing the eagle stirred memories that included the trip with Amy through the cave but quickly plunged into a dark abyss of painful, broken recollections of the drowning of her parents on the other side, the Trotts. Even she and Bryan rarely talked about it, but now the mental pictures came back of that terrible early morning years ago when their family was forced off a bridge and her parents died.

That's when she had first seen the eagle. The amazing bird had saved her and Bryan from an attacking dog and flown them from under the bridge to safety. It was hard not to experience again the grief of those moments. And now, following the high winds stirred up by the eagle, she was not only impressed once more with the power of the great bird, but also reminded of her present worries and fears, because her wise little sister here in Gloaming called the eagle's coming a portent, describing the winds as mighty deeds stirred up by the Ancient One. Obviously her father agreed and further interpreted these things as a signal to move forward in accordance with his views of the four thrones prophecy. All of it renewed her dread that someone, a warrior, would soon die.

Immersed in these thoughts, she returned to the middle of the camp for the evening meal and approached the table near her father's council tent that was reserved for the royal family and their friends. She and her sisters often met there with Amy, Lars, and Hamelin for supper and a review of the day's activities.

Charissa, however, was not at their usual table. After the eagle's strangely created windstorm, her father had returned to his large council tent and summoned Fearbane and his closest advisers on strategic military matters. Charissa had followed.

Layla found a place at the supper table where she could keep an eye on her father's tent. She hoped Charissa would soon join them, because they needed her analytical mind to help them think about the day's events.

Once everyone else was seated, the meal was served. It was simple fare—a few vegetables, some meat, bread, and water. They were eager to talk but needed to do so in private, not while servants lingered nearby and could listen in. So the conversation began with unimportant matters.

Sooner than Layla expected, there was movement around her father's tent. Most of the advisers streamed out, and Fearbane emerged with Charissa. They stood talking, and she seemed to be slowly shaking her head, but finally she shrugged. Fearbane pointed toward Layla and the others, and Charissa nodded and came their way.

As she approached, two servants came forward with her plate and drink and arranged the remaining food nearer her place at the table.

"Thank you. This will be quite enough for me, and now I need to talk to everyone else." The servants nodded and stepped away. Charissa then tersely related what she had heard—and stopped. Everyone looked surprised.

Eraina pushed her half-eaten plate of food toward the center of the table. "We're going to do what?"

Sophie chuckled, looked around the table, and winked. "A princess party sounds good to me."

Layla had taken a drink of water, but she quickly put her glass down. She didn't intend to bang it against the table, but the noise drew everyone's attention. "Well, it certainly doesn't to me."

Hamelin fidgeted. "I thought they were discussing battle strategies."

Lars picked up a napkin and touched the corners of his mouth with it. "Charissa, could you start again from the beginning and repeat what the plan is?"

"They want us to have a princess party tomorrow. It's part of their strategy."

Eraina leaned forward with both hands in front of her. "Strategy? I thought Father was on the verge of attacking! Now he wants to have a presentation of Layla as a princess? All of us do too, but—no offense, Layla—"

"None taken."

"I don't see how these two things fit together."

Charissa tilted her head to one side and shrugged. "I didn't admit it to Fearbane, but since Father is committed to an attack soon, this strategy actually does make sense once you think about it. Basically, the idea is that Father is going to launch an all-out attack against Landon—the coming of the eagle has convinced him it's time to act. But he needs time to ensure that our armies are fully prepared, our weapons ready, and our supply lines fully stocked and in place. And, of course, that the battle plans have been communicated to everyone."

"That makes sense," said Eraina. "All that takes time. But why a princess party? That's a huge event, and it takes time to arrange too."

"That's part of the reasoning. The first factor is timing, because it'll take some time to prepare to attack. But the other is to provide a cover. If we start a flurry of activity, immediately mobilizing everyone in the camp, it will attract attention. Landon will certainly detect it."

Amy tapped the table with her hand. "I see. So if we're planning a princess party, that will give Landon the impression that, even with a burst of activity over here, nothing threatening to him is going on. That we have other things on our mind. Is that it?"

Charissa nodded. "If we're making arrangements for a formal event, he won't be expecting an attack."

Lars picked up a piece of bread. "It wouldn't be very smart for anyone to launch an attack in these high winds anyway. Ever since the eagle came through, the swirling gusts haven't stopped."

Charissa finally took a small bite of food, but at the same time she glanced around the table and lowered her voice, even though no one else was around. "Exactly. He believes the eagle is helping us. With the winds blowing in every direction, Landon wouldn't anticipate anything threatening from us. We'll look like we're just preparing for a big party. But Father's planners say the winds are likely to die down late tomorrow, so our archers, our first line of attack, will be ready the next day. That's the plan."

Sophie patted Charissa's hand. "But there's still something about it you don't like."

Charissa frowned but then nodded slightly. "I just wish we had more information, that we were a little more sure of what we're doing."

"My big sister, you always want more facts. It's the way your mind works." She then pointed to the trees and other signs of the high winds. "These aren't just random gusts. They're here because the Great Eagle has stirred them up. I think Father was almost convinced to wait, but that's when Eraina spied the eagle and all of this happened. And these winds are still here. We may not know what it all means, but surely something is afoot."

Charissa looked at her little sister and put her other hand on top of Sophie's, which still lay over hers. "You're right. We said we would trust whatever Father decided, and he has decided. I certainly can't dispute that these winds are coming from the Ancient One's creature. Besides, whatever I think about the wind and the plan, at this point it doesn't matter. Everything is set."

Sophie clapped her hands and stood. "So what time is the party?"

Layla leaned forward. "Wait—" But her voice was drowned out by others shuffling their chairs and standing.

"About five o'clock tomorrow," said Charissa. "While some will be preparing for the party, others will be secretly getting weapons and supply lines in order. We'll have the presentation and further celebrations and then launch our attack early the next morning."

Eraina grinned. "I guess if there's going to be a princess party, we might as well enjoy it."

Layla groaned. The nightmare was happening, and her sisters were helping with the plans! "But—" And once again her words were covered, especially by Eraina, who was already taking charge of arrangements.

"Amy, you could help us get Layla ready. We can pick out

the clothes for her, but you should come along and watch us teach her the special curtsy and some other protocols, and then you can help her practice."

Layla tried again. "But—"

"No problem," said Amy. "I've recently flown with the eagle, learned how to ride lions and bulls, and kicked at a rat-snake. A few little curtsies should be a piece of cake."

Eraina wrinkled her eyebrows at Amy's expression involving cake and twisted her mouth. "Oh, don't worry. There will be plenty of cake, and you can have all you want. And, Lars, we need you to work with Hamelin, since he'll be Layla's escort. He'll need to learn a few of our special dance steps."

Eraina, Amy, and Sophie laughed, and even Charissa smiled. Hamelin exhaled and slumped his shoulders. Layla sat back down and put her face in her hands. She didn't want the others to see the tears forming in her eyes.

Chapter 20

The Princess Party: A Cape, a Crown, and a Chant

FROM EARLY THE NEXT MORNING UNTIL MIDAFTERNOON, Carr's camp teemed with activities, most of them devoted to the attack on Parthogen planned for the following day, though significant hours were also spent preparing for the princess party later that afternoon. Layla watched it all and could think of nothing else. If the attack failed, there would certainly be great bloodshed. If it succeeded, the four thrones could be filled and then—but she tried not to think about the prophecy that predicted death once the fourth throne was filled.

Her sisters—and even the king when he occasionally stopped by to check on his daughters—gave every appearance of blocking from their minds the preparations for war going on all around them. Carr encouraged Layla—telling her how her mother would have planned the ceremony and assuring her that it really would be very special—and her sisters worked on her hair, cosmetics, and clothes. Lars prepared Hamelin for his role, and Amy spent concentrated time with Layla, practicing the special curtsy, as well as the steps for the ceremonial dance.

Layla hoped for something—maybe by the eagle?—that would bring the plans to a surprising halt, but the presentation began as scheduled—just a few minutes after five o'clock. She and her sisters awaited the signal to begin their ceremonial walk from their tent to the presentation area. She peered through the opening and in the distance could see her father and Hamelin, her designated escort, just a few paces to his left, both of them facing the path she and her sisters would take toward them. Crowds of people gathered from all over the camp.

Her father was dressed in high royal attire, including his crown. A canvas awning had been erected and was held in place by royal guards to provide shade during the ceremony and to block as much as possible the high winds that continued to blow, especially now from the west.

The trumpets blew, announcing the beginning of the processional, and the people lining the walkway directed their attention to the sisters' tent. The flaps of the tent were ceremoniously opened by royal attendants, and Charissa, Eraina, and Sophia, dressed as princesses with their crowns in place, slowly began the march toward their father. After they covered half the distance, the three sisters stopped and turned back toward the tent, watching for Layla. The music swelled, and a trumpet fanfare blew again, louder and richer than the first.

Layla stepped into full view, and even from a distance, she could see her father stand straighter. His whole face broke into a smile, and she felt a hope rise within her that he could indeed recover his capital city and have all four daughters around him. His old age would then have some compensation for the years of grief he had spent after losing his wife and his city—and enduring the loss of Layla for twenty years. She slowly walked along the path her sisters had taken and passed them with smiles and nods, and at one point she stifled a puff of nervous laughter as she lowered her eyes, before catching herself and once again looking up toward her father. Everyone was staring at her, and she heard comments about the beauty of Carr's newly found daughter.

Though quartered in a military camp in the woods and deprived of all the comforts of their castle, the ladies-in-waiting and the sisters had managed to acquire the clothing, special oils, and cosmetics to make her radiantly beautiful. She hardly recognized herself, still thinking of herself as a Texas girl who usually wore blue jeans and plaid shirts, with little or no make-up and her long, quickly brushed brunette curls tied up in the back. And now she was stunningly dressed like a princess. She wore, at her sisters' insistence, their mother's full-length gown—royal blue with hints of ivory and pink thread that the full sun picked up—and white gloves and matching slippers. Her hair was twisted into a loose braid with a single curl on each side and interlaced with small white flowers and a chain of fine gold. Around her neck was a single strand of pearls.

She approached the area where her father stood, and her sisters followed, forming a three-person arc just behind her. Amy was also near the front but stood across from Hamelin on the other side of the processional walk.

Layla's name was announced by a finely dressed attendant, the lord chamberlain. His voice boomed, "Alathea Trott Collier Carr." The king smiled, and Hamelin watched her, looking at her father as her eyes began to glisten. "Daughter of His Majesty, King Carr, royal sovereign of Parthogen, and Her Majesty, the late Flora Carr, queen of these same lands. Also," continued the chamberlain, "daughter of Robert and Jessie Patricia Trott, great guardians of the princess in lands beyond the Atrium!" All those names together told the story of her life and made persons and places race through her mind.

And amid the joy and pageantry of it all, Layla felt a jarring stab of fear. She was actually here! Was this all a big mistake?

Bryan had told her not to come. He had said that if she filled the fourth throne, there was no telling what else could happen. That it could mean death to a warrior, maybe Hamelin or their brother, Michael, or both. What had she done? Then she looked ahead at Hamelin, who was smiling at her and waiting for her to approach. And her father, the king, was also waiting. He was older but still the man of her memories, the one who had held her in his lap in his library with all the books around, constantly laughing when he hugged her. And then her sisters giggled, and her mind snapped back.

The king maintained his dignity, but a smile of amusement began forming on his face as Layla hesitated at the beginning of her next step. Her sisters were trying, with facial expressions and their own slight body movements, to help her get through the coming high moment of the ceremony: the official, royal curtsy.

Layla glanced toward Amy, who gave her a nod, plus a wink and a smile that said, "Come on now, you can do it." Layla regained her balance. She moved her right leg fully behind her, lowered herself to her knee, extended her right hand toward Hamelin, and waited until he stepped over and likewise faced the king and took her right hand with his left.

Then to the surprise of all but Amy, she released Hamelin's hand and bent completely from the waist, extending her left and right arms fully while touching her face to her dress, which lay spread in front of her. The crowd cheered to see such a curtsy, strange and different but beautifully executed in complete deference to the king. The king beamed with wide eyes, the sisters clapped, and when Eraina let out a cheer, the entire crowd took permission from that and joined in. And over the cheers at one point, Layla could hear Amy yell, "Atta, girl! You *did* it— the *Texas Dip*! Just like the pageant at the West Texas Fair and Rodeo!" The cheering stopped as Layla gracefully rose to her feet, Hamelin again taking her right hand.

Her father stepped forward, and her sisters came closer from behind. They had in their hands a beautiful pink satin cape, which they placed around her neck and Carr fastened in front. The cape was made of the finest silk and had around its neck area what looked like a fluffy pillowed collar of pure white wool, which covered her neck especially in the back and to the sides.

The king then turned to his right to face an attendant who was extending toward him a crimson pillow, trimmed in gold, on which lay a crown, one identical to those worn by her sisters. The king reached out with both hands, took the crown with his little fingers held aloft, and turned back in a neat, easy pivot toward Layla. Once again she lowered herself but this time in a half-curtsy. Her father leaned forward and delicately placed the crown on her head, then stepped back. She raised her eyes to him and could see from his smile that she was now to stand. The king extended his right hand, his palm turned up, and she placed her left hand in it. And as he raised her up, he pulled her gently to his side, and she turned just as planned to face her sisters first and then the audience. Quiet *ahhhs* went up around the entire area.

"I now present to you," said the king, in a voice louder than any she had ever heard him use, "*Princess Alathea*! *First* daughter of the House of Trott! *Second* daughter of the House of Carr!" And then the king paused, but everyone knew he was not through. His eyes swept across the waiting, uplifted faces of the crowd and returned to rest on his four daughters. His chest swelled, and he focused again on Layla to finish his proclamation: "The *Fourth Princess* of the Kingdom of Parthogen!"

The audience erupted in cheers.

And from within the cheers, a chant arose, first from one voice, but quickly joined by others, and then the entire crowd, "*Four Thrones! Four Thrones! Four Thrones!*" Within seconds, it spread and reverberated throughout Carr's camp.

As soon as the crowd started chanting, light from somewhere around her made everything momentarily blur. Panic rolled over her stomach and chest and lodged in her throat. She felt warm, and her forearms glowed. Was that perspiration? Or...?

Hamelin! Where was Hamelin? Her jaw trembled. She instinctively pursed her lips and shut her eyes, but she couldn't stop the images in her mind's eye from rushing toward her. She saw something throwing off a glint of light. An arrow? A sword? She quickly opened her eyes, and there stood Hamelin just a few feet away, facing her, smiling and waiting. Whatever she had imagined had passed.

On cue, the musicians began playing rhythmic, gliding music. Her sisters did a kind of circling walk-like dance around her, holding hands, first in one direction and then in another. And then it was Hamelin's turn. Amy had given him lessons earlier in the afternoon, and now the moment presented itself. He stepped toward Layla, reached out his right hand, palm up, and she took it in her left hand with her palm down. Hamelin leaned over and whispered, "I wish Bryan were here; he should be doing this." Emotion filled her throat and nose and threatened her eyes with tears, but she held them back.

The music swelled into exactly what Amy had prepared them for, something like a minuet, but Amy had simplified the steps for both of them. They moved so that they stood side by side, Hamelin holding Layla's left hand in his right, shoulder high, their elbows bent. They put their outside hands on their hips and slowly walked forward to the music in minuet style, four small steps, and then dipped slightly, bending one knee with the other foot held aloft. They repeated the same process backing up but dipped slightly again after the first two steps and then after the fourth. The series repeated itself, and then they raised their right arms and touched hands palm to palm and walked promenade style in a circle, matching the rhythm of the music.

But the patterns of music then became broken and discordant. Strange, non-musical sounds filled the air—swishing noises followed by loud thumps that popped all around them. She glanced at the musicians. What was happening? Then the canvas awning, as if shredded by knives, exploded with ripping sounds, and screaming immediately followed as soldiers rushed to protect the royal family and honored guests.

Fearbane lifted his voice above the panicked shrieks. "To *cover*! To *cover*! We are *under attack*!"

Someone else, one of Fearbane's commanders, yelled, "To our planned positions?"

"*Yes*! But *pull back* by forty paces! The winds are high, and Landon's longbows are flying great distances! *Back*, Your Majesty! All of your family, *run* for cover!"

Layla ran, still holding Hamelin by the hand. She could see that her sisters, with Lars and Amy, were all being pushed to cover. She continued to hear screams and then more swishing and thudding of arrows as they flew and hit all around.

In the chaos, she stumbled and fell, and looked up as Hamelin bent over her to pull her to her feet. An arrow that otherwise would have hit her, had she not fallen, whizzed above her. She heard a sickening sound, and Hamelin groaned loudly. Someone—one of Carr's soldiers?—then scooped her into his arms and rushed toward cover. "*No*! Help *Hamelin*!" But her words were lost amid the noises and fog of war: shouts, screams, rattling armor, and weapons.

The last thing she saw before her view was blocked by soldiers and others rushing in all directions was someone holding Hamelin from behind, under his armpits, and dragging him away.

Someone was pulling on his arms, while a searing pain cut across his scalp and something warm streamed down his face. Shadowy faces...where was Layla?! Darkness filled his eyes.

Chapter 21

Waiting to Be Told

THE SOLDIER WHO RUSHED LAYLA TO SAFETY DEPOSITED her not so gently in one of the king's tents, far enough away from the battle lines to be safe. She immediately spied Amy, Eraina, Sophie and a few others already there and looked around frantically before rushing toward the opening.

"Hamelin's hurt! I've got to find him!"

Charissa entered just then. "Stay here! I've already sent someone to check on him." She then pointed to a nearby soldier assigned to guard their tent. "*You*! Take word to our ladies-in-waiting. Tell them we are all here and are in need of clothing fit for battle. Then make sure our horses are saddled, and fetch bows and arrows for my sisters. The ones they are accustomed to using."

He hesitated. Charissa glared. "*Now*!" He dashed away.

Charissa then turned to Layla and Amy.

"I'm sorry, but you're not trained in these weapons. We will make sure you have clothes suitable for movement, but for now, if fighting breaks out, you must stay to the rear, under the protection of soldiers who will be assigned to you."

Layla remained at the opening. "Charissa, please let me go check on Hamelin."

"My sister, I understand your concern. All of us share it. Hamelin is beloved by our family and all of Parthogen for what he has done. But the best thing we can do is prepare ourselves for the circumstances we now face. Hamelin is being cared for by the finest of our father's physicians. We cannot put you or those escorting you over there at risk, especially since you'll likely only be in the way."

Layla lowered her head and closed her eyes.

Charissa's voice softened. "I'll make sure I get a report as soon as possible." Amy walked over to Layla.

Charissa then turned to another soldier, who stiffened his posture. "Make sure those ladies-in-waiting get here safely— and soon! And get that report on Hamelin back to me!" The soldier raced away.

Eraina moved to a window of the tent that faced north and pulled the scarf over her head, holding it with both hands.

Sophie talked to another soldier, who nodded sharply and left.

Before long, several ladies-in-waiting rushed in with their arms full. They distributed the clothes Charissa had requested, and within minutes the girls had changed.

Everyone chatted in whispers while Charissa paced nervously, occasionally looking out the main door toward the large tent where she knew her father would be meeting with Fearbane and his leading commanders.

Soon two more soldiers came to their tent and were allowed in by Charissa. They spoke briefly with her before distributing bows and arrows and small shields for those who knew how to use them. Eraina took hers and quickly returned to the small window facing north. Charissa resumed walking in a tight circle, looking down, taking deep breaths, and rubbing her upper lip with her index finger. Long minutes passed.

Layla approached. "Charissa, is there any more news about Hamelin?"

"None. I'm sorry."

Another messenger appeared at the tent door.

"I have what you requested, Princess Sophia."

"Good. Bring it all in, and set it out on that big table." The soldier signaled to others outside, and within moments servants hurried in with bundles of food.

Sophie smiled. "I thought it would be a shame for all that special princess party food to go to waste. Besides, I think we're going to need our strength for what we may be facing."

"What do you think is going to happen next?" asked Amy.

"If I know my father, he'll soon be ordering a counterattack."

Eraina turned from the opening and walked closer to the group. "That's what I expect as well."

Charissa took a deep breath and pursed her lips but said nothing.

Sophie clapped her hands. "Come on. Let's get something to eat."

"Do you mind if we join you?" came a familiar voice at the door. At once they all turned. It was Lars. And standing next to him was Hamelin!

"Hamelin!" yelled Layla, and everyone rushed over to the two young men.

Lars was helping Hamelin, who had one arm around Lars's shoulder. His head was heavily bandaged, and the bandage showed signs of blood, especially high on the right side of his forehead. The two boys were escorted by a team of three soldiers, who stood there until Charissa sent them away.

"Are you okay?" said Eraina.

"I'm good." But he was obviously weak, his face pale.

Lars helped him move toward the table. "He got hit by an arrow. Fortunately it only grazed him. But it caught him right in the scalp line, and it bleeds a lot there. He's lost some blood, but the doctor says he'll be all right."

"I'm okay. Really. It looks bad, but I'll be fine."

"The doctor said he can't move around for a few days," added Lars.

"Good thing there's nothing much going on around here," muttered Amy.

Lars helped Hamelin sit. "If he does, it'll start bleeding again. They wanted him to stay where he was in the king's tent, but he insisted on finding all of you."

Layla came to Hamelin and put her cheek next to his on the side away from the wound. "I wish you had stayed where you were, but we're glad to know you're okay."

Eraina patted his shoulder. "And I'm glad you're here to learn what I've just seen. All of you, listen to this. It's about the eagle. I've been watching him."

Charissa turned from the main opening. "Where is he?"

"I saw him ascend out of his nest and head west. Right now, he's directly northwest of us, still a long way off, and climbing higher. But he's also circling."

"Circling?"

"Yes, at a high speed and in a tight spiral."

"Can you check again?"

Eraina went back to her window and peered again with the scarf over her head.

"There is something else. I see a cloud...the size of my fist... moving toward the eagle. Now more clouds are coming up out of the northwest...thunderclouds...they're building and the eagle is circling faster. It's like he's drawing the clouds toward himself. It's the strangest thing I've ever seen."

Eraina said nothing more for a few moments, then, "The clouds he's stirring up have turned into a whole bank of thunderheads, and there's lightning. The clouds are dark, and the eagle is still circling, but he's in the midst of the clouds. No, he's above the clouds, and now he's flying southeast, in our direction!"

"What about the clouds?" asked Charissa.

"They're following him, as if he's pulling them like a bridal train."

"What else?"

"Oh, my! It's not just clouds now. It's a whole wave of darkness in the northwest, from west to north, and it's breaking loose."

"What do you mean 'breaking loose'?" Charissa's voice was hurried.

"Rain! Rain is pouring out of the clouds, and the eagle is still pulling them toward us. It's a huge caravan! Everything from the mountain range south of Osmethan all the way to the Forest of Fears is getting a soaking! It's moving fast. If it gets all the way to us, it won't take long. And it looks like it's coming!"

At that moment, a soldier appeared at the opening of the tent. "*Princess Charissa!*"

Charissa huffed and abruptly spun toward the soldier. Her eyes betrayed her clear annoyance at hearing her name called in that way. "Yes?"

"I've been sent by the king. He requests that you take everyone to the farthest and most southern end of the camp."

"Why?"

"Why, my lady? It's...it's the king's command." The soldier swallowed hard. "He also says I'm to accompany you."

"And why does the king, my father, want us to leave this tent?"

The soldier remained silent, but he uneasily shifted his weight from one foot to the other.

"Why?" This time she spoke very slowly.

"My lady, there is a rumor..." He paused and glanced over his left shoulder.

"Yes, and the rumor is...?"

The words spilled out of the young soldier. "The rumor is there's going to be a counterattack. Within the hour."

"Remain here with everyone. No one is to leave!" She stared at the soldier. "Do you understand?"

"Yes, my lady." He nodded hard.

She turned and looked at her sisters and the others.

"All of you, stay here. I'm going to go speak with Father." She glanced at Hamelin. "And take care of his wound. He's starting to bleed."

Lars helped Hamelin to a bed. "Why don't you try to rest. We may have to fight soon."

Chapter 22

King and Daughter: A Family Struggle

C HARISSA STRODE INTO THE TENT WHERE KING CARR, Fearbane, and other commanders were talking in animated tones. The scene reminded her of bygone years when she had stood at her father's side, watching him point to strategic formations and listening as he taught her historic battle tactics. He glanced up when she entered but quickly looked away. The picture in her mind vanished, replaced by the stinging pain of her father's ignoring her, but she remained near the opening, several paces away from the war table.

The king pointed to the table and its maps and diagrams.

"Fearbane, review our situation! Where exactly do we stand?"

"We are still under attack, Sire, but we have suffered very few losses. We were able to get our people backed up farther east and south, and we are now outside the range of Landon's longbows, even with the high winds."

"What about our soldiers?"

"They're in a bit of disarray, Your Majesty, but the commanders are riding amongst the troops and restoring order. They are forming up within the wooded area. The main force is in the middle, with left and right flanks."

"How long before they are ready to counterattack?"

"Soon, Your Majesty. The sun is still high enough in the west to hamper our vision, but within another hour, it will be behind the city walls and low enough for us to begin. We will not have much light after that, but—"

"Good, Lord Fearbane. As soon as our men are in their battle positions, let me know, and watch for my signal to commence the counterattack, and—"

Charissa stepped toward the table. "Father, may I speak?"

"My daughter, we are short of time! As my oldest, I know you understand the cruelties of war. That's why I sent word for you to make sure that your sisters and our friends and servants are out of harm's way."

"They are all secure for now. But I must speak about other matters, Father. Because what you have asked me to do is not enough."

The king stiffened his shoulders. "Not enough? What do you mean?"

"My father, I 'understand the cruelties of war,' because, as your oldest, I have been trained in the arts of war."

"And that's why I asked you to—"

"Arts of war that you taught me as you would a son! Not the oldest daughter who only takes care of the younger children!" She stared at her father, holding his eyes with hers.

Carr's face darkened. He returned her sharp tone. "You evidently have more to say. So proceed."

"Sire," began Fearbane, "the time is short."

Charissa glared at Fearbane. "And some of it now *wasted* because you are interrupting!"

The king raised his hand to prevent Fearbane's response. "It's all right, Fearbane. We will let her speak."

"I will speak quickly and plainly. If my sisters and I are one day to rule this kingdom, then we must be involved in its defense."

"I agree, and I have listened to you. But we are now under attack and—"

"And you intend to launch an immediate counterattack! But I am asking—once again—to be heard. I have only a few questions, and if Commander Fearbane can satisfy my mind on a few points, then I will gladly do as you say and usher our family and people to the rear. But you trained me to ask questions, and I believe you should listen."

The king breathed in deeply but suppressed a sigh. He nodded to Fearbane.

"What is it, my lady?" asked Fearbane.

"First, what is the disposition of the wind? How strong is it?"

"It greatly favors Landon, my lady. The winds are blowing directly from the west, and their longbows have a great advantage."

"So we must stay outside their range."

"Obviously so, my lady."

"They have attacked us, but they have a superior defensive position, do they not?"

"The city, as your ladyship knows well, sits on a spot elevated from our position."

"Have they attacked us with anything more than longbows?"

"I'm not sure what your ladyship means."

"I mean, Master Fearbane, have they followed up the longbows? Have they sent infantry, foot soldiers? Has Landon let loose his wolves and dogs?"

He paused before answering. "No..."

"And why are they holding their position? What do you think they expect, Fearbane?"

"They expect we will fight back."

"And if we don't?"

"If we *don't*? Our men will be disheartened, and Landon will scorn us! And we will continue to be exiled from our city and our homes. This is the very moment our commanders and soldiers have been waiting for, for months. It's not the way we planned it, but it is here. And now we must fight."

"But what happens if we wait?"

"Wait?"

"Yes. What happens if we simply hold our positions and let them continue to volley their arrows, and perhaps even encourage them to continue, so long as we don't move close enough for full engagement?"

"I think waiting would be out of the question! The longer we wait, the more opportunity Landon has to be reinforced. For now, if we wait, his brother Tumultor and his forces will surely arrive from the north."

Suddenly lightning cracked outside, and its light was visible through the large tent opening. Charissa turned her head up slightly and to the side, listening and waiting. Within a few seconds, a loud thunderclap hit.

"And what happens, Master Fearbane, if the storm that accompanies that lightning reaches us with rain?"

"Then...then we will be fighting in the rain, my lady." Fearbane appeared to be growing impatient with this line of questioning, having to belabor the obvious. He looked at the king.

"Just a few more questions, Father, and I will be content. If it rains, what will happen to Landon's longbows?"

"They'll get wet." After he said this, Fearbane paused, his head cocked to the left, his eyes lifting slightly as he momentarily stared into space.

"And if our archers keep their bowstrings dry, will that be to our advantage?"

"Yes..."

At that moment, Eraina rushed into the tent. "Father," she

said breathlessly and without waiting for permission to speak, "I've been looking at the horizon from due north to the west, and a huge storm is rapidly heading our way. It has already dumped large amounts of rain between us and the mountain range south of Osmethan."

The king moved toward the opening of the tent and looked to the skies. "When will it be here?"

"It's coming at great speed. My guess is it will be here within half an hour. It's a massive thunderstorm."

Just then, although it was still well before sundown, the skies began to darken. The wind shifted from the west and continued more from the northwest. Lightning struck again in the storm clouds, and within a matter of only two to three seconds, a loud thunderclap followed.

Charissa moved to the opening and with one arm widened the flap. "Eraina, use your scarf to look toward Osmethan and tell us about Tumultor and his armies."

Eraina didn't need to be in the open air to see, but she quickly stepped outside, and Charissa and Fearbane followed. She spread the scarf and stood looking for long moments. "I see no signs of an army massing. In fact, I see Tumultor in his castle. He is laughing and dining with a few others." They returned to the tent, and Fearbane repeated her words to the king and the other commanders.

"Then this truly is a surprise attack," said Carr. "Landon in his arrogance has launched this attack on his own."

Charissa stepped within an arm's length of Fearbane. "So now, Commander Fearbane, what happens if we wait?"

"My lady, in battle, I have learned through the years not to hesitate. We have planned for this attack, and waiting makes us appear weak and indecisive."

"I understand what you're saying. Waiting can make you appear weak, and sometimes it creates inward feelings of helplessness. But waiting is a discipline, and it requires its own kind of courage. My friend, I too have learned over the years. I have especially learned to wait. As everyone in Parthogen knows to my shame, I was captured because I couldn't stand to wait even a few hours before having my morning bath. I couldn't endure a single bit of hardship. But once captured, I waited for weeks in an underground room of darkness, with very little water and almost no food. There was no one to hear me pound on the walls or cry. At first I waited because I had no choice, but later I waited because I could remember all of you. I then chose to wait, to bide my time, to look for just the right moment to act. And when I did, I escaped from Tumultor.

"But even then my learning wasn't done. After I escaped, I found myself alone in a dark cave. I waited for my rescuers to come, but they didn't. If I had waited longer, there's no telling what else might have happened, but I'll never know if rescue would have come from another source, because I finally gave up. My courage failed, and I decided I could wait no longer. And then I was captured again."

"I am sorry, my lady, to hear—"

"No, good Fearbane, it is not for you to be sorry. But I have learned that there are times to wait. And waiting can be a choice, a deliberate strategy."

"So what are you suggesting we do?"

"I say we remain out of range of their longbows. We prepare for this storm that is about to hit, and we keep our bowstrings dry. I say we stay close enough to keep them firing at us. In fact, Lord Fearbane, I am certain you can devise tactics that will draw their attention and their volleys of arrows but not actually lead us into a charge."

"Certainly I can, my lady, but then?"

"We wait more. That is, we wait until their arrows are depleted, their men are tired, their bowstrings are wet."

"And then?"

"When it stops raining, and the wind stops blowing, and just as the wings of the sun rise in the east..." Charissa looked around the room, paused, and, leaning in, peered directly into Fearbane's eyes. "And then we *attack*."

Fearbane stood motionless at first, but then a smile played at the edges of his mouth.

They held each other's stares for a moment, and Fearbane's cheeks reddened. He turned toward Carr. "This is for His Majesty to decide."

Carr's face softened, but his eyes remained fixed on Charissa. He moved from behind his table and walked toward her. She stood straight and waited for her father's approach. He stopped in front of her. She was almost as tall as he. She bowed her head ever so slightly, while he reached toward her with both arms and touched her elbows with his hands.

She raised her head and met his eyes. He smiled. The sting of his earlier avoidance of her faded away.

"You have spoken well, my daughter, my oldest." He gazed at her for several seconds and closed his eyes. When he opened them, he dropped his hands from her elbows and turned toward Fearbane.

"Commander Fearbane, I believe you said you could devise tactics that would correspond to the strategy my daughter has suggested?"

"I can, Your Majesty."

Carr looked around the room. "We have a revised battle plan. If you are in doubt as to its structure or tactics, or in need of clarification, consult Princess Charissa or Fearbane. All of you will work together to execute it."

The room was silent until Eraina stepped forward. "Father, I've continued to watch, and the storm—" Suddenly the entire area was lit with jagged bolts of lightning, followed immediately by rolling echoes of thunder. Rain began to fall, and then, still an hour before sundown, the sky fully darkened.

Eraina started again. "So now I'll keep an eye on Tumultor, but even if he musters his troops and comes this way, the rain will slow him down. I can explain it to everyone later, but I'm sure this storm is no accident. The eagle has brought these rains, just as he did the winds, and they are for our benefit."

Chapter 23

Watching and Waiting: Day One

LARS WASN'T MUCH FOR DOING NOTHING, THOUGH IT FELT like he was doing just that—nothing. A lot could be happening around him, but if so, he couldn't see or hear it. The wind and rain were too loud, and it was still dark. He stood, shifting his weight from one leg to the other, on an open-air platform well before sunrise. Eraina and Hamelin were there with him, but in those conditions, he felt like he was on his own. He figured Eraina was watching things with her scarf, and he had seen Hamelin sit down after they reached the platform. Probably his head was still hurting from the wound.

The platform was built at the southern and easternmost part of the open land between Carr's camp and the gates of Parthogen. If all went as planned, that area would serve as the main battlefield once the fighting started. But for now, nothing was happening. Except for the wind and rain. The structure stood eight feet high and ten feet square and had no walls, but it did have a roof to protect them from the rain—if it hadn't been for the gusting winds.

Lars stepped to the edge of it and looked as far as he could into the darkness and the storm, trying to make out the order and pattern of Carr's forces. Over the roar of the wind and rain, he could faintly hear the incidental clanging of armor as the soldiers took their appointed positions.

"I know Charissa's plan, but isn't there something we could be doing in the meantime? This feels like nothing!"

At that moment, Amy climbed the ladder built into the side of the platform. "This isn't nothing. The three of you are supposed to watch, wait, and be ready."

Lars couldn't help sighing. "We're definitely waiting."

Hamelin turned toward Amy. "Ready for what?"

"Anything. Eraina will use her scarf to find out what Landon may be planning and also see if and when Tumultor finds out what Landon has done and begins to marshal troops and come this way. When things start happening, be ready to use your special abilities."

Lars stepped away from the edge of the platform and wiped the dripping moisture from his forehead and eyes. "It still sounds like nothing to me."

"Look, I know I'm the newest one around here," said Amy, "and all I know about the world on this side is what I've read in the *Enchiridion* and learned from Layla and all of you. That's probably why they've asked me to be the messenger, because I have the least to add to any of the ideas and plans. But, for what it's worth, I think Charissa's strategies make sense. And even Fearbane now agrees."

"So what is the current strategy, besides watching and waiting? Here we are an hour before sunup, it's still raining, and the wind is blowing in our faces. What are our soldiers doing?"

"They are forming up into three evenly divided units, each facing to our left, toward the city walls."

"But still no signal to attack?"

"Right. All three units are supposed to stay just out of the range of the longbows. The idea is to stay close enough to attract attention but far enough away to avoid disaster. And always keep their bowstrings dry."

"So they haven't even strung their bows?"

"Nope. Not yet."

Lars blew out a short breath and looked toward the battleground. "Eraina, what do you see?"

"Like Amy said, our men are taking the field in their units but staying back. Landon's forces are stationed at the city walls, and they're ready, waiting for us to attack."

"What about Tumultor?"

Her gaze then swept all the way north toward Osmethan. "There's no sign that he's pulling together his forces. So it looks like we have some time before he starts this way."

Hamelin got to his feet. "What about the eagle? Can you still see him?"

"He's right above us. Ever since he brought the storm clouds from the far northwest, he has continued to hover over the storm. I don't know how he stays up there so long. It's as if he's riding the clouds."

"The rain has slowed down some," said Lars, "but it's steady. And the wind is still straight out of the west." They all fell quiet and watched. In spite of the dark cloud cover, faint signs of morning light began to gather back to their right, in the east, and they could tell that Carr's left, middle, and right flanks were now in position.

Hamelin breathed in and squared his shoulders. "It looks like everything's just about ready. Lars, you could show me some fighting techniques in case...you know..."

Lars nodded and stepped toward Hamelin.

Amy had begun to descend the platform ladder but stopped halfway. "Hamelin, how's your head?"

"It's okay. No more bleeding, and since all we're doing is watching, it should heal up pretty quick."

"Good. Layla was asking, so don't you and Lars get too rough and make it start. For now, I'll leave you three here in your observation spot. I'm sure I'll be back. Charissa, Fearbane, and the king are discussing battle plans."

"What are my other sisters doing?" shouted Eraina.

"Sophie's got Layla dressed in battle clothes. They've given her a quiver of arrows and a bow, and Sophie's trying to show her how to use them. So I'd say they're getting ready to fight."

Eraina rolled her eyes and groaned. "Just tell them I said to stay in the back!"

⸻◈⸻

Even though the three friends—Lars, Eraina, and Hamelin—were waiting for it, the sound of trumpets shattered the morning and sent chills up their spines. The sun was on the verge of breaking through the eastern horizon when the fanfare behind the right flank blew its call to battle. The soldiers in that flank perfected their lines, raised their shields, and took quick and sudden steps toward the city walls. Landon's defenders on the walls from all across the front, from south to north, ran quickly to their left, clustered on the middle and northern ends of the walls, and stretched their longbows.

After ten hard steps toward the city walls from the right flank, Carr's forces suddenly stopped. Landon's longbowmen let fly their arrows, and the sky, still gray in the west, became black with arrows in flight. Just as quickly, the right flank, with its shields held high, pivoted to the right and took quick steps in a diagonal retreat north and slightly northeast, away from the flying onslaught. Carr's commanders had measured the distances perfectly, and the arrows, even with the aid of the west wind, fell short.

The right flank continued its pivot clockwise toward the east and then, in parade-like maneuvers, turned back south as if marching toward the middle unit. A second volley of arrows from the longbowmen was released, ordered more out of frustration than calculation, and they too fell short.

The same thing happened at the other flank. A long and loud fanfare of horns blew, and though rain clouds masked the now rising sun, there was enough light for the defenders of the city walls to see what was happening—the sudden advance of Carr's left flank on their right. Landon's longbowmen hurriedly clustered more to the middle and south sides of the city walls.

Carr's left flank then made a similar kind of charging maneuver, shields raised, with the same result. The longbowmen let fly a first and then a second volley of arrows, but the due westerly wind created a crosswind for arrows shot to the southeast, and though their distance was slightly helped, once again the calculations by Carr's commanders were correct. As their men quickly pivoted in perfect unity to their left and backward, the deadly arrows—this time two and three and four volleys were fired—fell short.

And now the movement of the right flank, heading south, was matched by the movement of the left flank, which had just finished its counterclockwise maneuvers and was moving north. The two flanking units then met and spread out in formation behind the middle unit as trumpet blasts from all three units were sounded. The middle unit, supported from behind and also on both sides in close quarters, now charged forward with shouts and yells—five paces, then ten—and gave every appearance of making an all-out assault. Arrows from Landon's forces at the walls flew.

But once more Carr's units, disciplined by years of training, followed their commanders' instructions perfectly and, after some fifteen paces, stopped abruptly. Landon's long-bowmen had fired six volleys of arrows by the time the first arrows landed. Carr's middle unit had come dangerously close to the wind-aided edge of the range of the longbows, but even though a few arrows reached the first rank of the formation, the raised shields did their job, and the middle unit quickly split down its middle into two. Its right half raced diagonally, to the north and back to the east, and its left unit did the same, in the opposite direction, going south and then retreating to the east.

Then half of the right flank of Carr's forces moved toward the north and formed up with the half of the middle unit that had gone that direction. Half of the left flank did the same, moving south to form a full unit with the left half of the former middle. And the three units thus reformed themselves, left, middle, and right. As they made these moves, their maneuvers drew additional volleys from the walls, but once again the arrows fell no closer than the first ranks of Carr's forces, who easily deflected them with their shields. The wind continued to blow, and the rain stayed steady.

Hamelin wanted to clap. "Wow, did you see that?" Eraina and Lars nodded and looked at Hamelin and each other with broad grins.

Lars pumped a fist in the air. "Charissa's plan is working!"

Eraina held back a big smile, but it made the corners of her mouth twitch. "I'm sure we should give Fearbane some credit, and our well-trained soldiers."

A couple of hours passed, and there was no more movement from Carr's forces, so the three friends sat for a while, but the wind and rain kept them drenched. Just past midmorning, they stood, as it was evident that the soldiers were preparing for something else. Carr's forces took their positions in the original formations, left, middle, and right, with the left and right flanks angling slightly toward the city and the middle unit facing directly west.

Lars looked at the sky. "Has anything new developed, Eraina?"

"Nothing new. The eagle is still up there, and it looks like the wind and the rain are going to stay just like this."

"What about Tumultor?" asked Hamelin.

"Nothing there either. I keep looking long and deep all the way through the Forest to the mountain range and even on beyond that to Osmethan, and there are no signs of movement."

Though by now it was well past midmorning, the darkness of the clouds kept the sun covered, and the skies from east to west, north and south, alternated between gray and almost black.

Suddenly the loudest and longest trumpet blast thus far came from all sides and all units of Carr's armies. Eraina stepped forward, and the boys followed, as close to the action as the platform allowed. The king's longbowmen in the front held their bows aloft, but it was clear to Eraina—and it became clear to Lars and Hamelin when she pointed it out—that their bows were not strung. Once again, a feinting maneuver took place, but this time it was from all three units at once. They charged for ten paces and drew three quick volleys of arrows before they abruptly stopped and, without turning, reversed their steps, backing up in rapid formation, with perfect timing and discipline, no one tripping or falling.

The arrows from Landon's longbowmen fell short once again, but this time, instead of shifting, the three units did the same maneuver again, dangerously adding two more steps in their charge, and more volleys of arrows flew. Carr's men then repeated the same reverse movement, and the few arrows that barely covered the distance were deflected by the first ranks.

The three units then spread themselves wider north to south, ranks from the back moved to the sides, and the lines were longer and thinner, though not any closer. Then short, feinting, charging maneuvers took place again from all sides, complete with horns and shouts and angry voices. Once again, the longbowmen from the walls let fly their arrows, and another six volleys flew before the first hit the ground, and once again Carr's forces moved out and back and avoided the deadly shafts completely.

Lars almost laughed. "I wonder how many times they can do that."

"I don't know," said Eraina, "but it seems to work every time. Those guys on the wall are getting pretty edgy, I suspect."

Hamelin pointed toward Landon's archers. "Is there any chance they will run out of arrows?"

"Not for a while," said Lars. "They don't have an unlimited supply, but they will have huge stores of them, and they've probably got people already making new ones."

Carr's forces, still out of range of the longest arrows, settled down again and, while still alert, rested for a short stint and took on food and water. And even though they were soaked by the steady rain and the ground under their feet was muddy and sloshy, their spirits remained strong. Their voices could be heard over the wind and even occasional ripples of laughter.

Eraina chuckled. "They've already got some good stories to tell."

And so the day went. Carr's forces would form up, left, middle, and right. Using various techniques, beginning sometimes from the left and sometimes from the right, or sometimes with all three groups together, they would move aggressively and appear to charge, only to fall back just in time. Landon's forces on the walls had no choice but to take seriously each potential attack and let fly from their longbows, trying to take advantage of their elevated position and the wind blowing favorably for them.

Then after one last series of feints just at sundown, Carr's forces stood at ease and waited, relaxed in their formations. Landon's forces stayed on the walls as long as Carr's forces stayed in the field. The sky grew black, and all that could be detected of Carr's forces were the sounds of sword and shield occasionally touching. And then complete silence, except for the wind.

Then almost all at once and clearly upon some command, beginning from the south, where the left flank was, and moving all the way to the north, a wave of light emerged from Carr's men. The first few ranks of each unit had been given covered lanterns, and these were being lit in rapid succession. It quickly became clear to Landon's archers that Carr's full forces were still in place, evenly divided among all three units, left, middle, and right.

Carr's soldiers stood still as the first ranks held the lanterns high and the light from them shone both forward and back. Eraina, Lars, and Hamelin, from their position well behind the left flank, saw it all. Tension grew as Landon's forces watched. Then Carr's men began to shout. They held the lanterns above their heads for another long minute, while they continued to shout. Then, all at once, the lights were doused, the shouting stopped, and darkness covered the battlefield.

Eraina watched Landon's men on the city wall, and while they strained their eyes to see what was happening in the blackness in front of them and tried as hard as they could to listen, the only possible sound they could have heard was that of muddy boots sloshing as Carr's men made their way back to their encampment in the woods. It had been a successful day, but her father's troops looked exhausted. How long could they keep up this plan?

Chapter 24

Day Two: Osmethan

BRYAN WAS AWAKE. HE HAD SLEPT SOUNDLY THAT NIGHT, but now it was early morning, and all kinds of worries started racing through his head. Maybe he could just lie there and sort a few things out. But nothing was going to be easy. A lot of what he needed to do had to be accomplished in secret, and it had become hard to move around unnoticed. He and Romulus—especially Romulus, with his physique—had become recognized faces in Osmethan after the recovery of the sword from the Great Rock.

Romulus was given credit not only for pulling the sword but for getting the mysterious waters to flow again from the Rock. Now, as before, everybody who chose to—though the people in the elder quarter of the city would not—could drink the water that would keep them from aging. Bryan and Romulus both knew that Hamelin had been involved in pulling the sword, but Romulus was glad to take advantage of his celebrity status.

Several innkeepers had offered them free lodging, believing they would be good protectors from thieves and hooligans, and they had their choice of several places. Romulus picked one with the bedroom downstairs, near a door that led to the back alley, and the owners living upstairs, above the café.

Bryan rolled over in bed as he tried to figure out his next steps. So far, his trip to Gloaming had been somewhat successful, since he had found his brother, Michael—or Romulus, as he was known over here. Romulus also knew who he was, though neither of them admitted knowing who the other was.

But Bryan had so much more to do after finding his brother. He had sneaked into the flying chariot in Layla's place to protect not only her but also Michael and Hamelin. Both of them had been called warriors, and according to the *Enchiridion*, a warrior had to die as part of certain prophecies about the four thrones and the battle between Chimera and the Ancient One. Would they fight each other?

And now his brother and Hamelin had already skirmished briefly over the sword in the Great Rock, which set a bad tone for the future. The sword had originally been given to Hamelin, but now Romulus had it and not only thought the sword was rightfully his but also wanted the scabbard that went with it. And Hamelin likely had the scabbard. The two of them were on a collision path—unless he could do something about it.

Bryan sat up in bed. There was no way he was going to sleep. And he had even more to worry about. Michael seemed to be supportive of Landon, which meant he was also committed to supporting Chimera's other sons, Tumultor and Ren'dal. Hamelin, on the other hand, had been brought to Gloaming to fight against Chimera and his schemes, as carried out by his sons. Plus, Hamelin seemed sure that one of them, Ren'dal, held his parents captive in Ventradees.

But one good thing offered some hope. Hamelin was no doubt with his friends in Parthogen, quite a long way south of Osmethan. The distance itself would keep him and Romulus apart. All Bryan had to do, until he figured out a few other matters, was keep things that way. He got up and stretched. Some light was starting to come through the window, and then he noticed that Romulus's bed, on the other side of the room, was empty.

Bryan was almost dressed when he heard footsteps in the short hall that ran next to their room and connected the front of the inn to the back door. Romulus rushed in.

"Great, you're up. We've got to get going."

"No breakfast? You know I'm cranky when I don't eat."

"I'm not kidding. One of Tumultor's men has come to get us. Tumultor has just received a message carried by one of Landon's wolf dogs. Apparently the day before yesterday, in late afternoon, Landon launched a surprise attack on Carr's camp outside Parthogen. Tumultor is furious and says Landon was supposed to let him know what was happening and should never have done that without permission. The surprise attack apparently isn't going well, and now Landon needs help. Let's go."

Tumultor was still raging by the time Bryan and Romulus reached his quarters. "The idiot! This is the dumbest thing Landon's ever done—and there's a lot to pick from!"

Bryan usually let Romulus do the talking, but he couldn't stop himself. "But why would he do that? I thought he had the best position and would wait to be attacked."

"Because he's a fool! Always wanting to be the hero."

"Since he has the superior position, does he even need our help?" said Bryan.

Tumultor glared at Bryan. "If he's stupid enough to attack when he's occupying the higher ground, and stupid enough to do it without letting me know, then he's stupid enough to lose! Whatever, the plan has been that I would support him once the battle was engaged. His *job*—his *only* job!—was to let me know in time!" Tumultor slammed his hand down, open palmed, on a nearby table.

"So we have no choice. We will ride to his aid." Tumultor looked at Romulus, who looked at Bryan.

"Of course, my lord, we will ride with you, won't we, Bryan?"

Bryan tried not to hesitate, but it took him a second to clear his throat before saying, with an unsteady voice, "We will."

Tumultor turned and ordered his commanders to be ready to ride within two hours.

Bryan gave a sideways nod to Romulus, signaling that he wanted to speak in private.

"What is it?" asked Romulus, once they had walked away from the others.

"I'm not sure that it's smart for us to join in on this particular battle."

"But we have to go. We've already implied to Tumultor that we're on his side. Besides, I have the sword—"

"Think about it," said Bryan. "You have the sword, and obviously Tumultor's going to want you to use it, but you know good and well that you don't have the original scabbard yet. We both know that the sword is unusual, but it needs the scabbard. Don't you remember?"

"Of course I remember! I know that they belong together. But we do have the sword, and I intend to get the scabbard."

"That's just it," said Bryan. "Once the sword is resheathed, you can use it only once before you have to let it go."

"What?" Romulus stared at Bryan.

Bryan then realized that he had added more information

about the sword than Romulus had ever indicated he knew. Accurate information, but something he had learned from Hamelin's story back on the other side.

"How do you know so much?"

"Oh, uh…I've read your books too."

"I don't recall that part in the books. You'll have to show me the spot."

"Okay…if I can still find it."

"When we get back," said Romulus. "We have no time now."

"But maybe we should take the time! Going to war when you're not ready, and trying to use that sword when you don't know everything you should know about it, could be disastrous."

"Are you afraid, Big B?"

Bryan looked Romulus squarely in the eyes. "I do fear, Cousin, for you. If you are hasty."

"But I'm the warrior, right?" asked Romulus. "I've read the books too and just like the *Enchiridion* says, there is a warrior who will bear the sword. I have the sword, and so I must be—"

"But the time has to be *right*. It's not a question of courage, or even having the sword."

"But the *prophecy*—we *know* what everyone says about it, and about me."

Bryan could have added the words of their father in the file folder, and he wished he could say more, but he knew it wasn't the time to explain all that.

"Look, Romulus," he said, "even that's not enough. Anybody can read the prophecies, but you have to be sure the prophecies are talking about you. And besides, even if the prophecy is talking about you, you can't decide *when* the prophecy is supposed to be fulfilled. Good grief! Think! It's a *prophecy*! Even the people who first wrote it obviously didn't know when it would happen."

"Hmmm. You seem to know a lot about these things."

"They're obvious, don't you think?"

"Maybe," said Romulus. "But I know this." He looked around and lowered his voice even more, almost to a whisper. "Now is not the time for us to back away from Tumultor. We've got to go with him."

"I get it, and I'm going with you, no matter what. But be on the lookout. A prophecy is not a timetable. Even if you know what's going to happen, you don't know when."

Romulus looked around and spoke loud enough for all nearby to hear. "Very good, Big B. Glad to hear we're ready!" He slapped Bryan on the shoulder. "Ha! Let's go."

⸺⸺◉⸺⸺

Bryan and Romulus mounted their horses and took their assigned place near Tumultor at the head of a cohort of a hundred men, most of them fighters but some cooks and priests. They rode hard out of Osmethan toward Parthogen, but in spite of pushing the horses, the going was slow. The steady rain, falling since the previous day, meant their entire journey would be sluggish. What would have been two days of hard riding could likely be more. Bryan hoped for anything that would delay what seemed like an inevitable clash between Hamelin and Michael.

Chapter 25

Day Two:
Parthogen

EVERYONE WAS UP EARLY THE NEXT MORNING. ALL OF THE royal family and their friends from the other side had stayed in tents close to one another. Hamelin, Lars, and Eraina ate a cold breakfast, grabbed some food to take with them, and finished their final preparations to return to the raised platform. Charissa, Fearbane, and the king emerged from Carr's tent, where they had already reviewed battle plans for the day, but were still talking intently, their heads close together. Sophie and Layla finished breakfast and set out for the archery range with bows and arrows in hand.

Charissa stepped away from her father and Fearbane to talk to Amy. She then spied Layla. "Thanks for your help. We've already started setting up your idea, in case we need it."

"Sounds good, but not really mine. It's a strategy from an old battle story told on the other side." Charissa nodded, finished her conversation with Amy, several times pointing up and then north, and resumed her discussions with Fearbane and the king.

Amy approached Eraina, Lars, and Hamelin just as they set out. Hamelin paused. "Any new word for us?"

"Not new, but more urgent. Charissa says that the three of you have got to stay ready. Eraina, you've got to keep watching for anything and everything—from Landon's movements here, all the way to Osmethan to keep tabs on Tumultor. And be prepared to act if conditions change; anything related to Tumultor, the wind, or the rain. According to Charissa, these are the major factors."

Lars fidgeted. "So what are we supposed to do if anything changes?"

"Charissa's counting on the three of you to use your speed, Eraina's scarf, and Hamelin's strength for a special mission—once the full battle starts."

Lars shrugged. "We figured that much, but is there anything more specific you can tell us?"

Amy took in a deep breath and let it out. "I can now tell you *what* you're supposed to do when the time is right. It's just that I don't know—and I don't think anybody else does either—exactly *how* you're supposed to do it. But here's your job..."

<hr>

As the soldiers began to form up in their staging areas prior to returning to the battlefield, the three young people huddled together at the base of the platform and reviewed what Amy had said. Eraina's eyes widened as she whispered her thoughts. Lars slowly shook his head, and Hamelin took deep breaths as he listened.

It wasn't long before a commander's voice could be heard. "Positions, everyone! Go to your stations!" The soldiers moved rapidly toward their three units, and Eraina, Lars, and Hamelin mounted the platform. It was an hour before sunup, and still dark, but Eraina had no trouble using the scarf.

Hamelin watched her stare up and into the storm. "Anything different?"

"No. The eagle is still riding the clouds above us, and there is no obvious change in the weather. The wind is still coming from the west, and there's no sign of the rain letting up." Eraina then turned her attention to the north, toward Osmethan, and looked a long time.

Lars paced in a small circle. "Anything happening in that direction?"

Eraina used the scarf a little longer before she turned to the boys. No one else could have possibly heard, but she whispered anyway. "Tumultor and his men are still in Osmethan, but now they're rushing around, gathering up supplies and saddling horses. It won't be long before they're riding in our direction."

Hamelin looked Eraina squarely in the eyes. "Anything else?"

She knew why he was asking and hesitated. "Yes...there is something else... I could see Tumultor, and it was obvious he was ordering his commanders to round up their men for battle."

"What else?"

"I saw...standing near Tumultor—oh, Hamelin, I'm so sorry—I saw the one they call Romulus...and I saw Bryan. They're getting ready too...and it looks like they'll be with Tumultor when he comes."

⚬⚬⚬

Carr's three fighting units took their same positions an hour before sunup, while it was still dark. The soldiers in the front ranks of all three sections then lit their lamps and held them high. Landon's forces on the city walls could see the profiles of Carr's men. The archers on the walls stood at attention, watching, with longbows strung and supplies of arrows at the ready.

The wind and rain continued with no let-up as the opposing

forces were poised for the second full day of battle. As soon as the sun came up, the lanterns were extinguished, and with no trumpet call, Carr's armies moved quickly, repeating with some variations the tactics of the previous day and continuing to frustrate Landon's men.

All day long, with a break only at noon, the pattern of feinting, charging, withdrawing, changing places, and occasionally charging all at once continued. Carr's forces constantly tested the limits of Landon's longbows, with almost every charge taking them farther up the hill toward the city walls, only to retreat either north or south, with no clear pattern that could be anticipated by Landon's forces but always a well-prepared maneuver executed by Fearbane and his commanders.

On the platform, Eraina continued to watch, giving careful descriptions to Lars and Hamelin. They could see for themselves the charges and retreats of her father's forces, but she especially kept them updated on the progress of Tumultor's soldiers coming down from Osmethan. These reports were supplemented by descriptions of the eagle, who, apparently needing no rest, continued to ride the storm clouds above the battlefield. By the end of the day, the rains still fell, the wind did not let up in its strong west to east currents, and Tumultor's forces, though getting closer, were at least a day off at the pace they were going.

As the sun set, Carr's forces made one last collective charge, farther than they had ever gone up the hill toward the city walls, but the conditions in the air, the wetness of Landon's bowstrings, and the fatigue of the archers caused the arrows to fall just short of their intended targets.

Then, a half hour after sunset, Carr's forces once again regathered in their positions, equally divided among the three units, left, middle, and right, and the first ranks lit their lanterns and held them high above their heads. They all stood at attention, and, as before, the lights from the lanterns taunted Landon's troops with the fact that Carr's forces were evenly divided and in full strength. Their arrows had inflicted no damage.

The lanterns remained above the soldiers' heads until it was dark. Suddenly all were extinguished at the same time, and immediately there was noisy clattering and wild yelling. It was the sound of attack in battle—swords, spears, and shields clanging—but the actual distance charged was short, though the sounds of battle continued. The longbowmen at the walls let loose one last set of volleys, but the arrows landed in the empty, muddy field while Carr's forces marched back to their tents in the darkness.

Eraina checked on the eagle one more time before she and the others dismounted the platform. The great bird, above the clouds, above the rain, and above even the flashes of lightning, continued to circle and then to rest, sitting on the clouds as if he steered them like a chariot. For one brief moment, lightning illumined her vision, and she thought that the chariot of clouds gleamed like hot metal and resembled a throne.

But below, in the fields of battle in and around Parthogen, the winds continued to blow, and the rain fell steadily.

⚬

Tumultor and his men continued their furious ride toward Parthogen. At least they tried to. But the travel was slow—and frustrating. Mud kicked up into their faces by the horses and the crosswinds that hit them from right to left as they traveled mostly south made them curse the weather and their miserable conditions. Plus, the steady rain that had followed them now into their second day of hard riding, made it difficult and even dangerous to push the horses. In some places, they dismounted to walk their animals across slick and treacherous terrain.

But though the pace was slower than Tumultor wanted, he

made up for it with a relentless push to keep his troops moving forward. There was grumbling from the men, which made its way to Tumultor's commanders, but they were afraid to pass it on to Tumultor himself, and so they drove the horses and the men as hard as they dared.

And while Tumultor ignored the private pleas of his commanders to stop and sleep, the horses had to rest some, so Tumultor occasionally consented for his men, including Romulus and Bryan, to sleep for short periods, if they could, while enduring the driving wind and rain.

Hamelin, Lars, and Eraina made their way back toward the camp. As they approached the tent where Hamelin and Lars were staying, they could see a light on in Carr's quarters. They paused to glance inside and saw Charissa and Fearbane standing around the conference table, talking in hushed tones and pointing here and there to the drawings that represented their soldiers, the city, and their plans. Carr had dozed off in a chair in the corner. And then they spied Amy—just inside the opening, curled up in a ball, asleep. But no doubt waiting for more instructions, if any.

Eraina shook her head, and without a word, the three friends let her sleep. The boys went to their tent, and Eraina found Layla and Sophie in the girls' tent. They talked briefly, but her sisters insisted she get some rest. They knew that, one way or another, the days of sudden charges and quick retreats would soon end, and Eraina would then have dangerous work to do.

Chapter 26

Early on the Third Day

HAMELIN'S DREAMS THAT NIGHT INCLUDED FLASHING IM-ages of the Kaleys and others at the Fourth of July party back at the children's home. Roman candles exploded and illumined the starless sky in constellations of fire against a dark, billowing curtain of gathering clouds. He could hear the pops and cracks of lightning-aided fireworks followed by pounding rain, and then he heard a dog—but now many dogs and wolves—howling. Another Roman candle went off just above him, a blast that lit up the entire sky. And the barking grew louder, and the shower of light grew brighter. Mr. Kaley's voice shouted, "Keep your eyes peeled!"

He woke up, and it was all still there—the sounds of lightning and rain, the howling of dogs and wolves, and a bright light above his head. The light was outside the tent, but even the tent couldn't block it. Hamelin got up, stepped to the opening, and looked around. It was still raining, but lighter, and the wolfish howling, now that his head was outside the tent, seemed louder and not just coming from the city walls. The bright light behind a thin curtain of clouds was the globe of a full moon, and Buddy was there outside the tent some twenty feet away, baying at it, joining the distant chorus.

"*Buddy*! Be *quiet*!" Hamelin yelled in a loud whisper.

The wolf dog looked at him, cocked his head, and looked back to the moon. Then as a new round of howls from the city rolled through the night air, he barked—and ran toward Parthogen.

Hamelin looked over to Carr's tent, and the light was still on there. He walked over to the opening and stepped just inside. He could hear Charissa.

"So instead of one hour before sunup, it needs to be two—all the men, with the numbers I've described, in their positions. Make sure the left and the right flanks have plenty of lanterns. From what Eraina reports"—and then Charissa turned toward Eraina, who, to Hamelin's surprise, was there in the tent as well, dressed in men's clothes, like an archer. Hamelin had not noticed her at first, but now, as Charissa turned to look at her, they both saw him.

Charissa, however, never paused in what she was saying—"the clouds are thinning out...the time is approaching."

Fearbane was studying drawings on the table and looked up. "Yes, my lady. We will station the men, in exactly the strengths you have ordered."

Charissa again looked at Eraina—"Is that so, my sister? Do you still perceive that the clouds are lifting?"

"It seems so. The rain is slowing down, and earlier the moon was, at least for a few minutes, no longer obscured by the clouds."

"No doubt that's the reason Landon's dogs and wolves started howling," said Fearbane.

"Very good then," said Charissa. "In one hour's time we must get the men up and into their positions. Then, on my command, you'll know what to do."

"Yes, my lady—"

"But one more thing. Make *sure* the commanders very clearly instruct their men not to string their bows or uncover their arrows until told to. We've kept the strings and feathers dry all this time, so the last thing we want is to get them wet now. If the rain doesn't stop"—and here Charissa looked back at Eraina—"then we go to our alternate plans."

"But do we have time for that, my lady?" Fearbane turned toward Eraina. "Tumultor and his men are still coming. Is that not so, my lady?"

"It is. They continue to ride, but their pace is slow. Tumultor keeps pushing his men and his horses, but the rains have made their going treacherous. I don't see how they can get here before sundown. Indeed, it will probably be later."

"Then we'll still have some time if the opportunity is not there this morning," said Charissa. "But we dare not be indecisive...We cannot wait too long, though we must not be hasty." She looked again at Eraina, who nodded yes, and then to Fearbane, who not only nodded but bowed slightly.

"As you say, my lady. I wait upon your command."

He left just as Lars entered the tent. "I see I'm not the only one who couldn't sleep."

Charissa didn't smile. "I'm glad the three of you are here together. I know that Amy has already told you the general plan for what you're supposed to do. I wish I could give you closer instructions as to how you're going to manage to climb the wall and open the city gate at the right time, but that's your job. Eraina knows the layout of the city, so she will guide you to the gatehouse. In it are the ropes, pulleys, and animals that turn the wheel to open the gate.

"The special powers each of you has will be to your advantage, but the odds are against you. You will be severely outnumbered, though I promise you this. We'll do everything we can to pull

Landon's troops to our right flank, away from the southern end of the city walls, where you will have your best chance of entry."

"We know what we've got to do," said Hamelin. "If Eraina can guide us, Lars and I can get us over the walls. And then— well..." His voice trailed off, since he didn't know what they would find on the other side of the wall, between them and the gatehouse.

"I'll keep watching," added Eraina.

"And we'll stay together," said Lars.

They all looked at Charissa and hoped she would smile, but her face was unmoving, and her eyes connected intently with all of them. "Timing is critical, and everything will depend on you." She left.

Lars shrugged. "That was pretty clear. Still, I could use something to eat, even if it is my last breakfast." A faint smile played at his mouth.

Hamelin's eyes got wide, but Eraina rolled hers and gave Lars an amused smirk in return.

"Good idea. Never charge a city on an empty stomach, I always say. Besides, I've seen a few other things going on behind the walls, and I need to tell the two of you about them."

The three friends sat by themselves in the food tent near the king's quarters. On the table were bread, boiled eggs, and small pieces of sausage. Before anyone could take a bite, Hamelin asked, "So what else have you seen?"

"Strange things. Like Fearbane said, the full moon, brief as it was, had an effect on the dogs and the wolves. But it did something to Landon too."

Lars had just reached for some sausage, but he paused. "What?"

She leaned in and lowered her voice. "When all the howling started up, I scoured the city and especially the castle grounds, looking for Landon, and I found him in the middle of the courtyard—our father's courtyard!—and he was staring up at the moon, as it peeked through the clouds, baying at it. It was weird, but there he was, with all the other dogs and wolves gathered around him in a circle and howling."

"Sounds like the old legends of werewolves," said Lars.

"We've known he could communicate with them, and long ago there were rumors that he was a shape changer, a werewolf, but no one has ever seen that, and I certainly didn't. But it's evil, whatever he's doing with his creatures. It's not natural."

Hamelin stared at Eraina. "Buddy was howling this morning too. And then he ran off toward the city. Do you think he...?"

"All I focused on was Landon, and his strange behavior soon stopped, so I didn't watch long. Once the clouds covered the moon again, he barked instructions at his creatures, and they all ran back toward their pens."

"Have you seen anything else?" asked Hamelin.

"I have. I've been keeping an eye on the eagle as well, even before Landon's strange behavior. In fact—well, you decide for yourself. I was watching the eagle, and his flight patterns changed. Instead of circling as if he was holding the clouds by the force of his flying, he began to slash in and out of the clouds, and they parted, starting in the middle, and the moon briefly broke through. And that's when Landon and his creatures began to howl."

"Why would the eagle do that? It just makes Landon and his dogs worse." Eraina shrugged.

"So what's the eagle doing now?" asked Lars.

"I think it's time for me to check again." They all grabbed their food, and she led them outside the tent. The rain was still steadily falling. She gazed up, and her eyes began to track something. She pointed up.

"He's starting to circle again. It's like he's regathering the clouds."

"Is it going to rain more?"

"I don't know, but he's definitely pulling them back together." And within a matter of moments, a dark cloudy veil covered the sky, hiding all traces of the moon's light.

At that very moment, Charissa walked up with her bow in hand, a quiver of arrows on her back, and a ram's horn around her neck.

"I think it's time we go to your platform."

"We?" asked Eraina.

"Yes, I'm joining you. Strange things are happening."

So the four of them hurried off to the platform.

They passed Amy, and she fell in pace with them. "May I join you?"

Charissa put a hand on Amy's shoulder. "I need you to do something else. Go and tell Sophie and Layla to get their bows and arrows and stay near our father. Tell them that we have gone to the platform. And tell Fearbane that I said, with urgency, to be ready. Things are changing, and I want him to be prepared. It may not happen yet, but I have a feeling... Tell him to listen for the ram's horn, which will be my signal. He'll know what to do then."

Amy nodded and hurried away.

They made it to the platform and stood searching the skies. The soldiers were rushing all around them, getting into formation, first into their smaller units and then into larger divisions. It was completely dark, but there was no doubt that Landon's guards could hear their movements even from some four hundred yards away.

And then, climbing onto the platform, the four of them noticed it at once, though no one said anything. It had been raining for days, and the winds had been blowing and rushing, but suddenly everything stopped. In the quietness that followed, there was only the clattering of gear—swords, shields, and armor—as the soldiers took their positions.

Everyone looked at Charissa. Hamelin was amazed to see the difference in her. The first time he had seen her, she was a silly, talkative, soon-to-be bride in an upper room, scolding and shushing and laughing over jewelry and linens, shoes, and bridal wear. But now, standing there on the platform, hands on her hips, she looked more like a warrior than a princess.

Even Eraina was looking at her, and he thought he detected something in Eraina's eyes, either amazement, admiration, or some combination of both.

No one said anything to Charissa, because they could tell she was watching and thinking. She would speak when it was time to speak, and they would wait and listen.

The wind and the rain gave no sign of picking back up, and the stillness felt strange. Everyone stood motionless and quiet.

Charissa first looked northwest toward the city walls, but then her gaze swept from there to the north, where the left, middle, and right of Carr's forces were gathering. And then, more silence. The clanging of metal armor, of shields against swords and breastplates stopped, as soldiers stood still in their assigned positions.

Charissa turned to Hamelin, Eraina, and Lars. Her voice was quiet but not a whisper. Her words were clear and unrushed, but they had a sense of urgency about them. "The time has come. You know what you are to do. The moon is once again covered, the wind and the rains have stopped, and the men are in place. Go now to the southern end of the city walls, and use your gifts to get over. You'll have a head start. We will attract Landon's forces toward the north end of the walls. I'll give you as long as I can, but once we start our charge, there's no turning back. You've got to get the city gate open by the time our forces charge, before it's light enough for Landon's men to see what we're up to. He'll think we're coming from the north, but we'll be concentrated in the middle.

"Remember: everything will depend on opening that gate. If it's not up when we get there, we'll be leading our men to slaughter. If they get stopped just below Landon's archers, even soaked arrows, shot from wet bowstrings, will reach them with force. It will be a killing field."

She paused and then looked at Lars. "It's still dark, so you should remove your baggy clothes and wear only what allows you the greatest freedom to use your speed. It will, I sense, be tested."

Lars started to speak but then nodded and quickly ran away to his tent.

"But what of the rising sun..." began Eraina once Lars was gone, but Charissa shook her head slowly from side to side, as if to say, "Don't ask."

They all stood there in silence until Lars quickly returned and he picked up the conversation where they had left it. "How will we know when your command to charge the gate is near? We can't just wait to hear the horn. That'll be too late."

"Eraina will have to watch."

"But how will *you* know when to time your command to charge—that we're getting close enough to open the gate?" asked Hamelin.

"I won't. I have to manage the battle, watch the men, and trust that you'll be there in time."

"But—if you can't see..." said Hamelin.

"I'll have to know without seeing."

Eraina pulled the scarf off her neck. "Then you should take the scarf!"

"No. You will need it to direct Hamelin and Lars past Landon's men to the gatehouse. Besides, we don't know if the scarf can be given to another, or even if I could use it if I had it."

"But—"

"No, my sister. The scarf cannot be two places at once.

Guide your brave friends, and watch my face. I won't be able to see you, but you'll see me. I'll look toward our beloved city, and my face will tell you what we're doing, and when."

Eraina reached up and kissed her sister on the cheek. Charissa looked at her an extra second, and even in the dark Eraina could see the glistening in her eyes before she turned away.

"Now, off with you."

The three friends, in the darkness some thirty minutes before any sign of light would appear in the east, scrambled down the platform and ran due west, heading toward the southern end of the city walls—Lars, with the speed and balance of his feet and the strength that such speed gave his legs, Eraina in the middle with the scarf, and Hamelin, with the scabbard on his side and the gloves on his hands. They stayed together, holding hands, sprinting toward the walls of Parthogen.

Chapter 27

The Wall and the Scarf

THE CLOUDS HAD REGATHERED AND COVERED THE MOON. The darkness of the night—still before dawn, with no light showing from the east—made running to the southeast corner of the city walls the least dangerous portion of their mission. They reached that spot and stopped. They knew Charissa's final plan—and part of it was Layla's special strategy—so they now stood with their backs to the eastern wall, below the turret at the corner just above them, and looked toward the battlefield, waiting for Carr's forces to make the next move. The goal now was to draw Landon's forces away from the southern section of the wall to the other end. They hoped the plan would work. It had to.

From where they stood, Hamelin, Lars, and Eraina faced in the same direction as Landon's officers and longbowmen. Eraina could see what was happening, but the boys, like those stationed above them, strained their eyes for signs of Carr's forces moving in the dark. They soon heard what they couldn't see, the clanging of armored soldiers marching with shields and swords and the voices of men as Carr's three large units maneuvered toward their positions.

Everything then grew quiet, with only the occasional barking of one of Landon's dogs disturbing the silence—no wind, no night birds, and no rain falling.

All at once, a burst of light from the lanterns in the first ranks of each unit shattered the blackness of the eastern skyline and stretched across the battlefield from south to north. It was the same pattern that had been used previously, and it now appeared that all three of Carr's units were in place and equally filled out.

But the three friends knew different, that what was really before them, though Eraina alone could see it, was only the first few ranks of soldiers in each of the side divisions. The bulk of Carr's fighting force was stacked in the middle, even though the lanterns gave the impression that the three units were evenly divided—left, middle, and right.

Landon's soldiers spread across the entirety of the main eastern wall to counter what they thought was the same well-balanced opposition they had faced the previous two days. His lieutenants shouted along the lines, reminding their longbowmen to "watch out for their moves" or "be ready in every direction."

Silence. No wind, no rain, no movement of soldiers on the wall or in the open field. Hamelin took in a deep breath. The next steps would largely depend on him, but he had to wait...

The lights showing Carr's ranks suddenly went out, and chaotic noises from his forces exploded. Shouts in the darkness and the clanging of armor and weaponry filled the night air with the sounds of men rushing and maneuvering.

Suddenly lights flared across the front ranks of Carr's right flank as lanterns were lit all at once. The noise and clamor also rose up in that direction, and a soldier on the wall yelled out, "They're moving left! They're moving left!"

And then another voice of what was apparently a commander yelling, "Move north! They're massed on our left! Longbowmen, prepare!"

Hamelin and his friends could hear the running steps and voices of the soldiers above them, moving to the opposite side of the city walls for what appeared to be a potential attack from Carr's right. This was the cue for their next step.

First, the city wall. Their plan for scaling it was one they had used successfully in other situations. Though the walls were higher, some forty feet, they were also thicker and thus provided a wider area at the top on which to land. Hamelin would use his strength to throw Lars all the way to the top, where, with his balance, he would make use of the seven-foot-wide landing area and flatten himself in a prone position. If all was clear, the next step, certainly more dangerous, was to repeat the same toss with Eraina, with Lars there to catch her and make sure she landed safely. Last, it would be an easy matter for Hamelin simply to pinch the wall, making fingerholds with his grip, and pull himself up hand over hand to the top.

The two boys used a technique that would take advantage of Hamelin's strength and Lars's ability to jump. Hamelin overlapped his hands, palms up and waist high, and then faced his friend. With his back to the city wall and without a moment's hesitation, Lars placed his right foot in the pocket formed by Hamelin's hands, lightly touched his friend's right shoulder with his left hand, and pushed mightily with his right leg. In the same moment, Hamelin pulled up powerfully with his hands, and the Prince of Periluna launched skyward. The darkness of the night covered the leap and midair turn, and he landed silently on the wall with perfect balance.

Throwing Eraina would require a different technique and more power from Hamelin, but they knew what to do. She stepped toward him but then spied something on the ground to their left.

"Hamelin." Her tone was different.

"What?"

"A wolf dog. To your left. He's standing there, looking at us. Is that—?"

"Buddy! What are you doing here?! Don't worry, Eraina. He's my dog. Let's get you up there with Lars."

"Okay." They both glanced again at the white dog, who was still watching but then also let out a low growl.

"Take it easy, Buddy. Everything's okay. She's our friend." Hamelin reached toward Eraina.

"Here we go." She turned, and he put his right hand on her lower back and his left hand under her left leg just above the knee. "Get your balance. You'll know when I'm about to throw." From the corner of his eye, Hamelin saw Buddy crouch and show his teeth, but he kept going.

"Got it." Eraina spread her arms out for greater balance. "I'm ready."

Hamelin bent his knees, preparing to move his whole body up before thrusting his hands and arms skyward.

Just then Buddy jumped, extending himself toward Hamelin and Eraina.

"Yeow," said Eraina in a muffled cry. Hamelin quickly twisted his body to the side to avoid the dog's leap, but since he was holding on to Eraina, he didn't want to swat at the animal.

Eraina, in an instinctively defensive move, pulled both her hands and forearms up around her head, and the dog's body, though not hitting full force, nonetheless struck with a glancing blow off Hamelin's shoulders and back while the creature, still in midair, snapped his teeth at Eraina.

The bite missed her, but the canine snagged her scarf in his mouth before tumbling to the ground.

"Hey, what's going on down there?" Lars asked in a loud whisper. "I don't see any soldiers up here, but keep it down!"

But Eraina groaned, "Oh, *no*! He's got my *scarf*!"

"What?" came Lars's voice from above.

"Hey!" yelled Hamelin. "Come here, Buddy! What are you doing?! Stop!" He charged toward the dog, who, with the scarf still in his mouth, loped northward along the city wall. Hamelin managed to bend over and grab one end of the scarf as it trailed behind, and he held on.

Hamelin yanked, but Buddy held on, and the scarf tore right down the middle, along the length of the seam, with a sickening rip. Hamelin, now holding half of the scarf, panicked. He raced furiously after Buddy, but the dog began to scamper, and Hamelin remembered telling Lars not to chase the owl when they were in the waterless places. But maybe a dog...he directed his voice upward. "Lars, the scarf's torn! My dog has a big piece! And he's running toward the gate!"

"Hang on! I'll get it!" With that, Lars took two running steps northward along the city wall and jumped. He landed with a balanced, acrobatic roll and then was on his feet, racing at top speed after the dog.

Eraina dashed a few steps in that direction but stopped and fell to her knees. "Oh, no! It's my fault! It's *all* my fault...oh, *Hamelin*..."

He ran to her. "Don't worry. It's not your fault. I should have paid more attention. We just have to hope Lars gets back here soon with that piece of the scarf."

"But the *timing*... Charissa said our timing has to be perfect...*everything* depends on us!"

Hamelin watched Lars disappear into the darkness. He knew his friend could catch Buddy, but fighting a wild wolf dog, now back under the influence of Landon, and getting the half scarf out of his mouth was something else.

Chapter 28

A Felix Culpa

"So far," Charissa said, half out loud to herself, "it's going well." The plan she and Fearbane had devised was being implemented by the three units with complete precision. The goal had been to make the three groups of soldiers appear to be evenly distributed, though they were in fact stacked in the middle, with only a few ranks of soldiers on each side. Then they would use noise and the lanterns to make it appear that they were repositioning themselves to the north.

And the plan was working, so far. The soldiers at the top of the city walls had rushed toward their left and restationed themselves there, expecting the attack to come from Carr's right. She glanced back to the east, hoping she had not miscalculated the time of sunrise.

Her mind raced through the next steps. With their own arrows dry and well stocked, and with Landon's men now out of position and their bowstrings soaked, the risky assault up the middle just might work...but the gate would have to be rising by the time she gave the order.

The timing would have to be perfect, since the charge would need to start while it was still dark, to take advantage of her father's massed but unseen forces in the middle. Then, if everything went according to plan, the rising sun in the eyes of Landon's men on the walls would be to the advantage of her father's soldiers, not to mention their dry bowstrings. But if the gate didn't open and the engagement was prolonged, the sun in the eyes of Landon's archers wouldn't matter, because the mass of Carr's forces would be in close range on the ground directly below—and would be slaughtered.

Charissa decided she would ride one more time toward the front ranks of the middle unit, now still in darkness, though faint signs of light were barely peeking above the eastern horizon. She wanted to ensure that their forces were properly positioned and also encourage the commanders to be disciplined, to wait for her signal before charging.

She rode west toward the front lines, in the space just to the left of the middle division. As she approached the front, she saw movement, frenzied movement, ahead of her. And then she heard a sound—a yelping and snarling. She urged her steed toward the sound, which was now well in front of her first rank of soldiers. She was within range of Landon's long-bowmen, but the darkness protected her, and there was nothing happening to draw volleys from Landon's side.

She rode closer and detected the source of the noisy disturbance. There, directly in front of her, was a young man rolling around on the ground in a wild fight with a white dog who had a piece of cloth in his teeth...it was *Lars*! He was on his back, and the dog was on top, snarling. Lars had the sides of the dog's face and his ears in his hands and his legs wrapped around the dog's body in a powerful vise, but the dog was still using his upper body to butt his head at Lars.

Charissa drew her bow and took careful aim, but then—just

as Lars applied more pressure with his legs—the dog coughed out a gasping yelp, and the cloth fell away.

Lars loosened his legs, and the wolf dog twisted his body and head and pulled himself free. He scrambled toward the city walls.

Charissa dismounted and rushed over to Lars, now sitting up and breathing hard, with what looked like a piece of Eraina's scarf in his hand.

"Lars! Are you okay? Was that Hamelin's dog?"

"Yeah, I'm fine. Hamelin said it was his dog, but he's sure no friend. He grabbed and tore Eraina's scarf, or at least about half of it, so I didn't know what else to do except try to get it back to Eraina. Hopefully I can tie the two pieces together and it will still work. But now our *timing*! I'm sorry."

"Wait. Let me see that piece of the scarf." She put it around her neck and stuffed the ends into her vest, the kind that archers wore. Then she looked around, and her eyes widened as she glanced at the city walls and then back to her own forces. "I'm going to keep this."

"What?" said Lars. "But shouldn't—"

"Listen to me—I can *see* with it. And if I can see through this piece, then Eraina can see through the piece she's got. She still has the rest, doesn't she?"

"Yes, but Sue Ammi gave it to Eraina and said that it couldn't be given away."

Charissa's eyes widened. "Lars, she's not *giving* it to me! I'm *taking* it. Besides," she flashed the first smile Lars had seen on her face in many days, "I'm her *sister*. She's always taking *my* clothes! Now hurry! It's a fortunate mistake. Go back and tell her to watch for my face just as before, and I will keep an eye on all of you." With that, Charissa mounted her horse, and Lars raced back to the southeast corner of the city walls. The sun was not up, but the lower edge of the eastern sky was beginning to show hints of gray. The time to charge was near.

Eraina buried her face in her hands, though she also occasionally looked up, waiting in agony for Lars. Hamelin stepped closer to her and pressed what was left of the scarf into her hands. "We've got no choice. Lars isn't back with the other part of the scarf, and we have no idea when or even if he'll get it. Climb on my back, and I'll carry you up the wall."

Eraina looked at the torn-off remnant in her hands. "It's no good. What's the point of my going with you if I can't see anything? I'd only be in the way and slow you down. Timing is everything. You've got to go it alone."

"How do I get there—I mean, to wherever I raise the gate?"

"The gatehouse is easy to find. It's on this side of the city gate. It's a large walled-in area, but it's got its own doorway. Inside you'll find two oxen. They're yoked together to a huge horizontal beam connected to a wheel that uses ropes and pulleys to open the gate. All you have to do is drive the oxen around in their circle, and the gate will open. You won't have any trouble finding it...if you can get there."

"I can."

Eraina lowered her head and continued to look at the piece of torn scarf in her hands, and he patted her on the shoulder.

"Just wait here for Lars. Maybe he'll get back with the other piece and you can tie them together. That seam proves it's been torn before, so maybe it'll still work."

Eraina took a deep breath, almost a sob, and then added, "Without me to tell you when Charissa's charging, you'll just have to listen for it. When the sounds of war get close, open that gate. But probably you won't have to wait, now that I've slowed us down so much. That's all I know to tell you. Timing is..." But she didn't finish the sentence.

Hamelin nodded, turned to the wall, and began to climb, pressing his fingers into it, clenching it as a cat uses its claws to climb a tree. Within a minute, he was well above her, still surrounded by darkness.

⚬

Eraina had waited for what seemed like long minutes when she heard the sound of running steps coming up from her right. It was Lars! But there was nothing in his hands. She ran to meet him.

"Where's the scarf?"

"Where's Hamelin?"

"He's already gone over the wall."

"Why didn't you go with him?"

"Because I'm no help to him without the scarf!"

"Have you tried the piece of scarf you still have? To see if it works?"

Eraina's eyes got wide as she realized that she had only held her part of it in her hands. She placed it around her neck and looked in the distance and then through the city walls.

"Oh, my word!"

"What?"

"It *works*! It *still works*!"

"So what's the problem? That's great news, right?"

"Sure it is, but I just sent Hamelin over the wall thinking I couldn't help him, and all along it was right here in my hands. I should have gone with him!"

"It's not too late to help. Come on, get on my back, and I'll explain it to you. Your sister's got the other half of the scarf—"

"What?"

"Yeah, she's got it, and it works for her too! The scarf tore right along the seam—you remember that seam in the scarf?"

"Of *course* I remember the *seam*!"

"Well, she said that since you didn't give it to her, she could take it. And now, it turns out the scarf *can* be in two places at once! You and Charissa can watch each other, and that will speed things up. The timing can still work."

"If we can get the *gate* open! We're separated from Hamelin and—"

"No time for regrets! Climb on my back. It'll be slow going, but we can do it."

Eraina climbed up piggyback on Lars. She used her fingers to grasp the first fingerholds that Hamelin had left, while Lars put his toes in small places in the mortar. Slowly they started up the wall.

About halfway up, she leaned her head close to Lars's ear. "I can see Hamelin. He's on the ground, crouching behind a half-wall. It looks like he's got some of Landon's soldiers just around that corner to deal with. *Hurry*! We've got to catch up to him and help."

Chapter 29

Rushing the Gatehouse

HAMELIN REACHED THE TOP OF THE WALL AND FOUND HIM-self not far from a watch tower that provided different views of the surrounding grounds. He glanced through a narrow slit in the tower door before entering and spied a lone guard, an archer. The man had his back to Hamelin as he peered out another vertical opening toward the battlefield, where all the commotion seemed to be moving to the soldier's left.

Hamelin quietly stepped inside and, before the watchman knew what happened, subdued him with a quick chopping and pressure movement that Lars had taught him. He then stepped through an opening at the back of the tower and de-scended a spiral stairwell all the way to the ground. Before he emerged, he glanced around and could tell with the help of a nearby torch that there was no one in that area.

Hamelin paused to get his bearings. Stretching in front of him all along the inside of the city wall was an empty space about ten feet wide that allowed for easy movement, a corridor-like area that Eraina had called "the internal Pomerium." He was also glad to see that ahead of him and spaced at intervals along the Pomerium—from where he stood all the way to the main gate—there were lit torches mounted in the wall.

Also, here and there, which he hadn't thought about or Eraina hadn't mentioned, makeshift ladders had been leaned up against the wall for moving men and supplies up and down. Hamelin knew he could easily pass under these. Plus, as was obvious from the outside, though it looked different from the inside, he could see what Eraina had emphasized—that he would pass two more towers, located at intervals between the first tower where he had entered and the central tower that was next to the gatehouse.

He had no experience of what the inside of the gatehouse would look like, nor had he ever seen a mechanical system for raising this kind of gate, but Eraina had described it to him and Lars more than once during the preceding days. He had listened, but he had always counted on her being with him so he wouldn't have to know exactly what it all looked like or how it worked. He should have paid closer attention! A separate room this side of the gate...two oxen...pulleys and ropes. Did she mention a winch? Mr. Moore could explain that, but... He would just have to get there and see.

Some of what she had said about the gate came back to him. It was called a "portcullis," which just meant a big sliding gate in the middle with spikes on the bottom. "It's heavy," she had said, "and that's why it takes the pair of oxen to pull the whole contraption." She had also added something about pulling the ropes by hand, but the gate was so heavy that it would take twenty men to do it, which had been done once, it was said, but that was probably just a legend.

Hamelin took a deep breath. The two towers between him and the gatehouse bulged out internally as well as externally.

They were rounded as they faced outside the city walls, but the insides were rectangular, so they would give Hamelin, at least on this side, a partial wall to hide behind if he could just get to each one without being seen.

He ran for it, past one of the flickering torches, underneath a couple of ladders, and then into a dark corner formed by the near, inner side of the tower. Safe. He stood there for a moment and thought about entering this tower and going up the winding staircase to the wide and open platforms at the top of the wall so that he could run down them, but he dismissed that idea almost immediately. Down here he could see what was in front of him more easily, and even with most of the men and commotion above positioned to the north end of the city wall—which had been Charissa's plan—there would likely still be some on this end, so it was better to stay on the ground level.

Hamelin took another breath and intended to start his dash toward the next tower but pulled back when he saw a group of five men ahead and to his left, one of them holding a longbow. He had just in time caught their flickering shadows because of the light of the next torch down the inner wall. They were standing near the edge of the Pomerium and barely within radius of the closest torchlight, and he had nearly missed seeing them. He paused to think but decided he couldn't wait, since he was already behind schedule because of the incident with Buddy. So he had no choice. He'd have to go forward.

But instead of running, he decided the best thing to do was just walk, acting like he belonged there. He wasn't wearing Carr's colors, but neither did he have on Landon's. He hoped he could just bluff his way past the men. He walked along the Pomerium, glanced briefly at them to his left as he approached, and then looked straight ahead as if he had somewhere to go.

As he came level to the men, one of them glanced at him,

squinting his eyes. "Hey, *you*! *Boy*! What are you doing here? Shouldn't you be carrying supplies or something?"

Hamelin looked at the man and nodded but decided not to speak, afraid that his Texas accent would get him into worse trouble. He kept on walking.

"Hey, boy! I'm talking to *you*!" The man strode toward Hamelin. "Come here. Let me have a look at you. I don't recognize you. Who are your parents? What's your father's name?"

Hamelin paused, then took a couple of steps toward him, clearing his throat and smiling sheepishly.

By this time, the entire group was staring at him, and a second man had stepped forward next to the one who had first called to him.

Hamelin approached.

"I...I am..." As he spoke, he bowed, then took another step. By this time, he was almost between the two men.

The first man grabbed Hamelin's right wrist. "Stand up straight. Let me see your face."

From his bent-over position, Hamelin balled his two gloved hands into fists and suddenly raised himself upright, simultaneously yanking his fists upward at their heads. He caught both men in the chin at the same time, and they fell back as if shot from behind by an arrow, blood spurting from their mouths.

The sound of Hamelin's fists against their faces brought the other three to attention as they saw their two compatriots hit the ground.

"What the—?" said the one with the longbow. He approached quickly.

But Hamelin wasted no time. He jumped toward him and in one swift move jerked the bow away, then swung it like a baseball bat at the man's head, knocking him back and breaking the bow in the process. Hamelin crouched, preparing himself for an attack by the other two, but they thought better of it and fled into the darkness. Hamelin dropped the broken bow and ran toward his next destination, the gatehouse.

It was slow going, but with Lars's great balance and Eraina's sheer determination to stay on his shoulders by grasping the fingerholds Hamelin had left, they reached the top of the wall. Eraina saw the door to the tower open and could tell that a man's body was lying on the floor inside and that it wasn't Hamelin.

"Quick, in here," she hissed to Lars, and they scrambled inside and shut the door. Eraina pointed to the unconscious archer. "I'll take his bow and arrows, and you take his vest. It's got Landon's colors, and the bow and arrows are their design, even the feathers." She slipped the quiver over her shoulder and back, and Lars donned the vest as they hurried down the spiral staircase.

Just before reaching the bottom, Eraina stopped and looked for Hamelin.

"I see him."

"What's he doing?"

"He's running north along the wall. Heading toward the gatehouse! We've got to get there in time to help him!"

They emerged from the tower and ran down the Pomerium to the next tower and paused. Eraina nodded toward the three men who were sprawled on the ground, blood still flowing from their heads and faces, but pulled Lars after her at a brisk walk.

"Hamelin's been busy," Lars whispered.

"Hey," one of the men groaned, "you two, come over here. We need some help."

Eraina and Lars ignored them and kept going.

"I guess your colors worked," she muttered as they picked up their pace.

"So far, so good."

They started running again and came to the next tower, the last one before the gatehouse. As they paused by that tower, they heard loud voices above them on the platform.

"Keep moving to the left! The left! They're massing over there! Be ready to shoot!"

Eraina held up one hand, signaling to Lars that they should wait there at the tower. "I've got to see what's going on." She then grasped the scarf in both hands and looked hard through the walls toward the battlefield, searching for Charissa.

"I see her."

"What's happening?"

"She's using her scarf piece and looking at me! She's signaling." Eraina began to shake her head and slowly mouth the words, "No. Wait. We're not there!" She could see that Charissa was looking at her, pointing and saying something back.

"No!"

"What's she saying?"

Charissa grew increasingly impatient. It was still dark, but the sun's rays would soon crack the horizon. Using the trick with the lanterns, they had moved Landon's forces over to the right, but now they would have to start some form of engagement. First, the right flank would draw fire, even with only a few ranks of soldiers over there. Once volleys of arrows were being drawn to their right, and while it was still dark, she would have to move the mass of her soldiers, who were now in the middle, forward and closer in. It would put them in range of Landon's arrows, but it was a necessary risk to get them in position to charge the gate. It was muddy and uphill, but since the wind and rain had stopped, their dry bowstrings and Landon's wet ones gave them at least an equal range. They would have to move closer, however, while they still had the cover of darkness, if they were to get through the gate...if the gate was open.

Why doesn't Eraina look at me? I can see her. Why doesn't she look this way? Eraina! And then her inner words formed in her throat and burst from her lips. "Look at me!"

She could see her sister and Lars at the base of a tower. Eraina finally looked at her. Charissa held her right hand high and made a circling motion, followed by a forceful thrust of her arm to Carr's right flank. She then made another circling motion and threw her arm forward, pointing to the gate.

She watched Eraina, who was mouthing something, shaking her head. Did she say, "No. Wait"?

Charissa shook her head vigorously, slashing her hand side to side, palm down. She knew Eraina couldn't hear her and would have to read her lips, but even then she said it slow and loud. "We have to engage on our right! To get the men ready for the charge in the middle. The sun will soon be up, and they will see us." Charissa again signaled to her right and then pointed to the gate. "Now!"

Eraina again shook her head.

Charissa raised her right hand and met her sister's gaze as each one looked through her piece of scarf. And from that distance she mouthed three words as slowly and as clearly as she could, *"No. More. Delay."*

Chapter 30

The Rising Sun

HAT DID SHE SAY?" ASKED LARS.

"I couldn't make it all out, but her message was clear: she's moving ahead with her plans. Now. She's got to start the fight on Landon's left while it's still dark. The last thing she said was, 'No more...' something. Whatever it was, she's not waiting."

"Obviously not. The commotion around here is picking up."

Before they could move, dogs were everywhere, racing north along the Pomerium toward the left side of Landon's forces. Even the stairways of the towers were filled with them as those who had been above on the city walls came flooding down. Women and children also began to fill the area, carrying water and arrows.

As soon as Landon's dogs cleared the area, a lead archer with Landon's colors, followed by two others carrying supplies, rushed to the base of the tower where Lars and Eraina were standing.

"Hey, you two, what are you waiting on? Stop blocking the *stairs*! Get up there! *Go!*"

Eraina looked at Lars and froze for a moment before she signaled with her eyes, and they both charged up the stairs.

When they reached the wide space at the top of the wall, those following them rushed around them to the left.

Eraina leaned in to Lars. "I was about to say you should run ahead. We've got to help Hamelin." She tried to look below to find him but got bumped, as more archers at that very moment came pouring out of the same tower and charging along the platform to the left. The commander was shouting, "More *supplies*! More *arrows*! Get those shortbows up here as well! This is it! No more fakes and feints! They're coming from the left!"

The rush of Landon's men to the left forced Eraina and Lars along in the same direction, and they quickly found themselves approaching the middle of the wall, at the top of another stairwell that led down to the gatehouse and the Pomerium. Then came a shouted command from someone nearby. "Everyone, *stop*! Hold your positions!" The rush of archers to the left ceased, and Eraina stole a look toward the gatehouse.

Lars stepped closer. "Do you see him?"

"He's below us and—!" But the rest of her answer was drowned out by a frenzied scream from a field officer.

"*No! No!* Go *back*! Not the *left*! The middle! *Look*!" He pointed to the middle of the battlefield.

And there, with light now climbing on the eastern horizon, it was evident that the bulk of Carr's army was massed in the middle and already within a hundred and fifty yards of the city gate.

The field officer shouted again. "Longbows! They're finally in our range! Get ready..."

"*No! Let them come!*" cried another voice, obviously from someone of superior rank.

"But, sir!" came the other voice. "Shouldn't we order the longbowmen to take them at this distance?"

"No! These fools had planned on the cover of darkness, but they're too late! Let them get closer, if they dare. *Longbows, make room for the shortbows*! *Both of you, come to the front and wait on my command*!"

Landon's soldiers obeyed their commander's orders, and archers with bows of shorter range joined the longbows, arrows nocked and bowstrings taut. Waiting.

The ranking voice shouted again. "And *guard the gatehouse*—or better—*cut the oxen loose*! They'll never batter the gate down in time! Steady now. *Wait for my signal*! And when they're below us, we will *slaughter* them! *No mercy*!"

Hamelin could see the gatehouse just in front of him, but he heard the shouts from above, all of them. Landon's officers now knew that Carr's forces were coming up the middle. Hamelin also heard the command to guard the gatehouse, and within seconds he saw a soldier disappear inside the door that was only twenty yards in front of him and shut it. He heard the crossbolt slammed into place but knew he had no choice. This was no time for secrecy or cleverness. He raced to the wooden door and began to smash it with his fists to jar it loose from its hinges and make enough space to squeeze through.

Lars yelled to the ranking commander who had given the order to guard the gatehouse, "We'll go!" He grabbed Eraina's arm, and they stepped toward the stairwell.

At the same moment, another soldier came rushing by, a swordsman. Before going down, Lars stepped back, stuck out a foot, and tripped him. The man fell hard, face down on the platform.

"Hey, watch what you're doing over there!" someone shouted.

Lars yelled again, "We've got the gatehouse, sir!" The man he tripped was dazed and offered no resistance when Lars grabbed his sword and headed down the stairs, Eraina behind him.

The stairwell was just wide enough for people to come up and down two by two, but Lars used his feet and the strength of his legs to clear a path as they jostled and pushed their way to the bottom. It led into the Pomerium just outside the small wooden structure where the oxen and the mechanisms were kept. Lars held the sword above his head and turned in a half circle to look for Hamelin. Eraina saw the splintered door, nocked an arrow, and moved toward it.

———◉———

Hamelin, now inside the gatehouse, took in the scene. The soldier who had arrived just ahead of him had already used his sword to cut the straps binding the yoke around the outer ox.

"Who are you?" the man demanded. "What are you doing here?" He pointed his sword toward Hamelin, who crouched into a fighting posture and took a step toward him. The man shouted, "Get back! Get out of here!"

"Don't cut the other one loose!" yelled Hamelin back to him. "They've changed the orders!" But the soldier laughed and in the same moment slashed the remaining straps that bound the inner ox to the circular wheel.

"No one's getting in here to raise that gate. You must be one of Carr's!"

The soldier approached Hamelin and raised his sword. Then with a battle cry, he swiped it toward Hamelin, who jumped back and moved to his left, behind the outer ox. Landon's man then stepped forward and swung the sword again, Hamelin dodged once more, but the sword caught the outer ox on his flank and cut a deep gash.

The ox bellowed, and both oxen, now cut loose from the straps but still yoked to each other, reared slightly. The ox on the outside stumbled and tried to regain his balance but in the process bumped hard against Hamelin, who fell to the ground. With the animals still bellowing and Hamelin on his back, Landon's soldier gripped the handle of his sword with both hands and raised it above his head.

⟩⟨⟩⟨

Eraina heard the oxen and ran toward the battered opening. She reached it ahead of Lars and stuck her upper body through it just in time to see Landon's soldier prepare to plunge his sword into Hamelin's chest. Hamelin instinctively raised a gloved hand to deflect the tip of the sword, but she didn't wait to see if he could. In one motion, she drew and released, and the twang and a fleshy thud were instantaneous, followed by a scream. The feathered end of her arrow suddenly appeared in the upper portion of the man's chest.

Hamelin twisted his body toward the opening, where Eraina, with Lars just behind her, had already nocked another arrow and had the bowstring drawn.

"Move away, or the next one's through your heart! *Move!*"

The man was now on his knees with his left hand around the arrow, which had gone through his body, with only the feathered fletching visible at his chest and the point of the arrow sticking out his back.

Hamelin hurried over to him, snapped the pointed end of the arrow off, and was about to pull the feathered end from his chest.

"Wait!" yelled Lars. "Leave it in him for now, or he'll bleed more."

"Get over there." Eraina signaled to her right with her head.

The soldier groaned and crawled over to the far corner of the gatehouse.

"Face down and don't move!"

She and Lars scrambled through the opening while Hamelin grabbed the loose straps, tore them into three-foot strips, and tied the man's hands behind him. The prisoner offered no resistance, but Eraina kept an arrow pointed at him while also signaling to Lars. "Check outside. Make sure no one else is coming."

Lars, still wearing Landon's colors, ran back to the door and yelled to two soldiers rushing by. "Tell the commander everything is under control in the gatehouse. He can wait as long as he wants for Carr's men to get close. The straps on the oxen have been cut!"

The soldiers raced up the stairs to carry the message. Hamelin then lifted the door, now hanging lopsided by one of its hinges, and wedged it back into the opening as tightly as he could to provide some visual cover. He and Lars pulled the oxen away from their circular path around the wheel and its winch. They looked to Eraina for a signal.

She returned the arrow to her quiver and gripped the torn scarf in both hands, looking out toward the middle of the battlefield. She saw Charissa looking for her frantically.

The storm clouds had parted, and the sun was at that very moment breaking over the horizon. Eraina and Charissa locked eyes, and Eraina mouthed one word, "Wait." For good measure, she repeated it with her hand held up in a stop motion.

Charissa shook her head, but though her hand was raised with a horn in it, she didn't put it to her lips.

"*Hamelin*," yelled Eraina. "The *gate*! They're *coming*!"

Without a word, Hamelin jumped into the circular area, grabbed the horizontal bar that the oxen had been tied to, and began to push. At first there was no movement at all. Hamelin then backed up and again pushed, straining mightily with his arms up around his chest, the crossbeam in his hands, palms out, and leaning forward. He threw his whole body into the motionless bar for all he was worth. Blood began to seep from the wound in his scalp and roll down his forehead.

And the bar moved. Only slightly at first, but as he managed to take one small step, it moved more.

Lars jumped in beside him. "Every bit helps."

Then the two of them—Lars, Prince of Periluna, and Hamelin, the orphan boy from West Texas—strained with everything they had, and together they took another step. And then one more, and the pulleys creaked and twisted, and the ropes stretched to their maximum tautness—and the wheel in the middle began to turn. They took another step, this one faster, and gained momentum without pausing between steps, and the gate began to rise.

Eraina looked again and caught her sister's eye, and this time she yelled, "*Yes!*" and her head moved up and down. "*The gate is lifting!*" Eraina then looked toward the portcullis and, as if it could hear, yelled, "Come on, you ancient gate! Lift up your head!"

And looking back to her sister, Eraina could see—and then hear—that Charissa put the horn to her lips and let loose a blast.

And Charissa also shouted, to no one in particular, but Eraina could read her lips. And even in the throes of battle, those nearby could hear her.

"*The wings of the sun are climbing! Sound the trumpets! The gate to Parthogen is rising! Charge! Retake your city and your homes!*"

And then multiple horns sounded, and the offensive force of Carr's divisions surged from the middle toward the gate. By now, Hamelin and Lars strode at a brisk place, and Hamelin was turning the wheel by himself. Lars grabbed the sword and shield and ran back to the broken-in gatehouse door to guard the way. Only once did he have to engage someone who tried to squeeze in. There was chaos everywhere.

Shouts from the top of the wall were ordering the longbowmen to get out of the way, and inside the gates were cries to "bring more arrows" and "let the dogs loose," but it was too late. Confusion reigned as soldiers and servants scrambled in all directions and Carr's soldiers used the speed and greater number of their shortbows to overwhelm Landon's men upon the wall. And now the great city gate was high, and though the first ranks of Carr's soldiers stooped as they ran under it, by the time the tenth rank rushed through, the spikes of the portcullis were above the height of even the tallest man's head.

Hamelin, with blood flowing down his face and dripping off his nose, continued to turn the wheel for good measure, and Lars ran back inside to flip the lever that locked the winch in place to hold the gate open. Both boys then guarded the wedged door.

Eraina jumped, clapped, and held her arms aloft. "*Look! The eagle has scattered the clouds! The sun is rising! Look to the east! Look—*" And then she noticed something wrong with Lars. The sunlight covered his arms and face, and he wobbled. She steadied him and then led him over to a shaded area in the gatehouse.

She put her face close to his. "I didn't know you knew how to use that sword and shield."

He rolled his eyes. "I'm a *prince*! I've been trained..." And then he lost his breath.

"Yeah, you've been trained all right. To fight big worms."

Lars cracked open his eyes. "That was an amazing hit with that arrow. Right in his chest."

She turned her mouth down at the corners, cocked her head to one side, and gave a look with a bit of a question mark in it.

Lars took in a deep breath and let it out. "Would you really have struck him in the heart with the next arrow?"

She twisted one side of her mouth and raised her eyes a little. "Well, to tell the truth, I was aiming for his heart the first time. I just wanted him to know the next one would be closer."

Lars tried to roll his eyes again, just before they closed.

Chapter 31

Reclaiming Parthogen and Staying Alert

O NCE THE CITY GATE WAS RAISED, THE BATTLE TURNED INTO a rout. Landon's forces were not only low on supplies but exhausted, so they either surrendered or fled. The dogs had already raced northward to their pens and were lingering there, away from the main part of the city.

Using her half of the scarf, Charissa easily found Hamelin, Lars, and Eraina after the worst of the battle was over—still in the gatehouse. Eraina and Hamelin were helping Lars get to his feet.

Charissa laughed for joy when she found them. "I love your scarf!" The sisters ran to each other and hugged. Charissa then took a long look at Lars, who was bandaged all over his head and upper torso.

Eraina suppressed a chuckle. "He's okay."

"How did he end up like that?"

"It's a long story how we finally got here, but we each had our part, and in the end Hamelin and Lars took the place of the oxen and opened the gates!"

"That was mostly Hamelin," mumbled Lars, who was still trying to clear his head.

Hamelin kept a hand on his friend's elbow. "But you did all kinds of things at just the right moment."

Eraina patted his shoulder. "He just got a little too much exposure to the sun. But we stripped the clothes off a prisoner, and Hamelin tore them in long pieces. I know he looks like a mummy now, but at least his arms and head are covered."

Lars tried to smile through the opening for his mouth.

Charissa looked at the blood on Hamelin's face. "What about you?"

"Just the old arrow wound from the surprise attack. It started bleeding again."

Charissa gestured to some nearby attendants. "Hamelin needs a fresh bandage, and Lars needs proper covering. But here." She handed her half of the scarf back to Eraina. "I know I took it, but it seemed necessary at the moment."

"It was meant to be—torn right down the seam where it was originally mended." Eraina pushed her lips to the corner of her mouth and widened her eyes. "Would this be a good time to mention that I borrowed a piece of your favorite jewelry for Layla's princess party?"

"Not the same thing! Besides, I knew it already."

Eraina shrugged and handed the two pieces to Hamelin to tie together, at least until the scarf could be properly repaired.

Charissa called for a soldier to take care of their prisoner and then asked Eraina about Tumultor.

She wrapped the knotted pieces of scarf around her shoulders and peered to the north. "He's still coming, and all his forces with him. He probably doesn't know that the city has fallen."

"Even if he does, he'd still be coming to rescue Landon."

Eraina wrinkled her forehead and looked around. "So where is Landon?"

"I'm hoping you can tell me. He abandoned his troops, and no one came to his aid, not even his dogs, which actually worries me. They all went to the pens at the same time, so we think he's hiding nearby and still communicating with them."

Eraina nodded. "He's up to something and still has plans for them. No doubt they'll stay close as long as Landon is alive and somewhere in the city."

Hamelin pointed to Eraina's scarf. "Speaking of the dogs, can you see mine? Buddy? The white one?"

Eraina looked toward the pens. "I think I do. There's a big white dog barking at the rest, and they're staying put, at least for now. I hate to say it, but it looks like he's their leader again, probably listening to Landon."

"Which means we've got to find Landon," said Charissa, "so do your best to spot him."

"I will. It could take a while because there are lots of small places to hide all over the city and even throughout the castle." Charissa motioned to the attendants to take care of Lars and Hamelin. Eraina followed but looked back to Charissa. "I'll let you know as soon as I find Landon. He can't hide forever."

⸻ ◈ ⸻

Tumultor and his men, including Romulus and Bryan, continued their hard ride—sometimes walking—toward Parthogen. Tumultor was growing not only angrier but also more impatient. He also seemed more fearful, the longer it took. It was now early on the second day of their journey to Parthogen, though it was the third day of the battle. They still had a long day of riding ahead of them—and probably more on into that night. Word of Carr's feinting and bluffing tactics had reached Tumultor along the way, so he still hoped to reach the city before there was a counterattack.

But after sunup that morning, he got the news he feared.

One of Landon's dogs arrived with a written message attached to a collar. It was simple and brief—"The city has fallen to Carr. I'm hiding in city. Help."

Tumultor, mounted on his horse, cursed out loud as he read the note. His leading commander brought his horse near to Tumultor's.

"What's the news, my lord? Is it bad?"

"The city has fallen. My brother's alive but in hiding."

"So do we turn back?"

"*No*! I am a son of Chimera, and so is Landon. If he's in danger, I am under obligation to rescue him." He spurred his horse. "He's my brother, even if a *stupid* one!"

Lars needed more time to recover from his exposure to the sun, but after Hamelin got fresh bandages for his head wound, he and Eraina began walking around the battle-torn city. Eraina used the time to search for Landon, but the devastations suffered by the people on both sides of the battle captured their attention and emotions. The stains and stench of blood and animal waste added to the other gruesome sights Hamelin had never imagined he would experience.

The initial excitement of retaking the city, which restored Carr and his family to their castle and returned homes and freedom to the people, did nothing to soften the shock of destruction and dying all around him. Though he occasionally heard shouts of celebration and laughter when families were reunited, the agony-filled groans of the wounded were everywhere, matched only by the mournful cries of women and children as they discovered their loved ones injured or dead.

While growing up as an orphan in West Texas, Hamelin had dreamed—with only happy mental pictures—of one day finding his parents and leading a normal life with them in their own home. The possibility of suffering in order to see something great happen hadn't entered his mind. Certainly he had never considered the grief he now saw throughout Parthogen or the terrible price that some had paid to win their freedom.

An hour later, Lars joined them. In the weeks and months to come, the streets would need to be cleaned and homes and other dwellings repaired, but for now, the three friends helped with the wounded. Carr had ordered that soldiers on both sides were to receive care, and in spite of the ever present threat of more fighting with the approach of Tumultor, or even a sudden uprising brought on by Landon and his dogs, the king and his leaders, with help from the four princesses, their friends, and all others who could, joined in—while also remaining alert to the dangers.

As he worked, Hamelin remembered—and his stomach turned over—that everything around him had resulted from a single battle and they were nowhere near the end of the war with Chimera and his sons. He sat down for a moment to rest and caught sight of Eraina. She must have been thinking something similar, because as she worked, she also searched the city for Landon and gazed hard into the distance to watch for Tumultor and his forces. Even the battle for Parthogen wasn't over.

⸻ ◈ ⸻

Late that afternoon, Carr, Charissa, and Fearbane discussed the search for Landon and also how to counter Tumultor and his small but well-trained force when they drew near the city. Charissa passed on the information and suggested that she, her sisters, and their friends meet later that night in the castle.

The girls decided they could use the queen's bedroom, one of the few spaces that Landon and his dogs, thanks to Judith, had left alone. It was a large, spacious area, and with a few extra beds brought in and some quick cleaning by the servants, it was ready when the five girls gathered. They arranged a late supper and waited for Hamelin and Lars to join them.

By the time Hamelin and Lars arrived, the girls were sitting up in their individual beds, and the room had an unusual arrangement. In the middle was a long table full of breads, cheeses, meats, fruit, and nuts. On the other side of the table were the beds, arranged in a semicircle with the foot of each one toward the table and enough room between them to move about freely. Even though in bed, the girls wore trousers and shirts suitable for action. Charissa, Eraina, and Sophie had the beds from Hamelin's right to left, their bows and arrows nearby. Charissa also wore a short sword at her side. To Hamelin's left were Layla and Amy.

Layla and Amy didn't bother with having any weapons, but Layla—with a wink at Hamelin, to remind him that she hadn't forgotten West Texas—did have on the beautiful cape with the big collar she had received just three days earlier at her princess presentation. She wore it over her other clothes and obviously was enjoying it now, since she had been forced to change so soon because of the surprise attack.

Charissa directed the boys to sit opposite the five girls at the table, the door at their backs and to their right a floor-to-ceiling window with beautiful drapes. The window and drapes were partly open, with now no clouds to obscure the moonlight.

Lars looked around and chuckled. "You look like you're ready to fight."

Eraina pointed to the bows and quivers. "Charissa told us to be ready, and she keeps reminding me to watch for Tumultor. He and his men are only a couple of hours away, but it's late and they're stopping to water their horses. Father has sent scouts out as well, so we'll know if they stop for the night or continue to ride. And I'm still looking for Landon."

"Our soldiers are ready, for sure," said Charissa, "and now that we're back inside the city walls, we have the preferred elevated position. Tumultor at this point doesn't have the fighting force necessary to retake the city, but we can't let down our guard."

Hamelin nodded and instinctively tugged on his gloves. He then looked to Eraina. "And you're sure Bryan is with him?" He shot a worried glance at Layla as Eraina answered.

"Yes. He's not dressed like a soldier, but he's riding next to Romulus, who has Hamelin's sword at his side." She turned to her right and looked toward the last two beds. "We've promised Layla and Amy—and Father and Fearbane agree—that we will do everything we can to protect Bryan and Romulus, who could well be Michael."

Everyone fell silent. Finally, Sophie stood to the side of her bed and stepped toward the food table. "But all of us are here now. Our father is better than I've seen him in years, and we are back inside our beloved city. Let's enjoy these moments. Come to the table and eat."

Her suggestion calmed the tension in the air. Soon everyone was eating and talking, and remembering not only the losses they had witnessed but also the happy moments of families reunited and the people of Parthogen returning to their homes.

The food and conversation continued for almost an hour. The moon, full again that night, had risen high in the sky and could now be seen in all its glory. "I've never seen the moon look so full, almost powerful," said Amy.

Seconds later, the sounds of barking and baying came through the window, as if to prove her point.

Eraina gripped her scarf and scanned the castle grounds. "Those are Landon's wolf dogs. The moonlight stirs them." The howling and barking grew as more canines joined in.

Layla straightened her collar and cape. "Can we close that window? Those dogs are making me nervous."

Charissa stepped to the window, shut it, and pulled the drapes. "We can block their howling, but we have to stay alert. Until we find Landon, those wolf dogs won't scatter; and I can assure you that his brother Tumultor won't turn back."

Hamelin remembered the clashes with Tumultor months before, when he, Lars, and Eraina had crashed the wedding to rescue Charissa, and the vicious threats Tumultor had made to Charissa when they all hid behind the waterfall. He didn't look forward to meeting up with him again, especially with Romulus at his side, wielding the special sword.

Eraina continued to look—at first into the distance—but as she did, her attention seemed to move closer and closer in.

Chapter 32

What about Landon?

CHARISSA REMAINED AT THE WINDOW, DEEP IN THOUGHT. Landon's creatures continued to howl and bark. When she finally looked up, she asked Hamelin and Lars to follow her and warned everyone else to stay alert. She nodded at Eraina as an unspoken reminder to continue watching for Landon and Tumultor.

Once outside the room, she told Hamelin and Lars she was concerned about what Landon was now doing with his creatures—that they were away from their pens and gathering up near the castle—and wanted to talk more to Fearbane and her father. She and the boys found Carr and his commander in the king's suite, just down the hall on the same side as the queen's bedroom, with two soldiers stationed outside. The suite, already cleaned and polished, was appointed with ornate furniture and oriental rugs. The near area held a large tea table with chairs, an upholstered three-seat sofa, and book shelves on the wall to the left. The other area contained a bed, which dominated the far wall to the right, flanked by lamp tables, and a closet with a dressing table and full-length mirror. Both areas had a long window on the far wall. Fearbane was there, and the king ushered them in. Charissa had just started to explain her concerns when she heard a frantic voice calling her name.

At that very moment, Eraina burst into the room breathless. "Landon! I found Landon! I started over completely, searching the city and the castle grounds...and he was in the dog pens! Crouching down with his creatures all around him, helping him hide! I don't know how I missed him! But—"

"Is he still there?" interrupted Fearbane.

"Wait! Let me finish! Then only a few minutes ago he crept and crawled toward the castle and entered through the secret tunnel—you know, the hidden stairway that comes from outside the castle right up into Mother's wardrobe closet, in her special dressing room just the other side of the landing."

Fearbane strode to the door. "I'll take these two soldiers and go get him!"

"No. Stop! He's not there anymore! Just a minute ago he slipped out and raced down the stairs. He was heading toward the kitchen, and then I ran to find you."

Eraina paused and stared down the stairs and apparently even farther. "He's got a kitchen knife, and now he's moving toward the basement!"

Fearbane opened the door and barked to the soldiers, "Follow me!" He turned back to the king. "Your Majesty, please stay here. My men and I can find him and subdue him, but until we do, he is dangerous."

"You can certainly tie him up securely, but do him no harm. I want to negotiate with him before his brother gets here."

Fearbane nodded and dashed away. Hamelin and Lars stayed with the king, while Charissa and Eraina returned to the Queen's bedroom to update their sisters and Amy.

Everyone felt apprehensive for Fearbane and the soldiers

confronting a knife-wielding Landon, but Eraina, who began watching events unfold below them, soon laughed out loud. "What a coward! As soon as Fearbane and his two soldiers with swords and spears approached him, Landon ran to the very end of the basement—but there's no door there. He curled up in a ball against the far wall, and it looks like he was begging them not to hurt him."

"So what's happening now?" asked Sophie.

"The soldiers have plopped him in a chair at that very spot and tied his hands and feet. He's hanging his head. Fearbane is already on his way back, but he's left the two soldiers there to guard him."

Eraina smiled broadly, and everyone breathed a sigh of relief. Except Charissa. She stood quietly, hands on hips, listening.

Amy noticed. "So what is it, Charissa?"

"The dogs."

"I don't hear them anymore," said Layla.

"That's the problem. You don't hear them because they're not here. Where did they go?" Charissa looked at Eraina.

Within seconds Eraina had the answer. "They're racing toward the far end of the castle, just outside the basement wall where Landon is locked up."

Charissa quickly stepped toward the door but paused before leaving. "All of you, stay here, and be alert. Eraina, keep watching for Tumultor. I'll tell Father that we need to clear out those dogs before he negotiates with Landon."

⊷⊶⊷⦿⊷⊶⊷

Charissa strode down the hall to her father's bedroom and found him with Hamelin and Lars, still waiting for Fearbane. It wasn't long before the king's chief commander returned from his successful confrontation with Landon. He reported what had happened, and Carr was visibly pleased. Hamelin clapped his hands, and Lars laughed out loud, while Charissa quietly congratulated Fearbane.

"It has been a long time coming," she said, "but this monster is finally, at least for now, under our control."

"I sense a reluctance to celebrate, my daughter," said Carr, "and I understand why. There's still much to do. Tell me what in particular is now weighing on your mind."

"It's the dogs, Father. Less than an hour ago their barking and howling could be heard all around us, and especially on this end of the castle. But now, since Landon has been captured, Eraina tells me that the dogs have circled around the castle and gathered outside the far end of the basement, where Landon is tied up."

Carr rubbed his chin with his right hand. "I see your point. If the dogs are there, then Landon has summoned them, and if he has summoned them, then likely he has plans to use them."

"Sire, I can quickly send some soldiers to dispatch those dogs."

"I'm not worried about him using the dogs right now, given where he is and the fact that we are guarding not only the doors to the castle but also the only door to the basement—at the end away from him."

"Sire, as you know," said Fearbane, "my preference is that we execute him. His treasonous and murderous behavior truly justifies it, and it would greatly simplify our next steps."

Carr nodded and placed a hand on Fearbane's shoulder. "I understand your feelings. If he had died in battle, his death would indeed have served justice and been welcomed by us all, and Tumultor would have to lay all blame on Landon. But he is our prisoner, and he surrendered to us. We cannot justly execute him. And there's no time to put him on trial. His brother will be approaching soon. We've got to make the best deal we can under the circumstances. I think we should be willing to give Landon up to his brother in exchange for their withdrawal and promise never to attack Parthogen again."

"But Father, we all know that—"

"Of course, my daughter—we know that the word of neither of them has any value, but surrendering Landon to Tumultor might at least buy some time to reinforce our city and see what else the Ancient One has for us...before they come back."

"You're right, Father. And with those dogs gathering, time is of the essence. But should we first transfer him to your dungeon?"

"I don't want to take the time even for that. He's tied up now. I want to see him immediately and let him know what we're willing to do."

"Then of course several of us will accompany you, Father, starting with Fearbane and me."

Lars took a step closer. "Hamelin and I would like to join you as well."

Fearbane nodded. "I think it would be good for all of us to go, Your Majesty. I already have two soldiers down there. The seven of us should be enough for now, until we send a contingent to scatter those dogs."

⸺⸺◉⸺⸺

From the king's suite, they walked along a hall, down a beautiful winding staircase, through a ballroom of magnificent fixtures and furnishings—rugs, tables, tapestries, and tall windows—across a huge sitting room and then a smaller parlor, and finally through a grand entryway into another part of the castle.

They continued toward the far end of the castle, down a long corridor with guest rooms and smaller dining rooms on each side. They then came to the kitchen and proceeded just past it down a flight of steep stairs. As soon as the stairs ended at the basement floor, they could hear the dogs barking and yelping at the other end, where Landon was being held. The long, somewhat narrow space that then stretched before them grew darker toward the far end.

Hamelin could see various objects hanging on the walls, as well as shelves and storage areas containing brushes and brooms, bridles and bits, polishes and salves, and boxes and work tables—all needed to manage the running of the castle. There was even an area where old dishes and silver had been stored.

Along the way, they passed a room with a steel door, a few work areas, none of which had been used in a while, and several built-in storage closets. The walls were windowless, the only available light coming from irregularly placed torches on each side, and the flickering of the torches gave impressions of darting shadows all around them. But Carr strode toward the barking with Charissa, Fearbane, Hamelin, and Lars flanking him, two on each side.

Hamelin hoped the others couldn't tell how jumpy he was starting to feel. It didn't help that the darkness of the space was made creepier by the wild noises of the wolves and dogs, noises that grew louder and closer with every step. The only small point of relief, in spite of the frenzied creatures, came from the moonlight shining through a curtainless window at the far end of the basement. The window, about four feet high and two feet wide, faced them and looked to be halfway up the wall. The light helped some, though the noises from the dogs seemed concentrated around that window.

And why was there a window to the outside anyway, since the basement was underground? But then he remembered that the castle was built on elevated ground that sloped away from the central structures, so at the end wall just in front of them, the ground level outside was only a few feet above the floor level of the basement. Inside, the window was some ten feet up the wall, but outside, its lower frame was only about six feet above the ground.

But the main concern now was Landon. Where was he? And then, with shadows across his face and body, he came into view. He sat facing them at the end of the basement, his hands and feet bound with ropes to the arms and legs of a chair. Even in the darkness, it was evident that he was squirming against his restraints, twisting his head and upper torso toward the window.

As the king approached, the barking outside grew worse. Landon turned his head and stared at Carr, but then his eyes settled on Charissa and a sneer slowly curled his lips. "I caught you once, and I'll soon be giving you back to my brother Tumultor with my own hands."

Hamelin shot a look at Charissa and imagined how she felt. The stories of her humiliating capture years ago by Landon's rowdy soldiers, just after her morning bath, were widely whispered and known. Landon's mocking reminder, while he was still tied up as a prisoner, made it plain that he would be tough and cruel if it came to a fight.

On the other hand, this time Charissa likely wouldn't be so fragile.

Chapter 33

A Change

CHARISSA'S EYES NARROWED, AND IN AN INSTANT, SHE stepped forward, drew her sword, and slashed down on Landon's right wrist tied to the arm of the chair. Landon screamed, and his eyes bulged with panic, but she stopped the blade just as it penetrated the skin of his lower forearm and held it there. Drops of blood formed.

"Next time you see Tumultor, you better hope you have two hands to do anything with." She lifted the sword and stepped back. Blood ran down his wrist and dripped on the floor.

Landon shivered and then glared at her, but she met his gaze until he blinked and jerked his head toward the king. "You know you can't keep me like this."

Fearbane stepped closer to the king. "We'll keep you as long as we want and however we want."

As he did, the others also spread out in a line, with the king in the middle and Fearbane, Charissa, and the two soldiers to Carr's left, Hamelin and Lars on his right.

As if in response, the howling and barking outside grew,

and there were loud thumps against the wall, as the animals jumped and threw themselves against it.

"If your brother Tumultor comes for you, we'll hand you over," said Carr.

"You're not going to kill me?"

"No, though I can't argue with my daughter's willingness to send you back one-handed. Had you died in battle, we would not have lamented your loss, but now that you've been captured—hiding and cowering shamelessly, I might add—you are our prisoner. We will not kill you, but we will not let you go unless Tumultor promises to take you and agrees to certain conditions."

"He'll never agree to anything. He'll come, and if he doesn't, Ren'dal will come. You can't keep me here. You have no idea the powers you're up against."

"We know of your communication with wolves, and we know what evil ambitions Chimera gives Tumultor and especially Ren'dal."

"Then why are you down here talking to me? There's nothing to discuss."

"But there is. Master Fearbane, will you explain these things to the prisoner."

Fearbane looked directly at Landon. "We're back in our city and now the advantages of defending it are our own. We'll take our chances against your brothers. For now, His Majesty has agreed not to execute you, but there's nothing that will keep us from confining you to a small, dark place in the dungeon and hunting down your wolfish dogs. You know full well that these two young warriors have scattered them before and inflicted painful injuries on them. Unless you—by whatever dark means you use to communicate with them—silence them now and send them away from our city and kingdom, great harm will come upon them. Death, if necessary."

Landon looked at Hamelin and Lars and slowly nodded his head, but the smirk on his face was discernible even in the poorly lit conditions. The angry sounds outside grew, and Hamelin could now see the heads of dogs and their front legs scratching at the window behind Landon as they jumped toward it.

Hamelin shot a look to his right, toward Lars, and noticed that his friend's knees were bent slightly and he was ready to spring into action.

Landon's eyes darted between Carr and his people. His mouth twitched. "Let me see what I can do. Sometimes these creatures have a mind of their own, but I'll just..."

His chin dropped to his chest, and his breathing became deep as long seconds passed. The howling and barking of the wolfish creatures outside swelled. Some leaped high enough to bang their paws and heads against the window. Their teeth showed and, tongues out, their snarling slobber streaked the glass.

Landon shifted and leaned his head back, and his eyelids began to flutter. Then, with a startling outburst, he snarled and let out an agonized, full-throated howl. It grew in volume and pitch for long seconds.

Fearbane pulled on the king's arm. "Your Majesty! You must—" But it was too late.

With the howl at its highest pitch, drowning out whatever instructions Fearbane was trying to give, the head of a dog butted forcibly against the window, and the glass shattered with a boom. Within a split second, one of the dogs had his forepaws and head all the way up to his shoulders through the window and was ferociously snapping and barking. He fell back and disappeared, but a second later another dog, with a massive blue-gray head and white ears, made it, leaping and scrambling through the window and hitting the back of Landon's chair, knocking it over with him in it.

And then another dog jumped through the opening, and another, and within seconds the king and his protectors were face to face with a semicircle of canines, with Landon on the floor between them all.

Hamelin's gut tightened as he bent his knees, raised his gloved hands like fists, and prepared to punch, grab, and smash whatever came at him. Once it started, this would be no schoolyard fight. Landon's dogs were trained to tear them to pieces, but fortunately Buddy wasn't among them now.

Everyone was tensed, ready for attack, but the wolf dogs held their place, their heads and forelegs down, their fangs showing, ready to spring.

Fearbane spread his arms. "Hold back, Your Majesty. You must step away." He then took the king by the arm and firmly pulled him back and behind.

Charissa stepped into the space the king had occupied and pointed the tip of her sword toward the dogs.

In the meantime, Hamelin and Lars spread out, arm's length from each other. Lars went into a crouch, and Hamelin kept his arms and hands up, ready to fight.

The barking and snarling stopped, and Hamelin realized he had been holding his breath. He took a deep breath to steady himself. He knew Lars was just to his right, but he stole a look to his left to confirm where the others were now. To his immediate left was Fearbane, with the king behind him. Beyond Fearbane were Charissa and the two soldiers. All the animals held their position, heads and shoulders still down but their eyes turned upward.

And then, as if on cue, the dogs from just behind Landon and to his side slowly moved forward.

Fearbane still held his arms wide, making sure the king wouldn't come around him, and gave a quiet command to all. "Step back slowly. We must protect the king at all costs."

The dogs kept moving forward small step by small step, until they formed a protective fence in front of Landon, who was still tied to his chair, lying on the floor.

"Keep moving," said Fearbane steadily, and they all took another cautious step back.

Then two more dogs jumped through the window, but instead of falling into line with the others, they went straight to Landon and began to bite and chew through the cords. The dogs in front moved closer to each other. The large gray one with the white ears let out a low growl and was joined by a chorus of warning sounds from the others. The ropes around Landon's wrists were getting looser.

Then Landon himself began a low, moaning growl as his wrists became free and the dogs began to gnaw at the ropes around his feet, pulling on them and shaking their heads furiously from side to side.

"Back some more," said Fearbane, who obviously wanted to get all of them, and especially the king, out of the basement without bolting and encouraging the dogs to give chase.

An instant later, Landon's feet broke free. But instead of urging his dogs to spring forward and attack, he scrambled toward the back wall and positioned himself under the window. Hamelin didn't move. Was Landon going to try to climb out? Could the dogs help him do that? Surely the window was too high, and there were still shards of glass in the frame. But he remained there, raising his hands as if reaching for the sky. What was he doing?

The moon was high, and Landon stood at just the right angle for its light to hit him in the face. Was he going to start barking and baying at it as he had done before, to summon other dogs? Hamelin looked at the nearby creatures, wondering what they would do. They were crouched in a semicircle, forming a barrier between their master and the king's protectors. They bared their teeth and let out low warning snarls. But they stayed put. Long seconds passed.

Then Charissa took a half step forward while pointing her sword first at the dogs, then toward Landon. "Keep your concentration! The sons of Chimera are masters of deception. Be ready!" The dogs growled but didn't move. The room grew cold.

Hamelin felt his hands twitching and a chilling shiver starting at the top of his spine. He forced himself to stand at attention and focus on Landon.

It was barely detectable at first, but Landon slowly began to tremble. His torso, starting with his chest, shimmered and then suddenly expanded as if about to burst. His eyes stared vacantly in the direction of his dogs and then turned empty, glazed, and moist. His head and shoulders shook once and then shivered, and grotesque changes in his body erupted! His shape was shifting—his head narrowed in length, and all at once hair curled out of his cheeks and forehead.

Hamelin was sure the scene before him couldn't really be happening, but his eyes were telling him that a monstrous man-to-wolf transformation was taking place, though the morphing creature still stood on two legs.

The dogs crouched even lower, bared their teeth, and snarled.

Landon drooled and then looked wildly at his wolfish creatures and yipped out a series of sharp barks—and the dogs attacked.

The soldier on Fearbane's left quickly took on one of the dogs with his long spear. As the dog rushed and dodged, the soldier jabbed quickly but only nicked him, though he kept him at bay.

Another dog leaped straight at Charissa, who dispatched the creature with a single sword thrust that left it lying on the floor.

Holding the king behind him with his left arm, Fearbane yelled a warning to the two soldiers to Charissa's left, and they engaged two more dogs that shot forward to take up the fight.

On Hamelin's side of the room, the blue-gray dog made the mistake of jumping toward him first, only to receive a body blow from Hamelin's left arm as he delivered a roundhouse shot, followed by a right cross to the jaw that shattered teeth and immediately caused blood to spurt and drip.

Two other dogs came at Lars, one after the other, apparently thinking that the bluish dog could deal with Hamelin on his own. Lars gave the first one a sweeping body kick with his right leg and quickly spun around in a full 360-degree pirouette, catching the next dog in the throat with a left-footed knee kick that extended to chest high as Lars jumped into the air.

Fearbane now had the king pulled back several more paces, but Carr yelled, "Fearbane, don't abandon the others!"

"They're fine, Your Majesty!" He then called to his two soldiers, who were parrying and thrusting with one dog, to fall back and get the king out of the area.

Charissa stepped to her left and took over their opponent, a gray- and tan-mottled wolf that retreated two steps from the tip of her poised sword. Then all the remaining dogs did the same. Even the blue-gray dog managed to limp backward and retake his position in the middle of the formation, an arc that surrounded and protected Landon, who during the fighting had stayed under the window in the full moonlight.

And then in a final burst of frenzied, convulsive power, Landon's transformation was all but complete. His arms became giant forelegs, and his body lowered into a crouch; and just as he settled on all fours, he let out a howling shriek that was part man—but mostly wolf—and then leaped over the protective shield of his dogs toward Hamelin, who had momentarily glanced toward Charissa.

The other dogs froze in place as if under command.

The shape changer was still in midflight when Lars yelled, "*Hamelin!*" and at the same time jumped high in the air and landed a powerful kick just above Landon's left hindquarter, directly in his lower ribcage and belly.

The werewolf howled, but Lars's kick was from an angle and threw only the lower half of his body off target. His head was still near Hamelin, who at the last possible instant thrust both arms upward and caught Landon just above his shoulders, with his hands squeezing the fur and loose skin around his neck.

Though their heads were initially only inches apart, Hamelin maintained his grip and, with the force of his gloved hands, yanked the massive wolf out of the air in midflight and slammed the back of his head to the floor. Hamelin's instincts to fight were on fire, and for a furious split second he intended to squeeze Landon's neck until it snapped. But two voices went through his head. One was Carr's telling Fearbane earlier that they shouldn't kill Landon; and the other was the eagle's, when he told Hamelin he was out of control. Hamelin came to himself and held the perverted creature tightly but allowed him to breathe, even while Landon's powerful, hairy torso thrashed wildly—and dangerously.

"Help the boy!" yelled the king. "Don't let the creature bite him!"

Fearbane ran toward Hamelin, and Charissa rushed to Fearbane's left side to protect him.

Hamelin then further twisted Landon's neck and shoulders, and his body followed so that the werewolf's head was face down to the floor.

Lars remained crouched in a ready position in case the dogs on his side of the room decided to attack.

Fearbane came to Hamelin's left and placed the tip of

his sword at Landon's abdomen. "May I kill him *now*, Your Majesty? He is loose and no longer our prisoner! He's not even a man! He's a twisted beast who is attacking us. May I *kill* him?"

The king hesitated and then stepped toward the scene of the struggling werewolf held by Hamelin.

But the dogs in front of Lars began to crawl forward.

"Watch them, Son of Elwood," warned Carr. "They're coming toward you."

Lars had already seen them and was prepared. As the dogs moved closer, he widened his stance and pulled his right leg back, prepared to launch into a powerful kick.

But as Landon's head turned and tugged above Hamelin's vise-like grip, Lars unknowingly inched closer to the writhing creature.

Landon paused his straining for a moment but then suddenly jerked in one mighty thrust to his left and was now a mere handbreadth from Lars's left ankle and calf.

As the powerful werewolf pulled and stretched his upper body, the king saw it all and rushed forward. "*Look out!*"

Landon, with one last surge of strength, twisted his neck and opened his jaws to plunge his teeth into Lars. Carr leaped headfirst toward the small space between Lars's left leg and Landon's mouth and jammed his hand into the gap to deflect the werewolf's bite. The thrust of his hand, however, wasn't high enough on the werewolf's head.

Landon's crushing maw and teeth missed Lars but snapped down upon Carr's right hand and held him.

At that same moment, Landon's wolfish dogs all attacked.

"*Sire!*" screamed Fearbane as he rushed around Hamelin—who was still holding Landon—to rescue his king.

Charissa and Lars, in the chaos of the moment, furiously counterattacked. Charissa, enraged to see her father harmed, slashed and cut her way through a series of attacks, while Lars fought with a flurry of kicks, spins, and stomps. Together they drove the dogs against the far wall, wounding and bruising mouths, bodies, and legs, until the yelping and whining creatures limped from the basement as fast as they could, skirting everyone, including their master, who still clenched the king's hand in his mouth.

Hamelin did the only thing he knew to do. In one quick move, he released Landon's neck and shoulders but just as quickly grabbed his mouth with one hand above and another hand below and pulled the jaws apart, all the while keeping a downward pressure on Landon's head.

Fearbane pulled Carr free, but the hand was a bloody mess, torn and mangled.

The king groaned in pain, and Fearbane picked him up and rushed him toward the stairs. Charissa and the soldiers followed, sword and spear at the ready in case any wolf dogs, which were now in front of them, turned back to fight.

Hamelin quickly shifted his grip. Once he closed the werewolf's jaws, he held them closed with his right hand and placed his left hand powerfully on the animal's chest, flipping him onto his back while squeezing his flesh and pushing down with all his strength, driving the air out of his lungs. In that moment, he again considered killing Landon, but he felt the werewolf relent. Landon, though powerful, apparently knew he was held in a grip that he couldn't break.

Lars ran to the ropes that were still around the chair and on the floor. "I'll tie him up again!"

"No! He's too strong for those ropes."

"Then what do we use?"

Hamelin thought for a minute. "The chain."

"What chain?"

"The chain around my neck! I don't know what it's made of, but it's ancient and strong. Get it! Hurry!"

Lars came to Hamelin and pulled the chain up over his head. "Twist it and place it around his mouth all the way up to the top of his jawline."

Lars did just that and gave it one extra twist, careful not to get his own hands near the werewolf's teeth.

Hamelin, releasing his right hand from Landon's jaws, quickly used his strength in that hand to push the chain farther up and tighter around Landon's mouth. Then, using both hands, he dragged the werewolf by the shoulders into the space behind them, away from the window.

"Open that door over there," yelled Hamelin. "We've got to keep him out of the moonlight." He dragged Landon into the side room with the steel door. The room was dark, so there was no way to tell what else was in it, but the door was heavy. Hamelin shoved him in, slammed the door behind him, and dropped an iron bar across it into a slot.

"We need to get him to the dungeon," said Hamelin, "but that should hold him for a while. Will he change back?"

"I don't know," said Lars. "Let's hope he does. But the king... did you see his hand? He was protecting *me*!"

"I know, but Fearbane and Charissa have him now. Let's go find them. They may need us."

As they hurried away, Hamelin's legs and arms shook from both exhaustion and the intensity of the fight. But it was fear that magnified the quivering of his muscles. The king's hand! Landon had sunk his wolf teeth deep into the brave king. How could this have happened to the father of his friends?

Hamelin knew the werewolf legends from stories he'd read back in Texas. Here, however, old legends, including horror stories, came true. Could all this lead to death? Especially the death of a great king?

Chapter 34

The Eclipse

Hamelin and Lars raced toward the king's suite, where the door was closed. A loud groan came from the inside as they opened the door and looked in.

The king lay in his bed, his right arm extended and his hand in a basin of water while doctors attended him. His daughters were on the other side of his bed, with Amy and Fearbane at the foot of it.

Charissa, who stood at his left hand, saw Hamelin and Lars and waved them in.

They approached the king's bed, but his eyes were closed, and he groaned again. His clothes were bloody, as were his bed linens, and a maidservant came rushing in with a fresh basin of water and more towels. The doctors were working to stop the blood and dress the wounds on his mangled hand.

Hamelin and Lars slipped toward the bed and stood behind the four sisters.

Charissa looked at the boys and whispered, "Fearbane told us what happened."

Lars put his head down and could hardly look up.

Eraina turned to her left, where Lars was standing just behind her shoulder. "It's not your fault."

"But...he did it to protect me... I got too close..."

"It was all in the heat of battle, dear Lars," said Charissa.

Sophie reached over and patted him on the left shoulder. "You and Hamelin did all you could. Thank you." Lars kept his head down, shaking it slowly.

"I just didn't hold him tight enough," mumbled Hamelin. "I—"

"*No*," said Eraina. "Not another word. Our father loves you both, and we know from Fearbane that he refused to leave for his own safety. He did what he chose to do, which was to protect others. It's what he's always done."

The doctors were easing a mixture of powders, potions, and water down the king's throat. The maidservant was wiping his head with a cold towel, and he coughed, but within another minute, he took a deep breath, and his body relaxed.

The chief physician stepped back from the bed. "We've given him something that should help his pain. Right now he needs rest. It's a great trauma to be bitten by such a beast...we don't know..."

And everybody understood what the old physician didn't say—they didn't know what would happen when you're bitten by a werewolf. They knew, however, what the legends said.

"We'll have to see," he added. "For now, His Majesty appears comfortable. Maybe all of you should go get some rest."

The girls leaned down and kissed their father, one by one. Amy and Lars patted him on his left arm and filed out. Hamelin found it hard to move. What could he have done differently? Should he have killed Landon when he had the chance? He trudged a few steps toward the door but halted. He wasn't the last in the room.

Fearbane still stood at the foot of the bed, unwilling to leave. His hands were shaking. Finally, Fearbane took a deep breath, and with a sigh to suppress his rage, he stretched out a hand and touched his master's foot. The king stirred, looked to the end of the bed, and acknowledged his friend with his eyes. The great soldier nodded and settled back in a chair to guard his king. Hamelin left to join the others.

By the time Hamelin reached the queen's bedroom, the five girls had already entered, and Lars stood outside, waiting for him. They both mumbled at the same time. Lars said, "My fault," and Hamelin whispered, "Sorry." Lars touched his younger friend's shoulder, and they both stepped into the room.

The five girls were facing them in a semicircle, either sitting on the side of their beds or standing next to them. Charissa stood to Hamelin's right, closest to the window, and looked down, giving every appearance of thinking and not wanting to be bothered. Next, to his left were Eraina, then Sophie, Layla, and Amy. Eraina and Sophie kept their bows and arrows nearby, and Charissa had never removed her sword and sheath. Layla still wore her new princess cape, which almost looked silly now under the circumstances, but she slowly rubbed it with her head down, touching close to the spots around the neck where her father had fastened it. Amy lay back, but she was wide awake, watching and listening. The moon was high, and its light softened the room, even though the curtains remained drawn. The food was still there, but no one ate anything.

The sounds from the dogs had almost vanished since the attack, and now, instead of the occasional bark or howl, all was quiet. Had Landon silenced his dogs? Was he still communicating with them? Perhaps gathering them for an attack? Then, though no one had trimmed any of the lamps, the room started to grow darker.

"Is it clouding up again?" asked Amy.

Charissa took several steps toward the door but paused and turned as she reached it. "We have our minds on Father, but he would remind us to stay alert. A lot is happening all at once, and we have to be prepared and decisive. Our immediate problems are Landon and Tumultor. Eraina, see where Tumultor is and how much time we have until he's near the city."

Eraina spread the scarf over her head, grabbed the two ends, and peered out of the room, looking north.

⸺⸻◆⸻⸺

"How far are we now?" Tumultor barked to the commander riding on his left.

"Less than two hours away, sir. Maybe only an hour and a half." Tumultor raised his hand and signaled to stop.

"Have we had any other messages about Landon?"

The answer came from a soldier behind him, "No, my lord, nothing more."

"We'll give the men a little rest, water the horses, and then we'll make the last ride into Parthogen. When we get close, we'll send some messengers on ahead to tell Carr that we want to talk."

Bryan and Romulus stood together as the horses were watered and given a few handfuls of feed. Bryan looked up into the sky as they talked. "Pretty strange, isn't it?"

"It's all strange, but what bit of strangeness are you talking about?"

"The sky. Look at the moon—" He pointed upward to the full moon that had been following them in the darkness for the last several hours.

Romulus looked. "Hmmm. Yes, it is odd. It looks like..."

"An eclipse, at least a partial eclipse of the moon. I've been watching it for the last half hour. At first I thought I was seeing things, but it is some kind of lunar eclipse. At least a quarter of the moon has been covered."

Romulus smirked. "So it has. So what are you? Some kind of wise man or astrologer—maybe a diviner?"

Bryan chuckled. "No, but I do know—as you should know from your old books—that an eclipse of the moon can be a sign."

"What?"

"A sign. I'm sure you've read about them."

"Of course I have, but—"

"I'm just saying. All these odd things that have been happening, the magic sword, us meeting up with each other—hey, your whole life is strange—it makes me pay attention to these kinds of things." Bryan lifted his head and said in a slightly louder voice, "So when I see an eclipse of the moon, I pay attention. Who knows what it means?"

Others standing around heard Bryan's comment, which especially caught the attention of one of Tumultor's holy men. He quickly shuffled off to another holy man, who by his clothing and colors had a higher rank. They whispered together, and the greater holy man approached Tumultor's chief commander, who then brought him over to Tumultor. The three of them talked. Tumultor was clearly agitated, but the holy man looked determined, shaking his head and pointing to the moon.

Tumultor finally sighed with a loud groan and barked to his lieutenants. "We're stopping here! At least for a while. Don't anybody bed down yet, but we're going to see what these magi have to tell us."

When his men looked puzzled, Tumultor pointed to the moon. "They're telling me that something's going on up there, and we better know what it is before we go any farther. Some kind of omen." The soldiers nearby seemed glad and quickly tied their horses up and sat down.

"Are you kidding me?" said Romulus. "We're stopping

because there's a partial eclipse of the moon? What's going on here?" He stared at Bryan. "Why did you say that so *loud*?" Romulus shook his head, but the decision had been made. They were going to wait until the holy men had done their divinations and calculations. Bryan looked away, not wanting Romulus to detect his relief at the delay.

⸺⬦⸺

"What do you see, Eraina?" asked Sophie.

"They've stopped. I don't know why, because they don't seem to be making a camp for the night."

"Maybe they're resting their horses."

"Maybe, but Tumultor's been driving them hard for days now, and this is much longer than any other rest he's taken. If they keep coming, it won't take long, but for now they're just standing around. I'm not sure what they're doing." Eraina kept looking. "Hmmm."

"What is it?" asked Charissa.

"Tumultor is talking to some of his holy men, and they keep pointing up to the sky and...you know, what Amy said a minute ago was right—it is getting darker."

Hamelin stepped to the window and parted the curtains. "Hey, Lars, take a look at this."

Lars stood behind Hamelin. "It's an eclipse. At least a partial one so far. That must be what they're looking at."

Charissa and Amy joined the two boys, and all of them stared at the moon.

"The dark part is growing," said Amy. "You can see the shadows moving on the moon. I wonder how much of an eclipse it's going to be." No one answered. Silent minutes passed, and the darkness deepened. Then Amy pointed. "That's at least half an eclipse now. And it looks like it's still moving. It might be a pretty full one."

Charissa strode back toward the door. "Whatever the moon

does could affect the dogs. Keep watching Tumultor, Eraina, while Sophie and I go check on Father. We'll be back shortly, and then I want us to deal with Landon before Tumultor arrives."

Lars then glanced toward Hamelin and caught his eye. He tilted his head slightly toward the door, and when Charissa and Sophie left, the two young men stepped outside the room.

"Charissa is in a hurry and trying to get a lot of things done at once. Maybe we can help her."

"What do you have in mind?" asked Hamelin.

"By the time she gets back, we could have some important information for her—about Landon. The moon is covered up for now, and the dogs are quiet, but we don't really know if Landon will change back. There are different legends about how the changes happen. If he remains a wolf, or if he's still a werewolf at least for now, he's going to be really hard to handle. She wants to move him to the dungeon, which would be safer than keeping him where he is, but it'll take some soldiers and strong ropes, maybe even some chains, to control him, and that will all take time."

"I see what you mean. But if he's changed back to a man, that'll make things a lot easier."

"Right. So we could go find out and have that much information ready for Charissa, especially if Tumultor gets on the move again quickly."

"Good idea, but why don't I just go by myself and you stay here in case any surprises develop while I'm gone. You've got the speed to let me know if there's an emergency."

"Okay, but don't take any chances. Maybe just listen to see what kinds of noises he's making. All we want to know is whether he's still a wolf or if he's changed back to a man."

"I understand." Hamelin nodded and left.

He took a small torch and hurried through the castle down to the basement. It was still dark, but with no one else with him, it seemed even darker, and the darkness felt close and heavy on his shoulders. And it was quiet, no howling or barking, but the silence plus his memory of what had happened in this very space made his spine shiver again. His pace slowed as he approached the storage room where they had thrown Landon. He stuck his ear to the door and listened. Nothing. It was a thick door, and Hamelin knew that Landon could just be playing possum, waiting for someone to open it. If Landon had changed back to a man, he would be no problem to control, but...

He listened again. Was the door too thick? Had Landon passed out for lack of water or air? He and Lars hadn't thought about that. The king didn't want to harm him before handing him over to Tumultor... He again put his ear to the door but still couldn't hear anything. So he decided he would lift the bar, crack open the door, and step back. If Landon was in a wolf shape, he could at least hear his breathing—or maybe even catch a glimpse of him—but still be able to slam the door quickly. If he was a man, it wouldn't matter.

Hamelin placed the torch in a holder on the wall and tugged at the cuffs of his gloves. He then quietly raised the bar, slowly pulled the door open by a few inches, and stepped back. He looked into the darkness of the storage room. Nothing.

"Landon." No answer. He tried again, a little louder. "Landon." No growls. No steps. Not even breathing.

Then from what sounded like the back of the room, he heard a faint reply in the voice of a man, "Yes, what do you want?"

That was good news. He should be easy to handle. Hamelin closed the door and put the bar back in place. He had an idea...maybe he could save some additional time and get him to Fearbane's soldiers and then to the dungeon. It would be better than keeping him here, near a window that opened to the moon. He hurried back toward the end of the basement and couldn't help seeing along the way the signs of the recent fight with Landon and his dogs. The blood and bodies of wounded and slain mixed breeds were still there. Plus, the buzz of flies and...a small pool of blood where Landon had crushed the king's hand in his jaws. Hamelin's back and neck chilled, but he went on, avoiding the shards of broken glass as he retrieved some lengths of the rope that had bound Landon. He then returned to the steel door, lifted the cross bar, and slowly opened the door a foot wide. "Your brother Tumultor is on his way, and we're willing to hand you over to him. But I'm going to tie your hands, so come closer, and turn around."

"How do I know it's not a trick and you're not just going to kill me?"

"If we wanted to kill you, we could have done that already, and maybe I should have while you were a wolf. But the king didn't let us, so I'm not going to now."

"How is he?"

"He's hurt. His hand..."

"I'm sorry," came back Landon's voice, weakly, almost in a whine. "The moon did it. I couldn't help what happened after that."

"Yes, you could. You're bad no matter what your shape. When you were a man, you were communicating with your wolves and growling, and you were a man when you intentionally rushed over to the window. Don't make excuses."

"No, really, I'm *sorry*. I know I rushed to the window, and I know I can communicate with the dogs and the wolves, but I couldn't control that other thing..."

"Just come here, and turn around."

"You promise not to hurt me?" The voice was childlike.

Hamelin took a step closer and leaned in, trying to let his eyes adjust more to the darkness. "I promise."

Then out of the blackness came a blunt object that Hamelin saw only briefly. It crashed into the side of his head before he had time to get his hands up, and Landon rushed past him, pushing him even as he fell. He tried to focus, and the last thing he saw, before the blackness filled his eyes, was Landon, racing out the door that led to the stairs.

Chapter 35

# The Shape Changer

AFTER HAMELIN LEFT THEIR ROOM, ERAINA, LAYLA, AND Amy stayed propped up in their beds, but no one was sleeping. Lars returned to the window and parted the drapes. "How long do lunar eclipses last?"

Amy sat up straighter. "I don't know about over here, but on our side of the Atrium, it can vary a lot. From start to finish, an eclipse of the moon can be hours."

"But how long does a full eclipse last once it's total?"

"Oh, that varies as well. It depends on different factors, and I'm not sure what they are, but sometimes the full portion of an eclipse can be only ten or fifteen minutes."

"Interesting. It's pretty full right now, which is probably a good thing for however long it lasts."

Eraina rolled to the side of her bed. "Why is that?"

Lars let the curtains drop back in place. "Since Landon uses the moonlight to do his shape changing, the less of it the better. For now, he's locked up in a dark room in the basement until we get him to the dungeon. We're hoping he's already changed back so he'll be easier to handle."

Just then Charissa and Sophie returned, their faces suggesting bad news. Sophie brushed away a tear. "No change. Father is struggling."

Charissa shook her head and took a deep breath before she turned to Eraina. "Where is Tumultor now?"

"I've been watching the whole time you've been gone, and they haven't moved. His holy men continue to look at the eclipse."

"So we have at least two hours before they get here, but we need a plan. First, we have to be able to secure Landon, and I want to get that done and transfer him to the dungeon. I know we had no choice earlier after father was bitten, but where he is right now in the basement presents a risk, and we need to lessen the chances that his dogs can help him get free and create havoc in the castle or the city. After that, we can negotiate with Tumultor and get his agreement to take Landon."

"That all makes sense," said Sophie. "But I've got a couple of questions."

The room got quiet. Everyone knew that Sophie often had important questions at critical moments. "What if Landon doesn't turn back to human form?"

"But don't shape changers go back to their original form?" said Eraina.

"That's what the legends say, at least the ones I've read from the other side," added Layla.

Sophie tilted her head and turned her mouth down at the corners. "But he could still be a wolf when Tumultor gets here, and Charissa says we want him to take Landon...though I'm not as sure."

Charissa spread out both hands. "You're not sure if we want Tumultor to take Landon?"

"My sister, in some ways I'm surprised at you. I've heard from Lars and Eraina how you argued passionately with Father and Fearbane about matters pertaining to justice after Layla and I were attacked by Landon's dogs. That you stood your ground and insisted on justice for the sake of deterrence, justice for the sake of our family and our kingdom, and justice as a matter of maintaining our integrity. Now, when it's possible that our father may die, you're willing to negotiate Landon away? But if our father dies from this bite, then werewolf or not, Landon will have killed him. And if I know you, you'll want to see justice."

The silence in the room was heavy until Sophie spoke again.

"I'm sorry, my sister. I have the luxury of being the youngest and sitting more on the sidelines. I don't have the burden of decision-making that you do. No doubt there are many factors you must weigh and so much information you need. Forgive me. I'm sure it's the same burden Father has felt all these years."

Lars was still near the window, glancing out, but he took a step closer to both Charissa and Sophie.

"All of us need more information. So maybe some is on the way. Hamelin's gone down to the basement to see if he can hear anything, just to determine if Landon is still a wolf. If he's shifted back to a man, we can transfer him to the dungeon more easily. That'll give us more time to think about these other matters. Hamelin should be back any second."

An uninvited question filled Layla's head. *Is Hamelin alone in the basement with Landon?* A shadowy image of an old memory then pushed its way into her mind: it was the children's home and Hamelin was almost five...standing there on the porch about to cry as she left him to go to college. Her thoughts jerked back to the present, and her voice cracked. "Hamelin shouldn't be there by himself."

Charissa shot a quick look at Layla and then Eraina. "Check on Hamelin. He should be here by now."

Eraina quickly focused her attention downward, through the floors and walls toward the basement. She looked for long seconds, sweeping her head and shoulders side to side, her eyes searching and darting frantically. Suddenly she stood.

"Hamelin's lying on the floor! And there's no sign of Landon, whether wolf or man!"

Lars took a quick step toward the door but halted before taking a second one, stopped by the point of a long spear.

"Looking for me?" came a man's voice from the shadows just beyond the door. The one holding the other end of the weapon then crossed over the threshold. It was Landon.

"I hope you don't mind my borrowing this spear from the soldier who was guarding the king."

Landon made a jabbing motion toward Lars. "Back up. I don't want you trying any of your fast-footed tricks. I've got dogs waiting just outside Carr's room, and all it would take from me is one thought, and they'll be on him in a second. He wouldn't last long."

Eraina looked toward her father's room but kept her hands in her lap. Layla was careful not to watch her directly, since she didn't know if Landon knew of her sister's ability to see at distances or, if he did, that it was the scarf that enabled her to do it.

Eraina then casually glanced back at Charissa, who was now standing with her back to the window and watching her. She very slightly shook her head, signaling that Landon was lying.

Layla stood to the side of her bed. She clenched her fists to keep her hands from shaking, but her voice trembled. "What have you done to Hamelin?"

Landon shrugged. "Oh, don't worry about him. He's taking a little nap right now. I gave him a pretty good tap on the head. But I would guess he's still alive—but that's just a guess."

Charissa again glanced at Eraina, who looked into the basement. She took a deep breath and, when Landon wasn't looking, nodded a cautious yes back to Charissa.

Charissa blinked an acknowledgment and shifted toward Landon, while Lars backed up to her left. Both of them now stood between her bed and the window, facing Landon. Sophie slowly moved behind the table.

"So what do you want from us?" asked Charissa. "We have considered the pros and cons of executing you, but fortunately for you, our father has decided to give you over to Tumultor."

Landon smirked. "So your friend, the boy with such strength, told me. But that's actually not enough. I think I want a little more than that."

"What do you want?" asked Eraina before Charissa could respond.

"First of all," said Landon as he strode over toward the window, making Lars step away more as he poked the spear toward him, "I want to stand over here." He looked at the moon, which, though still mostly dark, had started to come out of the shadow of the eclipse. About an eighth of it was now showing.

"Don't you just love basking in moonlight?" he said with a sneer.

And then the changes that shifted him toward the body of a wolf started—the growth of hair, the pointing of his ears, and the lengthening of his face and mouth. Fearbane had told them all what had happened in the basement when Landon's body had suddenly morphed, but these alterations seemed slow and uneven, apparently matching the gradual and limited changes in the moon. Standing in the partial moonlight, he flickered sporadically from one stage of shape shifting to the next. For the moment, he retained mostly human features, his upright posture and a man's voice. Still, the transformation progressed, lurching forward in erratic starts and stops.

His upper torso shivered. "As I enjoy this moonlight, I'll tell you what else I want. I want one of you."

Charissa blew out a puff of air. "What do you mean?"

"Are you really so stupid? You should have married Tumultor when you had the chance."

"Over my dead body," said Eraina.

Landon shifted his darkening eyes toward her. "There's a smart girl. That's exactly what I mean! I need to kill one of you. It really doesn't matter which one. In fact, I'll leave it up to you. Now that the four sisters are back, but before you take the four thrones, all I have to do is kill one of you to stop the prophecy, retake my kingdom, and further my father Chimera's plan. So which one will it be?" His voice cracked from a high pitch to a growl.

Sophie laughed. Everyone looked at her with raised eyebrows, especially Landon, whose eyes began to slant as they took on a yellowish tint. "Is something funny?"

"You fool. How wrong can you be? It's true, we *are* four sisters, but how do you know that *we four* will occupy the four thrones? Right now our father is alive and sits on a single throne, and yet you were stupid enough to try to kill him. Why would you hasten our ascent, even if you're right about the prophecy?" Sophie laughed again, and as she finished, she snorted with disdain.

Landon narrowed his eyes and seemed surprised by the question. "He's an *old man*! He wouldn't live much longer anyway. And now that the fourth sister is back—oh, yes," he snarled and looked at Layla, "we know all about *you*!—the one whose return is sparking the famous prophecy about the four sisters and the four thrones, which I plan to stop! So, again, which one will it be? All I need to do is kill one of you."

Charissa took a half step toward Landon. "Are you *sure*? The prophecy actually refers to all of the *living* heirs. If you kill one of us, then three remain, and the three will still be all of the *living* daughters."

While Landon seemed to be thinking about that, an aura of light flickered around him, and his transformation toward a wolf-like appearance accelerated as the dark shadow eclipsing the moon continued to vanish.

Charissa drew her sword. "You seem to be puzzled—why don't you just go ahead and try to kill *me*? I'm the oldest. And by the way, how's your wrist doing? My sword is a little bloody, but still sharp."

"Don't try to taunt me. Besides, remember what I said about my dogs and your father. One move toward me, and he's finished."

"I doubt it. I think you're bluffing. I think you don't have any dogs near him at all. Our soldiers have chased them off. And I helped. Besides, even if you do, as you said, our father is old, and your bite will likely kill him anyway." Charissa positioned herself into a fighting stance.

"Not so fast!" interrupted Eraina. "It's true Charissa is the oldest, but that's the very reason you need to pick *me*. Besides," she continued with a barb in her voice, "I was there when Hamelin and Lars took care of your precious doggies just the other side of the Forest of Fears. I saw your big white wolf *humiliated* in a rock fight! I heard his bones cracking. So start with me!" Eraina reached for her bow and inched closer to Landon.

Sophie, still standing behind the table, waved her hands dismissively toward Eraina and Charissa. "Fine with me. Take either one of them. No point in starting with me, if you're not smart enough to figure out the prophecy—four *daughters* doesn't equal four *thrones*!"

All the girls laughed, and as she joined in, Layla felt her shaking stop. She could see what her sisters were doing—using confusion and misdirection as a tactic of war. They were well-trained, and she admired their wit and courage. She took a deep breath.

"Be quiet!" Landon growled as he remained in the moonlight and his shape shifting continued, though he was still upright. "Okay then—I'll just kill *all* of you."

Charissa raised her sword. "Go ahead, and try. But even if you succeed—which I doubt!—do you really think the four thrones will be *empty* just because you kill *us*? You obviously know nothing about royal families. We have plenty of jealous aunts, uncles, and cousins who will gladly come forward to take our place! Being part of a dynasty can be a very dangerous business."

Sophie chuckled loudest of all. "But we suppose you know all about family intrigue, being a son of *Chimera*! Nice *brothers* you have—where are they anyway?" The girls laughed again, and Lars slowly lowered himself into a crouch.

Landon's whole body convulsed, and he shrieked at the sisters. "Then we'll kill all your relatives too!"

Layla suddenly stepped to the foot of her bed. "If you're right about the four thrones, then killing us and our relatives is just too complicated! What you really have to do is—"

"*Layla!*" yelled Sophie. "Don't *explain* it to him!"

But before the girls could laugh again, Landon gave off a snarling howl. His head, arms, and upper torso morphed suddenly and fully into the body of a wolf, though he still stood on the legs of a man. The long spear fell to the floor, while his eyes turned red and slobber dripped from his open mouth. Fangs grew at the back of his snout. He shook his head and bared his teeth with a throaty growl. His voice changed, but his words were still understandable.

"I have a better idea. All I really have to do is give one of you my special venomous bite, one that changes you but doesn't kill. Then you'll be mine, a living heir who will never join your sisters on a throne!"

While Landon gaped at the defiant sisters, Lars swung into action. With lightning speed, he took one quick step toward Landon—whose trembling body was seized by the final throes of his change—and planted a powerful right kick into his abdomen. Landon fell in a heap, but the moonlight, now nearly full, poured down upon him. As he lay there, the aura that had flickered around him flashed for a long moment full and bright, and his legs and feet changed. His transformation into a massive wolf became complete.

Landon rose to a four-legged posture and prepared to jump toward Lars, who was ready to fight. Layla inched toward the door. The werewolf noticed her movements and snarled. Lars landed another kick, this time in the face. The powerful blow delayed him for a few more seconds, but Landon's eyes were now crazed and his instincts focused on the one daughter of Carr who had come to fill the fourth throne. He shook his head, and drool dripped from the side of his lower jaw. Lars kicked him again, and Layla bolted out the door.

⸺⸺ ◦《◎》◦ ⸺⸺

The creature growled at Lars and faked a jump toward him but dashed out the door.

Lars yelled to the others, "*Stay here*! I'm the only one fast enough to catch him!"

The girls looked at Charissa, who was already donning her bow and quiver full of arrows.

"What in the world is Layla *doing*?" yelled Eraina.

Sophie grabbed her bow and quiver. "Trying to save the *rest* of us! Besides, she's the only one who can't *shoot*!"

By this time, Charissa had reached the door. "Let's *go*!" she shouted, and her two sisters followed.

⸺⸺ ◦《◎》◦ ⸺⸺

Layla ran as fast as she could but was slowed by the cape still fastened around her neck. Why had she put that back on! If the werewolf came after her, she'd never outrun him! She got down the stairs but then heard the sound she was dreading—the wolf's claws clacking on the hardwood floor behind her. She ran across the ballroom toward its darkest part and then into the huge sitting room. She ducked behind the door, took in her breath, and waited. She fumbled with the tiny pair of hooks that held the cape around her neck but couldn't unfasten them. The clacking got louder as Landon kept coming across the ballroom floor and then into the sitting room. He raced past her.

He approached the opening to the next room, but instead of looking through it, he paused and lifted his head, sniffing the air. Layla tiptoed from behind the door and doubled back, but he must have heard her or smelled her. She ran toward the ballroom but knew from the frenzied clacking that he had changed directions and was scrambling after her.

Chapter 36

Knowing When

Hamelin's head swam with images of springing dogs and wolves, mixed with scenes of the rock fight he, Lars, and Eraina had with them. He could see himself picking up a huge rock and throwing it, but now he was the white wolf, and the rock was coming toward him. He tried to run away from it, but the rock hit him in the back of the head and knocked him down, leaving a huge lump on his head as he lay on the ground north of the Forest of Fears. It pounded. And the other dogs circled around to chew his ungloved hands, to finish him off. Hamelin could see the white dog creeping close to him—and feel the animal's hot breath on his neck. The dog put his wet nose and mouth near Hamelin's face, sniffing, but he didn't bite. He licked.

Hamelin rolled over and opened his eyes. He wasn't in the Forest of Fears, but a dog was there licking his face. Was that Buddy? Then he vanished. Hamelin tried to focus as he looked up into the blackness. How long had he been out, and where was he? The ground below didn't feel like dirt, but it did feel hard. And then he remembered. He had been hit in the head, and he was in the basement where they had locked up Landon.

He got to his feet and staggered toward the door. His head. Pounding. Hard to think. What had Landon done while he was out? He stumbled through the door, regaining something of his balance, and tried to concentrate. He headed toward the stairs that would take him up near the kitchen and along various dining rooms—if he remembered correctly—and then toward the ballroom. That was the way to the big staircase that would lead him back upstairs, where he hoped to find Lars and the girls.

He made it up the stairs, holding on to the banister, and staggered through the kitchen, down a long corridor, and across the grand entryway. He reached what he thought was the last big sitting room. And there in front of him, across the room, he saw a huge wolf. Was he seeing things? No—that was the werewolf Landon had turned into—running across the room and then dashing out the door that led toward the ballroom.

Hamelin moved as quickly as he could through the sitting room and then, in the greater light of the ballroom, came upon a scene of unfolding mayhem that he hoped was just a bad dream.

He shook his head, trying to focus his eyes in spite of the throbbing pain. His vision cleared, and what he saw took away his breath.

It was Layla, wearing her princess cape and running as fast as she could in the middle of the room—but her speed was no match for the werewolf.

The monster leaped, and just as Layla tried to move to her right to avoid him, he twisted his upper body toward the back of her neck, his mouth open and teeth bared. For a second, everything seemed to slow down as the creature flew toward Layla.

But then a growl and cry of pain both sounded as Landon's

deadly jaws closed on Layla's neck. Everything sped up again, but the thrashing tangle of wolf and woman was brief. Landon's strength prevailed as he dragged her to the floor, still clenching the back of her neck.

"*No!*" came a loud shout from the far side of the ballroom, back to Hamelin's left, as Charissa, Eraina, and Sophie charged into the room, each with her bow strung.

Landon raised his head in the direction of the three girls and momentarily let go of Layla's neck.

He stared at them—with Layla on the floor face down, pinned by his massive forelegs—and lifted his head and chest even higher, in defiance and apparent triumph. And then, just before he snapped his chest and head down again to take Layla by the neck, Hamelin heard the simultaneous twangs of three bowstrings, and three arrows—their feathers swooshing the air—plunged all at once into the werewolf's chest.

The shape changer let out a loud, yelping snarl and reared up on his back legs with his forelegs stretched out, the arrows not only lodged deep within his chest but protruding out his back.

The creature howled high and loud and long, his head, raised in the manner of a baying wolf; but he was also bathed by the moonlight beaming from the great windows high up the arched cathedral ceiling of the room. Layla rolled over on her back and tried to gain her feet, but the creature's rear legs still held her down.

Though stunned by the blow of the arrows, the wolfish torso grew even larger as his massive chest expanded, and the arrows, with the flexing of his entire physique, snapped and fell away when he shook his body like a wet dog.

Landon the werewolf now looked straight up toward the full moon, visibly soaking in its light and gaining new strength, as the eclipse had completely passed. He howled a long cry of triumph. He dropped his head toward Layla and sniffed at her neck, while he kept his blood red eyes on the three sisters. He snarled, shook his head violently, and then focused his predatory gaze on Layla. He lifted his head and chest one more time and opened his mouth. Drool dripped, and his fangs glistened.

And Hamelin knew. Just as SueSue said he would. The hammer. He reached into the scabbard with his left hand and pulled it out. In one motion, he transferred it to his right hand, and he could feel it growing to a size many times larger than the small hammer he had originally picked up in the Atrium. As he drew it back to throw, he could see out of the corner of his eyes that it took on a golden aura. He stretched both hammer and hand back in a full extension of his arm, with his weight on his right foot and the hammer touching almost to the floor. He then pushed off his right leg, shifting his weight forward as his left leg stretched out and his upper torso spun to face the wolf. His arm then whipped across his body, and he released the hammer—now as light to him as a baseball—toward the monstrous creature.

For a moment it seemed that his world stopped, as the three princesses to his left strained forward, trying to run to their sister—to fight Landon barehanded if they had to.

The werewolf, his body still extended upward prior to plunging his head and teeth downward, detected Hamelin's presence and turned his huge maw and torso toward him.

As the creature faced Hamelin, with his mouth open and teeth glinting in a snarl and his chest thrust out in a defiant posture, the hammer—in Hamelin's eyes in slow motion— flew its final few feet, tumbling head over handle, and crashed into the werewolf's body, its forged head striking his chest first and then continuing up toward his head.

The collision of hammer and creature shattered the shape changer in an explosion of light that flamed brilliantly for long seconds, leaving nothing but scattered, dying embers. The hammer, however, flew on toward the far wall, striking a thick wooden beam with a force that left a rounded imprint, before falling harmlessly to the floor, no longer shining, and back to its normal size.

The three girls rushed over to their fallen sister, crying as one, "*Layla!*"

They reached her just before Hamelin did and slid to the floor on their hands and knees, surrounding her.

Layla, still on her back, stared unfocused at her three sisters and then blinked. "Nice shots. But you really need to get better arrows."

They tried to smile, but the panic they felt covered their faces.

Charissa reached toward her. "Your neck. The werewolf bit you..."

Layla sat up quickly, loosened the princess cape from her shoulders, and let it drop. She felt the back of her neck, looked at her sisters, and winked. "All good."

They leaned over, looked at her neck, and, after a long, wide-eyed stare by all, collectively drew in their breath.

"The skin's not broken," whispered Eraina.

"Not a single tooth mark," said Sophie.

As the sisters stared in disbelief, Layla patted the cape and collar. "I think I became a princess, 'strictly speaking,' just in time!" They burst into laughter, and the three sisters fell on Layla, hugging her, and all of them rolled on the floor.

Hamelin had never seen a happier group of girls in all his life.

"*Hamelin!*" came a voice suddenly from the bottom of that pile. It was Layla.

The four princesses of Parthogen momentarily stopped their laughing. Layla sat up and looked at him. "You saved us!"

And then she and her sisters pulled Hamelin in and smothered him in a dogpile of hugs.

Chapter 37

Tumultor and Carr: Times of Turning

W HAT IS TAKING HIM SO LONG?" SNAPPED ROMULUS. HE was standing with Bryan next to the horses, ready to ride, but they continued to wait on the holy men. "An hour has passed!" His frustrations were spoken to Bryan, but others could hear. "We need to be riding, not waiting for them to consult the entrails of a goat. Look at them! All they do is look down at the animal they killed. Then they point to the moon. The next thing, just when you think they're done, a flock of birds flies by going north, and they start all over, talking and pointing."

Bryan tried to cool Romulus down. "You're right. I can't imagine what they think they're doing."

"You shouldn't have said anything."

"I sure regret it now. And I'm especially sorry for that goat." Bryan tried to hold back a grin.

Romulus snickered but then kicked a rock at his feet, picked up a dried stick from the ground, and threw it. "This old religion. It fails us!"

About that time, Tumultor gestured toward his commanders, Romulus, and Bryan, and they approached.

The priest spoke in solemn tones. "We have determined that this eclipse will be, from start to finish, more than two hours."

Romulus muttered to Bryan, "Yeah, and it took them an hour to figure that out."

The holy man went on. "It is an omen of fear for men at its coming but of great power for wolves at its passing."

Bryan could hear Romulus grumble under his breath, "What a genius."

Tumultor looked at his holy man and then toward the covey of lesser priests standing around him. They all nodded as if the high cleric had said something very profound.

Tumultor made a backhanded sweeping motion and then held his arm above his head. "The divining is done. The oracle portends good for Landon. On to Parthogen!" His interpretation sounded final, and everyone scurried to their horses.

The soldiers quickly mounted and gathered behind Tumultor, who led them away at a hard pace. Though the ground wasn't dry, the horses were rested and now able to move more rapidly, especially since the wind and the rain had ceased.

They rode for another half hour, before Tumultor signaled for a sudden stop. A bright light had appeared in the direction of the city. It was expected that they would see lights in the city, even at this late hour, since people would be working and tending the injured after the battle. But this light was different. It flashed in the area of the palace and grew into a ball of fire that rose, spread, and then exploded in a shower of brilliance. No debris was created by the explosion of light, but it lit up the main floor of the castle grounds and then held its glow for several seconds, before radiating out to half the city.

Tumultor glared at the chief of his holy men. "What was that?!"

His holy man could only shake his head and declare solemnly that it certainly was not a star and it was too low to be a comet.

Tumultor snorted in disgust and waved his hands over his head. "We will continue to ride. Watch for messengers from the castle as we get closer!"

But they had barely begun their hard pace again when a stream of dogs and wolves poured out of the city toward them. There was yelping and yipping, and among the dogs and wolves were also soldiers wearing Landon's colors, including wounded stragglers limping as fast as they could with the aid of their cohorts.

Tumultor slowed momentarily but continued toward the city.

Within another fifteen minutes, they encountered more strays and some soldiers. Significant numbers of Landon's packs—dogs, half dogs, and wolves—fled past them. One wolf, however, in particular ran with his head up, and Tumultor's commander suspected it was one of Landon's messengers.

The dog looked in Tumultor's direction, paused, sniffed, and looked again before running over to the commander, who jumped off his horse, then took the message from the animal's collar and handed it to Tumultor without reading it.

Tumultor let out a loud curse and yelled, "What?! The missing princess returned? And he didn't tell me? Ren'dal will—"

He abruptly turned his horse. "The *fool*! This is what he gets for launching an attack without my approval!"

"Do we continue to ride toward Parthogen?"

"*No!*"

"But, your brother—"

"My *brother* is *dead*! Killed by the boy warrior with the strength of Hercules!"

"Should we try to gather his men and his wolves?"

"*No*! His men can take care of themselves. There is no honor in defeat! And *I* don't talk to *dogs*!"

Tumultor spurred his horse back through his men and, without even a signal to his commanders, rode away toward Osmethan. Bryan and Romulus turned their horses to follow. Eventually word spread as to the exact phrasing of the message, and Bryan's heart sank to hear so much bad news all at once. Layla was in Parthogen! How did she get back? But more than that, how in the world could he possibly protect her and be riding with Tumultor? Which was already the problem he faced with Hamelin and Romulus. He was relieved to learn that the battle for the city was over and especially that Hamelin was still alive. But what would happen now? Tumultor would of course want revenge, but what would Romulus want to do about the young warrior who killed Landon, the man who had saved him from wolves when he was ten years old and abandoned? And then he wondered how Hamelin felt, knowing he had killed a man.

Sometime, somewhere, they would have to talk, and Bryan would need to give Romulus a "provable reason"—to use Romulus's words—not to trust Landon's story about his parents and their deaths. But that conversation could be risky for them all.

⚬⚬⚬

Lars and several of Carr's soldiers came running into the ballroom where Hamelin and the four sisters were laughing and hugging one another.

But there was no joy in Lars's voice. "Your father...he's getting worse...hurry!"

They rushed back to the king's bedroom, and there they found him still in the bed, looking deathly pale. Doctors were nearby, and Fearbane and Amy stood behind them. The room was upside down, with chairs and tables overturned, draperies shredded, and several wolves lying dead on the floor.

They stared in stunned silence, and Charissa motioned for everyone but the doctors to go back to the hallway. "What happened?"

Lars explained that he had run down the stairs after Landon, when the werewolf set out after Layla. He reached the ballroom and then heard a shout of distress from the courtyard, just outside the main entryway to the castle. Not knowing which direction Layla had gone, he ran out the main entry and into the courtyard, hoping to find her.

"There, just off to my right, was a single soldier, injured and surrounded by dogs, so I had to help him. I distracted the wolves by running at them and around them. They couldn't catch me, and I landed a few good kicks. Then Fearbane rushed in with his sword—"

"I wish I had been there earlier," said Fearbane, "but I was in His Majesty's room when I heard some commotion in the hall. I looked up in time to see Princess Alathea race by and the wolf—I recognized it as Landon—running after her, followed by Prince Lars. I rushed down the steps and heard snarling and howling outside the front entryway, and I assumed that Landon had headed that way. He evidently had sent a message to his creatures to gather up, and they were there in the courtyard. I wasn't about to let them enter the castle, because I knew they would be heading upstairs to find either the king or all of you. I ran into the courtyard, and Prince Lars was there engaging a pack of Landon's creatures.

"He was quite amazing," Fearbane continued. "Between the two of us, we fought them off successfully. But just when we thought we had them defeated, three of the creatures got by us and ran into the castle and up the stairs. Prince Lars—"

"I took off after them and caught them just as they entered

the king's room and was able to kick them off to the side. Fearbane came in a moment later, and we had a final show-down with those wolves." Lars pointed toward the bedroom. "It made quite a mess of things, but at least they didn't get to him. Or Amy, who was also in here."

"I waited for a while," Amy said, "but everything was going crazy, so I wasn't going to stay in the other room by myself. So I came here and walked in just before the dogs and Lars arrived. Probably not the best timing. I stood there frozen at first, but the dogs weren't interested in me. They wanted your father, but between Lars's kicks and Fearbane's sword, the dogs were no match. We were checking on your father when we saw an explosion of light."

"But the wolves didn't disturb our father?" asked Charissa.

"They never got to him, but the noise and chaos were terrible, and now he looks weaker than ever, so Lars ran to find all of you."

They all stared at the floor in silence. Finally, Amy whispered, "I'm afraid to ask, but where's Landon?"

"He's dead," said Charissa. "Hamelin—" But she stopped when Carr's doctors came into the hall.

"His Majesty's condition has taken a perilous turn. He is growing weaker. We're not sure..."

There was a sharp intake of breath from Layla and a stifled sob from Eraina. Charissa strode into his room, followed quickly by Sophie and everyone else. They stood around his bed and waited. His eyes were shut, his body still, and his breath shallow and faint. After several long minutes, he took a deep breath and seemed to relax.

The nurse who was bathing his brow looked up. "He's sleeping now. If you would like to get some rest, I can—"

"No," said Sophie. "We're not leaving him."

The four sisters, Fearbane, Hamelin, Lars, and Amy all

stationed themselves around his bed, sometimes standing, sometimes sitting. Always hoping. Hours passed.

Just as the sun began to rise, the king stirred. He opened his eyes, and the nurses quickly gave him water. He took a moment to focus on his children and friends who gathered around him. He smiled, and then one by one, he summoned them with his eyes and a slight wave of his left hand.

Hamelin had never been around someone so near death. He glanced at Layla to see what he was supposed to do.

She was gazing at her father, her eyes brimming with tears. Hamelin wondered how she could stand it. After losing the Trotts, and being gone for so long, she had finally found her family in Gloaming, though her mother over here was gone. And now she was losing her father. Would he find his parents in time, even to say good-bye?

The king spoke in low, whispered tones, but Hamelin was close enough to hear what he told each person. First, he motioned for Fearbane. The loyal commander tried to apologize for not helping the king in time, but Carr assured him that he had lived up to his name and that he, the king's soldier, was truly the bane of those who tried to strike fear in the hearts of his people.

Then Carr summoned Lars to his side and thanked him for protecting Eraina. "You must fight on for the good of Parthogen, Periluna, and all the Land of Gloaming. We are in your debt. Please tell your father I'll see him again in the land of hope."

Hamelin's heart beat faster as the king looked him in the eye and waved him closer with a weak hand. Hamelin leaned his head toward the king's pallid face.

"My young warrior, Layla told me that Hamelin Stoop is not your name by birth, but never doubt that you have made it a name worthy of a man. Thank you for fighting for my daughters and thus for Parthogen...for rescuing Charissa, protecting Eraina, restoring Layla to us, and bringing the healing waters to Sophie. Were it not for you, my family would not be reunited. Families must often travel to different places, but they should never be separated in heart. So do not give up your quest to find your family and learn your name...the search will tell you much about yourself. But in your haste to find your parents, do not give up the Ancient One's summons to save the Land of Gloaming. There will be no profit to you or anyone else if you search for them at too great a cost. We too are your quest. Remain loyal to the Ancient One, and one day you will find everything."

Hamelin heard the king's words but wasn't sure he understood them, so all he could do was nod as Carr pulled his forehead down and pressed it against his own. Then he released him and turned to Amy. Hamelin was too filled with emotion to listen well, but he heard the king express thanks for her friendship with Layla, praise her loyalty to Bryan, and say something about hope and watching.

Carr's words to his daughters were especially difficult to hear. He whispered, meeting each daughter's gaze as he said her name. "It has been a great joy of my life to see you live up to the names your mother and I gave to you. Sophia, all of us listen to you, because you are truly wise beyond your years. Eraina, though fierce and strong, you are well ordered, longing to see all put right, and thus you are a woman of peace and peacemaking. Alathea, your name means 'truth,' 'not to be forgotten,' and 'faithfulness.' You have been loyal to both of your families, and I promise you that your mother and I did not go a single day without remembering you—waiting and hoping for your return. And Charissa, daughter of grace, you have learned by suffering to overcome vanity. You have become a warrior who never allows your sense of justice to overwhelm the gift of mercy. I love you all, my daughters." He gave each of them a quiet kiss on the cheek while whispering private words that Hamelin couldn't hear.

The king then let his eyes linger on each of his children and friends. "Don't mourn for me. Know that I am truly happy to be with my family soon and to see my Flower." He then took a deep breath, closed his eyes, and went to sleep. And even in the sleep of death, his face revealed a man at peace with his past and his future.

A soft shimmer of light surrounded his body. Then, in an instant, he vanished, the sheets of his bed falling over the place he had been.

Hamelin, Layla, and Amy all started, and Hamelin looked at Lars. "What happened?"

"He died the death of the good. Just like Simannas."

All four sisters embraced and cried together around their father's bed.

Chapter 38

Next Steps

THREE DAYS LATER, FUNERAL SERVICES WERE HELD FOR King Carr. There was weeping and lamenting across his kingdom, and flowers and remembrances poured in from all the regions of Gloaming. Mourners of every class and rank came from towns and villages throughout the land.

Hamelin and his friends were especially struck by the words of King Elwood of Periluna, Lars's father, who was called upon to give a brief public eulogy for his friend. "I am honored to pay tribute to one of the greatest men I've ever known. Carr ruled with courage and wisdom, and all of us in Periluna lament his passing and join his friends and especially his four daughters in mourning his loss. Parthogen is the capital city of a legendary kingdom by the same name, and truly it has never had a king as noble as Carr. From his earliest days, it was predicted among those of us in royal families that he would one day be a great king. He worked hard, listened to his elders, and learned what it meant to be both a soldier and a leader. And we called him the 'warrior prince.'

"But we didn't anticipate that he would also become such a loving husband and father. And while his young queen Flora—whom he called 'my Flower'—persuaded him, once Princess Charissa was born, to delegate the front lines to his soldiers, as all kings must, he was always their example in courage and…"

Hamelin felt a chill in his back when he heard Carr described as a warrior. Words from the *Enchiridion* flashed through his mind: the fourth throne…a warrior dies. He glanced at Layla and saw her drop her head and bury her face in her hands, her shoulders shaking.

The solemn processions, speeches, and final ceremonies for the high king were followed by hugs and tears, joy and the laughter of remembrances. He had died the death of the good, so there was also feasting for all in the great city.

At the end of that very emotional day, the sisters and their three friends found themselves in a small parlor with two couches and three chairs arranged for conversation. After being with so many people all day, they needed to talk about things they could share only with one another.

The princesses told stories of their parents' great love for each other. They reminisced about their mother, and Charissa, as the oldest, told stories of them stretching as far back as she could remember.

"What did she look like?" asked Hamelin.

"Just look at Eraina," said Charissa.

Lars smiled and looked at Eraina. He mouthed the words "Little Flower" and winked.

Finally, the stories slowed down, and they sat quietly for a few moments before Eraina spoke, her voice troubled. "This is a terrible thing to think about, but it's bothering me, and I don't know who else to ask except all of you. We know that Landon's bite killed our father. But we also know that things could've been worse. You know…what we feared when we saw him bite Layla in the neck. It's why we were so relieved to see that the princess cape had saved her. But Father...it was a mercy that he died instead of...but what kept him from changing into...?"

No one replied, and Layla started a story. "I was wondering the same thing, and a memory of a conversation with Grandmother came back. It was right after Father's hunting dog bit me. The old nurse washed the gash and gave me a bandage, but it still really hurt. My face was swollen and throbbing. I went to Grandmother as soon as I could and asked her if I was going to die. She didn't laugh or make fun. In fact, she scared me. She said something like, 'There are some bites that can kill you, but this one likely won't.'

"I asked her how she knew that, and she held my face between her hands and said the power of goodness would protect me, because good is stronger than evil. So here's what I think—our father was good and died the death of the good. Landon's evil bite killed him, but it wasn't strong enough to change him."

Silent tears streamed down Charissa's face, Sophie pursed her lips and nodded, and Amy patted Layla's forearm.

"Thank you," said Eraina. "I'm so glad you remembered that story. It helps us."

"I'm glad to do something right...after..." Layla broke down in tears.

Eraina was the first to reach her. "Sweet sister, whatever is the matter? You've done many things right."

Amy came quickly and also stood next to Layla. "It's the prophecy, isn't it? You're worried that your coming..."

Layla looked at Amy with tear-filled eyes and nodded. She buried her face in her hands and wept softly. Amy and her sisters waited, saying nothing, but surrounded Layla, while Hamelin and Lars stayed near.

Layla finally looked up again.

"All of you know the story—that trackers on the other side chased Bryan and me and our parents, the Trotts, and pushed us off a road into an icy lake. Our parents drowned, but the trackers really weren't after them. They were after me. And now Father...he's the warrior prophesied to die when the four princesses... If only I hadn't come back..."

Sophie pulled a chair in front of Layla and took both her hands. "Layla, we'll never know what might have happened. But here's what we do know. If you hadn't come back, then our father never would have known the fulfillment of his hopes. All these years, he has mourned for you, and in these last days, having you back, he's been the happiest any of us can recall. I know what Father's choice would be—he would rather have you here, as he did, to see you alive, to see all of us together, if only for a few days, than to live for a thousand more years with the pain and grief of your loss. Layla, thank you for coming back. You've made all of us so happy. We don't know what else will happen, but your return is the greatest thing that's ever happened, even greater than recovering Parthogen. But now we have both you and Parthogen, and our father—'the warrior prince'—would have it no other way."

One by one, they embraced each other and went to their rooms to rest. But before long, Hamelin and Lars heard the girls' voices from their nearby bedroom, their whispered talk and their soft laughing and occasional crying. The boys got up from their beds, went back to the queen's bedroom, and knocked on the door.

At first there was silence, but the boys identified themselves, and then several voices at once said, "Come in." They entered and found the sisters and Amy with their beds pulled together as if they were all in one big bed. The boys sat nearby while the daughters told more stories of their father and mother on into the night.

———◆———

Hamelin and Lars were embarrassed to realize they had fallen asleep on the floor in the same room with the girls, so early that morning they slipped out before anyone could see. Later, everyone gathered in the smaller dining hall for breakfast. They ate and relived parts of the previous several days, but Hamelin was eager to talk about next steps, though he reminded himself not to rush things. Lars, however, soon asked what he wanted to know.

"What now?"

Eraina had just set down her cup of tea. "I've been wondering the same thing,"

Charissa pushed her plate away. "It is a fair question, and I've been trying to think it through, and here's what I'm sure of. Even though Tumultor has gone back to Osmethan, he won't take the death of his brother lying down. It won't surprise me if he starts mustering soldiers from all over his kingdom and, with the help of Ren'dal, marches back this way."

"And maybe not only here," said Lars. "He will still want to avenge losing the jewel of Periluna."

Layla leaned forward in her chair. "That all sounds right, but I think we have to consider more than Parthogen and Periluna." She paused, but no one interrupted. "I'm just depending on my reading of the *Enchiridion* and not any experience over here, but doesn't their overall strategy start with Chimera? And isn't his objective more than taking over all of the Land of Gloaming?"

"What do you mean?" asked Eraina.

"From what I've read, he emerged from the dark Pits where he was originally confined. To do that, he used something or someone called 'the Image,' and his goal, with the help of his sons, is to expand his empire beyond Gloaming."

"So what is there beyond the Land of Gloaming?" asked Lars.

Amy coughed softly, though it sounded a little like "ahem." She paused and then said, "There is the other side of the Atrium."

Eraina took a sip of tea and looked to Layla. "How would Chimera do that?"

"I don't think we can know, at least not at this point. But based on the *Enchiridion*, and from what Amy and I have seen in just a few days here, I believe any amount of evil and treachery against the Ancient One is possible for Chimera. And he will use Tumultor and Ren'dal to do it...and anyone else who will join him."

Hamelin and Layla glanced at each other. He felt certain they must be thinking the same things—about Bryan and the missing brother, Michael.

"So their next move could be a big one," Eraina said.

"I think Layla is right," said Charissa, "but in terms of strategy I don't expect them to make Landon's arrogant mistake of an ill-planned attack. Whatever they do, it may be surprising to us, but it will be well planned and coordinated."

"So they may not be back soon?" asked Hamelin.

"I think not. We're not threatening them at the moment. Besides, as Layla has said, they have larger objectives than Parthogen, or even Gloaming. I expect them to take some time planning, though we'll have to stay alert. Eraina of course will continue to watch Tumultor, which will give us some lead time if he starts our way."

"So what should we do next?" Hamelin hoped someone would mention his quest.

Eraina stood and walked a few paces away and then turned back to face the table.

"There is something big we haven't talked about yet, and I suspect it's because we're still grieving over our father. But there is the matter of the four thrones." Her voice was filled with emotion, but she continued. "Now that he's gone...we need to give a clear signal to our people about the succession of royal leadership. Charissa is the oldest and therefore should be named queen of Parthogen."

"I agree," said Sophie. "And furthermore—"

Charissa stood. "*No*! I don't agree. That's not what our father talked about or what the people expect, and it's certainly not what the prophecy says. It explicitly refers to four thrones, not one, not a queen, and not—"

"But that's because all of us—well, nearly all of us—" said Eraina, "probably thought of ourselves as occupying four princess thrones. Our father's death is something we never really considered. We assumed our father would still be alive as king and we as princesses would take four thrones—but always subordinate to him. And that's when Landon and his wolves would be overcome."

"Exactly. But now there's a twist in the story, and this doesn't look like the interpretation we've always had. Our beloved father has passed away, and we're in uncharted territory now. We'll have to adapt, but the prophecy still says *four* thrones."

"I'll admit," said Layla, "that I feel encouraged by all this conversation. So now maybe this shows that the four thrones left here in the castle by the mysterious envoy are not the ones intended by the prophecy."

Eraina stepped closer to the table. "But just because there can be only one queen doesn't mean that the four thrones won't be filled. Charissa takes one throne as a queen, and the rest of us occupy the remaining three as princesses, and that makes four."

Charissa frowned. "That's possible, but there's something

else that's bothering me, which makes me wonder if we really understand things properly."

Amy exhaled and muttered, "There's a lot about this I don't understand, so please go on."

"It's not the literal prophecy itself, which I suppose could work out to have either a queen and three princesses or four co-regents—with the four of us serving a shared queen-ship—but it's everything else that goes with the prophecy. It predicts not just that the wolves will be banished and our kingdom restored, but many other things. Layla, you've stud-ied the *Enchiridion*. Tell us more about them, about the other prophecies."

Layla rubbed her index finger across her mouth and looked up. "Well, that could be a long story. We had barely started talking about other prophecies when the eagle showed up, and we never finished. There's a lot to think about regarding the four thrones, as we all know, but they are only part of a pattern of special days to come. They fit into a bigger picture of restoration. One that includes the rescue of all of Gloaming, the defeat of Chimera, strange prophecies about a jewel, the sword that kills a usurper, the lifting of a curse, and the return of exiles. By the way, who are they? And I hate to mention it again, since we've had some bad days already, but we have to remember the prophecies about certain dark things we haven't yet seen—betrayal, a 'detestable thing,' the onset of the trem-ors, and the possible death of other warriors." Layla turned her palms up and shrugged. "I need to study more."

Charissa moved closer to Layla. "And that's partly my point too. There's truly a lot to think about. Landon is gone, but some of his dogs are still loitering around. And we know that Chimera is surely plotting and will no doubt use Tumultor and Ren'dal to continue his destructive work. We have our land back, for now, but there's so much else that hasn't happened.

It just doesn't seem like the time, until we know a lot more, to rush toward a coronation for any of us. In the meantime, we can let the people know that we are ruling together."

"It could take a lot of time, not to mention wisdom, to decipher all of this," said Sophie.

As soon as she mentioned wisdom, Lars sat up straighter. "SueSue." Everyone looked at him. "My father reminded me that she is called 'The Wise Woman' in the old stories. Why don't we go talk to her?"

Sophie stood. "A trip!"

Charissa tilted her head and squinted at Sophie.

"Who would go?" asked Amy.

Sophie waved her hand. "Count me in!"

"All of us are involved, and all of us certainly need to know our next steps," said Eraina. "But we'd be a big group, and it's a long way."

Charissa sat down again at the table. "Here are my thoughts. I will stay here. It's my responsibility. Fearbane of course will be here, but we'll stay ready to protect the city while we also guide the cleanup and prepare for the future.

"And, Layla and Amy, I recommend you both stay here since you are new to these lands." Layla nodded, and Amy let out a small sigh of relief.

"But I'll need you both to tell me more about the *Enchiridion* and help me plan."

Sophie sat down and leaned toward Charissa. "They could also practice their archery skills."

Charissa suppressed a smile. "Eraina, Lars, and Hamelin should go. And...perhaps Sophie..."

The youngest princess slapped the table. "Yes! And I have one request. May I take along a helper?"

Eraina sighed. "A *helper*? Who?"

"Allison, the gardener's daughter—she stayed with Layla at

my bedside, and she's more than a lady-in-waiting. She's also my friend."

Charissa cleared her throat. "The travel conditions can be difficult—"

"Oh, don't worry! Ali is tough."

"I wasn't worried about *her.*"

"Hooray! A trip! I've been staying here while all of you went out and had all the fun!" Eraina and Lars looked at each other, and Eraina rolled her eyes.

Charissa lifted a hand to get everyone's attention. "But there's one last thing that's very important. We are assuming that Tumultor won't come back here immediately, but we could be wrong. So while I agree this is an important trip—and Eraina, I know you need to go—you'll have to keep a careful eye out for Tumultor's movements, even as you travel. If you detect any signs of him gathering his forces, then you'll have to get word back to us."

"I've been watching him closely. So far, he doesn't seem to be doing anything. Just mostly staying by himself. He did send a messenger off somewhere to the east, but he's not mustering his soldiers."

Charissa turned to Lars. "With your speed, you can race back to bring us word to prepare. Which means that the others will be returning on their own. I'm sure that'll be fine, with Hamelin's strength and Eraina's ability to see distances, but it's still one less person for protection on the return trip."

Lars stood. "I can run here and still double back and meet them in the Forest."

"We'll see. But, Sophie, Eraina, and Hamelin, those are the possibilities. Your return trip could be dangerous."

They nodded their agreement, and so the preparations began. Eraina, who knew a lot about organizing things, would draft the plan for the trip, including schedules and all the supplies needed.

"We'll leave day after tomorrow," she announced.

Excitement energized their preparations as the team of five, including Ali, got ready to go to SueSue's house, the place of hospitality, special foods, and wise conversation.

Hamelin was disappointed that no one mentioned his quest, but a trip to SueSue's house brought him hope. There was always something new to learn from her.

Chapter 39

Avenging, Waiting, and Watching

TUMULTOR WASTED NO TIME IN SENDING A MESSENGER TO Ventradees to notify Ren'dal of Landon's death. Katris had never seen Ren'dal so angry. By the time the man had related the entire story—that the missing princess had returned, that Landon had launched a surprise attack, and that his death was at the hands of the strong young warrior—she feared Ren'dal was going to kill the messenger on the spot. She sent everyone out of the room while he raged.

"That *fool!*" he shouted. "I gave *explicit* instructions that I was to be informed about everything! Why didn't Tumultor have better control over him? And now the fourth princess has returned, and he launched an *attack*? And he's *dead*? He deserves it! Disaster always follows when people don't *obey my commands!*" He looked at Katris and said in a loud monotone, "I will avenge his death."

"But, Master, you mustn't harm the young warrior. Your father needs him to—"

"Not *him*, woman! But there are others who are close to

him. If I cause them pain, we will avenge Landon, and he will also be more willing to serve us!"

"Yes, my lord."

"Summon The Forty immediately."

"But, Master, The Forty? Surely they should be used only—"

"*Silence*! The forces of Gloaming may have impeded the mission of Landon, but they will not reverse what I have been commissioned to do. Summon The Forty, and let them know I have important work for them."

Katris nodded and left.

⸻ ◆ ⸻

Paul, Hamelin's second-grade friend, sat by himself on the front porch of the children's home. It was the end of July, and Paul had counted the days since Hamelin left. He sighed.

"Where is he?" he muttered out loud, though no one else could hear. "He should have told me more. I could help."

Paul looked around at the yard in front of him. To his left, several children from the home were swimming in the pool. The Kaleys sat beneath the two big oak trees, watching the swimmers. Mrs. Eastland stood next to the Kaleys, and the three of them were whispering. Mrs. Eastland dropped by the home a lot lately, and Paul could guess what they were discussing.

He could hear other children playing outside on the north side of the house. It was late afternoon, and supper was still an hour or more off. He looked around nervously, then stood.

This may be my chance. If no one is upstairs... He walked into the house and strolled toward the dining room. A couple of the workers were sitting at the tables, having some afternoon iced tea. Paul waved at them and then walked over toward the kitchen and stuck his head inside. There was Mrs. Parker, already getting things ready for the supper she would provide that evening. She looked up and saw him, and he waved and smiled before he ducked back out.

"You looking for someone?" she called out after him as the door swung closed.

He stuck his head back in the door. "No, ma'am. Just wondering what's for supper."

"Are you hungry already? It'll be a good supper. Don't you worry."

"Yes, ma'am." He backed away from the kitchen door and let it shut. Paul walked toward the stairs that led up to the boys' room. He looked around and was pretty sure no one noticed him going up. He entered the room and paused, looking down the long row of beds. No one was there.

He hurried down to the last bed on the left, Hamelin's. He glanced around again to make sure no one was watching. This would have to be quick. He opened the chest where Hamelin kept special things and looked inside. There wasn't a lot of stuff in it, so it didn't take him long to find an envelope with three pages. Paul couldn't read cursive, but he was pretty sure this was it. He recognized enough words to know that these were copies of the letter he had overheard them talking about. The letter from Hamelin's mother.

He took the pages and stepped quickly over to his own bed. He reached into a special box and removed his Polaroid camera. He carefully unfolded the pages on his bed and took a picture. The camera made a louder clicking sound than he wished for and a brighter flash as well. He looked toward the door, but he was still alone. As soon as the camera produced the first picture, he took another one, and then another. He laid the three undeveloped pictures on his bed, placed his camera back in the box, and took one more look at the door. He was still by himself. But then he heard some noise from below as the front screen door thwacked loudly, and he could hear boys' voices and their loud steps on the stairs. Somebody was coming!

He took the three pages and quickly folded them. He rushed over to Hamelin's box, opened it, and stuck the pages back in the envelope, trying to place the envelope under the same objects, but he wasn't sure. *Rats! I should have remembered where I found it.*

He hurriedly closed the lid and had just gotten back to his bed when three boys came rushing in.

"That swimming pool is awesome!" said one of them.

"Yeah," said another. "I'll bet there aren't many children's homes that have a pool like that!"

The boys began to change their clothes, and Paul casually picked up the pictures. He placed them in his box, being careful not to allow anything to touch the surfaces. It usually took a minute or two for the pictures to develop. He would come back and look at them later.

He strolled out of the room.

He wished he could read cursive. Maybe Mrs. Eastland would teach him.

* * *

SueSue, Johnnie, and Simon sat in rocking chairs on the wraparound porch, and Egg sat on the steps just in front of them. SueSue stopped rocking and stared south toward the Forest of Fears.

She stood but didn't move off the porch or back to the house. She continued to look south, and the others, who had learned to watch her, noticed that her gaze lifted.

"They are coming," she said.

"Who's coming?" asked Egg.

SueSue didn't answer. She took a step forward and continued looking, her head lifting as she raised both arms, as if to protect her eyes from the afternoon glare. "And troubles with them."

"What kinds of trouble?" asked Johnnie.

"In the storm clouds. The sword is flashing—lightning and thunder."

"I don't see anything," said Simon. "Are storms on the way?"

"The ground is shaking…terrible things…detestable—"

SueSue turned and stepped into the house. "Come with me."

"Egg," said Johnnie. "Don't leave the porch. We'll be right back—"

"No. Egg must come too." SueSue strode into the house and up the stairs. They followed her to the end of the first hall and turned left, passing their bedrooms at the tee where the two hallways intersected. SueSue then led them farther down the second corridor than they had ever been allowed to go.

The Wise and Hospitable Woman reached a dark spot at the end of the hall, where the house touched up against the mountain. She paused. "There are things about this old house that you need to know."

Look for the fifth book in the Hamelin Stoop series.

NOW THAT THE BATTLE OF PARTHOGEN HAS ENDED, REN'DAL wants revenge. How far is he willing to go to seize Gloaming once and for all? What is he willing to endure for the sake of power? Ancient prophesies loom over Hamelin and his friends as they discover a detestable thing, tremors, and danger lurking around every corner. Meanwhile, Paul begins to realize his role in the adventure is larger than he ever could have imagined. Will he be a key to shaping the future? Will anyone listen to what he has to say? And what about the prophecy of the warriors? Are Hamelin and Romulus doomed to face one another in a battle to the death?

- If you enjoyed *Hamelin Stoop: The Battle of Parthogen*, share it with your friends, small group, or book club.
- Mention Hamelin Stoop on social media using the hashtag #HamelinStoop.
- Review the Hamelin Stoop books at your online retailer.
- Join the "Readers and Fans of Robert B. Sloan" Facebook Group.
- Books can be purchased at all major online book sellers and at www.12GatesPublishing.com.

Acknowledgments

I HAVE TRULY ENJOYED WRITING THIS FOURTH INSTALLMENT in the Hamelin Stoop series. I wish the gaps were shorter between volumes, but at least this one wasn't as large as the gap between the previous two! I've had quite a few friendly questions about the publication date of this book, so it's very gratifying to know that the series is building up a devoted readership.

As to why I've enjoyed this book so much, I think it's partly because of the growth of the characters as they experience their own quests, as well as seeing the larger plot continue to develop. The entire series has multiple stories within stories, but I particularly hope the reader enjoys the variety of subplots, especially as these employ themes and symbolism from other ancient stories, as well as discovering how these varied myths come together in the formation of a larger story.

The process of writing can be an isolating experience, but as an author you're never truly alone. There are many who join your work in essential ways, so I want to acknowledge with gratitude the Houston Christian University Trustees for their gracious support alongside the many friends and family members who have continued to encourage me throughout the series. Plus, I am indebted to those who have offered superb technical advice on everything from copy editing to plot development.

Jennifer Crosswhite is a new professional friend who gave an earlier draft a thorough reading and made many substantively helpful suggestions. This book has benefited from her expertise.

Judy Ferguson has been with me from the very beginning

of this series, and once again she has supplied her remarkable technical proficiency to the processes of transcription, copy editing, and plot design. Judy has an amazing memory for detail, and not only can she spot a comma blunder at fifty paces, but she has the capacity to notice inconsistencies great and small over large swaths of text and story. I don't know where I would be with this series without Judy.

I also want to thank Angela Merkle. Not only has she created an outstanding cover and other artwork supportive of the series, but she has also been closely involved in matters related to plot development, point of view, and copy editing.

Angela works in different capacities for both Sue and me, so it was easy for us to agree that we wanted to dedicate this book to her in gratitude for her excellence and friendship.

I must also again, as for the other books in the Hamelin Stoop series, acknowledge the role of my grandchildren in the motivation for and development of these volumes. I've used a lot of the names of their parents and aunts and uncles—which has made reading the stories a lot more fun for them—and I've been amazed that the children, some by the time they reached nine years of age, but nearly all of them by the time they reached eleven, have read the books and then urged me to hurry up and finish the next one! I love them dearly and wish I could write enough books to dedicate one to each of them; but given the fact that we are now expecting grandchild number twenty-four, I don't think I have enough lifespan left!

As always, I take great joy in expressing the debt of love I owe to Sue, my wife of 53 years. Her virtuous determination, encouragement, support, and knowledge of the book building and book publishing business have made this endeavor possible.

I'm hoping that book five in this series will shorten the average gap between volumes. I'm well on my way but still have a lot to do. Again, to my readers, thank you for your patience. Stay tuned. The series continues.

About the Author

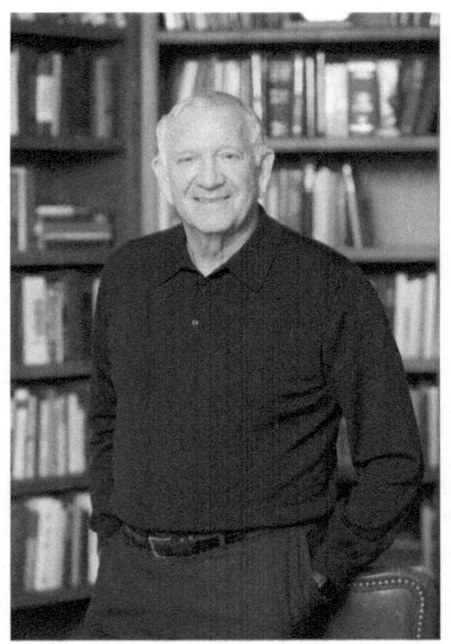

Having grown up in West Texas, Robert B. Sloan says the setting of the *Hamelin Stoop* series is near to his heart. He is married to his college sweetheart, Sue. With seven married children and over twenty grandchildren, they enjoy large family gatherings with good food and lively conversation around the table. Favorite family activities include playing games, writing and reading stories, and, of course, storytelling. Robert is also a university president and scholar.